Contents

Acknowledgments

Since I truly count my teachers and colleagues and students among my friends, I trust that my many various debts to them will have been acknowledged in my dedication. If I could, I would in each case take my dedication out of hiding and pay the personal thanks which are due. But for now I wish to express my profound esteem and gratitude to Germaine Brée who has been a unique inspiration and guide and friend to me in this work. Her own works on Camus are without equal, as is she, in my experience, without equal as a woman and scholar of vision, integrity, and warmth.

My special gratitude is due, as well, to Hugh Van Dusen, whose genial interest and support put this project on the tracks, as well as to Judy Stark who somehow reads my writing with patience and renders it in type without flaw. Finally, I give my children their space if not their wish, as they wonder still why I write philosophy. The truth is that they have entered this book and left their mark in more ways than they shall ever know.

Robert E. Meagher

Amherst, Massachusetts
Winter 1978

CAMUS' WRITINGS CITED

"Caligula" and Three Other Plays (hereafter, *Plays*)
Exile and the Kingdom (*Exile*)
The Fall (*Fall*)
A Happy Death (*Death*)
Lyrical and Critical Essays (*Lyrical*)
The Myth of Sisyphus and Other Essays (*Myth*)
Neither Victims Nor Executioners (*Neither*)
Notebooks 1935–1942 (*Notebooks I*)
Notebooks 1942–1951 (*Notebooks II*)
The Plague (*Plague*)
The Rebel (*Rebel*)
Resistance, Rebellion and Death (*Resistance*)
The Stranger (*Stranger*)
Youthful Writings (*Youthful*)

Preface

A preface, dictionaries tell us, is "something spoken or written as introductory or preliminary to a discourse, book, etc." Robert Meagher's book needs no introduction other than the quite excellent one he has provided himself. His purpose? "To display the unfolding of Camus' work" in such a manner that "the full range of his writings provides contextual insight into each individual work." It is his intent as "displayer" to exhibit a selection of texts whose interactions and exchanges will actualize for readers the affective-intellectual ambience of Camus' work, the source of his use of language. That for Camus the search for an adequate language was much more than an esthetic concern—though it was also that—is what Meagher has wished to make plain. He undertook the task because he felt that Camus was by now known almost exclusively as a minor existentialist, the proponent of a philosophy of "the absurd" illustrated in a couple of novels, *The Stranger* and *The Fall*, a grave distortion of the work. It is this kind of misconception that Meagher successfully challenges.

Prefacers, who have not themselves written the book they preface, have a privileged position only insofar as they are among its first readers. Their task cannot be to gloss what the author has said, but rather to awaken the readers' anticipation of what they may expect. Robert Meagher's book is not just another book on Camus. This discourse is highly distinctive and quietly persuasive. In the last two decades academic criticism has focused mainly—almost obsessively—on the linguistic texture and structural characteristics of written texts: on the *how* rather than on the *why* and *what* of writing. It has tended to eliminate the author as the source of the works that carry his signature, and to abstract them from his personal experience and situational context. Marxist-inspired criticisms, which, on the other hand, probe the sociohistorical dimensions of a literary text, read it largely in terms of the determining boundaries of class-consciousness. Camus' work has received its large share of diverse critical readings, some of them rich in suggestiveness, but all too often bewildering to the noninitiated readers because of their technical vocabulary and abstract methodology. Meagher's text is free of any such terminology; it is addressed to the "common reader," yet does not condescend.

A philosopher by training, well versed in the texts of the western intellectual tradition, both Hellenic and Biblical, Meagher has an acute sense of language. His book on Augustine explored the tensions that underlie the Augustinian discourse and define the framework of the changing perceptions of an era and the conflicts and problematics to which they give rise. He approaches Camus in the same way. Starting with a small cluster of familiar words which Camus cited as basic to his world he first explores their connotations and resonances in the Hellenic tradition to which Camus refers. He can thus explain their hold on Camus' imagination and the force with which they hold sway in a work that from that base develops with dramatic intensity.

The book is carefully crafted. Framed by a thoughtful introduction and a brief concluding statement, it is divided into three sections, each one introduced by an essay and followed by a selection of texts. The continuity of the analysis is assured by short transitional passages that link the sections one to the other. The effect is of a continuum, of "unfolding" as Meagher suggests. The sections are grouped under the aegis of the three mythical figures—Sisyphus, Prometheus, and Nemesis—who embody the "governing myths" that give Camus' work its impetus. To them Meagher restores their full legend and complexity, so that they invite the kind of scrutiny and questioning which leads to an exploration in depth of their relation with the texts selected and to one another. Although they are obviously not replicas of one another, and although Camus' fictional characters do not replicate them, they are interconnected and reinstated as central to and inseparable from the dynamic of the total work, its inner dialectic. It is that inner dialectic and the parameters with which it operates that Meagher clarifies and delineates.

The texts displayed are more than an anthology in the current sense of the word. They have at least two functions: as evidence to validate the displayer's point of view; to serve as a matrix for further readings. They are taken from the diverse genres Camus cultivated and are for the most part synchronic for each section, whereas the sections follow the chronological pattern of publication. Meagher's essay is a diachronic weaving of the separate parts into a whole. This is a case where one could say that the medium is the message. For what the pattern conveys is indeed fundamental to Camus' outlook. No one of the mythical figures eliminates the other. They do not represent mutually exclusive viewpoints, but rather differing animating attitudes each qualified and limited by the other. It is the power of mental attitudes physically inscribed in ways of confronting reality that Camus explored: the power and the limits—not in the black and white, either/or alternative that sparked the dismaying ideological violence of the time, but in that "turn of the screw" of which I. A. Richards spoke, "one turn of the screw away, slight the shift in position, vast the consequences."[1] How does Prometheus become Caesar? What do the writings of Camus in their variety and apparent fragmentation reveal of their author's deep desire to "think his way through" the conflicts, the tensions, the uncertainties, the difficulties in which he was enmeshed?

This is a particularly timely question in the twenty years that have gone by since Camus' death; our outlook and situation have changed. Those of us who belong to Camus' generation received the work piecemeal and read it against a dismaying background of violence. It was closely identified with his personality. In the highly

charged emotional climate of the mid-century, and in spite of
Camus himself that personality became a quasi-legendary exemplary figure. Three years after Camus' death, Susan Sontag expressed
with particular appositeness the quality of feeling Camus had quite
generally inspired: "Kafka arouses pity and terror, Joyce admiration,
Proust and Gide respect, but no modern writer that I can think of,
except Camus, has aroused love. His death in 1960 was felt as a
personal loss by the whole literary world."[2] Affection was the feeling Camus inspired in his friends though not familiarity, so great
was a reserve due in part to a desperate need to husband his
strength.[3]

True there were notable exceptions. Ideological confrontations in
the fifties—with their either/or intransigencies—were not suited to
Camus' dialectic of restraint and limit. His discomfort in regard to
the myth of a Russian Socialist Utopia, prevalent in leftist circles;
his stance in the Algerian war whose polarization he thought could
be avoided opened him to merciless attack. Impartiality was not the
hallmark of those years where Paris intellectuals were concerned.
And the attack was sustained after his death, the image of Camus in
the role of "conscience of his time" which he had not sought had
its other face: the guilt-ridden face of the moralistic "petit
bourgeois" of Marxist stereotyping. Thence the tendency to
moralize all Camus' work in terms of a kind of black-and-white
morality play with the author cast in the role of self-righteous
judge: a man of "Noble Feeling" rather than "Noble Act" (Sontag,
p. 57). This partial and "ad hominem" judgment obscured the very
quality of the work which Meagher sets out to recapture, its sometime precarious inner dynamic.

The restraints he imposed on his polemical writings and the cold
irony that they sometimes communicate made him a ready target
for often ill-informed opponents. It was his very effort not to project
his "I" upon a human theater so charged with human distress that
led him to sacrifice certain areas of his awareness and sensibility
—his humor and self-irony, his devastating sense of human postur-

ings and his unlimited capacity for self-illusion and justification.

Now, once again, the ideological climate in Paris has shifted as a new generation faces up to the realities of Gulag. Camus now looks rather like a precursor, whose political integrity and courage are no longer impugned. There is a new surge of interest in Camus, both in his sociopolitical concepts and in his more properly literary creations. As the "new" and "new new novel" run their course, critical interest is turning once again to questions of linguistic context and meaning. Camus does not play literary games; but like most of his greater contemporaries he is not satisfied to use already elaborated forms. He hammers out his own, fully aware of the fact that in themselves they offer a cryptic language carrying conceptual implications and communicating—indeed defining—meaning.

It is a measure of Meagher's understanding of and interest in Camus that in his essay he has recaptured the tone of friendly intimacy that Sontag described while fully maintaining the objective distanced perspective time now allows him. Whereas for Camus' first readers the personality often sustained the interest in Camus' work, for a new generation it is the work that sustains interest in the personality of the man.

The position of today's readers in relation to the work has also changed. Virtually all that Camus wrote is now available in print: all Camus published in his lifetime, and texts that appeared posthumously. Camus was not a prolific writer to be sure, but neither is the full corpus of his work slight, more particularly in light of the difficult internal and external circumstances of its elaboration. The very variety of the forms it presents—from genre to genre and within each genre—tends to promote either fragmentary readings or clearly reductive ones such as Sartre's early influential reading of *The Stranger* in terms of *The Myth of Sisyphus*. So it is not merely to rid the work of critical encrustations that Meagher has chosen his manner of presentation but to bring about a shift in critical focus. As reader he views Camus' work holistically, from outside. All its various expressions he sees as skillfully fashioned "shards," evoking thereby the images of the critic as archaeologist reconstructing some precious vase from its parts. A modest claim and one does not push. He does not claim to possess the full design, or the single "meaning." He is not chiefly concerned with the mythic figurative and thematic interplay that modulate the complex movement of Camus' creative search for a language to vehicle the inner modifications or questionings of his thought.

It seems plausible to consider that for Camus each work was a "speech act" whose resonance rebounded to former such acts as well as to future ones. Thence perhaps the occasional references linking work to work: In *The Stranger*, Meursault's reading in prison of the scenario later developed by Camus in *The Misunderstanding*; a reference to Meursault in *The Plague*; and in *The Rebel* and *The Just Assassins*, two versions, one discursive, the other dramatized, of an episode in the activities of a group of Russian terrorists. The little we know of the novel he was writing at the time of his death points to the recovery and reintegration of the autobiographical fragments of his first essays.

From another point of view readers today, Meagher suggests, stand at the center of a circle that was never closed. There the voice of *The Stranger*, his world of sea, sun and sand, fire and water, looks across at the drizzle and concentric canals from which the *Judge-Penitent*'s voice addresses his silent interlocutor, while *The Renegade*'s soundless self-martyred dirge echoes in the waterless desert. Each of these figures is self-enclosed in his own rhetorically contrived space, mythical figurations of the conflicting drives that give Camus' plays their momentum. They do not cancel each other out. Moving across genre—from the discursive mode to the lyrical via the fictional and dramatic, the aphoristic and autobiographic—Meagher has set himself the task of pursuing the emergent creative patterning. He supplements each source of information by another, cross-referencing, one might say, so as to disengage Camus' authentic voice from those of his many textually created personae, a voice that of necessity both encompasses and qualifies all the others. The complexities of Camus' work have become more visible to those of us who are familiar with recent methods of critical analysis. Meagher's essay is subtle yet direct, scholarly yet accessible to the common reader. It does not lay claim to passing some kind of final judgment on the work; nor does it overstress its importance. But it furnishes a fresh and welcome approach to a deeper understanding of the quality and validity of Camus' work.

Meditating in *Beyond* on the present trends in criticism, I. A. Richards distinguished between the "relatively mechanical techniques" of contemporary scholarship and the "inner testimony" that informs our selection and weighing of the "outer evidence" they bring. "What we have to fear," he writes, "as theory follows theory and interpretations expandingly outdo one another—is that the whole enterprise of trying to understand great works will suffer disparagement." "What are we doing," he asks, "in trying to understand any great work?" And he suggests that only through the integrative force of that inner perception can we attain our goal, which is to join literature and life: "We must, I think, agree," he concludes, "that it is just from such invitations to integrative perceptions that all the finer moral texture of living derives" (*Beyond*, pp. 38–39). Robert Meagher's book is just such an invitation.

Germaine Brée

NOTES

1. *Beyond* (New York: Harcourt Brace Jovanovich, 1973), p. 163.

2. "Camus's Notebooks" in *Against Interpretation* (New York: Farrar, Straus & Giroux, 1966), p. 63.

3. It is only very recently that Herbert Lottman's documented biography of Camus (Doubleday, 1979) has provided an account of the serious handicaps under which he struggled. Although not always entirely reliable, and at times blurred by too much detail, it brings welcome new information, correcting a number of distortions.

Foreword

This volume has been prepared with one wish in mind: that the voice of Albert Camus might speak to our times with renewed clarity and fullness. Such wishful thinking is, indeed, both presumptuous and self-effacing. Presumptuous, in that a certain colleagueship with Camus must have been assumed in this project, necessarily without his consent. And self-effacing, in that the sole striving herein is to be utterly faithful to his words and to his silences. One might with some appropriateness regard this volume as a theatrical mask, frozen in a single expression, thought to be essential, and constructed so as to project and to amplify the voice which sounds through it. But why, one might ask, would anyone imagine that the eloquence of Camus requires added clarity and fullness?

The fact was and is that Camus has long been misunderstood, not in the refinements of his thought but in its boldest assertions. This most unwarranted shadow of misapprehension brought no small pain to Camus while he lived and brings some portion of the same pain to all who would preserve his memory. There is, indeed, lasting irony in the fact that this man, a journalist by profession, whose words are so without pretense and indirection, should find himself at such bedeviled cross-purposes with his readers. Neither an academic nor an intellectual, by birth or by training, he was not inclined to deal in obscurities. The palate of his mind never relished the labyrinthian delicacies of consummately refined but pointless discourse. Most contemporary philosophers are engaged in what can only be described as an elaborate stall, while, by contrast, Camus knew and felt with the sure grasp of silent instinct

what required to be said; and he set about saying it with all the
lucid passion which he could summon. He crafted no technical
language to spare his writings the rough test against everyday experience and plain talk. He stumbled into his one technical coin-
age, "the absurd," and regretted the lapse ever after. When once
asked to list his favorite words, he offered the following: the world,
pain, earth, mother, human beings, the desert, honor, poverty,
summer, and the sea. It is difficult to fathom how a literature com-
posed of such plain, pedestrian elements could be read so often
askew from its deepest purposes. And yet epithets such as "existentialist," "negative," "pessimistic" loiter around Camus' works
wherever they are read and discussed. Only yesterday I met a student whose mentor had recommended that she read *The Stranger*
as an antidote to her too positive outlook, naive beyond her years.
That such a pretentious violation should occur at all is maddening;
but that it should be managed at the hands of Camus is doubly so.
No hands could be more ill-suited and unwilling for such a felony
than those of Camus.

Camus is misread for many reasons. In part, it is a function of
the company which he has been made to keep. Most notably,
Camus and Sartre have been wedded, by the arrangements of
chance and history, in the minds of most readers, despite the fact
that, by their own admission, they have nothing in common with
each other (cf. *Lyrical*, p. 345). Less notably, Camus and Heidegger are commonly linked, the one to the other. And yet one can no
more imagine Heidegger a journalist than Camus a fascist, which
marks only the beginning of their differences. In fact, one might
claim that Camus did not belong to his time, no matter the care
with which he addressed its concerns. There is truth in the comment of R.-M. Albérès, cited by M. Lebesque in his biography of
Camus: "Camus is a selective writer who, by temperament, belongs
to a line of descent rather than to a period. There are some on
whom the hue of the literature of their times does not rub off and
Camus is one of these. You could explain the whole of Camus by

imagining that the years 1895–1933 had not existed." Above all we must understand that Camus wrote, so to speak, out of doors, beneath a sky and on the edge of a sea which must have looked very much the same to Odysseus, to Aeneas, to Plotinus, to Augustine, and to his own unknown father, Lucien Camus, as it did to himself. The Algerian coastal city of Oran, built with its back to the sea, was to Camus a source of amusement and of some slight scorn. Camus never wrote with his back to the sea. If we keep that one item in mind, we will never altogether misunderstand him.

Camus' imagination, the well from which his words are drawn, is not modern, much less European, still less postwar existentialist. Instead, by his own account, it is Mediterranean, which denotes neither simply a place, nor simply a time, but rather a timeless inner landscape, a rugged finite terrain, bordered by foreign, uninhabitable expanses: the sea, the sky, the desert. He may have had in mind these worldly infinities and the still stranger and more impenetrable infinities imaged therein when he wrote that "there are mysteries it is suitable to enumerate and meditate" (*Notebooks II*, p. 67). These natural borders describe the limits of thought and of art, as Camus understood them. He never ventured far into sea, or sky, or desert but thinks thoughts native to their common shore. He is neither mystic nor metaphysician; his instinctive concerns are the more worldly yet spiritual concerns of art, ethics, and politics, the ancient concerns of informing the material of human making and doing with the measure of beauty and right. When asked to give more precise coordinates for this Mediterranean civilization to which his own writings belong, Camus made frequent reference to classical Greece, not as preserved in museums and ruins but as remembered and reborn in the heart. Camus was not a Graecophile, and surely not a classicist. Rather, he spoke of himself as having a "Greek heart" and claimed that of all the worlds known to him he felt most at home in the world of Greek myth. If we are, then, to hear his words with the tones and overtones which he meant them to have we must stand where he stands, between desert, sea, and sky, in a land rid of one God yet visited by gods and demigods. Camus wrote, as we shall see, under the auspices of Sisyphus, Prometheus, and Nemesis; and it is right that we should read him under those same auspices.

Thus far we have noticed only one reason for Camus' being so widely misread, namely that he is read out of context, or, rather, out of his own appropriate context, which he describes as Mediterranean and Greek. But there is another related reason for the chronic confusion haunting his works. He is read quite selectively with the assumption that the customary selections adequately speak his mind. Nearly everyone who reads Camus reads *The Stranger*; a few then go on to read *The Plague*. And occasionally *The Fall* is read. Those who concern themselves with Camus' philosophy mostly limit their investigations to *The Myth of Sisyphus*. And so the case is rested. Authors are seldom done justice by an exclusive reading of their earliest works; but this is especially true in Camus' case. For his work unfolds in cycles according to a conscious design. No one work or cycle of works was ever intended to state his mind. The movement from his earlier writings to his later writings not only reflects the necessarily unforeseeable change and growth found in most any author's career; rather, it also represents a conscious dialectic in which a position is asserted with a view toward its later contradiction. Thus, in *The Stranger* and in *The Myth of Sisyphus* a vision is presented which is to all or most appearances existentialist, only to be overthrown and surpassed in *The Plague* and in *The Rebel*. Camus asserts existentialism so as to overcome it; he directs his mind toward it so as to direct his mind against it. However, when only *The Stranger* and *The Myth of Sisyphus* are considered, a process becomes a product; and Camus becomes a captive existentialist, forever, it would seem.

To display the unfolding of Camus' works, such that the full range of his writings provides contextual insight into each individual work, is the task of this entire volume and cannot be the responsibility of its foreword. However, even in these most preliminary remarks, something more might well be said of the peculiar movement and development informing Camus' works. I have called the movement "dialectical"; and what I have in mind in saying this is a quite ancient understanding of what it means to pursue the truth by "thinking one's way through" (*dia-legein*) to the truth. The dialogues of Sokrates and the *De Trinitate* of Augustine are splendid examples of dialectical thinking. In simplest terms, thinking is assumed to proceed from image to image; and even when truth is imaged, it is imaged always imperfectly, always fragmentarily. In every true image, or in every image of the truth, something of the truth is glimpsed and something of the truth is obscured. Thus every true word or thought is a partial truth; for every image both is and is not what it images. This two-sidedness of thinking requires that every image or thought be both affirmed and denied, reaffirmed and again denied. Only in saying both "yes" and "no" to a partial truth is one being utterly faithful to the character of process or becoming inherent in all would-be truthful thinking. This discipline of ascent from partial truth to partial truth, from image to image, from affirmation to denial to affirmation, a discipline common to many metaphysical and mystical traditions, clearly underlies the movement from one governing myth to another in Camus' work—from Sisyphus to Prometheus to Nemesis—a movement with no end of its own yet always discontinued somewhere, sometime by the caprice of chance or necessity or providence of which we know both too much and nothing. In short, truth is no more of a piece for us than a shattered vase. Countless edges matching only now and then. Pieces, crucial shards, always missing. All we possess are relative truths—from one perspective true, from another perspective false—one edge matches, another doesn't. Our work lies in turning each truth, each image, each shard around and around again in our hands, picking them up and putting them down. Faithfulness would seem to lie in losing track of none of them. Camus knew well the maxim of Plotinus that all sin lies in abstraction. Why else would he have explained his love of the

Greeks by saying that in the end they exclude nothing, that they leave room for everything?

"That the voice of Albert Camus might speak to our times with renewed clarity and fulness." In order that this might be accomplished nothing more need be added than what has too often been removed: the Mediterranean landscape, the Greek line of descent, the gods and demigods, the disciplined movement from "yes" to "no," never halted, never still, save in death. Thus, under the governing images, the ruling deities and heroes, of his work —Sisyphus, Prometheus, and Nemesis—the full circuit of Camus' thought will be traced in this volume not so as to replace whole works with selections but rather to suggest the necessity and the fruitfulness of embracing the full scope of Camus' writings. And yet it must be acknowledged plainly that this volume too proceeds through images and offers partial truths regarding Camus. The mask of Camus herein is Greek in its features, philosophical in its commitments, uncritical in tone. It is my hope and not my fear that this mask, once worn, will be removed and set aside in favor of what it has served both to disclose and to conceal.

Albert Camus

Introduction

The task of this introduction is to describe an appropriate context for the reading of Camus' works. What is called for is, in theatrical terms, a set; and theatrical terms are, indeed, singularly proper to the corpus of Camus' works, which were never far removed from the concerns of classical drama. The set must be simple, its back to mountains and desert, facing the sea, and open to sun and sky. As Camus' thinking unfolds, it moves toward midday, when shadows are sharp but short, serving to outline the figures which cast them. The lines drawn here and now, which will block out the play of our thoughts, must be bold and decisive. I will draw three such lines across this as yet blank stage. I will introduce three categories of thought essential both to the corpus of Camus' writings and to that of ancient Greek literature, three fundamental concerns bonding the one to the other and revealing their essential kinship: nature, necessity, and friendship.

NATURE

The Greek word which informs this particular inquiry is the word *physis*, from which our own word "physician" is derived. In fact, the concern to study and to understand the "nature" of things seems to have had its origin in early Greek medical science. The method practiced was one of careful observation and insight; for nature was something to be seen, something revealing itself to the eye. However, mere observation must be distinguished here from

the insight which may or may not accompany it. I discover an area
of discoloration on my arm. Upon closer observation, I notice
slight swelling. It is sensitive to the touch. Before me is a phenome-
non, an appearance, a symptom or a set of symptoms. I know
something to be red, swollen, and sore; but I do not yet know what
it is. I know neither its cause nor its likely outcome. Consequently,
I don't know whether to be alarmed or heedless. If it requires treatment, and this too is an open question, I would not know how to
treat it: with heat, with cold, with rest, with activity, with fasting,
with drugs. Should it be soaked, rubbed, lanced, left alone, or amputated? My observations—that it is red, swollen, and sore—
respond to none of these queries. I bring my symptoms to a physician and the physician usually finds them familiar, calls them by
name, and tells me what to do. What I have brought, aside from
my arm, is observation, while what the physician brings is insight.
And this insight is largely a function of experience. I have never
seen such a thing before and the physician has seen just such a
thing many times before, often enough to recognize it again.

After all, our bodies and their symptoms are not altogether
unique. I have a human body and you have a human body and everyone I know has a human body, even though I have mine and
you yours and they theirs. I know my body, in this case as red,
swollen, and sore; but the physician knows, or is striving to know
the human body. This is finally what distinguishes the physician
from the layperson, whom the Greeks call an *idiōtēs* (whence our
"idiot"), which simply means one who lives in one's own world, in
this case in one's own body. In Greek usage, the *idiōtēs* is the
private person, while the physician is the public or common person, the one who knows not merely this one body which he or she
inhabits—this most private of spaces allotted uniquely, one to
each—but the human body, allotted to us all, in common.

But what could this mean—"the human body"—which is not
private but public or common? Everywhere we look, the human
body is either this body or that body, either yours or mine. No,

upon reflection, not everywhere is this the case; for when we peer into thought and speech, the human body exists always in common, always in such a way as it is both yours and mine. Indeed, the only possible mode of possessing the human body is in knowing it. It is always common or public, never diminished as it is shared; for it is exclusively an object of inner sight which holds all things in common. "Let us therefore notice," writes Herakleitos, "that understanding is common to all men. Understanding is common to all, yet each man acts as if his intelligence were private and all his own."[1] So long as I observe my own body without any understanding of the human body, my observations are mere idiosyncrasies, inexperienced and unknowing. It is as if I were in a deep sleep, dreaming a private reality all my own, unbeholden to the laws and forces of a world beyond this one dream of mine. "We share a world when we are awake," again we listen to Herakleitos; "each sleeper is in a world of his own."[2]

The physician, then, is one who is awake to a common world in which we live a common life. This heightened, more experienced, more penetrating vision of the physician is not, however, unmindful of the particular, the private, and the unique. In medical practice, this means that distinctions must be drawn between male and female, young and old, tall and short, robust and frail, strong-willed and weak-willed, type A and type B, and so on, indefinitely. But always there is the striving to discern the generic, to read the emerging pattern or form which will guide one's hand and one's healing arts more surely in the future. "Nature," says Herakleitos, "loves to hide."[3] And the physician must ferret out nature from its countless concealments. Each such disclosure, in turn, sheds light upon the common human space which human beings cohabit.

Already we are, in these reflections, well beyond the relatively confined investigations of the medical physician. Clearly, the physician is already in our eyes a paradigm. For there is, it would seem, a nature to everything, a pattern, a form, an emergent order behind every symptom and every movement in this ever-changing world of which Herakleitos says, "Everything moves, nothing is still."[4] In fact, the passion of the physician to understand what always remains in the midst of endless change did reach to every corner of inquiry and endeavor in ancient Greece. Thus Thales, Anaximander, Anaximines, Demokritos, Parmenides, and Herakleitos strove to discern the primary elements, forces, and processes which underlie and account for the myriad unfoldings of the cosmos. They sought to know the nature of the whole, of all things. In similar fashion, Solon, the sixth-century Athenian poet and political reformer, studied the *polis*, the city-state, inquiring into its nature, as if it were an organism whose good and ill health, whose birth and death, behaved according to laws which may be known and taught. And Thukydides, in writing his great history of the Peloponnesian war, writes not for the sake of his own generation who had themselves endured and survived the war; rather, he writes a history which, he tells us, shall last forever, so convinced is he that he has perceived and chronicled a timeless, essential conflict. In his eyes, the war between Sparta and Athens, no less than the plague whose story he also tells, followed a fixed course in its unfolding. Indeed, he labored to observe and to note the symptoms of both pestilences with a physician's care so that they might be recognized, better understood, and perhaps even diverted when they appear again, as he is certain they shall, in their own good time. So also in the drama of Aischylos, Sophokles, and Euripides, as well as in the sculpture of, for example, Polykleitos, Praxiteles, and Phidias, there is the same achieved transparency to the generic. The individual is never lost, always only transcended and illumined, measured and placed in an enduring perspective.

This near obsession with the nature of things represented for the Greeks, however, more than a mere ephemeral contagion. It represented the proper and most serious work of human being. It is no mere idiosyncrasy of the Greeks to inquire into the one at the source of all multiplicity, the still and perfect order behind all movement and change. Instead, Aristotle argues that

> All men by nature desire to know. An indication of this is the delight we take in our senses; for even apart from their usefulness they are loved for themselves; and above all others the sense of sight. For not only with a view to action, but even when we are not going to do anything, we prefer seeing (one might say) to everything else. The reason is that this, most of all the senses, makes us know and brings to light many differences between things.[5]

To know something, then, to know its nature, is to bring to light its differences from other things. We must know a thing's beginning and its ending, its every edge. To know what something is not is to know what it is; and to know what something is is to know what it is not. In short, knowledge of nature is knowledge by contrast, knowledge of borders or limits. Consequently, there can be no such knowledge of what is infinite and eternal. Knowledge of nature is knowledge of things which come into being and pass out of being. The very word "nature" (*physis*) is derived from the word meaning "to bring forth," "to grow," and "to come into being." The nature of a thing describes the course of a thing's becoming, the course of its unfolding. And among all beings which dwell in a state of becoming, among all beings which are born and which die, among all beings whose natures are possible objects of observation and insight, it would seem most incumbent upon human beings to know themselves. "Know thyself," the Delphic Oracle enjoins. No maxim is more central to Greek thinking. Thus Sokrates, when asked to comment upon the natures of other more obscure and remote beings, explains that he has no time for such concerns:

> And I'll tell you why, my friend. I can't as yet "know myself" as the inscription at Delphi enjoins, and so long as that ignorance remains it seems to me ridiculous to inquire into extraneous matters. Consequently I don't bother about such things, but accept the current beliefs about them, and direct my inquiries, as I have just said, rather to myself, to discover whether I really am a more complex creature and more puffed up with pride than Typhon, or a simpler,

gentler being whom heaven has blessed with a quiet, unTyphonic nature?[6]

Self-knowledge here means knowledge of one's human nature rather than knowledge of one's personal uniqueness. "The soul grows according to its own law,"[7] writes Herakleitos; and those who know themselves know that law beyond any awareness they may have of their own private inclinations and addictions. Indeed, the attainment of self-knowledge, knowledge of human nature, is all the more urgent and crucial for human beings, because they must choose whether to act in accord with their nature or to act in defiance of it. According to Greek understanding, human nature is a nature unlike any other in that it accommodates personal freedom. For animals and plants, the line between what is natural and what is unnatural divides the possible and necessary from the impossible; whereas, for human beings, nature distinguishes the appropriate from the inappropriate. In brief, human nature dictates propriety and not possibility. The ways of most every being are rooted deep in instinct. Whales and falcons, much less poplars and rhododendrons, know nothing of the leisure and imaginative space in which human beings consider their alternatives. And the alternatives may differ vastly, one from the other. The choice is seldom reserved for each of us to make in our full maturity. Instead it is largely a matter of rearing, of education. Here too the range of possibilities spans our wildest imaginings and the stakes could not be higher, as Plato suggests in his *Laws*:

> Now human being we call a gentle creature. But in truth, though it is wont to prove more godlike and gentle than any other, if it but have the right natural endowments and the right schooling, let it be trained insufficiently or amiss and it will show itself more savage than anything on the face of the earth.[8]

Augustine formulates quite simply and pointedly the question we have reached; and his response too could not be more Greek, or Mediterranean.

> Why, then, is the soul admonished to know itself? This, I believe, is
> the reason: so that it might reflect upon itself and live in accord with
> its own nature.[9]

After all, human freedom is not absolute and extends only so far as
the choices we make. The consequences of our choices are beyond
our freedom and our control. The harvest of a life lived in accord
with "the law of the soul" is not the same as the outcome of a life
of violation. "All is disgust," writes Sophokles, "when one leaves
his own nature and does things which misfit it."[10] To know and to
live in accord with human nature is to yield the force of one's own
will to the energy (*energeia* in Greek), the being-at-work, within
one, to will to become no more and no less than what one is. This
is essential Greek wisdom; and its reward is happiness or well-being, whose meaning is to us more foreign than we may suspect.
Now, so as to hint at the meaning of happiness as the end or fruition of human *physis*, and so as to bring to a close these reflections
on nature, I cite two ancient Greek accounts of happiness, the first
a Homeric hymn and the second a dramatic chorus from Euripides'
Hekyba.

The Hymn to the Earth

The mother of us all,
the oldest of all,
hard,
    splendid as rock

Whatever there is that is of the land
                it is she
                      who nourishes it,
              it is the Earth
                    that I sing

Whoever you are,
howsoever you come

                    across her sacred ground
            you of the sea,
            you that fly,
it is she
        who nourishes you
    she,
        out of her treasures
                            Beautiful children
                            beautiful harvests
                                are achieved from you
                            The giving of life itself,
                            the taking of it back
                            to or from
                                any man
                                    are yours

The happy man is simply
                            the man you favor
the man who has your favor
                        and that man
                                has everything

        His soil thickens,
        it becomes heavy with life,
        his cattle grow fat in their fields
        his house fills up with things

These are the men who govern a city with good laws
            and the women of their city,
                the women are beautiful
                                    fortune,
                                    wealth,
                                        it all follows

        Their sons glory
                in the ecstasy of youth
        Their daughters play,

they dance in the flowers,
   they skip
      in and out
   on the grass
      over soft flowers

It is you
   the goddess
it is you who honored them

Now,
mother of gods,
    bride of the sky
       in stars
 farewell:
but if you liked what I sang here
give me this life too
    then,
    in my other poems
        I will remember you[11]

Ten thousand men possess ten thousand hopes.
A few bear fruit in happiness; the others go awry.
But he who garners day by day the good of life,
 he is happiest. Blessed is he.[12]

NECESSITY

Nature, in this case human nature, is known by contrast, by setting appropriate possibilities off apart from inappropriate ones. To
disclose the arc of human *physis*, its coming-to-be, its peculiar excellence and well-being, and its ceasing-to-be, must mean to discern the limits of human being. And, for the Greeks, these limits
are, above all, the limits of freedom and power. It is for a fatal ig-

norance of precisely these limits that Dionysos lashes out at
Pentheus in *The Bacchai*:

> You do not know
> the limits of your strength. You do not know
> what you do. You do not know who you are.[13]

These are not three distinct accusations; rather, they are a single accusation. The unknowing of those who are blind to the limits of
their power and thus their freedom moves in upon and covers their
thoughts and words and deeds like a dense fog. With visibility so
low, limits are discovered only as one will opposes and crashes into
another will with blind and deaf inevitability. Tragedy is made of
such collisions and of the rude and often too late awakenings which
then ensue. The innate wisdom of the chorus speaks, always helpless, always unheeded:

> unwise are those who aspire,
> who outrange the limits of man.
> Briefly, we live. Briefly,
> then die. Wherefore, I say,
> he who hunts a glory, he who tracks
> some boundless, superhuman dream,
> may lose his harvest here and now
> and garner death. Such men are mad,
> their counsels evil.[14]

No one, least of all the Greeks, would claim that freedom and
power are at any point meted out in equal shares to all, men and
women, regardless of the conditions of their birth. Such is a child's
dream, with everything, indeed everything, against it. Instead,
there are the privileged; and there are the cursed. In religious
categories, there are the saved and the damned. And, between
these two extremes are more gradations than we could count. Nevertheless, there is no one so privileged, so free or so powerful, to
elude the arrow of these words: "You cannot always have your way
where you should not."[15] This reminder, appropriately enough, is

spoken by Death to Apollo, who is arguing, in the opening lines of the *Alkestis*, for one single exception to the most harsh and relentless of human limits, the necessity (*anagkē*) of mortality. No one is to be exempted. Here is necessity at its egalitarian best. Here the footing is indeed equal. Human being, human nature is shaped by necessity, by compulsion and restraint, by not being given one's way, by feeling one's power drain from one as from a shattered basin, and one's freedom snapped as easily as a twig. And nowhere is the grip of necessity, the human limit, more recognizable than in the face of death. In Euripides' *Alkestis* we find the great ode to necessity. Necessity, we hear, and already know, is implacable.

> I myself, in the transports
> of mystic verses, as in study
> of history and science, have found
> nothing so strong as necessity,
> nor any means to combat her,
> not in the Thracian books set down
> in verse by the school of Orpheus,
> not in all the remedies Phoibos has given the heirs
> of Asklepios to fight the many afflictions of man.
>
> She alone is a goddess
> without altar or image to pray
> before. She heeds no sacrifice.
> Majesty, bear no harder
> on me than you have in my life before!
> All Zeus even ordains
> only with you is accomplished.
> By strength you fold and crumple the steel of the Chalybes.
> There is no pity in the sheer barrier of your will . . .
>
> Even the sons of the gods fade
> and go in death's shadow.[16]

Even the sons of heaven go darkened in death. No epithet for human beings is more profound or telling than the Greek *thanatoi*, the "deathful ones," mortals. Not to be aware or mindful that one is going to die is to be a fool with all of the perils and havoc which folly carries in its wake. To "know thyself" is first of all things to know that one is born to die. Whence the colloquial advice of the drunken, braying Herakles to a servant in the house of Admetos:

Come here, I'll tell you something that will make you wise.
Do you really know what things are like, the way they are?
I don't think so. How could you? Well then, listen to me.
Death is an obligation which we all must pay.
There is not one man living who can truly say
if he will be alive or dead on the next day.
Fortune is dark; she moves, but we cannot see the way . . .
We are only human. Our thoughts should be mortal. . . .[17]

But what does this mean: to think mortal thoughts? For Herakles, the answer is simple. Seize the day. Pay special attention to Aphrodite. Now there's a sweet goddess, he tells us. Put gloomy thoughts aside. Drain the cup and be glad. This too, so far as it goes, is solid Greek wisdom, barely distinguishable, of course, from the innate sensuality and good sense of any people who have preserved the art of enjoying themselves in the grip of a hard life. But must we not go further? The human spirit craves more even when it is most besotted and momentarily content. What more does this mean: to think mortal thoughts? Again we proceed best by contrast. The Greek vision of human being sees us poised precariously between two foreign possibilities to which we are nevertheless drawn. "Human being lies mid-way (en mesō) between gods and beasts and inclines toward both," writes Plotinus, explaining further that: "Some human beings become like gods and others become like beasts. Most, however, remain in the middle."[18] This middle realm describes the proper sphere of ethics and politics, the common public domain. "He who is unable to live in the city," teaches Aristotle, "or who has no need because he is sufficient for himself, must be either a beast or a god."[19] Here, then, are our alternatives: the bestial, the divine, and the human.

Any consideration of these possibilities must necessarily turn back upon our earlier reflections. For these three orders of being—gods, mortals, and beasts—represent a spectrum of freedom and power, tyranny and oppression. At the summit dwell the gods, *athanatoi*, the deathless ones, exempt from the most bitter necessity of death. Free of this fatal limit, they are amoral, callous, insensitive, and cruel. Mercurial in their passions, their loves and hatreds, capricious in their exercise of power, shallow in their delights and in their sufferings, the gods are uncomprehending of human tragedy, because they finally know the price of nothing. Their rootless wills—seldom denied, dependably petty and vain, shockingly interchangeable and thus never ultimately frustrated—afford them their only scale of values. The odor of sacrifice—human and bestial—the odor of destruction, waste, and rot—is sweet to the gods. At the other extreme are the beasts, dumb and helpless, without even the wit or voice for supplication. They feed, convey, and entertain humans; their blood is spilled and their blackened smoke rises to the gods and wins favor with them for human wishes and whims. Their being is one of sheer instrumentality with no effectual, therefore legitimate, will of its own. They are utterly crushed by *anagkē*. Nothing moves, nothing stirs in the beast on whom the grip of necessity is nothing less than total.

These two extremes—the life of the gods and the life of the beasts—are not, however, genuinely accessible to human beings. What is alone possible is to incline toward and thus to approximate the one or the other. Human beings cannot become gods, nor can they become beasts; but they can indeed come to bear a striking resemblance to the one or to the other. And it was in the tyrant and in the slave that the Greeks recognized the most blatant human likeness to god and to beast, respectively. The arrogant Athenian generals put these extremities quite plainly to the Melians whom they were about to annihilate: "The strong do what they have the power to do and the weak accept what they have to accept."[20] On the one hand, near-absolute power, the license to act with impunity; on the other hand, near-absolute weakness, the necessity of suffering without recourse. Tyrants do whatever they please; slaves bow to whatever comes along. This is precisely the gamut of being, the ascending scale of freedom and power, which Thrasymachos presents in the dialogue known as *The Republic* and which Sokrates eventually challenges with his image of the divided line later in the same dialogue. What matters most here is, however, that even Thrasymachos realizes that human power and human weakness are never, in fact, absolute. Unqualified power is unattainable and unqualified weakness is unnecessary. The slave's options of assassination and suicide are enough to strip tyrants of their would-be divinity.

Even if the pursuit of personal power and freedom will inevitably end in compromise, Thrasymachos argues that self-assertion should always go the limit. This, he would say, is simply the law of our being. In proclaiming this same law or inclination Athenian imperialism developed its own convenient theory to support the practice to which it was committed. Of course, there was and is nothing novel in either. Again we may listen to the Athenian generals at Melos, a gang of would-be divinities lording it over their fellow humans and doing their level best to have a clear conscience in doing so. Surely this is the consummate greed, to covet both mammon and virtue, both plunder and purity:

> Our arms and actions are perfectly consistent with the beliefs men hold about the gods and with the principles which govern their own conduct. Our opinion of the gods and our knowledge of men lead us to conclude that it is a general and necessary law of nature to rule wherever one can. This is not a law that we made ourselves, nor were we the first to act upon it when it was made. We found it already in existence, and we shall leave it to exist for ever among those who come after us. We are merely acting in accordance with it, and we know that you or anybody else with the same power as ours would be acting in precisely the same way.[21]

Anyone with power acts in accord with power. This is the precise claim of all tyrants or would-be tyrants. In fact it is mere pretext and ploy. But it requires to be heard out. The claim is that all mortals long insatiably to be gods, possessing divine, that is absolute, power and freedom. All necessity, every impediment to freedom, is bitter and insufferable. And what clearer, more intransigent barrier to this divine avocation could there be than the presence of other beings with the same calling, the same blind craving to be god? We are antipolitical by nature. The presence of others like ourselves spells the ultimate frustration of our own coming-to-be. The city is necessarily at war, a war of each against each, of all against all, in which every warrior weighs fundamental passion against fundamental passion, desire against fear: desire of the best possible fate (the near-divinity of the tyrant) against fear of the worst possible fate (the near-death of the slave). There never is peace, only truce, the precarious balance of powers frustrated in their designs. Hot war cools; cold war blazes up again. Always the powerful doing what they can and the weak suffering what they must. This is the prospect presented to us as the law of our individual and collective nature and summarized in the bold amoral assertion of Thrasymachos: "Every man, when he supposes himself to have the power to do wrong, does wrong." [22] In elaboration of this assertion, Thrasymachos tells a story, the legend of Gyges the Lydian, who might be any one of us and in whom all of us are to see ourselves and others essentially imaged.

> They relate that he was a shepherd in the service of the ruler at that time of Lydia, and that after a great deluge of rain and an earthquake the ground opened and a chasm appeared in the place where he was pasturing, and they say that he saw and wondered and went down into the chasm. And the story goes that he beheld other marvels there and a hollow bronze horse with little doors, and that he peeped in and saw a corpse within, as it seemed, of more than mortal stature, and that there was nothing else but a gold ring on its hand, which he took off, and so went forth. And when the shepherds held their customary assembly to make their monthly report to the king about the flocks, he also attended, wearing the ring. So as

he sat there it chanced that he turned the collet of the ring toward
himself, toward the inner part of his hand, and when this took place
they say that he became invisible to those who sat by him and they
spoke of him as absent, and that he was amazed, and again fumbling
with the ring turned the collet outward and so became visible. On
noticing this he experimented with the ring to see if it possessed this
virtue, and he found the result to be that when he turned the collet
inward he became invisible, and when outward visible, and becoming aware of this, he immediately managed things so that he became
one of the messengers who went up to the king, and on coming
there he seduced the king's wife and with her aid set upon the king
and slew him and possessed his kingdom.[23]

Nowhere is this dream of power divine more prevalent than in
youth. Surely this, in part, accounts for the Greek obsession with
youth. For one terribly brief but glistening moment it seems and
feels that one will never die and that one may thus entertain the
visions of a burgeoning god. In this one adolescent instant, desire
knows no bounds and all fear is put aside. It is indeed no wonder
that youth dominate the corpus of Greek tragedy, as they surely do.
We need think only of Antigone, Orestes, Neoptolemos, Hippoly-
tos, Elektra, Iphigenia, Kassandra, and Makaria to give flesh to this
image of illusion and immanent tragedy. Youth is that time of life
when the human soul is most nakedly disclosed—its kinship with
the earth, the beast, the titan, and the god—and when the heart-
rending struggle or *agōn*, the "wrestling match," infused in its
hybrid blood hurls it into its most essential conflicts. Youth are
prone to the most sublime or atrocious acts. Neither is tolerable.
You cannot always have your way where you should not. No lesson
comes with more pain to youth. It is indeed in youth that mortal
thoughts stand in sharpest contrast to every nerve and fiber of our
being. But we learn by contrast and when youth is broken the lesson of the species is learned as nowhere else.

FRIENDSHIP

The Athenian generals at Melos claimed to possess more than superior power over the Melians. They claimed to be not only pre-eminently powerful but also preeminently wise. For they spoke of having discovered the law of our being and instructed the Melians accordingly. A human being is always either powerful or weak with respect to another human being, either master or slave. Our own peculiar balance of power and weakness defines our proper and necessary activity at any moment. Masters do as their power per-mits; slaves do as their weakness argues. The weak yield, acquiesce, give up as much ground as they cannot hold. The powerful act pridefully; and the weak act shamefully. This was the privileged in-struction of the Athenian warlords, a teaching surely refuted by the Melians who that very day endured annihilation and yielded not at all. This same teaching is likewise challenged strongly by Greek in-stinct, custom, and literature.

In the *Iliad*, Homer describes the mixing of human goods and ills in a great mixing bowl. Each life is poured, in part from the urn of good fortune and in part from the urn of ill fortune. The parts are, of course, unequal from one life to another. Some lives are remarkably blessed, others doomed; some are privileged, others oppressed. Clearly, there is no denying the existence of this drastic inequality between individual human beings. And we would appear forced to conclude from this that human beings whose lots in life are cast so unequally have nothing in common and can never be friends. For all friendship, as the Greeks understand friendship, resides in *koinonia* or commonality. There is an ancient Greek proverb to the effect that "friends have all things in common." Thus Aristotle, in his essay on friendship in the *Nichomachean Ethics*, explains that when one party is either much the superior or the inferior of the other or "when one party is removed to a great distance, as God is, the possibility of friendship ceases."[24]

How far are human beings, in fact, set apart from one another? It would seem that the rich and the poor, the powerful and the weak, the young and the old, men and women, east and west, north and south, black and white are everlastingly prone to misunderstand and to mistreat one another. The Greek theatre, a model of the political cosmos, reflected all such human differences and their attending chauvinisms in its seats of power, its platforms of privilege, its conventional gestures of command and of supplication, its stylized robes and masks, which made king and commoner, man and woman, citizen and slave, Greek and barbarian, young and old immediately recognizable. The grids and categories of Greek theatre left no significant human distinction unmarked, no significant human distance unmeasured. Indeed, the Greek theatre describes a ladder of freedom and oppression, each human being receiving the dread burden of necessity from above and handing it on to the next one below. Each time the weight of imposition grows until the lowest mortals are utterly crushed, reduced to crawling like slavish beasts, while lords and kings sit high above them in cruel indifference.

In the Greek theatre, however, human beings are placed at desperate odds with each other only so that they might, against all those odds, reach up in supplication or reach down in compassion and embrace in friendship. The distances between one human being and another human being are exactly delineated and measured in Greek drama only with a view toward the overcoming of those distances. And in play after play we witness just such an overcoming. In Greek literature, the instances of human beings' reaching to embrace across the widest imaginable human divisions and distances are too numerous to recount and too unmistakable to slip our notice, if only we look. Here we are at the heart of Greek tragedy. "If any man should fall support him with your hands,"[25] sings the chorus of old broken men in the *Herakles*. And it is no one less than Herakles himself who is struck down by Hera's wrath, driven mad and made unknowingly to slaughter his own family. "Necessity," we are told, "breaks even the strong." [26] It was a once-strong voice which cries out now:

> I am bewildered. Where could *I* be helpless?
>   Help! Is there some friend of mine, near or far,
> who could help me in my bewilderment? [27]

And, from afar, a friend does come to share Herakles' grief, "a rival weight" [28] to counterpoise his downfall. The one offers his hand to the other and they are yoked in love. Just so, in the *Philoktetes*, it is only with the support of his magic bow, the token of an old friendly act, and with the assurances of a young, faltering but friendly boy that the aged and embittered Philoktetes is able to prop himself up and sustain his human stature. The callow Neoptolemos and the despairing Philoktetes reach across the barriers of several betrayals old and new to a bond of care and trust. But no leap is more astounding than that encountered in the last book of the *Iliad* when, after the dreadful carnage and rage of the days and years now past, Priam and Achilles weep together, the one weeping for his own son whom he sees in his son's slayer and the other weeping for his goddess mother whose grief over his own impending death, he sees, will be deathless. The broken king and the scourge of Troy, in their overwhelming sadness, their eyes washed with tears, sighted with a special clarity, wonder at one another. A moment of recognition which brings us to the very center of Greek wisdom. Wisdom comes with suffering; not only one's own but that too of others. When Aithra stands weeping for seven foreign women who have lost their sons in battle, making their grief her own, Theseus, her son, upbraids her, saying: "Their troubles should not make you moan. You do not belong to them" (literally, you do not share the same birth, or nature). [29] Yet, after a savage battle, this same Theseus is seen lifting the slain warriors onto biers for burial, soiling himself with the pollution of the dead. Is this foul work fit for a king? The response we are given says it all: "How can our common ills be shameful to us?" [30]

Finally, the distances between human beings are negligible. And human strife is sheer misadventure. The spaces between human beings come to nothing when measured against the space between human beings and gods, between mortals and immortals. Metaphysical oppression may provide a precedent and a pattern for political oppression; but finally the former renders the latter inexcusable. The human lot is a harsh one without being made still harsher by one's fellows. We may recall the pleading of Adrastos, a king who had seen enough of the suffering which human beings inflict on one another:

> O wretched mortals,
> Why do you slaughter each other with your spears?
> Leave off these struggles; let your towns take shelter
> In gentleness. Life is a short affair;
> We should try to make it smooth, and free from
>   strife.[31]

"He needs no friends," writes Euripides, "who has the love of gods. For when god helps a man, he has help enough."[32] However, the Greeks lived mostly without the assurance of divine love or help; and in this they are not alone. Only from one another could they hope to receive the simplest and most profound of graces: good-will. This is the essence of friendship (*philia*), the bond of the city and the balm of a difficult life. *Philia* may be translated variously to evoke its many dimensions: friendship, love, care, good-will, recognition, kindness. And "what is there more kindly," writes Aischylos, "than the feeling between host and guest?"[33] Indeed, in the ritual practice of hospitality, we may glimpse friendship in its most elemental expression.

The rites of hospitality reward generously anyone who would reflect upon them. And even in these quite cursory reflections, we must not fail to notice one crucial detail. Guests are not required, indeed they are not permitted, to identify themselves until after they have accepted the offer of hospitality, bathed, put on clean clothes, and supped. The stranger must not be unmasked until host and guest are one in the bond of hospitality. This required anonymity assures that host and guest act toward one another as human beings in an essential relationship unillumined or, perhaps, unobscured by their personal identities. This simple giving and receiving of the most fundamental goods of life in the face of necessity must remain untouched and unqualified by issues of race, class, business, sex, family, religion, and politics. These distinctions are, after all, also masks which often render human beings all but unrecognizable to one another. Here, when guest kneels to host in supplication and when host bends to guest in the washing of feet, the human bond is stripped to bare essentials. There is an ancient Celtic proverb to the effect that "one who bids me to eat wishes me to live." Here is friendship, good-will, human sympathy and love in crystalline form. Here without alloy, is human being, mutually recognized and mutually affirmed.

The guest is, at first, a suppliant, needy, and dependent. The guest's needs are the most essential human needs: food, warmth, shelter, clothing, and companionship, which correspond to the essential resources of any host, rich or poor. The guest, by the defining necessities of being a stranger and a wayfarer, is cast in the posture of the suppliant. And the host—walled, roofed, warmed, provisioned—is in a relative position of power. Nevertheless, the ritual requirements dictate that hosts bend to guests, wash their feet, and attend to their needs. Hospitality dispels the inequalities of fortune and necessity which mark off host from guest; for no distinctions are more fortuitous and readily reversed than are these. Today's guest is tomorrow's host; today's host tomorrow's guest. Necessity breaks even the strong. The sons of heaven too go darkened in death. The Greeks have but one word for both guest and host, *xenos*, "stranger." Language best makes no distinction where necessity does not. Besides, there is more truth to human unity than to human diversity. We are—for one another—shelter, nourishment, warmth, and care. Guest requires host and host requires guest; and both are one. In the bond of hospitality we glimpse the human bond in its most simple and self-revealing form. *Politeia*, the political bond, is merely an expansion of this same care and good will. The city which forgets how to care for the stranger has forgotten how to care for itself.

"Man is by nature," writes Aristotle, "a political animal."[34] There is no instinct or conviction more Greek than this one. And if we understand its significance with appropriate clarity and scope we will see that in these words our three thematic concerns converge: nature, necessity, and friendship. To say that human being is naturally political is not to speak of unscrupulous cunning, deception, and self-aggrandizement. These distortions must come home to roost elsewhere. To say that human nature is political is to say that our essential possibilities require human interaction for their realization. Because we are many we are possible. Resident here is the assurance that our lives are enabled, enhanced, and graced by the presence of other human beings, rather than undercut, threatened, and denied by them. Nothing is more Greek than the embracing of the human consortium, the web of human kinship in the earth, in life, and in death. Nothing is more Greek than the simple instinct to cherish the company of others, the simple, hopeful predisposition in favor of human companionship. "No one," writes Aristotle, "would choose the whole world if it meant enjoying it alone."[35] The Greeks clung to the conviction that we have arms above all not to inflict or to ward off blows but to embrace one another.

Here we have it. A set, a frame of mind, a landscape. As such it must now slip back and become the ground against which our reflections on Camus will unfold. But it will never be out of sight, whether it is ever focused upon or not. Clearly, the central categories for our interpretation of Camus' thought are now present: nature, happiness, youth, necessity, limits, suffering, oppression, solidarity, compassion, and friendship. How close do these categories bring us to Camus' concerns? I believe they bring us about as close as we may come to a man whose silences were as deep as his words. In his last interview before his death, on December 20, 1959, Camus was asked what he felt had been neglected in his work. He is said to have answered impatiently: "The dark part, that which is blind and instinctive in me."[36] What is blind and instinctive, one's heart, must necessarily remain somehow dark, but not entirely. Camus used to say he had "a Greek heart" and we are already on our way toward an understanding of what this could mean: to have a Greek heart.

NOTES

1. Herakleitos, in "Herakleitos: The Extant Fragments," tr. Guy Davenport, *The American Poetry Review* 7, no. 1 (1978): 14, #2.

2. *Ibid.*, #15.

3. *Ibid.*, #17.

4. *Ibid.*, p. 15, #20.

5. Aristotle, *Metaphysics*, 980 a 22–28, tr. W. D. Ross, in *The Basic Works of Aristotle*, ed. Richard McKeon, New York: Random House, 1941.

6. Plato, *Phaidros*, 230 a, tr. R. Hackforth, in *Plato/The Collected Dialogues*, ed. Edith Hamilton and Huntington Cairns, Bollingen Series, no. 71, New York: Pantheon, 1961.

7. Herakleitos, *op. cit.*, p. 16, #45.

8. Plato, *Laws*, 766 a, tr. A. E. Taylor, in *Collected Dialogues*, *op. cit.*

9. Augustine, *De Trinitate*, 10.5.7, translation mine.

10. Sophokles, *Philoktetes*, 902–903, tr. David Grene, University of Chicago Press, 1957.

11. "The Hymn to the Earth," in *The Homeric Hymns*, tr. Charles Boer, Chicago: Swallow, 1970, pp. 5–6.

12. Euripides, *Hekyba*, 906–911, tr. William Arrowsmith, University of Chicago Press, 1958.

13. Euripides, *Bacchai*, 396–401, tr. William Arrowsmith, University of Chicago Press, 1959.

14. *Ibid.*, 396–401.

15. Euripides, *Alkestis*, 63, tr. Richmond Lattimore, University of Chicago Press, 1955.

16. *Ibid.*, 962–990.

17. *Ibid.*, 779–785, 799.

18. Plotinus, *Enneads*, 3.2.9–11, translation mine.

19. Aristotle, *Politics*, 1253 a 28–29, tr. Benjamin Jowett, in *Basic Works*, *op. cit.*

20. Thucydides, *The Peloponnesian War*, tr. Rex Warner, Baltimore: Penguin, 1954, p. 360.

21. *Ibid.*, p. 363.

22. Plato, *Republic*, 360d, tr. Paul Shorey, in *Collected Dialogues*, *op. cit.*

23. *Ibid.*, 359d–360a.

24. Aristotle, *Nicomachean Ethics*, 1159 a 4–5, tr. W. D. Ross, in *Basic Works*, *op. cit.*

25. Euripides, *Herakles*, 122–123, tr. William Arrowsmith, University of Chicago Press, 1956.

26. *Ibid.*, 1396.

27. *Ibid.*, 1105–1107.

28. *Ibid.*, 1206.

29. Euripides, *The Suppliant Women*, 292–293, tr. Frank William Jones, University of Chicago Press, 1958.

30. *Ibid.*, 768.

31. *Ibid.*, 949–954.

32. Euripides, *Herakles*, 1338–1339, *op. cit.*

33. Aischylos, *The Libation Bearers*, 702–703, tr. Richmond Lattimore, University of Chicago Press, 1953.

34. Aristotle, *Politics*, 1253 a 2, in *Basic Works*, *op. cit.*

35. Aristotle, *Nicomachean Ethics*, 1169 b 18, translation mine.

36. Albert Camus, *Essais littéraires*, Paris: Gallimard, 1962, p. 1925, translation mine.

ONE

Sisyphus

O my soul, do not aspire to
immortal life, but exhaust
the limits of the possible.

—Pindar

Our first concern is necessarily with beginnings, with the soil and the stuff from which everything else in Camus comes to be. "Every artist," writes Camus, "keeps within himself a single source which nourishes during his lifetime what he is and what he says."[1] Camus traces his own origins back to his first published essays, written in his twenty-second year, and still further back to the world of poverty and sunlight to which those earliest writings were so revealingly, even if clumsily, faithful (1). Poverty and the sun—already we find here the duality and the struggle which course through Camus' thinking from beginning to end, without resolution. Always light and always shadow. Always the warmth of passion wedded to cold indifference.

> What is more complex than the birth of thought? The right explanation is always double, at least. Greece teaches us this, Greece to which we must always return. Greece is both shadow and light. We are well aware, aren't we, if we come from the South, that the sun has its black side?[2]

And yet we cannot speak appropriately of dualism in Camus' work; for he speaks always of one world, a world of both poverty and sunlight, of a single sky from which both beauty and indifference descend upon mortals. "What more can I hope for," asks Camus, "than the power to exclude nothing and to learn to weave from strands of black and white one rope tautened to the breaking point?"[3] Like Augustine, who in this and in many other matters may be said to have been his mentor, Camus lived on the very edge

of a fundamental dualism without ever giving way to the release
from contradiction which dualism promises.

We must turn now to what Camus has called "the birth of
thought." At first, the largesse of sensual grandeur and the stran-
gling grip of poverty are not ideas nor images nor words. They are
sheer experience, bestowed and known in silence. And for this,
their silence, they are not less real nor less true. Camus never knew
the voice of his father; and his mother was mute. Born into a dense
and rich silence, Camus was not inclined to doubt the presence or
the stature of feelings, bonds, or truths which are left unspoken.
Herein lies his first and perhaps most profound difference from
Sartre, who entitled his autobiography *The Words*, and in which he
says of himself: "I began my life as I shall no doubt end it: amidst
books."[4] Camus, on the other hand, nearly avoided books altogether. His mother was unable to read and Camus' studies were
met at home with curious indifference. In fact, Camus told of his
frightening great-uncle, the head of the clan, that he had threatened to shoot anyone who would dare to teach young Albert Latin.
Each day, between home and school, Camus would journey from
one world to quite another. While Sartre learned from his grandfather's library what it might mean to think of "nothingness," Camus
learned from his mother, with her simple tangible certainties drawn
in close around her, what it might mean to think of "nothing."[5]

Ideas spring easily and prolifically into our minds from books.
When one begins with formed words, with an ever-flowing stream
of conversation and reading, it is silence that is difficult to attain.
The fullness of silence is emptied until silence is known as mere
pause or absence or inadvertence. And yet, when one begins with
silence, words emerge slowly, laboriously so. They must be
uprooted from the dark soil of experience and carefully transplanted
in what Sokrates knew to be the less sustaining, less enduring world
of written language.[6] Words born of silence are few and precious to
those who bear them. "We live with a few familiar ideas," writes
Camus.

> Two or three. We polish and transform them according to the socie-
> ties and the men we happen to meet. It takes ten years to have an
> idea that is really one's own—that one can talk about. This is a bit
> discouraging, of course. But we gain from this a certain familiarity
> with the splendor of the world. Until then, we have seen it face to
> face. Now we need to step aside to see its profile.[7]

To form an image, an idea, a word—the three are not separable
in ancient Greek understanding—is to step aside from experience,
to turn the world askance without losing sight of it, without losing
touch with it altogether. This is what it means, in simplest terms,
to abstract—which would seem to be the essence of art—to see no
longer face to face but in profile. Looking face to face, our eyes
meet; we are personally and uniquely engaged, seer in seen. Often
we glimpse our own immediate reflection or effect. To view in
profile, however, is to see from a greater personal distance, at some
remove from the private and the particular. One approaches the essential, the nature of the seen object. Camus himself describes "a
taste for *expression* as evidence of decadence," and goes on to comment that "Greek sculpture starts to decline as soon as the statues
begin to smile and have an expression in their eyes."[8] Indeed, ar-
chaic Greek art prefers the profile (or, in sculpture, the cow-eyed
stare, which is its three-dimensional equivalent); and this is not a
preference born of limited technical capacity but a substantive preference for the impersonal, the objective, or the essential. And this
same preference is evident in Camus' thinking. He admires Greek
drama whose "aim," he says, "was not to create *a character*";[9] and,
in introducing his own dramatic works, he confesses to "liking only
one kind of play."

> After a rather long experience as director, actor, and dramatist, it
> seems to me that there is no true theatre without language and style,
> nor any dramatic work which does not, like our classical drama and
> the Greek tragedians, involve human fate in all its simplicity and
> grandeur.[10]

In short, Camus strove to be an "objective writer,"[11] whose work would not be an activity of self-expression but rather one of disclosure, of bearing witness. "A work of art," writes Camus, "is a confession, and I must bear witness."[12] And that to which he must bear witness is nothing less than what he has called "human fate in all its simplicity and grandeur." Such a witness will require that he turn his own experiences askance, that he know both poverty and the sun in profile. He must find images in which every element of individuality has been crushed like so many grapes and in which humanity has been distilled to a point of transparent clarity. Clearly, Camus thought himself to have found such images in Greek myth (2). Here his own most silent instincts found voice with a balance and a resonance which he was otherwise helpless to give them. When Camus says that "a man's work is nothing but this slow trek to rediscover, through the detours of art, those two or three great and simple images in whose presence his heart first opened,"[13] surely he must have in mind, at least on one expansive level, the three mythical figures of Sisyphus, Prometheus, and Nemesis, who served as the patrons and paradigms for his entire literary and philosophical endeavor. And we too, in tracing that endeavor, must have these three images in mind. First, Sisyphus (3).

Sisyphus, the legendary founder of Ephyra (later Corinth), which he is supposed to have built as a base for his piracy and brigandage, is something of a rogue, to be sure. According to one tradition, Sisyphus is the actual father of Odysseus, as the result of his having raped Antiklea, the wife of Laertes, who is usually reputed to be the father of the wily hero of Troy. Indeed, Odysseus' epic cunning and wile would be quite easily explained if he were the son of Sisyphus, whom Homer describes as "the craftiest of mortals." After all, it is not everyone who manages to trick Hades (Pluto), lord of the dead, from the underworld and shackle him under the sun so that no one can die. And like most famed tricksters he adds insult to injury. Even when Ares rescues Death and mortals resume mortality, Sisyphus foremost among them, he tricks Death a sec-

one time. Prior to his death, Sisyphus instructs his wife Merope to neglect his funeral libations when he is gone. Then, in the underworld, he complains to Persephone, the captive wife of Hades, that he is not receiving his due. In fact, he persuades her to grant him a brief reprieve so that he might return to life and see that the proper libations are poured. Of course, as soon as he sees again the light of day, his pledge to return at once to death is worth not a penny. Sisyphus turns his back on death and on the gods; and he resumes his less than fully admirable life, which he nevertheless treasures.

Mortals never write the last chapter, however. The gods always have their way in the end; for they have all the power. Hermes (Mercury) is sent to drag back Sisyphus to death and to a peculiar necessity specially designed for him, from which there can be no literal escape. A trick for the trickster. When Odysseus descends among the hordes of the dead, he gives us an account of Sisyphus' fate, which he then witnesses.

> Also I saw Sisyphus. He was suffering strong pains, and with both arms embracing the monstrous stone, struggling with hands and feet alike, he would try to push the stone upward to the crest of the hill, but when it was on the point of going over the top, the force of gravity turned it backward and the pitiless stone rolled back down to the level. He then tried once more to push it up, straining hard, and sweat ran all down his body, and over his head a cloud of dust rose.[14]

It is upon this bizarre punishment that Camus focuses his attention; for he discerns herein an image of human fate. In Camus' own recounting of the myth, all of the essential elements— Sisyphus' cunning, "his scorn of the gods, his hatred of death, and his passion for life," his eluding of death and his forced return, his endlessly repetitive ascents and descents of the cursed hill with his rock—all of these mythical elements are fired afresh, melted down, and re-cast. "Myths," says Camus, "are made for the imagination to breathe life into them";[15] and in saying this he is describing his own endeavor to tell again this story and to fire again our imaginations with a glimpse of human fate, its simplicity and its grandeur.

There is clearly a parallel in Camus' rendering between, on the one hand, Sisyphus' return to life from the underworld upon the pretext of seeing to his proper funeral rites and, on the other hand, Sisyphus' return to the foot of the hill to shoulder his rock still another time. As Camus retells this myth, both returns become returns to life. They are fused together to provide a single complex image. In both instances, Sisyphus resumes and thus reaffirms life after having encountered death in profile—at once his own death and Death itself—whether in the underworld or in the rock makes no matter. Both, after all, are images of mortality. The certainty of death and of its implications—namely, that in death nothing remains of one's efforts and energies and commitments, that in death one is simply undone—this certainty is indeed a crushing truth, which we will explore further in our reflections on the absurd. It is this truth that Sisyphus is forced to encounter and to which he is yoked. When Sisyphus is dragged back to the underworld and, later, made to shoulder his rock, he does not literally die. He is dragged into and condemned not to death but to an awareness of his death. The issue here is not death but mortality. Plants and animals first live and then die. Human beings live and die at once when they live and die consciously. Consciousness permits us to die imaginatively before we die in fact and thenceforth to live with a view toward death. Once consciousness is expanded to encompass death and thus life in the face of death, we have a new choice to make.

The choice is not, however, whether to die or not to die. Death is chained only in stories, and then only briefly. Death is a matter of necessity and not of choice. Our choice is whether to grant or to deny to death its supposedly necessary implications, its pretentions, its assumed airs. Camus, perhaps surprisingly, speaks of possible victory and explains that "crushing truths perish from being acknowledged";[16] but the meaning here requires a subtle human

squint to be seen. The victory over death is no more literal than
was Sisyphus' encounter with death. The victory is moral, not literal. We may recall the Melians before the Athenian generals. The
force of the Athenians was irresistible; but their claims, their airs,
were quite deniable. The Melians knew that their annihilation was
certain; their grip on their own lives would never suffice. But their
integrity was another matter. In fact, they refuted the Athenians by
choosing death before degradation. Similarly, once Iphigenia realizes that there is no hiding from the entire Greek army and from
her decreed doom, she sees before her a choice and makes it. She
no longer pleads for a life which necessity will never allow her. Instead, she turns to Klytemnestra and says:

> And now hear me, Mother,
> What thing has seized me and I have conceived
> In my heart.
>   I shall die—I am resolved—
> And having fixed my mind I want to die
> Well and gloriously, putting away
> From me whatever is weak and ignoble.[17]

We find the same fate and the same human splendor in the story
of another youth whose loveliness crests at the very moment when
she must die. Like Antigone and Iphigenia, Polyxena shall be still
another bride for death. Again we see the passion for life and the
hatred of death at their fullest pitch while confronted with the inex-
orable. Face on with death, human rebellion must take the de-
vious, cunning path of scorn which to all but the knowing conscious eye passes for a too easy acceptance. The eye needs practice
in discernment and with this in mind we would do well to study
the figure of Polyxena. By the vote of the full assembly of Greek
warriors, the epitome of false pride and arrogant imperialism, Polyxena, the beautiful young daughter of Hekyba, is to be sacrificed
as a victim on the grave of Achilles. Once it is clear that there is to
be no such thing as pity she takes the only course there is and walks

to her death. She will not be dragged and she will have nothing to
do with slavery. As we listen to Talthybius' account of her last minutes we must try to imagine her happy.

> The whole army of the Greeks,
> drawn up in ranks, was present at the execution,
> waiting and watching while Polyxena was led
> by Achilles' son slowly through the center of the camp
> and up the tomb. I stood nearby, while behind her
> came a troop of soldiers purposely appointed
> to prevent her struggles . . .
> Then, [the son of Achilles]
> grasping his sword by its golden hilt, he slipped it
> from the sheath, and made a sign to the soliders
> to seize her. But she spoke first:
> "Wait, you Greeks
> who sacked my city! Of my own free will I die.
> Let no man touch me. I offer my throat
> willingly to the sword. I will not flinch.
> But let me be free for now. Let me die free.
> I am of royal blood, and I scorn to die
> the death of a slave."
> "Free her!" the army roared,
> and Agamemnon ordered his men to let her go.
> The instant they released their hold, she grasped her robes
> at the shoulder and ripped them open down the sides
> as far as the waist, exposing her naked breasts,
> bare and lovely like a sculptured goddess.
> Then she sank, kneeling on the ground, and spoke
> her most heroic words:
> "Strike, captain.
> Here is my breast. Will you stab me there?
> Or in the neck? Here is my throat, bared
> for your blow."[18]

Greek drama is indeed replete with human victims. And it is
those very victims, the slaves, the utterly weak and helpless, who

find the crack, the eye of the needle, through which human pride
is saved. "Every beautiful thing has a natural pride," writes Camus,
"in its own beauty."[19] Mortals are, indeed, beautiful things; and
nowhere is their pride more resplendent than in their mortality,
when it is conscious. Iphigenia truly shines when she commands
her mourners to dance rather than to grovel and weep, as does
Polyxena when she bares her breasts in defiance of Agamemnon
and his male rabble. Here is human pride in its most rarefied yet
demotic form. Here is human royalty which is the common inheri-
tance of all who will not be slaves. Euripides in all his plays seeks
to wrest virtue and heroism once and for all from the gods and the
warlords, from the privileged and the powerful, and to bestow them
upon the disinherited and the doomed, in whom human fate and
beauty are transparently manifest. This same commitment to the
democratization of human excellence lies at the origins and the
center of Camus' work. Sisyphus must be understood as a paradigm
whose scorn for the gods, whose hatred of death, and whose passion
for life may be glimpsed wherever the arc of human *physis*, the living of death, and the dying of life, are conscious. At first we must
focus our attention here and overlook the rest. For Sisyphus is
indeed a rogue and the many metamorphoses of Sisyphus in
Camus' writings contain too their unsavory elements. For example,
Camus does not, to be sure, commend Meursault or Caligula to us
in every respect. Their truths are partial truths, whose truth, however, is to be our first, though not final, concern.

These first partial truths revealed by the most fundamental stirrings of consciousness pervade Camus' early writings. A close look
anywhere will disclose the face of Sisyphus, his beloved world, his
hateful rock, and his supreme scorn. We need only survey his writings (as in selections 4–21) to sense how it is that Camus proposes
to give flesh to this ancient myth. And there is little purpose to my
choreographing the reader's movement through those passages. Let
it suffice instead to trace again the simplest contours of the image of
Sisyphus and of his truths as they unfold in the passages cited.

The kingdom of Sisyphus is of this world (4), a kingdom of finite possibilities, a kingdom whose limits are first known instinctively. The limits of the humanly possible are as close and as inescapable as one's own body. Our bodies are our first teachers (5–6); and the first truths are identical with breath and blood, sense and passion. Before anything else, truthfulness is immediacy, the immediate giving way to the flow of what is simply, immediately given, the giving way to desire, to love, and to their altogether worldly objects (7–8). Human love appropriately limits itself to the possible; for it is inevitably limited to the possible. All else is delusion. To love what is proper to others or what only a life hereafter might afford (9) or even to love immoderately beyond the counsels of balance and harmony are all to love wrongly. Envy (10), hope, and excess (11) all violate the appropriate scale of human desire and love. For all its explicit hedonism, Camus' affirmation of sense and passion is inherently ascetic. From the outset he requires of himself and of us a rigor which may be described as a keeping of strict human kosher. The kingdom of Sisyphus is not only of this world but is, more pointedly, a kingdom of mortals where human attention is focused upon the human (12). If there is another, divine being and kingdom, they too shall have to heed and respect human mortality (13). The task is to exclude nothing (14) and thus to include everything—gods, beasts, and mortals—without confusion (15).

The limits of the human are not, however, simply coincident with the limits of the body. The mind too—with its movements of imagination, thought, and will—belongs to the kingdom of this world. The mind too possesses its certainties and its passions. Now the mind is the human organ of invention (which means both discernment and creation); and necessity is the mother of invention. It is indeed the mind which brings human beings face to face with their ultimate necessity, death. Human beings are called mortals not because they die once but because they die over and over in their imaginings. Human beings are called mortals not because they are going to die but because they know that they are going to die and live accordingly. It is indeed in that "accordingly" that wisdom resides. But the mind, like the body, has its own peculiar temptations to delusion and excess, which it must overcome. In fact, body and mind tend to balance one another's distortions when each is given its due (16–17).

Although the body may well catch the scent of its own lurking death and although the mind is no stranger to life, it might be argued that Camus both finds life to be at first richer without consciousness and finds consciousness to be sheer illusion without consciousness of death. Without drawing permanent lines which would assuredly falsify such matters, Camus seems to assign life to the body and death to the mind. And the truth in such a designation would be that human nature and thus human tragedy are nowhere so poignant as in youth when, even if only for an instant, one's body is unmindful of anything but the life with which it overflows while one's mind is obsessed with thoughts of death. In such moments, whatever their catalyst, life and death, mind and body collide. Like two poles of fundamentally opposing current, as soon as they are crossed they shower the human sky with a dancing fire. "There is no love of life," writes the young Camus, "without despair of life."[20] Herein lies the constitutive human contradiction which is all but unendurable (18–22). But endure we must; for therein lies our nature, our beauty, and our pride.

At this point where human will creates an alternative between literal victory and literal defeat, a place to stand between divine exemption and bestial subjection, human art and human wisdom converge; and human being reveals itself as the consummately tragic work of art. The fuller the life, the happier the life and, paradoxically, the happier the death. The fuller the life, the more heightened the tragedy when life goes darkened in death with its eyes and arms opened wide (23). The sheer fact of death empties life, pours it out until there is no more; but the consciousness of death brings life to fruition, ripens it to bursting, like a fruit on the vine. Indeed, Camus saw around him life being lived just so, poi-

gnant with tragedy and death (24). And there is no more serious
work than this. "I feel certain," writes Camus, "that the true, the
only, progress of civilization, the only one to which a man devotes
himself from time to time, lies in creating conscious deaths."[21]
Such a man was Patrice Mersault, the central figure in Camus' first
novel, to which we must now turn our attention.

Once he had decided at the age of twenty-two that he must
write, just as he must swim, at the insistence of his body, Camus
very soon began to plan his first novel. At this point his vision and
his talent were fresh and unformed. Several years later he was to
write that "the true work of art is the one which says least."[22] And
indeed it may be said of his first attempted novel, A Happy Death,
that it says too much. Herein the young author endeavored to spill
out in one story all that was on his mind and in his heart and the
result was unwieldy and dissatisfying. In fact, so great was Camus'
dissatisfaction with this first novel, which contained within it the
germs of so much of his later work, that he decided against its
publication. Instead, he chose the longer, more careful route of
slowly unfolding his vision and his art in successive works and
stages. Nevertheless, we may find in this first major work, however
embryonic it may be judged to be, a clarion statement of his first
and foundational concerns and insights.

Before deciding upon the title A Happy Death (La Mort
heureuse), Camus had called his projected work A Happy Life (La
Vie heureuse). The change of title is quite appropriate and telling
for reasons which will become evident in time. Now, we may take
note of a not so evident point of reference for this change. In both
titles the focus is clearly upon happiness; and it is a commonplace
in ancient Greek literature that no one may be called happy until
he or she is dead. Before death one may be called fortunate; but
only in death may one be said to be happy. "In every matter," says
Solon to Croesus, "we must mark well the end; for oftentimes God
gives men a gleam of happiness, and then plunges them into

ruin."[23] We must recall here the words which Camus (appropriately but inaccurately) attributed to Oedipus: "All is well." Only of the happy may it be said that all is well; and only in death may this be said with assurance. The crucial insight here is that what the Greeks understood as happiness is not an ephemeral feeling but an enduring quality. The happy life is the life that possesses a certain rightness of which each one is the worst judge in one's own case. We see the happiness or the rightness of others' lives more easily than we see our own.[24] Happiness is a virtue or excellence which a being possesses and displays, a well-being which is beheld rather than felt. And the well-being of human nature requires both completion and objectivity for its assessment. Finally, only in death is this completion and objectivity achieved.

Strictly speaking, there is, then—for the Greeks and, I propose, for Camus—no such thing as a happy life. There is, however, such a thing as a life consumed by the desire and the striving for happiness. Such a life was Patrice Mersault's; but not at first. Mersault begins as a nondescript white-collar worker in Algiers, absorbed in making a living and satisfied with whatever his routines offer him: a lunch with Emmanuel, a cigarette on his balcony, a night with Marthe. He says yes to everything but nothing matters. Fortunately, however, he finds a mentor. Roland Zagreus, a man of considerable wealth and of even more considerable passion, points out to Mersault: "You live badly. Like a barbarian."[25] They shatter one another's illusions. Both men are unhappy. Zagreus has an excuse in his two amputated legs; but Mersault is without excuse for his unhappiness. Zagreus puts the matter clearly: "You, Mersault, with a body like yours, your one duty is to live and be happy."[26] All that is lacking, Mersault thinks, is freedom, to be free from the exhausting round of work and rest required simply to maintain himself. In his own words:

> Even now, if I had the time . . . I would only have to let myself go. Everything else that would happen to me would be like rain on a

stone. The stone cools off and that's fine. Another day, the sun
bakes it. I've always thought that's exactly what happiness would
be.[27]

In part, Mersault is unhappy because he has little money and
must work for what he has. But he is also lacking inwardly. His
own will for happiness and his own revolt against necessity have not
yet caught flame. Finally, the proddings of Zagreus and the sight of
utter human desolation in the person of Cardona the barrelmaker
bring him to his own despair and to the passion for life which is its
natural child. Mersault rebels (25); and the logic of rebellion
begins. The demand of happiness silences all else (26–27). His
murdering Zagreus is itself barely noticed: "The next morning,
Mersault killed Zagreus, came home, and slept all afternoon." This
quest for life and happiness is solitary; and, quite inadvertently, the
conclusion is drawn that for one to live another must die. The only
misery of any note is apparently one's own.

There can be no question here of tracing Mersault's journey
toward a happy death, except to point out that it is circular. After
still another "brutal manifestation of life,"[28] he returns home to
the same sun and the same sea but with new resolve and with an
ever-deepening consciousness (28). His quest turns inward, always
reaching toward his impersonal ideal of a stone, warm in the sun
and cool in the rain. He comes to love Lucienne. He watches her
wed her gestures to the world (29) and he seeks to match his own
gestures to hers (30). In the midst of a beauty, love, and friendship
which had always been present but had never been fully embraced,
Mersault opens himself to a simple communion with all that is
(31–34). He excludes nothing and gives way to his natural well-
suitedness to the world. The thin gauze between will and world,
between inner and outer reality, begins to dissolve. His consciousness
is sheer release to the sun, its warmth, its revealing brilliance, its
blinding glare, its indifference, and its black side. Nothing else
matters now but a vast will and consciousness which dwell as one
within him. And in his giving way to these, Mersault finds exactly

what he thought he would find: happiness in human terms (3 5–36).

"Strive not, dear soul," says Pindar, "after a deathless life." [29] If not deathless, then deathful. The abandonment of Mersault is finally just that, abandonment. "Mark the end," writes Solon; for therein lies the mettle of human happiness or well-being. As Mersault approaches his death, which he describes as an "accident of happiness," [30] a tremendous hope and a tremendous despair join hands. [31] Mersault dies (37). The swimmer loses his buoyancy and sinks into the warm sea. He becomes a stone, warm in the sun, cool in the rain, lonely in the cold earth. Sisyphus and his rock are one.

"When we are stripped down to a certain point," writes Camus, "nothing leads anywhere any more, hope and despair are equally groundless, and the whole of life can be summed up in an image." [32] It is just such an image—bare and elemental—which Camus wished to present in his first novel. His first words were to be grounded in silence and were to say as little as possible. If Camus was to be assured of the truthful movement of his thought and speech, he must begin in the beginning and proceed with slow care. In these terms A *Happy Death* was a failure and required that he begin again. Patrice Mersault and his vast consciousness are stripped down to a point, without extension. In *The Stranger* Camus reaches back with his imagination to "point zero," [33] to the hypothetical absence of consciousness, incarnate. Meursault is indeed an image, a being of our imagination, an experiment of thought, as close as we are able to come to a zero point, a living, mindless rock. Or, better yet, a human beast, innocent and untamed.

Camus, many years after writing *The Stranger*, lamented of himself that he had "ceased to have any but brief emotions, devoid of the long echo that memory gives. The sensitivity of dogs," he suggests, "is like that." [34] If we press such a state to its limit and remove from it the element of conscious exasperation, I suspect that we approach the pristine condition in which Meursault moves and has his being. Meursault lives the life of his body to its limits, a life of always immediate sensuality. He knows nothing either of regret or of hope.[35] The past and the future are as nothing to him; for they exist only in imaginative consciousness. As Augustine points out with brilliant clarity in Book Eleven of his *Confessions*, without imaginative consciousness, the past does not exist because it is no longer, the future does not exist because it is not yet, and that present which may not be divided into past and future does not exist because it is without extension. In short, without imagination and consciousness, time does not exist and thus neither does the self, which is inherently temporal. Meursault moves from discrete moment to discrete moment, like a rock, now warm in the sun, now cool in the sea, now desirous, now satisfied. "The body knows nothing of hope (or, we may add, of despair). All it knows is the beating of its own heart."[36] Meursault's life is the life of his body with a layer of mood or feeling so thin as to be transparent to the state of his body.[37]

Meursault's near mindlessness is not, however, a matter of sheer deprivation. Rather, Meursault's life displays an undeniable fulness and integrity. The world that bestows itself on him, moment by moment, and in which he indulges without question or qualm, is lavish and benign. It is sufficiently pleasant, varied, and undemanding that he is never once driven beyond it to imagine alternatives. The simple truth which bears witness to itself in Meursault's life is that the force of sensual nature may suffice to move and to shape a human life. Meursault is buoyed up, carried along, and delighted in life as a swimmer in the sea. Here is point zero and its truth: human beings are sensual animate beings. A partial truth, to be sure; but Camus discloses its truth first and its partiality second, lest we fail to give this fact its due or fail to notice it at all. Camus' creation of Meursault brings all the strange excitement of discovering a fragment of some ancient, misplaced treasure, a mere shard from which we may nevertheless project the remaining whole and which in itself is lovely. Indeed, Meursault is a fragment of a once and future ideal race, one initial episode in Camus' unlikely odyssey back, or forward, towards an image of human nature.

Meursault's pre-lapsarian contentment is, however, too good to be true, given what we know of the whole truth. The "balance of the day," the "spacious calm of this beach," Meursault recalls, "on which I had been happy"[38] was shattered by an altogether inadvertent act, no more premeditated or voluntary than the pulsing of his heart which had long accommodated itself to the rhythm of the sun. Unfortunately, the act is, in this instance, murder. Yet with even more honesty may it be said of this Meursault that he killed "in the innocence of his heart."[39] No logic prompts Meursault to this act which possesses no motive whatsoever. Apparently stones are not only warmed in the sun; they are also led to kill. The murder simply happens to Meursault as it does to the Arab, though with admittedly different consequences. The Arab is dead and Meursault is undone.

As in A *Happy Death* the turning point here is an act of murder. Once again the sun-soaked earth and the murder of another human being are embraced without pause. However, in *The Stranger*, this act marks the beginning of Meursault's "undoing."[40] (Actually the word here is *malheur*, "unhappiness.") Meursault loses his earlier happiness and must find another. It would perhaps not violate Camus' meanings if we were to think of part one of *The Stranger* as entitled "Natural Happiness" and part two as entitled "Conscious Happiness," which will be consummated, as we would expect, in a conscious or happy death. We cannot possibly follow here with any closeness Meursault's undoing, his unhappiness, nor his attainment of a new and fuller happiness. If we read the selections from *The Stranger* with both Sisyphus and Patrice Mersault in mind our own thoughts will surely find their proper course. For now, these present comments must be brief.

With the murder of the Arab, Meursault rapidly loses his innocence, or, more precisely, he loses his innocent state; for he is as yet unconscious and thus incapable of recognizing his deed or himself in his deed. At first it is only the most immediately personal consequences of his act which strip him of his once oblivious contentment, his earlier happiness. He is driven from his finite paradise and confined to a cell which is sensually neither benign nor lavish. Thus he is driven from immediacy quite literally because each immediate moment now contains so very little. He discovers consciousness by default (38). Sensually deprived, Meursault must look elsewhere for fullness. He stumbles upon time or rather temporality when his imagination, like a sleeping limb, begins to stir. His discoveries (inner time, memory, fiction, sleep, dreams) are childish in their proportions and may strike us as merely playful.[41] Indeed, we might easily pass over these first movements of consciousness unless we pause and realize what it is that we are witnessing: the emergence of consciousness from point zero. Meursault discovers his inner life as unwittingly as if he had found a flight of stairs in what had always appeared to be a one-level home. He turns one corner after another in what proves to be a vast labyrinthian world. We may recall the words of Augustine which Camus must have known well:

> I have become a problem to myself, like land which a farmer works only with difficulty and at the cost of much sweat. For I am not now investigating the tracts of the heavens, or measuring the distance of the stars, or trying to discover how the earth hangs in space. I am investigating myself, my memory, my mind.[42]

This labor, or play—it is both—bears its first splendid fruit when Meursault, after overhearing the same conversation for months, recognizes in it his own inner voice. Now he not only thinks but he knows his thoughts. Like someone who had never gazed into a pond or a mirror before, Meursault experiences his first moment of self-consciousness. The well is struck and now there is no holding it back.

"So I learned," reflects Meursault, "that even after a single day's experience of the outside world a man could easily live a hundred years in prison."[43] From these words it is clear that Meursault has overcome the despoilment of his sensual life wrought by his imprisonment. But this victory is a mere prelude to his ensuing struggle with a far more crushing truth, the certainty of his imminent death. There are no exceptions to the guillotine's deadly accuracy. Finally Meursault permits himself no illusions; and with the stripping away of all illusions of immortality, Meursault becomes universal. The valence of each detail in this story grows before our eyes as we approach myth. The cell walls expand to enclose us all. The world which Meursault found and still finds so unsparing in its gifts is lethal in the end. In being made to stand before a judge and witnesses, before his friends, strangers, and members of the press, to be told that he is going to die, Meursault is, in fact, privileged. The sentence is universal; what is unique to him is that the State has at its own expense choreographed a moment of consciousness which brings him to the brink of wisdom. The well is struck, the sky darkens and sends its densest rains, consciousness becomes now a rising, swelling river. Consciousness and death, freedom and necessity race toward one another with no prospect of prize. Any victory will be as subtle as an apparition.

In his struggle with the priest (39), whom he sees as the agent of delusion, Meursault dons the mask of Sisyphus and gives voice to his passion for life, his hatred of death, and his scorn for the gods. The priest, and we too, are caught in a flood. Meursault speaks of a slow persistent breeze blowing against him and we feel the fatal burden gathering its mass. He walks into and against it, conscious of who he is, of how he has lived his life and why. He pits his few certainties against death. He lived indifferently, he killed indifferently, and he dies indifferently. He has matched his movements to the apathy which moves the sun and the stars. The sky has been both benign and indifferent toward him, one day setting before him a table fit for a god and the next day bending his neck to the blade as if he were a dumb beast fit for slaughter. So it is; and so has he been in his life, one day amiable, the next day deadly. Like

life itself, he meets with no complaints; and then for no reason at
all he changes his ways and is cursed for it. Yes, he and the universe are brothers. Let the others howl in rage. Tomorrow they will
go to the sea and laugh, as he too would, if he could.

We have witnessed in Camus' earliest novels the rise of consciousness from sensuality, the birth of thought and its struggle with
the most primitive of truths. Now we must consider the same event
as presented in the earliest of Camus' philosophical essays, *The
Myth of Sisyphus*. It was Camus' custom to explore each myth and
its proper concerns in several literary forms: fiction, essay, and
drama. Camus is masterfully lucid in his essays; and very little
commentary is required here to provide the context and connections which will allow his own words to speak to us straight on.
Camus describes the often quite pedestrian origins of consciousness
(40) and reminds us of the feel of those first stirrings. This emergent
consciousness at once poses a question, an issue to be decided: either we follow the path of consciousness or we turn aside or back
away from it. The patterns of avoidance are many, various, and
quite accessible. Whatever their pretext or peculiar form Camus
calls all such courses suicidal. The path which remains faithful to
the first data of consciousness, the first certainties of the mind, is,
on the other hand, arduous and harrowing.

The mind's most elemental certainties are at first truisms, things
which are as profoundly unknown as they are obvious: I live and
die; I crave living and I die anyway. If consciousness dwells along
with these truisms they become truths, living certainties which stalk
and haunt any life not long ago unmindful and content. What
Camus calls "the absurd" now looms, which he describes as our essential impossibility or contradiction. The absurd has no one for-
mulation or face. Rather, the absurd refers to our essential ill-
suitedness to this world wherever and whenever we encounter it.
The inalienable human calling is to pursue happiness; and yet the
necessary conditions for human happiness or well-being prove
always to be twofold and mutually exclusive. Every metamorphosis

of the absurd repeats this central contradiction. Augustine came to this very same insight and saw in our impossibility not an essential flaw but the mark of sin. And Camus seems never to have ceased considering this claim. For the most part, however, he draws back from such an idea. He was troubled enough by his own assertion of a human nature while professing ignorance of its source, without his going on to assert a primordial human sinfulness.

The mind seeks order, makes distinctions, measures, sorts, accepts and rejects possibilities. Sokrates once suggested that the mind cannot act with seriousness unless it assumes that some possibilities (arguments, works of art, deeds, lives, ideas, etc.) deserve more respect than others. And the mind does insist on taking itself seriously. All of the mind's movements—logical, aesthetic, ethical, and metaphysical—rest on its assumed capacity to discern real unevennesses in things. And yet Camus suggests that this assumption is without support and that the mind is cosmically alone and unwarranted in its concerns. The mind writes in sand at water's edge. It makes its distinctions as one might make a sound: to fill the void, to break an infinite silence, to hear itself. As soon as the mind is silent again, the silence is again infinite. No echo, no resonance, no response are forthcoming, ever. The mind seeks and requires rapport; but there can be no rapport between the rational and the irrational (41–42). Nevertheless these two most unlikely mates are wedded to each other in a fortuitous yet altogether necessary bond which Camus calls the absurd and which, he argues, must be preserved and pursued (43). The mind must understand its world in human terms, which is to say that it must be happy in its world in human terms. If what the mind must do cannot be done, then it must insist on being undone. The human ear is able, after all, to hear something being affirmed when a negation is negated. When the mind denies its own denial, something in it is affirmed. And to this it must cling (44).

The one initial temptation which must be resisted and which constitutes the first philosophical question is suicide, the dissolution of absurd consciousness however one manages it, whether by faith, metaphysics, routine, distraction, or a revolver. The first truthful assertion is the defiant finite assertion of consciousness and will in the face of their infinite denial. Wisdom and happiness, whatever else they entail, mean survival. The absurd hero is, then, first of all a survivor. Authentic consciousness is first of all self-consciousness. And will is self-assertion. If one's sole duty is to survive, then the only ethical criterion is a quantitative one: more life is better than less life. This is where matters stand with Camus' first absurd heroes. Like Sisyphus they are estimable. But they are also unacceptable. We cannot help but notice that they are all murderers. Surely this qualifies their innocence somewhat. Are we not meant to be disturbed by Meursault's wishing for "howls of execration" at his execution? Perhaps a part of us is in that very crowd of onlookers, howling or not. And what of Caligula, who is surely the most outrageous, and possibly the most winning, of the sons of Sisyphus?

In Caligula the ancient dream of the philosopher-king becomes a nightmare. In him power and absurd wisdom converge. "Men die; and they are not happy."[44] Of this much he is certain; and he sets out to permit no one in his empire any illusions to the contrary. He teaches the doctrine of the absurd not as a provisional, partial truth but as the whole truth, and carves it into law. He forgets the sun, shuns the body's demands and its truths. Instead, it is to be the moon, the impossible, or nothing. And when mortals drive such bargains it is always nothing and never the moon which they must settle for in the end. Indeed, mark his end (45). The murderous happiness of Caligula is less than convincingly happy.

Throughout the cycle of Sisyphus, Camus' absurd heroes are on the verge of a new discovery, a new truth, which is nevertheless reserved for Prometheus to herald and to embody. Of them all, Jan, the hero of *The Misunderstanding*, comes the closest to it. We may recall the story which Meursault says he must have read a thousand times (38). His concern is not simply for his own happiness but also for the happiness of his sister and mother. He leaves behind the sea, the sun, and even his young wife, for a time, to embrace his sister and mother, to join his will for their happiness to theirs. His gesture is one of love and of hospitality. He acknowledges the claim which others' desires and deprivations have upon him. In Jan's gracious plan we glimpse a wider and more fully human consciousness in what has been a long night of near nihilism; but it never dawns. True to Sisyphus, he conceals his goodwill and his true purposes with a touch of trickery. Indeed, the words which he wished to utter were nearly beyond belief even if stated in the simplest, most straightforward manner possible (46). The margin of misunderstanding is very slim in such matters, too slim for any but the most direct, unambiguous gestures and words. For now, Martha's conviction that in the present order we are never recognized stands fast; and the final word is still "No" (47–48). But the present order may be overturned, if a true rebel were to come along. For now "absurdity is king"; "but," writes Camus in his *Notebooks*, "love saves us from it."[45] We must await Prometheus, rebel, and lover of humankind.

NOTES

1. Camus, *Lyrical*, p. 6.
2. *Ibid.*, p. 357.
3. *Ibid.*, p. 169.
4. Jean-Paul Sartre, *The Words*, tr. Bernard Frechtman, Greenwich, Conn.: Fawcett, 1964, p. 25.
5. Cf. Camus, *Youthful*, pp. 243–244.
6. Cf. Plato, *Phaedrus*, 274d, ff., in *Collected Dialogues, op. cit.*
7. Camus, *Lyrical*, pp. 76–77.
8. Camus, *Notebooks I*, pp. 28–29.
9. *Ibid.*, p. 207.
10. Camus, *Plays*, p. x.

11. Cf. Camus, *Lyrical*, pp. vi, 159.

12. Camus, *Notebooks I*, p. 4.

13. Camus, *Lyrical*, p. 17.

14. Homer, *The Odyssey of Homer*, XI.593–600, tr. Richmond Lattimore, New York: Harper & Row, 1965, p. 183.

15. Camus, *Myth*, p. 89.

16. *Ibid*, p. 90.

17. Euripides, *Iphigenia in Aulis*, 1373–1377, tr. Charles R. Walker, University of Chicago Press, 1958.

18. Euripides, *Hekyba*, 521–526, 541–566, tr. William Arrowsmith, University of Chicago Press, 1958.

19. Camus, *Lyrical*, p. 69.

20. *Ibid*., p. 56.

21. *Ibid*, p. 77.

22. Camus, *Notebooks I*, p. 103.

23. Herodotus, *The Persian Wars*, 1.30–33, tr. George Rawlinson, New York: The Modern Library, 1942; cf. also Aristotle, *Nicomachean Ethics*, 1100a 3–9, in *Basic Works, op. cit.*

24. Cf. Aristotle, *Nicomachean Ethics*, 1169b 34, in *Basic Works, op. cit.*

25. Camus, *Death*, p. 27.

26. *Ibid*., p. 26.

27. *Ibid*., pp. 38–39.

28. *Ibid*., p. 51; cf. pp. 69–70.

29. Pindar, *Pythian Odes*, III. 61–62, translation mine.

30. Camus, *Death*, p. 131.

31. Cf. *ibid*., p. 133.

32. Camus, *Lyrical*, p. 37.

33. Cf. Camus, *Notebooks II*, p. 20.

34. *Ibid*., p. 141.

35. Camus, *Lyrical*, p. 94.

36. Cf. Camus, *Stranger*, p. 127.

37. Cf. *ibid*., p. 80.

38. *Ibid*., p. 76.

39. Camus, *Death*, p. 136.

40. Cf. Camus, *Stranger*, p. 76.

41. *Ibid*., p. 98.

42. Augustine, *Confessions*, X.16, tr. R. S. Pine-Coffin, Baltimore: Penguin, 1961.

43. Camus, *Stranger*, p. 98.

44. Camus, *Plays*, p. 8.

45. Camus, *Notebooks I*, p. 93.

Readings

1

As for myself, I know that my source is in *The Wrong Side and the Right Side*, in the world of poverty and sunlight I lived in for so long, whose memory still saves me from two opposing dangers that threaten every artist, resentment and self-satisfaction.

Poverty, first of all, was never a misfortune for me: it was radiant with light. Even my revolts were brilliant with sunshine. They were almost always, I think I can say this without hypocrisy, revolts for everyone, so that every life might be lifted into that light. There is no certainty my heart was naturally disposed to this kind of love. But circumstances helped me. To correct a natural indifference, I was placed halfway between poverty and the sun. Poverty kept me from thinking all was well under the sun and in history; the sun taught me that history was not everything. I wanted to change lives, yes, but not the world which I worshiped as divine. I suppose this is how I got started on my present difficult career, innocently stepping onto the tightrope upon which I move painfully forward, unsure of reaching the end. In other words, I became an artist, if it is true that there is no art without refusal or consent.

In any case, the lovely warmth that reigned over my childhood freed me from all resentment. I lived on almost nothing, but also in a kind of rapture. I felt infinite strengths within me: all I had to do was find a way to use them. It was not poverty that got in my way: in Africa, the sun and the sea cost nothing. The obstacle lay rather in prejudices or stupidity. These gave me every opportunity to develop a "Castilian pride" that has done me much harm, that my friend and teacher Jean Grenier is right to make fun of, and that I tried in vain to correct, until I realized that there is a fatality in human natures. It seemed better to accept my pride and try to make use of it, rather than give myself, as Chamfort would put it, principles stronger than my character. After some soul-searching, however, I can testify that among my many weaknesses I have never discovered that most widespread failing, envy, the true cancer of societies and doctrines.

I take no credit for so fortunate an immunity. I owe it to my family, first of all, who lacked almost everything and envied practically nothing. Merely by their silence, their reserve, their natural sober pride, my people, who did not even know how to read, taught me the most valuable and enduring lessons. Anyhow, I was too absorbed in feeling to dream of things. Even now, when I see the life of the very rich in Paris, there is compassion in the detachment it inspires in me. One finds many injustices in the world, but there is one that is never mentioned, climate. For a long time, without realizing it, I thrived on that particular injustice. I can imagine the accusations of our grim philanthropists, if they should happen to read these lines. I want to pass the workers off as rich and the bourgeois as poor, to prolong the happy servitude of the former and the power of the latter. No, that is not it. For the final and most revolting injustice is consummated when poverty is wed to the life without hope or the sky that I found on reaching manhood in the appalling slums of our cities: everything must be done so that men can escape from the double humiliation of poverty and ugliness.

(*Lyrical*, 6–8)

2

The world in which I am most *at ease:* the Greek myth.

(*Notebooks II*, 249)

3

The gods had condemned Sisyphus to ceaselessly rolling a rock to the top of a mountain, whence the stone would fall back of its own weight. They had thought with some reason that there is no more dreadful punishment than futile and hopeless labor.

If one believes Homer, Sisyphus was the wisest and most prudent of mortals. According to another tradition, however, he was disposed to practice the profession of highwayman. I see no contradiction in this. Opinions differ as to the reasons why he became the futile laborer of the underworld. To begin with, he is accused of a certain levity in regard to the gods. He stole their secrets. Ægina, the daughter of Æsopus, was carried off by Jupiter. The father was shocked by that disappearance and complained to Sisyphus. He, who knew of the abduction, offered to tell about it on condition that Æsopus would give water to the citadel of Corinth. To the celestial thunderbolts he preferred the benediction of water. He was punished for this in the underworld. Homer tells us also that Sisyphus had put Death in chains. Pluto could not endure the sight of his deserted, silent empire. He dispatched the god of war, who liberated Death from the hands of her conqueror.

It is said also that Sisyphus, being near to death, rashly wanted to test his wife's love. He ordered her to cast his unburied body into the middle of the public square. Sisyphus woke up in the underworld. And there, annoyed by an obedience so contrary to human love, he obtained from Pluto permission to return to earth in order to chastise his wife. But when he had seen again the face of this world, enjoyed water and sun, warm stones and the sea, he no longer wanted to go back to the infernal darkness. Recalls, signs of anger, warnings were of no avail. Many years more he lived facing the curve of the gulf, the sparkling sea, and the smiles of earth. A decree of the gods was necessary. Mercury came and seized the impudent man by the collar and, snatching him from his joys, led

him forcibly back to the underworld, where his rock was ready for
him.

You have already grasped that Sisyphus is the absurd hero. He *is*,
as much through his passions as through his torture. His scorn of
the gods, his hatred of death, and his passion for life won him that
unspeakable penalty in which the whole being is exerted toward ac-
complishing nothing. This is the price that must be paid for the
passions of this earth. Nothing is told us about Sisyphus in the underworld. Myths are made for the imagination to breathe life into
them. As for this myth, one sees merely the whole effort of a body
straining to raise the huge stone, to roll it and push it up a slope a
hundred times over; one sees the face screwed up, the cheek tight
against the stone, the shoulder bracing the clay-covered mass, the
foot wedging it, the fresh start with arms outstretched, the wholly
human security of two earth-clotted hands. At the very end of his
long effort measured by skyless space and time without depth, the
purpose is achieved. Then Sisyphus watches the stone rush down
in a few moments toward that lower world whence he will have to
push it up again toward the summit. He goes back down to the
plain.

It is during that return, that pause, that Sisyphus interests me. A
face that toils so close to stones is already stone itself! I see that
man going back down with a heavy yet measured step toward the
torment of which he will never know the end. That hour like a
breathing-space which returns as surely as his suffering, that is the
hour of consciousness. At each of those moments when he leaves
the heights and gradually sinks toward the lairs of the gods, he is
superior to his fate. He is stronger than his rock.

If this myth is tragic, that is because its hero is conscious. Where
would his torture be, indeed, if at every step the hope of succeeding
upheld him? The workman of today works every day in his life at
the same tasks, and this fate is no less absurd. But it is tragic only at
the rare moments when it becomes conscious. Sisyphus, proletar-

ian of the gods, powerless and rebellious, knows the whole extent of his wretched condition: it is what he thinks of during his descent. The lucidity that was to constitute his torture at the same time crowns his victory. There is no fate that cannot be surmounted by scorn.

If the descent is thus sometimes performed in sorrow, it can also take place in joy. This word is not too much. Again I fancy Sisyphus returning toward his rock, and the sorrow was in the beginning. When the images of earth cling too tightly to memory, when the call of happiness becomes too insistent, it happens that melancholy rises in man's heart: this is the rock's victory, this is the rock itself. The boundless grief is too heavy to bear. These are our nights of Gethsemane. But crushing truths perish from being acknowledged. Thus, Œdipus at the outset obeys fate without knowing it. But from the moment he knows, his tragedy begins. Yet at the same moment, blind and desperate, he realizes that the only bond linking him to the world is the cool hand of a girl. Then a tremendous remark rings out: "Despite so many ordeals, my advanced age and the nobility of my soul make me conclude that all is well." Sophocles' Œdipus, like Dostoevsky's Kirilov, thus gives the recipe for the absurd victory. Ancient wisdom confirms modern heroism.

One does not discover the absurd without being tempted to write a manual of happiness. "What! by such narrow ways—?" There is but one world, however. Happiness and the absurd are two sons of the same earth. They are inseparable. It would be a mistake to say that happiness necessarily springs from the absurd discovery. It happens as well that the feeling of the absurd springs from happiness. "I conclude that all is well," says Œdipus, and that remark is sacred. It echoes in the wild and limited universe of man. It teaches that all is not, has not been, exhausted. It drives out of this world a god who had come into it with dissatisfaction and a preference for futile sufferings. It makes of fate a human matter, which must be settled among men.

All Sisyphus' silent joy is contained therein. His fate belongs to him. His rock is his thing. Likewise, the absurd man, when he contemplates his torment, silences all the idols. In the universe suddenly restored to its silence, the myriad wondering little voices of the earth rise up. Unconscious, secret calls, invitations from all the faces, they are the necessary reverse and price of victory. There is no sun without shadow, and it is essential to know the night. The absurd man says yes and his effort will henceforth be unceasing. If there is a personal fate, there is no higher destiny, or at least there is but one which he concludes is inevitable and despicable. For the rest, he knows himself to be the master of his days. At that subtle moment when man glances backward over his life, Sisyphus returning toward his rock, in that slight pivoting he contemplates that series of unrelated actions which becomes his fate, created by him, combined under his memory's eye and soon sealed by his death. Thus, convinced of the wholly human origin of all that is human, a blind man eager to see who knows that the night has no end, he is still on the go. The rock is still rolling.

I leave Sisyphus at the foot of the mountain! One always finds one's burden again. But Sisyphus teaches the higher fidelity that negates the gods and raises rocks. He too concludes that all is well. This universe henceforth without a master seems to him neither sterile nor futile. Each atom of that stone, each mineral flake of that night-filled mountain, in itself forms a world. The struggle itself toward the heights is enough to fill a man's heart. One must imagine Sisyphus happy.

(*Myth*, 88–91)

4

I am happy in this world for my kingdom is of this world.

(*Notebooks I*, 9)

5

To know your body's limits—that's the true psychology.

(*Death*, 39)

6

The body . . . teaches us where our limits lie.

(*Notebooks I*, 71)

7

The misery and greatness of this world: it offers no truths, but only objects for love.

Absurdity is king, but love saves us from it.

(*Notebooks I*, 93)

8

It begins not in love but in the desire to live. But is love so far off when, after climbing up through the wind to the great square house above the sea, two bodies cling close together, while from the far horizon the soft breathing of the sea rises to this room cut off from the rest of the world? The marvel of night, when the hope of love is one with the rain, the sky, and the earth's silences. Exact balance of two beings joined together by their bodies, and made alike by a common indifference to everything which is not this moment in the world.

(*Notebooks I*, 165)

9

The man who loves *on this earth* and the woman who loves him
with the certainty of finding him again in the hereafter. Their loves
are not on the same scale.

(*Notebooks I,* 107)

10

In their company it is not poverty, or destitution, or humiliation
that I felt. Why not say it? I felt and I still feel my nobility. In the
presence of my mother, I feel that I belong to a noble race: the one
that envies nothing.

(*Notebooks II,* 255)

11

It is legitimate to glory in the diversity and quantity of experience—and especially in the life of the senses and the surrender to
passionate impulses—only if one is completely disinterested in the
object of one's desires.

There is also the leap into material things—and many men who
glory in the senses do so only because they are slaves to them.
Here, too, they embrace the vulture which is eating them away.

Hence the absolute necessity to have gone through the experience of chastity, for example, and to have been ruthless with oneself. Before any deliberately thought-out enterprise aimed at glorify-
ing the world of immediate experience, a month's asceticism in
everything.

Sexual chastity.

Mental chastity—prevent your desires from straying, your
thoughts from wandering.

One single, unchanging subject for meditation. Reject everything else.

Work continuously, at a definite time, with no falling off, etc.,
etc. (Moral training and asceticism too.)

Find excess within moderation.

(*Notebooks I*, 162, 85)

───⁓{⁓───

12

The greatest saving one can make in the order of thought is to accept the unintelligibility of the world—and to pay attention to man.

(*Notebooks II*, 86)

───⁓{⁓───

13

Secret of my universe: imagining God without human immortality.

(*Notebooks II*, 12)

───⁓{⁓───

14

Pascal: Error comes from exclusion.

(*Notebooks II*, 42)

───⁓{⁓───

15

Regarding M. I don't refuse a path leading to the Supreme Being,
so long as it doesn't avoid other beings. To know if one can find
God as the outcome of one's passions.

(*Notebooks II*, 73)

16

You know, a man always judges himself by the balance he can
strike between the needs of his body and the demands of his mind.

(*Death*, 36)

17

An Athenian proverb put the man who could neither read nor
swim in the very lowest class of citizens.

(*Notebooks I*, 206)

18

Few people realize that there is a refusal that has nothing to do
with renunciation. What meaning do words like future, improve-
ment, good job have here? What is meant by the heart's progress? If
I obstinately refuse all the "later on's" of this world, it is because I
have no desire to give up my present wealth. I do not want to
believe that death is the gateway to another life. For me, it is a
closed door. I do not say it is a step we must all take, but that it is a
horrible and dirty adventure. Everything I am offered seeks to deliver man from the weight of his own life. But as I watch the great
birds flying heavily through the sky at Djemila, it is precisely a certain weight of life that I ask for and obtain. If I am at one with this
passive passion, the rest ceases to concern me. I have too much
youth in me to be able to speak of death. But it seems to me that if
I had to speak of it, I would find the right word here between horror and silence to express the conscious certainty of a death without
hope.

    We live with a few familiar ideas. Two or three. We polish and

transform them according to the societies and the men we happen
to meet. It takes ten years to have an idea that is really one's own—
that one can talk about. This is a bit discouraging, of course. But
we gain from this a certain familiarity with the splendor of the
world. Until then, we have seen it face to face. Now we need to
step aside to see its profile. A young man looks the world in the
face. He has not had time to polish the idea of death or of nothingness, even though he has gazed on their full horror. That is what
youth must be like, this harsh confrontation with death, this physical terror of the animal who loves the sun. Whatever people may
say, on this score at least, youth has no illusions. It has had neither
the time nor the piety to build itself any. And, I don't know why,
but faced with this ravined landscape, this solemn and lugubrious
cry of stone, Djemila, inhuman at nightfall, faced with this death
of colors and hope, I was certain that when they reach the end of
their lives, men worthy of the name must rediscover this confrontation, deny the few ideas they had, and recover the innocence and
truth that gleamed in the eyes of the Ancients face to face with destiny. They regain their youth, but by embracing death. There is
nothing more despicable in this respect than illness. It is a remedy
against death. It prepares us for it. It creates an apprenticeship
whose first stage is self-pity. It supports man in his great effort to
avoid the certainty that he will die completely. But Djemila . . .
and then I feel certain that the true, the only, progress of civilization, the one to which a man devotes himself from time to time,
lies in creating conscious deaths.

What always amazes me, when we are so swift to elaborate on
other subjects, is the poverty of our ideas on death. It is a good
thing or a bad thing, I fear it or I summon it (they say). Which also
proves that everything simple is beyond us. What is blue, and how
do we think "blue"? The same difficulty occurs with death. Death
and colors are things we cannot discuss. Nonetheless, the important thing is this man before me, heavy as earth, who prefigures my
future. But can I really think about it? I tell myself: I am going to

die, but this means nothing, since I cannot manage to believe it and can only experience other people's death. I have seen people die. Above all, I have seen dogs die. It was touching them that overwhelmed me. Then I think of flowers, smiles, the desire for women, and realize that my whole horror of death lies in my anxiety to live. I am jealous of those who will live and for whom flowers and the desire for women will have their full flesh and blood meaning. I am envious because I love life too much not to be selfish. What does eternity matter to me. You can be lying in bed one day and hear someone say: "You are strong and I owe it to you to be honest: I can tell you that you are going to die"; you're there, with your whole life in your hands, fear in your bowels, looking the fool. What else matters: waves of blood come throbbing to my temples and I feel I could smash everything around me.

But men die in spite of themselves, in spite of their surroundings. They are told: "When you get well . . . ," and they die. I want none of that. For if there are days when nature lies, there are others when she tells the truth. Djemila is telling the truth tonight, and with what sad, insistent beauty! As for me, here in the presence of this world, I have no wish to lie or to be lied to. I want to keep my lucidity to the last, and gaze upon my death with all the fullness of my jealousy and horror. It is to the extent I cut myself off from the world that I fear death most, to the degree I attach myself to the fate of living men instead of contemplating the unchanging sky. Creating conscious deaths is to diminish the distance that separates us from the world and to accept a consummation without joy, alert to rapturous images of a world forever lost.

(*Lyrical*, 76–78)

19

The same men at Fiesole who live among red flowers keep in their cells the skull that nourishes their meditations. Florence at their windows and death on their tables. A certain continuity in despair can give birth to joy. And when life reaches a certain temperature, our soul and blood mingle and live at ease in contradiction, as indifferent to duty as to faith.

(*Lyrical*, 100)

20

For the path that leads from beauty to immortality is tortuous but certain. Plunged deep in beauty, the mind feeds off nothingness. When a man faces landscapes whose grandeur clutches him by the throat, each movement of his mind is a scratch on his perfection. And soon, crossed out, scarred and rescarred by so many overwhelming certainties, man ceases to be anything at all in face of the world but a formless stain knowing only passive truths, the world's color or its sun. Landscapes as pure as this dry up the soul and their beauty is unbearable. The message of these gospels of stone, sky, and water is that there are no resurrections. Henceforth, from the depths of the deserts that the heart sees as magnificent, men of these countries begin to feel temptation. Why is it surprising if minds brought up before the spectacle of nobility, in the rarefied air of beauty, remain unconvinced that greatness and goodness can live in harmony. An intelligence with no god to crown its glory seeks for a god in what denies it. Borgia, on his arrival in the Vatican, exclaims: "Now that God has given us the papacy, let us hasten to enjoy it." And he behaves accordingly. "Hasten" is indeed the word. There is already a hint of the despair so characteristic of people who have everything.

Perhaps I am mistaken. For I was in fact happy in Florence, like many others before me. But what is happiness except the simple harmony between a man and the life he leads? And what more legitimate harmony can unite a man with life than the dual consciousness of his longing to endure and his awareness of death? At least

he learns to count on nothing and to see the present as the only
truth given to us "as a bonus." I realize that people talk about Italy,
the Mediterranean, as classical countries where everything is on a
human scale. But where is this, and where is the road that leads the
way? Let me open my eyes to seek my measure and my satisfaction!
What I see is Fiesole, Djemila, and ports in the sunlight. The
human scale? Silence and dead stones. All the rest belongs to history.

    And yet this is not the end. For no one has said that happiness
should be forever inseparable from optimism. It is linked to love—
which is not the same thing. And I know of times and places where
happiness can seem so bitter that we prefer the promise of it. But
this is because at such times or places I had not heart enough to
love—that is, to persevere in love. What we must talk of here is
man's entry into the celebration of beauty and the earth. For now,
like the neophyte shedding his last veils, he surrenders to his god
the small change of his personality. Yes, there is a higher happiness, where happiness seems trivial.

(*Lyrical*, 101–102)

21

Millions of eyes, I knew, had gazed at this landscape, and for me it
was like the first smile of the sky. It took me out of myself in the
deepest sense of the word. It assured me that but for my love and
the wondrous cry of these stones, there was no meaning in anything. The world is beautiful, and outside it there is no salvation.
The great truth that it patiently taught me is that the mind is
nothing, nor even the heart. And that the stone warmed by the sun
or the cypress tree shooting up against the suddenly clear sky mark
the limits of the only universe in which "being right" is meaning-
ful: nature without men. And this world annihilates me. It carries
me to the end. It denies me without anger. As that evening fell
over Florence, I was moving toward a wisdom where everything

had already been overcome, except that tears came into my eyes and a great sob of poetry welling up within me made me forget the world's truth.

It is on this moment of balance I must end: the strange moment when spirituality rejects ethics, when happiness springs from the absence of hope, when the mind finds its justification in the body. If it is true that every truth carries its bitterness within, it is also true that every denial contains a flourish of affirmations. And this song of hopeless love born in contemplation may also seem the most effective guide for action. As he emerges from the tomb, the risen Christ of Piero della Francesca has no human expression on his face—only a fierce and soulless grandeur that I cannot help taking for a resolve to live. For the wise man, like the idiot, expresses little. The reversion delights me.

But do I owe this lesson to Italy, or have I drawn it from my own heart? It was surely in Italy that I became aware of it. But this is because Italy, like other privileged places, offers me the spectacle of a beauty in which, nonetheless, men die. Here again truth must decay, and what is more exalting? Even if I long for it, what have I in common with a truth that is not destined to decay? It is not on my scale. And to love it would be pretense. People rarely understand that it is never through despair that a man gives up what constituted his life. Impulses and moments of despair lead toward other lives and merely indicate a quivering attachment to the lessons of the earth.

(*Lyrical*, 103–104)

~~

22

There are moments when I don't believe I can endure the contradiction any longer. When the sky is cold and nothing supports us in nature. . . . Ah! better to die perhaps.

(*Notebooks II*, 143)

‿‿

23

To increase the happiness of a man's life is to extend the tragic nature of the witness that he bears. A truly tragic work of art (if it does bear witness) will be that of a happy man. Because this work of art will be entirely wiped out by death.

(*Notebooks I*, 98)

‿‿

24

Probably one has to live in Algiers for some time in order to realize how paralyzing an excess of nature's bounty can be. There is nothing here for whoever would learn, educate himself, or better himself. This country has no lessons to teach. It neither promises nor affords glimpses. It is satisfied to give, but in abundance. It is completely accessible to the eyes, and you know it the moment you enjoy it. Its pleasures are without remedy and its joys without hope. Above all, it requires clairvoyant souls—that is, without solace. It insists upon one's performing an act of lucidity as one performs an act of faith. Strange country that gives the man it nourishes both his splendor and his misery! It is not surprising that the sensual riches granted to a sensitive man of these regions should coincide with the most extreme destitution. No truth fails to carry with it its bitterness. How can one be surprised, then, if I never feel more affection for the face of this country than amid its poorest men? . . .

In Algiers no one says "go for a swim," but rather "indulge in a swim." The implications are clear. People swim in the harbor and go to rest on the buoys. Anyone who passes near a buoy where a pretty girl already is sunning herself shouts to his friends: "I tell you it's a seagull." These are healthy amusements. They must obviously constitute the ideal of those youths, since most of them continue the same life in the winter, undressing every day at noon for a frugal lunch in the sun. Not that they have read the boring sermons of the nudists, those Protestants of the flesh (there is a theory of the body quite as tiresome as that of the mind). But they are simply "comfortable in the sunlight." The importance of this custom for our epoch can never be overestimated. For the first time in two thousand years the body has appeared naked on beaches. For twenty centuries men have striven to give decency to Greek insolence and naïveté, to diminish the flesh and complicate dress. Today, despite that history, young men running on Mediterranean beaches repeat the gestures of the athletes of Delos. And living thus among bodies and through one's body, one becomes aware that it has its connotations, its life, and, to risk nonsense, a psychology of its own. . . .

This race is indifferent to the mind. It has a cult for and admiration of the body. Whence its strength, its innocent cynicism, and a puerile vanity which explains why it is so severely judged. It is commonly blamed for its "mentality"—that is, a way of seeing and of living. And it is true that a certain intensity of life is inseparable from injustice. Yet here is a race without past, without tradition, and yet not without poetry—but a poetry whose quality I know well, harsh, carnal, far from tenderness, that of their very sky, the only one in truth to move me and bring me inner peace. The contrary of a civilized nation is a creative nation. I have the mad hope that, without knowing it perhaps, these barbarians lounging on beaches are actually modeling the image of a culture in which the greatness of man will at last find its true likeness. This race, wholly cast into its present, lives without myths, without solace. It has put all its possessions on this earth and therefore remains without defense against death. All the gifts of physical beauty have been lavished on it. And with them, the strange avidity that always accompanies that wealth without future. Everything that is done here shows a horror of stability and a disregard for the future. People are in haste to live, and if an art were to be born here it would obey that hatred of permanence that made the Dorians fashion their first column in wood. And yet, yes, one can find measure as well as excess in the violent and keen face of this race, in this summer sky with nothing tender in it, before which all truths can be uttered and on which no deceptive divinity has traced the signs of hope or of redemption. Between this sky and these faces turned toward it, nothing on which to hang a mythology, a literature, an ethic, or a religion, but stones, flesh, stars, and those truths the hand can touch.

To feel one's attachment to a certain region, one's love for a certain group of men, to know that there is always a spot where one's heart will feel at peace—these are many certainties for a single human life. And yet this is not enough. But at certain moments everything yearns for that spiritual home. "Yes, we must go back there—there, indeed." Is there anything odd in finding on earth that union that Plotinus longed for? Unity is expressed here in terms of sun and sea. The heart is sensitive to it through a certain savor of flesh which constitutes its bitterness and its grandeur. I learn that there is no superhuman happiness, no eternity outside the sweep of days. These paltry and essential belongings, these relative truths are the only ones to stir me. As for the others, the "ideal" truths, I have not enough soul to understand them. Not that one must be an animal, but I find no meaning in the happiness of angels. I know simply that this sky will last longer than I. And what shall I call eternity except what will continue after my death? I am not expressing here the creature's satisfaction with his condition. It is quite a different matter. It is not always easy to be a man, still less to be a pure man. But being pure is recovering that spiritual home where one can feel the world's relationship, where one's pulsebeats coincide with the violent throbbing of the two o'clock sun. It is well known that one's native land is always recognized at the moment of losing it. For those who are too uneasy about themselves, their native land is the one that negates them. I should not like to be brutal or seem extravagant. But, after all, what negates me in this life is first of all what kills me. Everything that exalts life at the same time increases its absurdity. In the Algerian summer I learn that one thing only is more tragic than suffering, and that is the life of a happy man. But it may be also the way to a greater life because it leads to not cheating.

Many, in fact, feign love of life to evade love itself. They try their skill at enjoyment and at "indulging in experiences." But this is illusory. It requires a rare vocation to be a sensualist. The life of a man is fulfilled without the aid of his mind, with its backward and forward movements, at one and the same time its solitude and its presences. To see these men of Belcourt working, protecting their wives and children, and often without a reproach, I think one can feel a secret shame. To be sure, I have no illusions about it. There is not much love in the lives I am speaking of. I ought to say that not much remains. But at least they have evaded nothing. There are words I have never really understood, such as "sin." Yet I believe these men have never sinned against life. For if there is a sin against life, it consists perhaps not so much in despairing of life as in hoping for another life and in eluding the implacable grandeur of this life. These men have not cheated. Gods of summer they were at twenty by their enthusiasm for life, and they still are, deprived of all hope. I have seen two of them die. They were full of honor, but silent. It is better thus. From Pandora's box, where all the ills of humanity swarmed, the Greeks drew out hope after all the others, as the most dreadful of all. I know no more stirring symbol; for, contrary to the general belief, hope equals resignation. And to live is not to resign oneself.

(*Myth*, 104, 105, 106, 111, 112, 113)

25

. . . he closed his eyes on the despair that rose within him like a tide for the first time in a long while. Today, in the face of abjection and solitude, his heart said: "No." And in the great distress

that washed over him, Mersault realized that his rebellion was the
only authentic thing in him, and that everything else was misery
and submission.

(*Death*, 53)

~~{~~

26

. . . he stopped and took a deep breath. Millions of tiny white
smiles thronged down from the blue sky. They played over the
leaves still cupping the rain, over the damp earth of the paths,
soared to the blood-red tile roofs, then back into the lakes of air and
light from which they had just overflowed. A tiny plane hummed
its way across the sky. In this flowering of air, this fertility of the
heavens, it seemed as if a man's one duty was to live and to be
happy.

(*Death*, 7)

~~{~~

27

He recognized in himself that power to forget which only children
have, and geniuses, and the innocent. Innocent, overwhelmed by
joy, he understood at last that he was made for happiness.

(*Death*, 84)

~~{~~

28

On the third day he left Genoa for Algiers.

All during the crossing, staring at the water and the light on the
water, first in the morning, then in the middle of the day, and then
in the evening, he matched his heart against the slow pulse of the
sky, and returned to himself. He scorned the vulgarity of certain
cures. Stretched out on the deck, he realized that there could be no

question of sleeping but that he must stay awake, must remain conscious despite friends, despite the comfort of body and soul. He had to create his happiness and his justification. And doubtless the task would be easier for him now. At the strange peace that filled him as he watched the evening suddenly freshening upon the sea, the first star slowly hardening in the sky where the light died out green to be reborn yellow, he realized that after this great tumult and this fury, what was dark and wrong within him was gone now, yielding to the clear water, transparent now, of a soul restored to kindness, to resolution. He understood. How long he had craved a woman's love! And he was not made for love. All his life—the office on the docks, his room and his nights of sleep there, the restaurant he went to, his mistress—he had pursued singlemindedly a happiness which in his heart he believed was impossible. In this he was no different from everyone else. He had played at wanting to be happy. Never had he sought happiness with a conscious and deliberate desire. Never until the day . . . And from that moment on, because of a single act calculated in utter lucidity, his life had changed and happiness seemed possible. Doubtless he had given birth to this new being in suffering—but what was that suffering compared to the degrading farce he had performed till now?

(*Death*, 80–81)

~~~

29

. . . at that moment she seemed to Patrice to wed her gestures to the world.

(*Death*, 98)

~~~

30

All of this made him linger over Lucienne's hand when he said goodbye, and made him see her again, inviting her to take long

walks at the same silent pace, offering their tanned faces to the sun
or the stars, swimming together and matching their gestures and
their strides without exchanging anything but the presence of their
bodies.

(*Death*, 99)

31

The world always says the same thing. And in that patient truth
which proceeds from star to star is established a freedom that re-
leases us from ourselves and from others, as in that other patient
truth which proceeds from death to death. Patrice, Catherine,
Rose, and Claire then grew aware of the happiness born of their
abandonment to the world. If this night was in some sense the figure of their fate, they marveled that it should be at once so carnal
and so secret, that upon its countenance mingled both tears and the
sun. And with pain and joy, their hearts learned to hear that double lesson which leads to a happy death.

It is late now. Already midnight. On the brow of this night
which is like the repose and the reflection of the world, a dim surge
and murmur of stars heralds the coming dawn. A tremulous light
descends from the sky. Patrice looks at his friends: Catherine sitting
on the parapet, her head tipped back; Rose huddled on the deck-
chair, her hands resting on Gula; Claire standing stiff against the
parapet, her high, round forehead a white patch in the darkness.
Young creatures capable of happiness, who exchange their youth
and keep their secrets. He stands beside Catherine and stares over
her glistening shoulder into the bowl of the sky. Rose comes over to
the parapet, and all four are facing the World now. It is as if the
suddenly cooler dew of the night were rinsing the signs of solitude
from them, delivering them from themselves, and by that tremulous and fugitive baptism restoring them to the world. At this moment, when the night overflows with stars, their gestures are fixed

against the great mute face of the sky. Patrice raises an arm toward the night, sweeping sheaves of stars in his gesture, the sea of the heavens stirred by his arm and all Algiers at his feet, around them like a dark, glittering cape of jewels and shells.

(*Death*, 102–103)

32

. . . to establish himself in a routine which would henceforth require no further effort, to harmonize his own breathing with the deepest rhythm of time, of life itself.

(*Death*, 118–119)

33

What mattered was to humble himself, to organize his heart to match the rhythm of the days instead of submitting their rhythm to the curve of human hopes.

(*Death*, 120–121)

34

And just as the swimmer advances by the complicity of his arms and the water which bears him up, helps him on, it was enough to make a few essential gestures—to rest one hand on a tree-trunk, to take a run on the beach—in order to keep himself intact and conscious. Thus he became one with a life in its pure state, he rediscovered a paradise given only to the most private or the most intelligent animals. At the point where the mind denies the mind, he touched his truth and with it his extreme glory, his extreme love.

(*Death*, 122)

35

What matters—all that matters, really—is the will to happiness, a kind of enormous, ever-present consciousness.

(*Death*, 128)

36

He gripped Catherine's shoulder and shook his head, sprinkling water into her face. "You make the mistake of thinking you have to choose, that you have to do what you want, that there are conditions for happiness. What matters—all that matters, really—is the will to happiness, a kind of enormous, ever-present consciousness. The rest—women, art, success—is nothing but excuses. A canvas waiting for our embroideries."

"Yes," Catherine said, her eyes filled with sunlight.

"What matters to me is a certain quality of happiness. I can only find it in a certain struggle with its opposite—a stubborn and violent struggle. Am I happy? Catherine! You know the famous formula—'If I had my life to live over again'—well, I would live it over again just the way it has been. Of course you can't know what that means."

"No."

"And I don't know how to tell you. If I'm happy, it's because of my bad conscience. I had to get away and reach this solitude where I could face—in myself, I mean—what had to be faced, what was sun and what was tears . . . Yes, I'm happy, in human terms."

(*Death*, 128–129)

37

In January, the almond trees bloomed. In March, the pear, peach, and apple trees were covered with blossoms. The next month, the

streams gradually swelled, then returned to a normal flow. Early in
May, the hay was cut, and the oats and barley at the month's end.
Already the apricots were ripening. In June, the early pears appeared with the major crops. The streams began to dry up, and the
heat grew more intense. But the earth's blood, shrinking here on
the coast, made the cotton bloom farther inland and sweetened the
first grapes. A great hot wind arose, parching the land and spreading brushfires everywhere. And then, suddenly, the year changed
direction: hurriedly, the grape harvests were brought to an end.
The downpours of September and October drenched the land. No
sooner was the summer's work done than the first sowing began,
while the streams and springs suddenly swelled to torrents with the
rain. At the year's end, the wheat was already sprouting in some
fields; on others plowing had only just been finished. A little later,
the almond trees were once again white against the ice-blue sky.
The new year had begun in the earth, in the sky. Tobacco was
planted, vines cultivated and fertilized, trees grafted. In the same
month, the medlars ripened. Again, the haymaking, the harvest-
ing, the summer plowing. Halfway through the year, the ripe
fruits, juicy and sticky, were served on every table: between one
threshing and the next, the men ate the figs, peaches, and pears
greedily. During the next grape harvest, the sky grew overcast. Out
of the north, silent flocks of black starlings and thrushes passed
over—for them the olives were already ripe. Soon after they had
flown away, the olives were gathered. The wheat sprouted a second
time from the viscous soil. Huge clouds, also from the north,
passed over the sea, then the land, brushing the water with foam
and leaving it smooth and icy under the crystal sky. For several
days there were distant, silent flashes in the sky. The first cold spells
set in.

During this period, Mersault took to his bed for the first time.
Bouts of pleurisy confined him to his room for a month. When he
got up, the foothills of the Chenoua were covered with flowering
trees, all the way to the sea's edge. Never had spring touched him
so deeply. The first night of his convalescence, he walked across

the fields for a long time—as far as the hill where the ruins of Tipasa slept. In a silence violated only by the silky sounds of the sky, the night lay like milk upon the world. Mersault walked along the cliff, sharing the night's deep concentration. Below him the sea whispered gently. It was covered with velvety moonlight, smooth and undulating, like the pelt of some animal. At this hour of night, his life seemed so remote to him, he was so solitary and indifferent to everything and to himself as well, that Mersault felt he had at last attained what he was seeking, that the peace which filled him now was born of that patient self-abandonment he had pursued and achieved with the help of this warm world so willing to deny him without anger. He walked lightly, and the sound of his own footsteps seemed alien to him, familiar too, no doubt, but familiar the way the rustling of animals in the mastic bushes was familiar, or the breaking waves, or the rhythm of the night itself in the sky overhead. And he could feel his own body too, but with the same external consciousness as the warm breath of this spring night and the smell of salt and decay that rose from the beach. His actions in the world, his thirst for happiness, Zagreus' terrible wound baring brain and bone, the sweet, uncommitted hours in the House above the World, his wife, his hopes and his gods—all this lay before him, but no more than one story chosen among so many others without any valid reason, at once alien and secretly familiar, a favorite book which flatters and justifies the heart at its core, but a book someone else has written. For the first time, Mersault was aware of no other reality in himself than that of a passion for adventure, a desire for power, a warm and an intelligent instinct for a relationship with the world—without anger, without hatred, without regret. Sitting on a rock he let his fingers explore its crannies as he watched the sea swell in silence under the moon. He thought of Lucienne's face he had caressed, and of the warmth of her lips. The moon poured its long, straying smiles like oil on the water's smooth surface—the sea would be warm as a mouth, and as soft, ready to yield beneath a man's weight. Motionless now, Mersault

felt how close happiness is to tears, caught up in that silent exultation which weaves together the hopes and despairs of human life.
Conscious yet alienated, devoured by passion yet disinterested,
Mersault realized that his life and his fate were completed here and
that henceforth all his efforts would be to submit to this happiness
and to confront its terrible truth.

Now he must sink into the warm sea, lose himself in order to
find himself again, swim in that warm moonlight in order to silence what remained of the past, to bring to birth the deep song of
his happiness. He undressed, clambered down a few rocks, and entered the sea. It was as warm as a body, another body that ran down
his arms and clung to his legs with an ineffable yet omnipresent
embrace. Mersault swam steadily now, feeling the muscles of his
back shift with each stroke. Whenever he raised an arm, he cast
sheaves of silver drops upon the sea, sowing under this mute and
vivid sky the splendid harvest of happiness; then his arm thrust back
into the water, and like a vigorous plowshare tilled the waves,
dividing them in order to gain a new support, a firmer hope. Behind him, his feet churned the water into seething foam, producing
a strangely distinct hissing noise in the night's silence and solitude.
Conscious of this cadence, this vigor, an exultation seized Mersault; he swam faster and soon realized he was far from land, alone
in the heart of the night, of the world. Suddenly he thought of the
depths which lay beneath him and stopped moving. Everything
that was below attracted him like an unknown world, the extension
of this darkness which restored him to himself, the salty center of a
life still unexplored. A temptation flashed through his mind, but he
immediately rejected it in the great joy of his body—he swam
harder, farther. Gloriously tired, he turned back toward the shore.
At that moment he suddenly entered an icy current and was forced
to stop swimming, his teeth chattered, his movements lost their
harmony. This surprise of the sea left him bewildered; the chill
penetrated his limbs and seared him like the love of some god of
clear and impassioned exultation whose embrace left him power-

less. Laboriously he returned to the beach, where he dressed facing
the sky and the sea, shivering and laughing with happiness.

On his way home, he began to feel faint. From the path sloping
up toward his house, he could make out the rocky promontory
across the bay, the smooth shafts of the columns among the ruins.
Then suddenly the landscape tilted and he found himself leaning
against a rock, half-supported by a mastic bush, the fragrance of its
crushed leaves strong in his nostrils. He dragged himself back to the
house. His body, which had just now carried him to the limits of
joy, plunged him into a suffering that gripped his bowels, making
him close his eyes. He decided tea would help, but he used a dirty
pan to boil the water in, and the tea was so greasy it made him
retch. He drank it, though, before he went to bed. As he was
pulling off his shoes he noticed how pink his nails were, long and
curving over the fingertips of his bloodless hands. His nails had
never been like that, and they gave his hands a twisted, unhealthy
look. His chest felt as though it were caught in a vise. He coughed
and spat several times—only phlegm, though the taste of blood
lingered on his tongue. In bed, his body was seized by long spasms
of shivering. He could feel the chill rising from every extremity of
his body, meeting in his shoulders like a confluence of icy streams,
while his teeth chattered and the sheets felt as if they had been
soaked. The house seemed enormous, the usual noises swelled to
infinity, as if they encountered no wall to put an end to their
echoes. He heard the sea, the pebbles rolling under the receding
wave, the night throbbing behind his windows, the dogs howling
on distant farms. He was hot now, threw back the blankets, then
cold again, and drew them up. As he wavered between one suffering and another, between somnolence and anxiety, he suddenly
realized he was sick, and anguish overwhelmed him at the thought
that he might die in this unconsciousness, without being able to see
clearly. The village steeple chimed, but he could not keep count of
the strokes. He did not want to die like a sick man. He did not want
his sickness to be what it is so often, an attenuation, a transition to

death. What he really wanted was the encounter between his life—a life filled with blood and health—and death. He stood, dragged a chair over to the window and sat down in it, huddling in his blankets. Through the thin curtains, in the places where the material did not fall in folds, he saw the stars. He breathed heavily for a long time, and gripped the arms of his chair to control his trembling hands. He would reconquer his lucidity if he could. "It could be done," he was thinking. And he was thinking, too, that the gas was still on in the kitchen. "It could be done," he thought again. Lucidity too was a long patience. Everything could be won, earned, acquired. He struck his fist on the arm of the chair. A man is not born strong, weak, or decisive. He becomes strong, he becomes lucid. Fate is not in man but around him. Then he realized he was crying. A strange weakness, a kind of cowardice born of his sickness gave way to tears, to childishness. His hands were cold, his heart filled with an immense disgust. He thought of his nails, and under his collarbone he pressed tumors that seemed enormous. Outside, all the beauty was spread upon the face of the world. He did not want to abandon his thirst for life, his jealousy of life. He thought of those evenings above Algiers, when the sound of sirens rises in the green sky and men leave their factories. The fragrance of wormwood, the wildflowers among the ruins, and the solitude of the cypresses in the Sahel generated an image of life where beauty and happiness took on an aspect without the need of hope, a countenance in which Patrice found a kind of fugitive eternity. That was what he did not want to leave—he did not want that image to persist without him. Filled with rebellion and pity, he saw Zagreus' face turned toward the window. Then he coughed for a long time. It was hard to breathe. He was smothering under his blankets. He was cold. He was hot. He was burning with a great confusing rage, his fists clenched, his blood throbbing heavily under his skull; eyes blank, he waited for the new spasm that would plunge him back into the blind fever. The chill came, restoring him to a moist, sealed world in which he silenced the animal rebellion, eyes closed, jealous of his thirst and his hunger. But before losing consciousness, he had time to see the night turn pale behind the curtains and to hear, with the dawn and the world's awakening, a kind of tremendous chord of tenderness and hope which without doubt dissolved his fear of death, though at the same time it assured him he would find a reason for dying in what had been his whole reason for living.

When he awakened, the morning had already begun, and all the birds and insects were singing in the warmth of the sun. He remembered Lucienne was coming today. Exhausted, he crawled back to his bed. His mouth tasted of fever, and he could feel the onset of that fragility which makes every effort arduous and other people so irritating in the eyes of the sick. He sent for Bernard, who came at once, quiet and businesslike as always. He listened to Mersault's chest, and then took off his glasses and wiped the lenses. "Bad," was all he would say. He gave Mersault two injections. During the second, Mersault fainted, though ordinarily he was not squeamish. When he came to, Bernard was holding his wrist in one hand and his watch in the other, watching the jerky advance of the second hand. "That lasted fifteen minutes," Bernard said. "Your heart's failing. The next time, you might not come out of it."

Mersault closed his eyes. He was exhausted, his lips white and dry, his breathing a hoarse whistle. "Bernard," he said.

"Yes."

"I don't want to die in a coma. I want to see what's happening—do you understand me?"

"Yes," Bernard said, and gave him several ampules. "If you feel weak, break this open and swallow it. It's adrenalin." As he was leaving, Bernard met Lucienne on her way in. "As charming as ever."

"Is Patrice sick?"

"Yes."

"Is it serious?"

"No, he's all right," Bernard said. And just before he was out the door: "One piece of advice, though—try to leave him alone as much as you can."

"Oh," Lucienne said, "then it can't be anything."

All day long, Mersault coughed and choked. Twice he felt the cold, stubborn chill which would draw him into another coma, and twice the adrenalin rescued him from that dark immersion. And all day long his dim eyes stared at the magnificent landscape. Around four, a large red towboat appeared on the sea, gradually growing larger, glistening with sunlight, brine, and fish scales. Perez, standing, rowed on steadily. Mersault closed his eyes and smiled for the first time since the day before, though he did not unclench his teeth. Lucienne, who had been fussing around the room, vaguely uneasy, threw herself on the bed and kissed him. "Sit down," Mersault said, "you can stay."

"Don't talk, you'll tire yourself out."

Bernard came, gave injections, left. Huge red clouds moved slowly across the sky.

"When I was a child," Mersault said laboriously, leaning back on the pillow, his eyes fixed on the sky, "my mother told me that was the souls of the dead going to paradise. I was amazed they had red souls. Now I know it means a storm is coming. But it's still amazing."

Night was beginning to fall. Images came. Enormous fantastic animals which nodded over desert landscapes. Mersault gently swept them away, despite his fever. He let only Zagreus' face appear, a sign of blood brotherhood. He who had inflicted death was going to die. And then, as for Zagreus, the lucid gaze he cast upon his life was a man's gaze. Until now he had lived. Now he could talk of his life. Of that great ravaging energy which had borne him on, of that fugitive and generating poetry of life, nothing was left now but the transparent truth which is the opposite of poetry. Of all the men he had carried beside himself, as every man does at the beginning of this life, of all those various rootless, mingling beings, he had created his life with consciousness, with courage. That was his whole happiness in living and dying. He realized now that to be afraid of this death he was staring at with animal terror meant to be afraid of life. Fear of dying justified a limitless attachment to what is alive in man. And all those who had not made the gestures necessary to live their lives, all those who feared and exalted impotence—they were afraid of death because of the sanction it gave to a life in which they had not been involved. They had not lived enough, never having lived at all. And death was a kind of gesture, forever withholding water from the traveler vainly seeking to slake his thirst. But for the others, it was the fatal and tender gesture that erases and denies, smiling at gratitude as at rebellion. He spent a day and a night sitting on his bed, his arms on the night table and his head on his arms. He could not breathe lying down. Lucienne sat beside him and watched him without speaking a word. Sometimes Mersault looked at her. He realized that after he was gone, the first man who put his arms around her would make her soften, submit. She would be offered—her body, her breasts—as she had been offered to him, and the world would continue in the warmth of her parted lips. Sometimes he raised his head and stared out the window. He had not shaved, his red-rimmed, hollow eyes had lost their dark luster, and his pale, sunken cheeks under the bluish stubble transformed him completely.

His gaze came to rest on the panes. He sighed and turned toward Lucienne. Then he smiled. And in his face that was collapsing, even vanishing, the hard, lucid smile wakened a new strength, a cheerful gravity.

"Better?" Lucienne asked in a whisper.

"Yes." Then he returned to darkness between his arms. At the limit of his strength and his resistance, he joined Roland Zagreus for the first time, whose smile had so exasperated him in the beginning. His short, gasping breath left a moist cloud on the marble of the night table. And in the sickly warmth rising toward him from the stone, he felt even more distinctly the icy tips of his fingers and

toes. Even that revealed life, though, and in this journey from cold
to warm, he discovered the exultation which had seized Zagreus,
thanking life "for allowing him to go on burning." He was overcome by a violent and fraternal love for this man from whom he
had felt so distant, and he realized that by killing him he had consummated a union which bound them together forever. That heavy
approach of tears, a mingled taste of life and death, was shared by
them both, he realized now. And in Zagreus' very immobility
confronting death he encountered the secret image of his own life.
Fever helped him here, and with it an exultant certainty of sustaining consciousness to the end, of dying with his eyes open. Zagreus
too had had his eyes open that day, and tears had fallen from them.
But that was the last weakness of a man who had not had his share
of life. Patrice was not afraid of such weakness. In the pounding of
his feverish blood, though it failed to reach the limits of his body,
he understood that such weakness would not be his. For he had
played his part, fashioned his role, perfected man's one duty, which
is only to be happy. Not for long, no doubt. He had destroyed the
obstacle, and this inner brother he had engendered in himself—
what did it matter if he existed for two or for twenty years? Happiness was the fact that he had existed.

The blanket slipped from Mersault's shoulders, and when Lucienne stood up to cover him, he shuddered at her touch. Since
the day he had sneezed in the little square near Zagreus' villa to
this moment, his body had served him faithfully, had opened him
to the world. But at the same time, it lived a life of its own, detached from the man it represented. For these few years it had
passed through a slow decomposition; now it had completed its tra-
jectory, and was ready to leave Mersault, to restore him to the
world. In that sudden shudder of which Mersault was conscious,
his body indicated once more a complicity which had already won
so many joys for them both. Solely for this reason, Mersault took
pleasure in that shudder. Conscious, he must be conscious, he
must be conscious without deception, without cowardice—alone,

face to face—at grips with his body—eyes open upon death. It was a man's business. Not love, not a landscape, nothing but an infinite waste of solitude and happiness in which Mersault was playing his last cards. He felt his breathing weaken. He gasped for air, and in the movement his ruined lungs wheezed. His wrists were cold now, and there was no feeling in his hands at all. Day was breaking.

The new day was cool, filled with the sound of birds. The sun rose quickly, and in a single leap was above the horizon. The earth was covered with gold, with warmth. In the morning, sky and sea were spattered with dancing patches of blue and yellow light. A light breeze had risen, and through the window a breath of salt air cooled Mersault's hands. At noon the wind dropped, the day split open like ripe fruit and trickled down the face of the world, a warm and choking juice in a sudden concert of cicadas. The sea was covered with this golden juice, a sheet of oil upon the water, and gave back to the sun-crushed earth a warm, softening breath which released odors of wormwood, rosemary, and hot stone. From his bed, Mersault received that impact, that offering, and he opened his eyes on the huge, curved, glistening sea irradiated with the smiles of his gods. Suddenly he realized he was sitting on his bed, and that Lucienne's face was very close to his. Slowly, as though it came from his stomach, there rose inside him a stone which approached his throat. He breathed faster and faster, higher and higher. He looked at Lucienne. He smiled without wincing, and this smile too came from inside himself. He threw himself back on the bed, and felt the slow ascent within him. He looked at Lucienne's swollen lips and, behind her, the smile of the earth. He looked at them with the same eyes, the same desire.

"In a minute, in a second," he thought. The ascent stopped. And stone among the stones, he returned in the joy of his heart to the truth of the motionless worlds.

(*Death*, 137–151)

38

Except for these privations I wasn't too unhappy. Yet again, the whole problem was: how to kill time. After a while, however, once I'd learned the trick of remembering things, I never had a moment's boredom. Sometimes I would exercise my memory on my bedroom and, starting from a corner, make the round, noting every object I saw on the way. At first it was over in a minute or two. But each time I repeated the experience, it took a little longer. I made a point of visualizing every piece of furniture, and each article upon or in it, and then every detail of each article, and finally the details of the details, so to speak: a tiny dent or incrustation, or a chipped edge, and the exact grain and color of the woodwork. At the same time I forced myself to keep my inventory in mind from start to finish, in the right order and omitting no item. With the result that, after a few weeks, I could spend hours merely in listing the objects in my bedroom. I found that the more I thought, the more details, half-forgotten or malobserved, floated up from my memory. There seemed no end to them.

So I learned that even after a single day's experience of the outside world a man could easily live a hundred years in prison. He'd have laid up enough memories never to be bored. Obviously, in one way, this was a compensation.

Then there was sleep. To begin with, I slept badly at night and never in the day. But gradually my nights became better, and I managed to doze off in the daytime as well. In fact, during the last months, I must have slept sixteen or eighteen hours out of the twenty-four. So there remained only six hours to fill—with meals, relieving nature, my memories . . . and the story of the Czech.

One day, when inspecting my straw mattress, I found a bit of newspaper stuck to its underside. The paper was yellow with age, almost transparent, but I could still make out the letter print. It was the story of a crime. The first part was missing, but I gathered that its scene was some village in Czechoslovakia. One of the villagers had left his home to try his luck abroad. After twenty-five years, having made a fortune, he returned to his country with his wife and child. Meanwhile his mother and sister had been running a small hotel in the village where he was born. He decided to give them a surprise and, leaving his wife and child in another inn, he went to stay at his mother's place, booking a room under an assumed name. His mother and sister completely failed to recognize him. At dinner that evening he showed them a large sum of money he had on him, and in the course of the night they slaughtered him with a hammer. After taking the money they flung the body into the river. Next morning his wife came and, without thinking, betrayed the guest's identity. His mother hanged herself. His sister threw herself into a well. I must have read that story thousands of times. In one way it sounded most unlikely; in another, it was plausible enough. Anyhow, to my mind, the man was asking for trouble; one shouldn't play fool tricks of that sort.

So, what with long bouts of sleep, my memories, readings of that scrap of newspaper, the tides of light and darkness, the days slipped by. I'd read, of course, that in jail one ends up by losing track of time. But this had never meant anything definite to me. I hadn't grasped how days could be at once long and short. Long, no doubt, as periods to live through, but so distended that they ended up by overlapping on each other. In fact, I never thought of days as such; only the words "yesterday" and "tomorrow" still kept some meaning.

When, one morning, the jailer informed me I'd now been six months in jail, I believed him—but the words conveyed nothing to my mind. To me it seemed like one and the same day that had been going on since I'd been in my cell, and that I'd been doing the same thing all the time.

After the jailer left me I shined up my tin pannikin and studied my face in it. My expression was terribly serious, I thought, even when I tried to smile. I held the pannikin at different angles, but always my face had the same mournful, tense expression.

The sun was setting and it was the hour of which I'd rather not speak—"the nameless hour," I called it—when evening sounds were creeping up from all the floors of the prison in a sort of stealthy procession. I went to the barred window and in the last rays looked once again at my reflected face. It was as serious as before; and that wasn't surprising, as just then I was feeling serious. But, at the same time, I heard something that I hadn't heard for months. It was the sound of a voice; my own voice, there was no mistaking it. And I recognized it as the voice that for many a day of late had been sounding in my ears. So I knew that all this time I'd been talking to myself.

(*Stranger*, 98–101)

39

It was at one of these moments that I refused once again to see the chaplain. I was lying down and could mark the summer evening coming on by a soft golden glow spreading across the sky. I had just turned down my appeal, and felt my blood circulating with slow, steady throbs. No, I didn't want to see the chaplain. . . . Then I did something I hadn't done for quite a while; I fell to thinking about Marie. She hadn't written for ages; probably, I surmised, she had grown tired of being the mistress of a man sentenced to death. Or she might be ill, or dead. After all, such things happen. How could I have known about it, since, apart from our two bodies, separated now, there was no link between us, nothing to remind us of each other? Supposing she were dead, her memory would mean nothing; I couldn't feel an interest in a dead girl. This seemed to me quite normal; just as I realized people would soon forget me once I was dead. I couldn't even say that this was hard to stomach; really, there's no idea to which one doesn't get acclimatized in time.

My thoughts had reached this point when the chaplain walked in, unannounced. I couldn't help giving a start on seeing him. He noticed this evidently, as he promptly told me not to be alarmed. I reminded him that usually his visits were at another hour, and for a pretty grim occasion. This, he replied, was just a friendly visit; it had no concern with my appeal, about which he knew nothing. Then he sat down on my bed, asking me to sit beside him. I refused—not because I had anything against him; he seemed a mild, amiable man.

He remained quite still at first, his arms resting on his knees, his eyes fixed on his hands. They were slender but sinewy hands, which made me think of two nimble little animals. Then he gently rubbed them together. He stayed so long in the same position that for a while I almost forgot he was there.

All of a sudden he jerked his head up and looked me in the eyes.

"Why," he asked, "don't you let me come to see you?"

I explained that I didn't believe in God.

"Are you really so sure of that?"

I said I saw no point in troubling my head about the matter; whether I believed or didn't was, to my mind, a question of so little importance.

He then leaned back against the wall, laying his hands flat on his thighs. Almost without seeming to address me, he remarked that he'd often noticed one fancies one is quite sure about something, when in point of fact one isn't. When I said nothing, he looked at me again, and asked:

"Don't you agree?"

I said that seemed quite possible. But, though I mightn't be so sure about what interested me, I was absolutely sure about what didn't interest me. And the question he had raised didn't interest me at all.

He looked away and, without altering his posture, asked if it was because I felt utterly desperate that I spoke like this. I explained that it wasn't despair I felt, but fear—which was natural enough.

"In that case," he said firmly, "God can help you. All the men I've seen in your position turned to Him in their time of trouble."

Obviously, I replied, they were at liberty to do so, if they felt like it. I, however, didn't want to be helped, and I hadn't time to work up interest for something that didn't interest me.

He fluttered his hands fretfully; then, sitting up, smoothed out his cassock. When this was done he began talking again, addressing me as "my friend." It wasn't because I'd been condemned to death, he said, that he spoke to me in this way. In his opinion every man on the earth was under sentence of death.

There, I interrupted him; that wasn't the same thing, I pointed out, and, what's more, could be no consolation.

He nodded. "Maybe. Still, if you don't die soon, you'll die one day. And then the same question will arise. How will you face that terrible, final hour?"

I replied that I'd face it exactly as I was facing it now.

Thereat he stood up, and looked me straight in the eyes. It was a trick I knew well. I used to amuse myself trying it on Emmanuel and Céleste, and nine times out of ten they'd look away uncomfortably. I could see the chaplain was an old hand at it, as his gaze never faltered. And his voice was quite steady when he said: "Have you no hope at all? Do you really think that when you die you die outright, and nothing remains?"

I said: "Yes."

He dropped his eyes and sat down again. He was truly sorry for me, he said. It must make life unbearable for a man, to think as I did.

The priest was beginning to bore me, and resting a shoulder on the wall, just beneath the little skylight, I looked away. Though I didn't trouble much to follow what he said, I gathered he was questioning me again. Presently his tone became agitated, urgent, and, as I realized that he was genuinely distressed, I began to pay more attention.

He said he felt convinced my appeal would succeed, but I was saddled with a load of guilt, of which I must get rid. In his view man's justice was a vain thing; only God's justice mattered. I pointed out that the former had condemned me. Yes, he agreed, but it hadn't absolved me from my sin. I told him that I wasn't conscious of any "sin"; all I knew was that I'd been guilty of a criminal offense. Well, I was paying the penalty of that offense, and no one had the right to expect anything more of me.

Just then he got up again, and it struck me that if he wanted to move in this tiny cell, almost the only choice lay between standing up and sitting down. I was staring at the floor. He took a single step toward me, and halted, as if he didn't dare to come nearer. Then he looked up through the bars at the sky.

"You're mistaken, my son," he said gravely. "There's more that might be required of you. And perhaps it *will* be required of you."

"What do you mean?"

"You might be asked to see . . ."

"To see what?"

Slowly the priest gazed round my cell, and I was struck by the sadness of his voice when he replied:

"These stone walls, I know it only too well, are steeped in human suffering. I've never been able to look at them without a shudder. And yet—believe me, I am speaking from the depths of my heart—I *know* that even the wretchedest amongst you have sometimes seen, taking form against that grayness, a divine face. It's that face you are asked to see."

This roused me a little. I informed him that I'd been staring at those walls for months; there was nobody, nothing in the world, I knew better than I knew them. And once upon a time, perhaps, I used to try to see a face. But it was a sun-gold face, lit up with desire—Marie's face. I had no luck; I'd never seen it, and now I'd given up trying. Indeed, I'd never seen anything "taking form," as he called it, against those gray walls.

The chaplain gazed at me with a sort of sadness. I now had my back to the wall and light was flowing over my forehead. He muttered some words I didn't catch; then abruptly asked if he might kiss me. I said, "No." Then he turned, came up to the wall, and slowly drew his hand along it.

"Do you really love these earthy things so very much?" he asked in a low voice.

I made no reply.

For quite a while he kept his eyes averted. His presence was getting more and more irksome, and I was on the point of telling him to go, and leave me in peace, when all of a sudden he swung round on me, and burst out passionately:

"No! No! I refuse to believe it. I'm sure you've often wished there was an afterlife."

Of course I had, I told him. Everybody has that wish at times. But that had no more importance than wishing to be rich, or to swim very fast, or to have a better-shaped mouth. It was in the same order of things. I was going on in the same vein, when he cut in with a question. How did I picture the life after the grave?

I fairly bawled out at him: "A life in which I can remember this life on earth. That's all I want of it." And in the same breath I told him I'd had enough of his company.

But apparently, he had more to say on the subject of God. I went close up to him and made a last attempt to explain that I'd very little time left, and I wasn't going to waste it on God.

Then he tried to change the subject by asking me why I hadn't once addressed him as "Father," seeing that he was a priest. That irritated me still more, and I told him he wasn't my father; quite the contrary, he was on the others' side.

"No, no, my son," he said, laying his hand on my shoulder. "I'm on *your* side, though you don't realize it—because your heart is hardened. But I shall pray for you."

Then, I don't know how it was, but something seemed to break inside me, and I started yelling at the top of my voice. I hurled insults at him, I told him not to waste his rotten prayers on me; it was better to burn than to disappear. I'd taken him by the neckband of

his cassock, and, in a sort of ecstasy of joy and rage, I poured out
on him all the thoughts that had been simmering in my brain. He
seemed so cocksure, you see. And yet none of his certainties was
worth one strand of a woman's hair. Living as he did, like a corpse,
he couldn't even be sure of being alive. It might look as if my
hands were empty. Actually, I was sure of myself, sure about everything, far surer than he; sure of my present life and of the death
that was coming. That, no doubt, was all I had; but at least that
certainty was something I could get my teeth into—just as it had
got its teeth into me. I'd been right, I was still right, I was always
right. I'd passed my life in a certain way, and I might have passed it
in a different way, if I'd felt like it. I'd acted thus, and I hadn't
acted otherwise; I hadn't done x, whereas I had done y or z. And
what did that mean? That, all the time, I'd been waiting for this
present moment, for that dawn, tomorrow's or another day's, which
was to justify me. Nothing, nothing had the least importance, and I
knew quite well why. He, too, knew why. From the dark horizon
of my future a sort of slow, persistent breeze had been blowing
toward me, all my life long, from the years that were to come. And
on its way that breeze had leveled out all the ideas that people tried
to foist on me in the equally unreal years I then was living through.
What difference could they make to me, the deaths of others, or a
mother's love, or his God; or the way a man decides to live, the fate
he thinks he chooses, since one and the same fate was bound to
"choose" not only me but thousands of millions of privileged people who, like him, called themselves my brothers. Surely, surely he
must see that? Every man alive was privileged; there was only one
class of men, the privileged class. All alike would be condemned to
die one day; his turn, too, would come like the others'. And what
difference could it make if, after being charged with murder, he
were executed because he didn't weep at his mother's funeral, since
it all came to the same thing in the end? The same thing for
Salamano's wife and for Salamano's dog. That little robot woman
was as "guilty" as the girl from Paris who had married Masson, or

as Marie, who wanted me to marry her. What did it matter if Raymond was as much my pal as Céleste, who was a far worthier man? What did it matter if at this very moment Marie was kissing a new boy friend? As a condemned man himself, couldn't he grasp what I meant by that dark wind blowing from my future? . . .

I had been shouting so much that I'd lost my breath, and just then the jailers rushed in and started trying to release the chaplain from my grip. One of them made as if to strike me. The chaplain quietened them down, then gazed at me for a moment without speaking. I could see tears in his eyes. Then he turned and left the cell.

Once he'd gone, I felt calm again. But all this excitement had exhausted me and I dropped heavily on to my sleeping plank. I must have had a longish sleep, for, when I woke, the stars were shining down on my face. Sounds of the countryside came faintly in, and the cool night air, veined with smells of earth and salt, fanned my cheeks. The marvelous peace of the sleepbound summer night flooded through me like a tide. Then, just on the edge of daybreak, I heard a steamer's siren. People were starting on a voyage to a world which had ceased to concern me forever. Almost for the first time in many months I thought of my mother. And now, it seemed to me, I understood why at her life's end she had taken on a "fiancé"; why she'd played at making a fresh start. There, too, in that Home where lives were flickering out, the dusk came as a mournful solace. With death so near, Mother must have felt like someone on the brink of freedom, ready to start life all over again. No one, no one in the world had any right to weep for her. And I, too, felt ready to start life all over again. It was as if that great rush of anger had washed me clean, emptied me of hope, and, gazing up at the dark sky spangled with its signs and stars, for the first time, the first, I laid my heart open to the benign indifference of the universe. To feel it so like myself, indeed, so brotherly, made me realize that I'd been happy, and that I was happy still. For all to be accomplished, for me to feel less lonely, all that remained to hope was that on the day of my execution there should be a huge crowd of spectators and that they should greet me with howls of execration.

(*Stranger*, 144–154)

40

All great deeds and all great thoughts have a ridiculous beginning. Great works are often born on a street-corner or in a restaurant's revolving door. So it is with absurdity. The absurd world more than others derives its nobility from that abject birth. In certain situations, replying "nothing" when asked what one is thinking about may be pretense in a man. Those who are loved are well aware of this. But if that reply is sincere, if it symbolizes that odd state of soul in which the void becomes eloquent, in which the chain of daily gestures is broken, in which the heart vainly seeks the link that will connect it again, then it is as it were the first sign of absurdity.

It happens that the stage sets collapse. Rising, streetcar, four hours in the office or the factory, meal, streetcar, four hours of work, meal, sleep, and Monday Tuesday Wednesday Thursday Friday and Saturday according to the same rhythm—this path is easily followed most of the time. But one day the "why" arises and everything begins in that weariness tinged with amazement. "Begins"—this is important. Weariness comes at the end of the acts of a mechanical life, but at the same time it inaugurates the impulse of consciousness. It awakens consciousness and provokes what follows. What follows is the gradual return into the chain or it is the definitive awakening. At the end of the awakening comes, in time, the consequence: suicide or recovery. In itself weariness has something sickening about it. Here, I must conclude that it is good. For everything begins with consciousness and nothing is worth anything except through it. There is nothing original about these remarks. But they are obvious; that is enough for a while, during a sketchy reconnaissance in the origins of the absurd. Mere "anxiety," as Heidegger says, is at the source of everything.

Likewise and during every day of an unillustrious life, time carries us. But a moment always comes when we have to carry it. We live on the future: "tomorrow," "later on," "when you have made your way," "you will understand when you are old enough." Such irrelevancies are wonderful, for, after all, it's a matter of dying. Yet a day comes when a man notices or says that he is thirty. Thus he asserts his youth. But simultaneously he situates himself in relation to time. He takes his place in it. He admits that he stands at a certain point on a curve that he acknowledges having to travel to its end. He belongs to time, and by the horror that seizes him, he recognizes his worst enemy. Tomorrow, he was longing for tomorrow, whereas everything in him ought to reject it. That revolt of the flesh is the absurd.*

A step lower and strangeness creeps in: perceiving that the world is "dense," sensing to what a degree a stone is foreign and irreducible to us, with what intensity nature or a landscape can negate us. At the heart of all beauty lies something inhuman, and these hills, the softness of the sky, the outline of these trees at this very minute lose the illusory meaning with which we had clothed them, henceforth more remote than a lost paradise. The primitive hostility of the world rises up to face us across millennia. For a second we cease to understand it because for centuries we have understood in it solely the images and designs that we had attributed to it beforehand, because henceforth we lack the power to make use of the artifice. The world evades us because it becomes itself again. That stage scenery masked by habit becomes again what it is. It withdraws at a distance from us. Just as there are days when under the familiar face of a woman, we see as a stranger her we had loved

---

* But not in the proper sense. This is not a definition, but rather an *enumeration* of the feelings that may admit of the absurd. Still, the enumeration finished, the absurd has nevertheless not been exhausted.

months or years ago, perhaps we shall come even to desire what
suddenly leaves us so alone. But the time has not yet come. Just
one thing: that denseness and that strangeness of the world is the
absurd.

Men, too, secrete the inhuman. At certain moments of lucidity,
the mechanical aspect of their gestures, their meaningless pan-
tomime makes silly everything that surrounds them. A man is talking on the telephone behind a glass partition; you cannot hear him,
but you see his incomprehensible dumb show: you wonder why he
is alive. This discomfort in the face of man's own inhumanity, this
incalculable tumble before the image of what we are, this "nausea," as a writer of today calls it, is also the absurd. Likewise the
stranger who at certain seconds comes to meet us in a mirror, the
familiar and yet alarming brother we encounter in our own photo-
graphs is also the absurd.

I come at last to death and to the attitude we have toward it. On
this point everything has been said and it is only proper to avoid pa-
thos. Yet one will never be sufficiently surprised that everyone lives
as if no one "knew." This is because in reality there is no experience of death. Properly speaking, nothing has been experienced but
what has been lived and made conscious. Here, it is barely possible
to speak of the experience of others' deaths. It is a substitute, an
illusion, and it never quite convinces us. That melancholy conven-
tion cannot be persuasive. The horror comes in reality from the
mathematical aspect of the event. If time frightens us, this is because it works out the problem and the solution comes afterward.
All the pretty speeches about the soul will have their contrary convincingly proved, at least for a time. For this inert body on which a
slap makes no mark the soul has disappeared. This elementary and
definitive aspect of the adventure constitutes the absurd feeling.
Under the fatal lighting of that destiny, its uselessness becomes evident. No code of ethics and no effort are justifiable *a priori* in the
face of the cruel mathematics that command our condition.

(*Myth*, 10–12)

41

The mind's deepest desire, even in its most elaborate operations, parallels man's unconscious feeling in the face of his universe: it is an insistence upon familiarity, an appetite for clarity.

(*Myth*, 13)

42

In this unintelligible and limited universe, man's fate henceforth assumes its meaning. A horde of irrationals has sprung up and surrounds him until his ultimate end. In his recovered and now studied lucidity, the feeling of the absurd becomes clear and definite. I said that the world is absurd, but I was too hasty. This world in itself is not reasonable, that is all that can be said. But what is absurd is the confrontation of this irrational and the wild longing for clarity whose call echoes in the human heart. The absurd depends as much on man as on the world. For the moment it is all that links them together. It binds them one to the other as only hatred can weld two creatures together. This is all I can discern clearly in this measureless universe where my adventure takes place. Let us pause here. If I hold to be true that absurdity that determines my relationship with life, if I become thoroughly imbued with that sentiment that seizes me in face of the world's scenes, and that lucidity imposed on me by the pursuit of a science, I must sacrifice everything to these certainties and I must see them squarely to be able to maintain them. Above all, I must adapt my behavior to them and pursue them in all their consequences. I am speaking here of decency. But I want to know beforehand if thought can live in those deserts.

I already know that thought has at least entered those deserts. There it found its bread. There it realized that it had previously been feeding on phantoms. It justified some of the most urgent themes of human reflection.

From the moment absurdity is recognized, it becomes a passion, the most harrowing of all. But whether or not one can live with one's passions, whether or not one can accept their law, which is to burn the heart they simultaneously exalt—that is the whole question.

(*Myth*, 16–17)

43

I can therefore say that the Absurd is not in man (if such a metaphor could have a meaning) nor in the world, but in their presence together. For the moment it is the only bond uniting them. If I wish to limit myself to facts, I know what man wants, I know what the world offers him, and now I can say that I also know what links them. I have no need to dig deeper. A single certainty is enough for the seeker. He simply has to derive all the consequences from it.

The immediate consequence is also a rule of method. The odd trinity brought to light in this way is certainly not a startling discovery. But it resembles the data of experience in that it is both infinitely simple and infinitely complicated. Its first distinguishing feature in this regard is that it cannot be divided. To destroy one of its terms is to destroy the whole. There can be no absurd outside the human mind. Thus, like everything else, the absurd ends with death. But there can be no absurd outside this world either. And it is by this elementary criterion that I judge the notion of the absurd to be essential and consider that it can stand as the first of my truths. The rule of method alluded to above appears here. If I judge that a thing is true, I must preserve it. If I attempt to solve a problem, at least I must not by that very solution conjure away one of the terms of the problem. For me the sole datum is the absurd. The first and, after all, the only condition of my inquiry is to preserve the very thing that crushes me, consequently to respect what I consider essential in it. I have just defined it as a confrontation and an unceasing struggle.

And carrying this absurd logic to its conclusion, I must admit that that struggle implies a total absence of hope (which has nothing to do with despair), a continual rejection (which must not be confused with renunciation), and a conscious dissatisfaction (which must not be compared to immature unrest).

(*Myth*, 23)

44

Now the main thing is done, I hold certain facts from which I cannot separate. What I know, what is certain, what I cannot deny, what I cannot reject—this is what counts. I can negate everything of that part of me that lives on vague nostalgias, except this desire for unity, this longing to solve, this need for clarity and cohesion. I can refute everything in this world surrounding me that offends or enraptures me, except this chaos, this sovereign chance and this divine equivalence which springs from anarchy. I don't know whether this world has a meaning that transcends it. But I know that I do not know that meaning and that it is impossible for me just now to know it. What can a meaning outside my condition mean to me? I can understand only in human terms. What I touch, what resists me—that is what I understand. And these two certainties—my appetite for the absolute and for unity and the impossibility of reducing this world to a rational and reasonable principle—I also know that I cannot reconcile them. What other truth can I admit without lying, without bringing in a hope I lack and which means nothing within the limits of my condition?

If I were a tree among trees, a cat among animals, this life would have a meaning, or rather this problem would not arise, for I should belong to this world. I should *be* this world to which I am now opposed by my whole consciousness and my whole insistence upon familiarity. This ridiculous reason is what sets me in opposition to all creation. I cannot cross it out with a stroke of the pen.

What I believe to be true I must therefore preserve. What seems to me so obvious, even against me, I must support. And what constitutes the basis of that conflict, of that break between the world and my mind, but the awareness of it? If therefore I want to preserve it, I can through a constant awareness, ever revived, ever alert. This is what, for the moment, I must remember.

(*Myth*, 38)

∿

45

CAESONIA: You're still a boy, really; you've a whole life ahead of you. And, tell me, what greater thing can you want than a whole life?

CALIGULA [*rising, looks at her fixedly*]: You've been with me a long time now, a very long time.

CAESONIA: Yes. . . . But you'll keep me, won't you?

CALIGULA: I don't know. I only know that, if you're with me still, it's because of all those nights we've had together, nights of fierce, joyless pleasure; it's because you alone know me as I am. [*He takes her in his arms, bending her head back a little with his right hand.*] I'm twenty-nine. Not a great age really. But today when none the less my life seems so long, so crowded with scraps and shreds of my past selves, so complete in fact, you remain the last witness. And I can't avoid a sort of shameful tenderness for the old woman that you soon will be.

CAESONIA: Tell me that you mean to keep me with you.

CALIGULA: I don't know. All I know—and it's the most terrible thing of all—is that this shameful tenderness is the one sincere emotion that my life has given up to now. [CAESONIA *frees herself from his arms.* CALIGULA *follows her. She presses her back to his chest and he puts his arms round her.*] Wouldn't it be better that the last witness should disappear?

CAESONIA: That has no importance. All I know is: I'm happy. What you've just said has made me very happy. But why can't I share my happiness with you?

CALIGULA: Who says I'm unhappy?

CAESONIA: Happiness is kind. It doesn't thrive on bloodshed.

CALIGULA: Then there must be two kinds of happiness, and I've chosen the murderous kind. For I *am* happy. There was a time when I thought I'd reached the extremity of pain. But, no, one can go farther yet. Beyond the frontier of pain lies a splendid, sterile happiness. Look at me. [*She turns toward him.*] It makes me laugh, Caesonia, when I think how for years and years all Rome carefully avoided uttering Drusilla's name. Well, all Rome was mistaken. Love isn't enough for me; I realized it then. And I realize it again today, when I look at you. To love someone means that one's willing to grow old beside that person. That sort of love is right outside my range. Drusilla old would have been far worse than Drusilla dead. Most people imagine that a man suffers because out of the blue death snatches away the woman he loves. But his real suffering is less futile; it comes from the discovery that grief, too, cannot last. Even grief is vanity.

You see, I had no excuses, not the shadow of a real love, neither bitterness nor profound regret. Nothing to plead in my defense! But today—you see me still freer than I have been for years; freed as I am from memories and illusion. [*He laughs bitterly.*] I know now that nothing, *nothing* lasts. Think what that knowledge means! There have been just two or three of us in history who really achieved this freedom, this crazy happiness. Well, Caesonia, you have seen out a most unusual drama. It's time the curtain fell, for you.

[*He stands behind her again, linking his forearm round* CAESONIA's *neck.*]

CAESONIA [*terrified*]: No, it's impossible! How can you call it happiness, this terrifying freedom?

CALIGULA [*gradually tightening his grip on* CAESONIA's *throat*]: Happiness it is, Caesonia; I know what I'm saying. But for this freedom I'd have been a contented man. Thanks to it, I have won the godlike enlightenment of the solitary. [*His exaltation grows as little by little he strangles* CAESONIA, *who puts up no resistance, but holds her hands half opened, like a suppliant's, before her. Bending his head, he goes on speaking, into her ear*] I live, I kill, I exercise the rapturous power of a destroyer, compared with which the power of a creator is merest child's play. And this, *this* is happiness; this and nothing else—this intolerable release, devastating scorn, blood, hatred all around me; the glorious isolation of a man who all his life long nurses and gloats over the ineffable joy of the unpunished murderer; the ruthless logic that crushes out human lives [*he laughs*], that's crushing yours out, Caesonia, so as to perfect at last the utter loneliness that is my heart's desire.

CAESONIA [*struggling feebly*]: Oh, Caius . . .

CALIGULA [*more and more excitedly*]: No. No sentiment. I must have done with it, for the time is short. My time is very short, dear Caesonia. [CAESONIA *is gasping, dying.* CALIGULA *drags her to the bed and lets her fall on it. He stares wildly at her; his voice grows harsh and grating.*] You, too, were guilty. But killing is not the solution. [*He spins round and gazes crazily at the mirror.*] Caligula! You, too; you, too, are guilty. Then what of it—a little more, a little less? Yet who can condemn me in this world where there is no judge, where nobody is innocent? [*He brings his eyes close to his reflected face. He sounds genuinely distressed*] You see, my poor friend. Helicon has failed you. I won't have the moon. Never, never, never! But how bitter it is to know all, and to have to go through to the consummation! Listen! That was a sound of weapons. Innocence arming for the fray—and innocence will triumph. Why am I not in their place, among them? And I'm afraid. That's cruelest of all, after despising others, to find oneself as cowardly as they. Still, no matter. Fear, too, has an end. Soon

I shall attain that emptiness beyond all understanding, in which the heart has rest. [*He steps back a few paces, then returns to the mirror. He seems calmer. When he speaks again his voice is steadier, less shrill.*]

Yet, really, it's quite simple. If I'd had the moon, if love were enough, all might have been different. But where could I quench this thirst? What human heart, what god, would have for me the depth of a great lake? [*Kneeling, weeping*] There's nothing in this world, or in the other, made to my stature. And yet I know, and you, too, know [*still weeping, he stretches out his arms toward the mirror*] that all I need is for the impossible to be. The impossible! I've searched for it at the confines of the world, in the secret places of my heart. I've stretched out my hands [*his voice rises to a scream*]; see, I stretch out my hands, but it's always you I find, you only, confronting me, and I've come to hate you. I have chosen a wrong path, a path that leads to nothing. My freedom isn't the right one. . . . Nothing, nothing yet. Oh, how oppressive is this darkness! Helicon has not come; we shall be forever guilty. The air tonight is heavy as the sum of human sorrows.

(*Plays*, 70–73)

46

"The whole misfortune of men comes from the fact that they don't use a simple speech. If the hero of *The Misunderstanding* had said: 'Well, here I am and I am your son,' the dialogue would have been possible and not at cross-purposes as in the play. There would have been no tragedy because the height of all tragedies lies in the deafness of the protagonists. From this point of view, Socrates is the one who is right, against Jesus and Nietzsche. Progress and true nobility lie in the dialogue from man to man and not in the Gospel, a monologue and dictated from the top of a solitary mountain. That's

where I stand. What balances the absurd is the community of men
fighting against it. And if we choose to serve that community, we
choose to serve the dialogue carried to the absurd against any policy
of falsehood or of silence. That's the way one is free with others."

(*Notebooks II*, 125–126)

47

MARTHA: No, no! What concern of mine was it to look after my
brother? None whatever! And yet now I'm an outcast in my
own home, there is no place for me to lay my head, my own
mother will have none of me. No, it wasn't my duty to look
after him—oh, the unfairness of it all, the injustice done to
innocence! For he—he now has what he wanted, while I am
left lonely, far from the sea I longed for. Oh, how I hate him!
All my life was spent waiting for this great wave that was to lift
me up and sweep me far away, and now I know it will never
come again. I am doomed to stay here with all those other
countries, other nations, on my left hand and my right, before
me and behind; all those plains and mountains that are
barriers to the salt winds blowing from the sea, and whose
chatterings and grumblings drown its low, unceasing sum-
mons. [*In a lower tone*] There are places to which, far as they
may be from the sea, the evening wind brings sometimes a
smell of seaweed. It tells of moist seabeaches, loud and with
the cries of seagulls, or of golden sands bathed in a sunset glow
that has no limit. But the sea winds fail long before they reach
this place. Never, never shall I have what's due me. I may
press my ear to the earth but I shall not hear the crash of icy
breakers, or the measured breathing of a happy sea. I am too
far from all I love, and my exile is beyond remedy. I hate him,
yes, I hate him for having got what he wanted! My only home
is in this gloomy, shut-in country where the sky has no hori-

zons; for my hunger I have nothing but the sour Moravian
sloes, for my thirst only the blood that I have shed. That is the
price one must pay for a mother's love!

There is no love for me, so let her die. Let every door be
shut against me; all I wish is to be left in peace with my anger,
my very rightful anger. For I have no intention of rolling my
eyes heavenward or pleading for forgiveness before I die. In
that southern land, guarded by the sea, to which one can escape, where one can breathe freely, press one's body to another's body, roll in the waves—to that sea-guarded land the
gods have no access. But here one's gaze is cramped on every
side, everything is planned to make one look up in humble
supplication. I hate this narrow world in which we are reduced
to gazing up at God.

But I have not been given my rights and I am smarting from
the injustice done me; I will not bend my knee. I have been
cheated of my place on earth, cast away by my mother, left
alone with my crimes, and I shall leave this world without
being reconciled.

(*Plays*, 124–125)

~~

48

MARTHA: Yes, I am going, and it will be a relief for me, as well.
Your love and your tears are odious to me. But before I go to
die, I must rid you of the illusion that you are right, that love
isn't futile, and that what has happened was an accident. On
the contrary, it's now that we are in the normal order of
things, and I must convince you of it.

MARIA: What do you mean by that?

MARTHA: That in the normal order of things no one is ever recognized.

MARIA [*distractedly*]: Oh, what do I care? I only know that my heart is torn to shreds, and nothing, nothing matters to it except the man you killed.

MARTHA [*savagely*]: Be silent! I will not have you speak of that man; I loathe him. And he is nothing to you now. He has gone down into the bitter house of eternal exile. The fool! Well, he has got what he wanted; he is with the woman he crossed the sea to find. So all of us are served now, as we should be, in the order of things. But fix this in your mind; neither for him nor for us, neither in life nor in death, is there any peace or homeland. [*With a scornful laugh*] For you'll agree one can hardly call it a home, that place of clotted darkness underground, to which we go from here to feed blind animals.

MARIA [*weeping*]: I can't, oh, no, I can't bear to hear you talk like that. And I know he, too, wouldn't have borne it. It was to find another homeland that he crossed the sea.

MARTHA [*who has walked to the door, swings round on her*]: His folly has received its wages. And soon you will receive yours. [*Laughing as before*] We're cheated, I tell you. Cheated! What do they serve, those blind impulses that surge up in us, the yearnings that rack our souls? Why cry out for the sea, or for love? What futility! Your husband knows now what the answer is: the charnel house where in the end we shall lie huddled together, side by side. [*Vindictively*] A time will come when you, too, know it, and then, could you remember anything, you would recall as a delightful memory this day which seems to you the beginning of the cruelest of exiles. Try to realize that no grief of yours can ever equal the injustice done to man.

And now—before I go, let me give a word of advice; I owe it to you, since I killed your husband. Pray your God to harden you to stone. It's the happiness He has assigned Himself, and the one true happiness. Do as He does, be deaf to all appeals, and turn your heart to stone while there still is time. But if you feel you lack the courage to enter into this hard, blind peace—then come and join us in our common house. Good-by, my sister. As you see, it's all quite simple. You have a choice between the mindless happiness of stones and the slimy bed in which we are awaiting you.

[*She goes out.* MARIA, *who has been listening in horrified amazement, sways, stretching out her arms in front of her.*]

MARIA [*her voice rising to a scream*]: Oh, God, I cannot live in this desert! It is on You that I must call, and I shall find the words to say. [*She sinks on her knees.*] I place myself in your hands. Have pity, turn toward me. Hear me and raise me from the dust, O Heavenly Father! Have pity on those who love each other and are parted.

[*The door opens. The* OLD MANSERVANT *is standing on the threshold.*]

THE OLD MANSERVANT [*in a clear, firm tone*]: What's all this noise? Did you call me?

MARIA [*gazing at him*]: Oh! . . . I don't know. But help me, help me, for I need help. Be kind and say that you will help me.

THE OLD MANSERVANT [*in the same tone*]: No.

(*Plays*, 132–134)

TWO

Prometheus

And openly I pledged my
heart to the grave and suffering land, and often in
the consecrated night, I
promised to love her faithfully until death, unafraid,
with her heavy burden of
fatality, and never to de-
spise a single one of her
enigmas. Thus did I join
myself to her with a mortal
cord.

—Hölderlin

Prometheus, son of Iapetos the Titan and of Klymene (or, according to a variant tradition, Themis, "Earth the Wise") was himself something of a trickster. Once, at Mekone (later Sikyon), when immortals and mortals met to determine the due of the gods, Prometheus wrapped the choicest portions of the sacrifice in the stomach of an ox and covered a bag of bones and worthless scraps with a delectable but thin layer of fat. These two options were then offered to the high god Zeus, who soon found himself in possession of a teasing slab of fat and an otherwise inedible bundle of garbage. With Prometheus as priest, the gods receive a blasphemous token and his beloved mortals receive the earth's abundance. And, when the rage of Zeus refuses fire to mortals, Prometheus stealthily undermines the divine prohibition and brings to earth the glowing embers of a divinely kindled fire wrapped in a hollow stalk. From these and many other tales told of Prometheus, two qualities emerge as unmistakably Promethean: a commitment to cunning and a commitment to humanity.

In the cosmic civil war between the Titans and the Olympians, Prometheus is said to have preferred and proposed cunning over sheer brutal might. This he learned, according to Aischylos' account in *Prometheus Bound*, from his primordial mother Earth. "She my mother," explains Prometheus,

> who holds the judgement seat,
> Even Earth, that entity with many names,
> Had often told me, yea had prophesied
> The way of it, how not in physical strength
> But cunning guile the victory should lie.[1]

111

Clearly, "Prometheus of the intricate and twisting mind,"[2] as Hesiod names him, chooses guile when its alternative is all-crushing might, which is the case as he confronts the Titans, or even Zeus; but toward mortals he is direct and unqualified in his compassion and beneficence. When Zeus "plotted out the pattern of his kingdom," relates Prometheus to the chorus in *Prometheus Bound*, "Man alone, poor suffering man, meant nothing."[3] Once the chaotic violence of the Titans was driven deep into Tartarus, the regime of Chronos was replaced not with the architecture of reason and justice but rather with fresh but familiar tyranny, still another reign of capricious favor and disfavor. And human beings were so squarely in the disfavor of Zeus that he was contemplating their elimination. Then, in the face of Zeus's tyranny and his policy of genocide, Prometheus rebelled and championed the human cause.

Prometheus' rebellion against Zeus and his goodwill toward mortals find their consummate expression in his thieving of fire from heaven and his delivering it to human hands and purposes. With the gift of fire, Prometheus bestows upon mortals all of the arts: from the writing of words and numbers to animal husbandry, to medicine, to augury and sacrifice. Aischylos sums up the gifts of Prometheus in one word: *technē*, which means the making of something, the transforming of material so that something becomes what it was not. To look at a tree and to see not a tree but lumber and, still further, to see a table, and then to let this projected image guide the forceful movement of one's hands in the felling of the tree, the stripping of the bark, the splitting and cutting of the wood to size, and the pegging of the boards into place: all of these activities represent an exercise in *technē* or art. And the most fundamental instrument, the most elemental transforming power for art would seem to be fire, which transforms flesh into meat, ore into metal tools and weapons, wood into warmth, and water into steam. The power to cause the particles of matter to move ever more rapidly is the foundational power not only for ancient art but for modern technology and this power is first glimpsed and held in the kindled flame. There too, in the simplest flickering flame, we may see both the perils and the precariousness of this power: if not controlled, it might consume everything; if not itself nourished and protected, it might go out.

If we consider the activity described a moment ago which began with a tree and ended with a table, the appropriateness of the name *Pro-metheus*, "Fore-thinker," becomes evident. But there is more to this name than first appears. To make anything at all requires "pro-vision," an eye for the well-suitedness of material to project, an eye for the details and the proper sequence of construction. But the word *pro-metheomai* from which *Prometheus* is derived means not only to think ahead but also to provide for and to care about. Actually, the full valence of Prometheus' name would be better served by translating it as "Provider." Thus, when Prometheus says of his boon to humankind that "I made him conscious and intelligent,"[4] we must have in mind a consciousness and an intelligence which reaches beyond craft and skill to care and compassion. After all, "craft (*technē*) is far weaker than necessity."[5] What mortals may accomplish is always less definitive than what they must suffer. However many flames one might kindle and feed, the inner flame cannot be forever or long sustained. Even the sons of heaven go darkened in death. Mortal strength must always yield to mortal weakness; and craft must open into helpless care. Thus we come to realize that Prometheus' most remarkable gift to human beings is not fire but sympathy. Sympathy too, it seems, is a matter of forethought; for it is the response of the heart to the perception of life as a whole, the perception that men, poor suffering men, die and are not happy.

It is, then, for his "human-loving disposition,"[6] for his "excessive love for humankind,"[7] that Prometheus is crucified on a massive rock by Zeus. For giving sympathy he has become an object of sympathy; the pitier has become himself an object of pity. Prometheus, a god, deathless and divinely privileged, attends to the suffering of human beings, mortal and cursed. No wider chasm

presents itself to imagination than this one: for an immortal to show
consideration for the condition of mortals. Every leap which
human compassion would require seems slight by comparison.
Prometheus willingly sets aside his divine prerogatives and assumes
the yoke of necessity; he suffers what he must suffer if he is to attend to the sufferings of others. In fact, no art requires a more
reaching imagination or a more adamantine will than the art of
care and compassion. When consciousness grows sufficiently to
consider not only one's own suffering but also that of others, not
only one's own peculiar station but the human condition, then
consciousness may be said to be deathless and thus divine. There is
a tradition which tells that it was Prometheus who lifted human
beings from their four legs and taught them to walk upright, delica-
tely balanced on two feet of clay but lifting their heads boldly to the
sun and the sky. If so, then it would seem that human pride and
rebellion and nobility lie in forethought, in providing for oneself
and for others, in invention but, even more, in sympathy.

The theme of vicarious suffering winds through the tale of Prometheus like a rich and fruitful vine. Prometheus attends to human
suffering; and when, in turn, he is brought low under Zeus's wrath,
he turns to the chorus of Titans, his brothers: "I plead with you, I
plead. Take on my load who now do suffer."[8] And this they do
with such loyalty that when threatened by Hermes, the Deputy of
Zeus, their leader responds for them all:

> Beside him I prefer to stay
>   Whate'er the peril or the hurt.
> Never a trust to undermine—
>   I learned that lesson long ago,
> Nor would to any other sin
>   Sooner my fierce derision show.[9]

Io too, the wandering woman, tells her own painful tale and listens
to that of Prometheus, thus entering this same thicket of suffering
and sympathy. Finally, in the prophecies of Prometheus, we follow

the line of fellowship still further. One day the magic arrows of Herakles will both fell the cursed eagle which so torments Prometheus and wound Cheiron who, in turn, will offer to die in Prometheus' stead, thereby winning release for them both from their agonies. Herakles too will one day plead to be put out of his misery; and, when the shepherd boy Philoktetes grants him this most minimal of graces, he will reward him with the sacred bow, a token of friendship which will sustain Philoktetes through his bitter years of betrayal and which he will one day offer in friendship to the callow son of Achilles in gratitude for his loyalty and compassion.

Once the seed of human fellowship is sown, it grows up a sturdy and prolific vine. When Titan strength weakens itself and embraces mortal haplessness, the human heart is quickened with a spirit of rebellion and faithfulness titanic in its strength and subtlety. Clearly, Prometheus founds and stands at the head of a new race of human Titans who challenge the callous, petty gods with the upright stature of their deeds and with the gracious reach of their consciousness and care. With Prometheus, they refuse to "shape [their] character anew, to fit new tyranny in heaven."[10] Instead, they will be able to say with him: "Long since I looked the issue full in the face,"[11] and their consequent resolve will be as impossible to dissuade as an ocean wave.[12] Such is the lineage which Camus claims for his own heroes and heroic principles in the second stage of his thought's unfolding. Again the struggle is finally between will and rock, between wit and indifference; but Prometheus, unlike Sisyphus, is not alone. In retrospect, now on Mount Aetna with Prometheus, it is clear that all was not well with Sisyphus. He was a murderer at howling odds with his fellows, an "idiot," living a life and enduring a fate all his own, or so it seemed.

As we have seen, Sisyphus and his many counterparts in Camus' early writings come to the realization that they are "made for happiness,"[13] and that "all that matters, really, is the will to happiness, a kind of enormous, ever-present consciousness."[14] Indeed, to Patrice Mersault "it seemed as if a man's one duty was to live and to be happy." [15] But this simplicity of vision and resolve is only a matter of "seeming," a mere semblance. The human condition, its possibilities, its necessities, and its demands are a good deal more complicated than they first appear to absurd consciousness. I am not alone in the will to happiness; nor am I alone in my unhappiness. In addition to my sufferings, there are the sufferings of others like me (1), except that the times of our lives are mostly out of sequence. As I was being born, someone else was dying. When my soul quakes with grief and dread, others laugh heartily. My winter is another's summer; and my feasting, another's starving. At first glance we humans have little in common outside of the narrow circles into which we are drawn by chance and some small choice. A second glance, which will reveal the essential consortium of human living and dying, requires no little imagination and insight. Such wisdom, if it comes at all, comes with suffering and age (2).

"When anyone's soul," writes Plato, "feels a keen pleasure or pain, it cannot help supposing that whatever causes the most violent emotion is the plainest and truest reality, which it is not." [16] Thus it is not surprising that Camus' early heroes, face to face with death, regard death, and more particularly their own personal death, died always alone, as the plainest and truest reality, which it is not. Indeed, Plato again reveals the obvious, when, in the *Protagoras*, [17] he points out that what is nearest to one's eyes always appears greater than what stands far off. For this very reason he suggests that what saves our life from ruinous misapprehension and mischoice is the art of measurement (*metrētikē technē*), which overcomes the power of appearance and allows us to give to each reality its due, regardless of its proximity to or remoteness from us. Without this art, the pleasures and pains of others would possess the sole relevance of mirroring our own pleasures and pains. Our own immediate desires and fears, delights and sufferings would be unquestionably prior to all else. Our isolation would be final. This very isolation enwraps Camus' early heroes and drives Martha to the despairing lament that in this life no one is ever recognized, ever given one's due, by anyone else.

This art of measurement, the assigning of human attention and value to beings and events according to their respective worth (*timē kat'axian*) is the essence of human practical wisdom or what the Greeks called *sōphrosunē*, prudence or moderation. It is the opposite of *hybris*, the arrogant estimation of all things as they bear upon one's own immediate desires and fears. And yet nothing comes as easily as *hybris*; no assumption is more readily made than the assumption that things are as they appear, that things are simply what they are for me. Perhaps only the havoc and the human wreckage brought about by acting on such an assumption can persuade us to question it. Limits are usually first discerned in their transgression. Even then, wisdom comes slowly, if at all. For what could be more difficult than to weigh one's own pleasures and pains, one's own living and dying, no more heavily than another's? To know and to act in accord with the scale of things irrespective of where one stands in their midst is, it seems, a god-like feat, or at least the gift of a god. This art, the art of measure, is the consummate gift and example of Prometheus who, though a god, sought to assure human being its due.

It is to the Greeks that Camus points all those who would learn more of measure and of *sōphrosunē*. In ancient Greek literature the tragic, or absurd, character of human fate reaches its most poignant expression. For never is human being more essentially contradicted, more impossible, than when it endeavors to exclude nothing and to do justice to each possibility. By comparison, Camus found the strivings of his own contemporary Europe to be narrow and exclusive, lacking in all due sense of measure and proportion. In his essay "Helen's Exile," Camus describes the range and the depth of modern *hybris*. Blinded to all else by the proximity of certain social injustices, we seek an all-consuming equity, without remainder. We turn our backs on beauty and thirst after righteousness. The natural universe becomes no more to us than the plastic scene for historic endeavor. We attend only to what we might do and to what we might alter, failing any longer to wonder at what bestows itself upon us apart from all our makings and doings. What is beyond our conceivable control is of no interest and thus of no account. We pretend that our cities, our plans, our deeds, and our hopes are erected upon a surface so cleared of natural forces that only our wills decide their outcome. On account of this, their characteristic pretense, Camus does not hate his times; instead, he questions them.

"Admission of ignorance, rejection of fanaticism, the limits of the world and of man, the beloved face, and finally beauty" (3): this is where Camus would have us look to Prometheus and the Greeks. This cluster of qualities and commitments indeed defines the core of Camus' second series of writings. One truth cannot be allowed to obscure another. No matter how closely one attends to the pallor of tyranny and oppression, one must not forget to savor the sun's brilliance. Even if it breaks one's revolutionary stride and delays the movement of history, one must lie in the sun as well as march against despots. Quite simply, there is beauty in the world and there is suffering in the world. Neither is more real or more true than the other. Perhaps there is no denying that the human soul longs to be one, to love single-mindedly and single-heartedly; but here too human being is essentially contradicted and impossible. Nature and history are not to be reconciled (4). Natural beauty draws us into immediacy and indulgence, while historical change requires that we sacrifice the present, what is, for what shall or might be. Only fanaticism, whether self-indulgent or self-righteous, avoids this contradiction; and this only for a time. The lie, the denial, the pretense inherent in all fanaticism eventually goes awry in the direction of its own peculiar prejudice.

The issues here are simple and straightforward. This world is beautiful and to live in this world is to live with its beauty (5–7). This world is also ridden with oppression which one must oppose. And the unity which we nonetheless seek must be grasped only in the approximating reach of finite human consciousness and will, only in the lucid resolve to exclude nothing essential. For, as Camus puts it so plainly: "nothing is true that forces one to exclude" (8). We would surely mistake Camus' sense of the balance to be struck in one's life, however, if we were to imagine a daily diet with equal portions of swimming and political action. There are times of one's life as well as historical periods which require very little sacrifice, while others demand almost everything. His youth in Algiers and his mature manhood in occupied France made quite disparate demands upon Camus, and appropriately so. Truth lies in responding unevenly to the uneven demands of the moment. The darker the times the more one must attend to their illumination through deeds and words which may bring some light; and the more brilliant the day the more one must pause and revel in its shining. There is no recipe for right measure, only outer limits which dictate that neither the sun nor suffering are ever to be forgotten altogether. We must never stray so far from either that we grow fanatically unable or unwilling to find our way back.

Camus himself in his own life provides us with a telling suggestion of this striving for measure. For example, his years in the Resistance so saddened and sickened his heart, so accustomed his eyes to darkness, that he truly wondered whether the sun would ever again bring anything but pain to him. Day by day he lived under the unlimitedly demanding realization that to attend even to one's own survival was to hold back what the situation required. One reality—Nazi tyranny—all but defined his care and attention. Responsive to the darkest of times, he lived a long exile, a long winter, in the midst of which he never forgot summer or the sea. And when the fascist plague was at last lifted, he went home, to come alive again, to take up beauty again in his arms and in his heart. "I discovered once more," he tells us, "that one must keep intact in oneself a freshness, a cool wellspring of joy, love the day that escapes injustice, and return to combat having won that light" (8). Camus speaks of an "inner way," which never ceases to identify and to oppose human cruelty and dishonor and which at the same time is resolved to seek out the light, to face it directly and somehow, before one dies, to name it. This inner way is again the way of measure, the practice of the most benign and most humanizing of all arts (9).

Before turning to Camus' major Promethean works, *The Plague* and *The Rebel*, wherein the art of measure is practiced with systematic discipline, we would do well to scan Camus' other writings of this period, which in general may be said to comprise the years 1945–1951. In so doing we shall attain a gathering appreciation of the many varied dimensions and expressions of the commitment to exclude nothing and to give to each thing its due. First, however, we must notice that from the outset Camus' Promethean writings are concerned with right action. Sokrates once pointed out that all serious thought is premised on the assumption that some opinions are more respectable than others;[18] and, similarly, it may be claimed that all serious action is premised on the assumption that some deeds are more respectable than others. Sisyphus left us with a purely quantitative measure: more life is better than less life. But this measure alone is clearly unequal to the task of assigning honor and contempt appropriately to the deeds and lives of individuals. According to a purely quantitative ethic, the longevous despot outshines as well as outlives those who are as weak as they are just. A purely quantitative ethic would commend the tyrant Zeus and his henchmen over against the benevolent and long-suffering Prometheus. Camus realizes that in our times it is virtue, the good deed, which requires formal defense (10); and in *The Rebel* he will make his case.

The ethic of Sisyphus and of the absurd hero does, it must be granted, possess its partial truth. All else being equal, more life is better than less life. But "all else" is not equal, argues Camus. All deeds, he claims, are not equivalent. It is one thing to inflict suffering and another to endure it. Goodwill and hostility, wanton cruelty and the healing arts, are not equal. Camus realizes how fundamental are these claims, these judgments; and yet he finds little support for their assertion as anything more or other than the assertion of private preference. Neither faith, nor society, nor a common sense of human nature any longer provide a ready common measure for the shared assessment of freedom's options (11). Existentialism (12–13) does no more than offer elaborate theoretical foundation for modern theories of absolute freedom which prove to be quite interchangeable with equally absolute denials of freedom. If the individual will is its own measure, then it possesses no measure at all apart from the cyclopean eye of history. In the end, Existentialism is able to commend only one value, sincerity, the lowest common denominator of every assessable life, mere consistency, which is in itself no virtue at all.[19]

Both Christianity and Marxism, Camus recognizes, possess and promulgate distinct visions of human action which claim to judge words and deeds in accord with a transcendently valid measure. In both cases Camus understands these visions to be visions not of the present but of the future, either of the end of time or of the end of history. Both are possessed of a grand hope the status of which cannot be a matter of knowledge but only of belief. Marxism no less than Christianity finally lays claim to revelation; and for this reason Camus considers them both to be religions (14). For Christians and for Marxists, true enough, all actions are not equivalent; some lives are eminently commendable while others fall under the most intransigent condemnations. Both Christianity and Marxism have their saints: in the former case, one who suffers every insult and injury, even death, with a view toward the coming heavenly kingdom; and, in the latter case, one who is willing to overturn and destroy whatever and whomever may stand in the path of the inevitable classless society. In short, the Christian ethic proposes the victim, the martyr as its measure, while the Marxist proposes the executioner, the revolutionary. Camus finds both unacceptable (15). Both deny the present, refuse it its due. Both deny the natural will to live, the preference for more life rather than less, which cannot decide everything but which cannot either be altogether effaced.

Christianity and Marxism, as Camus sums up their claims and demands, together offer us but two options: to be destroyed or to destroy. We are asked to choose between God and history (16); and to both the odor of sacrifice is sweet. We are asked either to relinquish or to dispatch life for something we shall never see, which Camus regards as madness and as a deadly form of love (17–18). Being given a choice between being a victim and being an executioner is like being given no choice at all (19). "What to do between the two?" (20), asks Camus. He sees that he cannot affirm God nor can he choose history absolutely. His inner way must lie somewhere between the divinization of history and the creation of history, somewhere between the excessive hopes of Christianity and Marxism, but nevertheless shy of Existentialist nihilism. There is no avoiding history; for "we are in it up to our necks."[20] And besides, in itself "history is simply man's desperate effort to give body to his most clairvoyant dreams."[21] After all there is much that is unacceptable in the present order of things; and the pursuit of justice entails the pursuit of change. Camus' only caution is that our dreams be human dreams, lucid and limited, neither blind nor blinding (21). And there is no more modest dream, optimistic in its own fashion(22), than that which Camus proposes: "to fight within history to preserve from history that part of man which is not its proper province."[22]

What Camus has in mind to save from history is nature, primarily human nature, the sheer givenness of human life and of intrinsic human purposefulness. Nature, however elusive and undefinable, must be the basis for our rejection of tyranny and oppression; without this affirmation, all of our denials are utterly arbitrary (23). But whence nature, whence this givenness? Camus has no answer here and seems aware of the implications of this unknowing (24). Nature, like the light behind us guiding the steps of consciousness, remains nameless, affirmed, acted upon, yet never directly known. Herein lies the most telling of Camus' silences, which we will explore further in our discussion of *The Rebel*.

This much Camus does know: that the meaning of human nature resides in community. Only in common with others is the truth and the meaning of human being disclosed. In other words, Camus is convinced that human nature is essentially political. His avowed concern is with those who live outside of any immanent kingdom,[23] deprived of the gracious consolations of either sacred or secular faith, namely, with the damned (25). The human community is the community of those who are given life and made to die in silence, without understanding and without reprieve. Human solidarity is the solidarity of those who one day celebrate gratuitous life and another day mourn gratuitous death and who meanwhile battle for meaning and measure (26). Human nature is what we have in common and is thus inseparable from "the sea, rains, necessity, desire, the struggle against death . . . the things that unite us all" (27) . . . "everyday life with the most possible light thrown upon it" (28). Art and rebellion draw upon the same source and employ the same compassionate imagination which discloses the essential human consortium (29) and seeks to strengthen human complicity (30).

Each time that Camus speaks of "the community of suffering, struggle, and death,"[24] we may assume that his own imagination is replete with memories of the Resistance, which represents as close an embodiment as Camus himself may have witnessed of community as he envisioned it should be. In his "Letters to a German Friend" (31–33), he contrasts the measured aims of the Resistance against the immoral, reckless, Faustian ambitions which the Germans brought to their historic misadventure. The very word "Resistance" describes the conservative posture of Camus' comrades who realized that violent, historical struggle has no rewards to offer. Instead, they found history demanding a long detour from which they hoped for nothing beyond a return to the joys of peace and goodwill which they had been forced to set aside. They fought not for *the* future as they or anyone else would presume to fashion it, but rather, more moderately, for *a* future,[25] a chance to begin again. Although the sword of the Resistance fighters was surely blunted and slowed by their unwillingness to despair of human integrity, their spirit in the end prevailed. From those years of inner and outer combat Camus claims to have learned this much for certain: "contrary to what we sometimes used to think, the spirit is of no avail against the sword, but . . . the spirit together with the sword will always win out over the sword alone" (31) (34).

The spirit is itself of no avail against the sword. This lesson was perhaps the one which Camus learned most painfully and most reluctantly. He found himself forced to the conclusion that one cannot change or overthrow a murderous regime without risking murder. This is the central, gnawing question for Camus throughout his Promethean writings, "the only really serious moral problem" (35): "to find out whether I can kill or let others be killed" (36). This was no remote or idle query for a member of the Resistance; rather, it was of necessity the first item of business, a business for which Camus found himself dreadfully ill-suited (37). What could be imagined more contradictory than Prometheus, the lover of humankind, as a murderer? Yet this was the contradiction which Camus was compelled not only to imagine but to embody. He was all too conscious of the fact that historical change for the better comes by all but imperceptible stages and always at a staggering price (38). History plunges those who enter it into all but unbearable compromise and contradiction. No one, he urges, is to be pushed into so ambiguous an endeavor (39). One fights, and risks killing, for a half-truth or, perhaps, a quarter-truth (40). One must simply keep in mind that what one is fighting is a lie and that the quarter-truth is liberty which one can only hope will one day catch fire (41). Meanwhile, against all doubt and weariness we are to support one another with the clearest words spoken from the heart and to sustain a calm hope.

We turn now to Camus' major Promethean works, first *The Plague* and then *The Rebel*. In the face of works so rich and carefully crafted, this brief commentary must inevitably appear thin and merely suggestive. Even the quite substantial selections appended hereto and to which these remarks aim at providing some preliminary guidance are themselves mere intimations. It cannot be otherwise. And with these limits clearly acknowledged we may resume.

The Plague is set in the North African coastal city of Oran in the year 194–. The precise date is for the reader to supply; and, in fact, the city of Oran itself is quite interchangeable with any number of other cities. It is described as "completely modern," [26] preoccupied with commerce, getting rich, and the usual weekend pastimes of "love-making, sea-bathing, going to the pictures." [27] Oran is a town without a soul; and it covers its own vacuousness with a mesh of habit lest anyone fall into unfamiliar and fatal thoughts. It is a town asleep.

The first unusual event is the death of a rat on a second-floor landing, soon followed by three more in the hall; and, within days, the streets are littered everywhere with dead vermin. But these deaths serve as mere portents. In fact, at the sight of the first dead rat the author's imagination leaps at once to thoughts of human suffering and of impending human death. It is only a matter of time before the plague itself makes the same leap. Two weeks pass; the rats disappear and the first human plague victim dies. "You must picture the consternation of our little town," writes the author of the plague journal, "hitherto so tranquil, and now, out of the blue, shaken to its core, like a quite healthy man who all of a sudden feels his temperature shoot up and the blood seething like wildfire in his veins." [28]

The first plague death marked the end of bewildering portents and the beginning of a state of seige. "There have been as many plagues as wars in history; yet always plagues and wars take people by surprise." [29] As the word "plague" is uttered for the first time in Oran, the citizens set about singly and collectively developing patterns of avoidance. Even when the state of plague is proclaimed, no one really acknowledges the disease and its implications. Nevertheless certain conditions fail no one's notice: the city gates are closed and sealed off; all correspondence with the outer world is forbidden; and, within, the stench of death rises. Oran becomes overnight a city in exile. One word begins to characterize its life: separation. There is no reason or compassion to the lines which the plague now draws. Those within the city are separated from those without; loved ones are unable to return and visitors are unable to leave. The plague-stricken are separated from those as yet uncontaminated. Of course, the dead are separated from the living. And, finally, for those who keep a haunted inner vigil and each day await death, if only in their imaginations, the separation slips inward and estranges them from their own lives. "Hostile to the past, impatient of the present, and cheated of the future, we were much like those whom men's justice, or hatred, forces to live behind prison bars."[30]

Repeated parallels, such as the one above, to *The Stranger* are unmistakable in *The Plague*. Indeed, one might argue that *The Plague* is simply *The Stranger* "blown large," the story of an individual expanded into the story of a city. Both stories begin with a life of unreflective contentment which is suddenly shattered by the intrusion of an alienating, exiling force. What then ensues is a process of decisive awakening, a gradual coming to consciousness. One by one the plagued citizens come to recognize conditions and necessities which preceded and endure beyond the exceptional circumstances presently occasioning this heightened awareness. Thus, in *The Stranger*, Meursault realizes only that he is to die and the implications of that fact which single him out from no one. Similarly, in *The Plague*, it is acknowledged that the plague is no more than the established order, the reign of death under which all mortals live by definition, and the reign of terror which some crazed mortals inflict upon others in that arena which Camus vaguely terms "history," where one, it seems, is always either master or slave, executioner or victim, have or have-not. "That's why everybody in the world today looks so tired; everyone is more or less sick of plague."[31] "But what does that mean—'plague'? Just life, no more than that."[32] The condition and quality of our lives are determined, after all, not only by the treatment we receive from the indifferent sky but also by the treatment we receive from one another. Two orders clearly impinge upon our lives, the order of the universe and the order of the state, nature and history. Both tend to be lethal. The plague stands as an embracing metaphor for human affliction and suffering whatever its source or form.

What advances *The Plague* beyond *The Stranger* is primarily the introduction of human plurality and of history. The prison cell widens to encompass a city and red-robed judges wreak as much havoc as fate itself. We must have in mind both the universe and occupied France, as well as Spain and Algeria, or, perhaps, Vietnam and Chile, if we are to realize the full valence of this allegory. Death and suffering are unjust whether we endure them from above or from a fellow's hands. "All executioners," wrote Camus in *The Myth of Sisyphus*, "are of the same family."[33] The first task is to realize that the plague is in our midst and the next task is to combat it. *The Plague* is a chronicle focused on the taking up of these two essentially human and essentially communal tasks. What we find in its pages is a chronicle of conversion stories much like those which fascinated the young Augustine and to which he added his own in due time, except that Augustine was converted to faith, while Camus' figures are converted to clear-sightedness and compassion. One by one they come to realize that "everybody's in the same boat,"[34] and that "now that plague was among us, it was up to them to do whatever could be done to fight it."[35] The path they take is described simply as "the path of sympathy."[36] It is claimed to be a road neither for heroes nor for saints but rather for those with a "common decency"[37] which endeavors, "so far as possible, not to join forces with the pestilences."[38]

No one's conversion is so attentively traced in *The Plague* as that of Paneloux, the priest. His is perhaps the most public voice in the

city of Oran as it is depicted to us; and that would be reason alone
for the stakes' being so high in this case. But there seems to be still
another more substantial reason for the attention paid to Paneloux.
He sees his calling to be one of striving for sanctity; and, indeed,
there are those who wonder whether he may be a saint. This issue
is critical; for *The Plague* is very clearly a book about callings, con-
versions, and sanctity. Camus is manifestly concerned with the justification of good deeds, the measuring of lives, and the articulation
of an ethic. He realizes with Aristotle that to say that one action is
better than another, one must have some conception of the good
and of the best, which means some conception of sanctity. This
question is raised explicitly in a conversation between the book's
two central characters, Rieux and Tarrou:

> "It comes to this," Tarrou said almost casually; "what interests me
> is learning how to become a saint."
> "But you don't believe in God."
> "Exactly! Can one become a saint without God?—that's the prob-
> lem, in fact the only problem, I'm up against today." [39]

The first plague sermon of Paneloux (42) is preached to a vast
congregation swelling beyond the cathedral walls. Paneloux stands
high above the anxious crowd and accuses them of sin, assuring
them that they have deserved the plague. They are to fall on their
knees, own their sins and their sins' deserts, repent, and leave the
rest to God. Finally, they are to rejoice; for the plague itself marks
the path to their salvation. Only the blind will fail to see in the
plague the healing embrace of a loving God. This consoling hope,
however, which cautions inaction and commends the helpless victim, is hardly congenial to Tarrou and Rieux, who exhaust their
arms and their hearts daily in struggling against the plague (43).
Rieux comments that Christian recitations are often inexperienced
and unthinking. When confronted with suffering, however, Christians
frequently give in less tamely than they say they will; and, like their
faithless fellows, they rise above themselves. Indeed, Paneloux will

soon give proof to Rieux's account. Gradually the inescapable lesson of human suffering is learned in Oran wherein the plague becomes the concern of all. Whatever transcendent faiths or private loves may have blinded individuals to this common concern, the number of the converted grows, each of whom comes to realize that "there can be no true goodness nor true love without the utmost clear-sightedness" (44). No one is pushed to rebel: each one is left to find his own way in his own time.

Before tracing further the conversion of Paneloux, we would do well to notice briefly another conversion, that of Rambert, the journalist. From the outset Rambert is obsessed with one desire: to escape the plague city and so to be reunited with his distant lover. He regards himself as a stranger having no common cause with Oran and having an inalienable right to pursue his own private happiness. All his thoughts are strategies of flight, which, at first, fail him and which he himself eventually relinquishes of his own accord. "For nothing in the world," explains Rieux, "is it worth turning one's back on what one loves. Yet that is what I'm doing, though why I do not know" (45). In fact, Rambert makes room for a more expansive love, which contradicts yet never refutes the intimacy to which he will one day return. For now, his former devotion is "refined to a pale abstraction;"[40] but he does not forget.

The turning-point for Paneloux comes with the death of a young child. Here the contrast between what his heart believes and what his eyes see is absolute and all but untenable. He no longer understands and yet he suggests that "perhaps we should love what we cannot understand" (46). Rieux thinks and loves quite otherwise; but what is clear and crucial to him is that they work together in a common struggle which is unaffected by either belief or disbelief. Paneloux has witnessed human suffering and learned its lesson. He will try now to relieve suffering before pointing out its excellence. In league with the plague-fighters, Paneloux too will fight against Creation as he finds it, even as he continues to believe in Creation as the perfect work of God. He begins to live an eternal contradiction (47), which finds full expression in his second and last plague sermon (48).

Paneloux does not launch his second sermon at the congregation from a position of profound distance and privilege; rather, he speaks always of "we" in a voice gentler and more thoughtful than before. One image lies now at the center of his words and of his life: the image of Christ crucified, an image of ultimate contradiction. For no contradiction is more absolute than that of the "god-man," the immortal-mortal, embraced yet abandoned in death by his father. According to tradition, Christ on the cross both enjoyed the vision of the blessed and sank into despair. Faith and sight, inner reality and outer appearance, time and eternity stand at an infinite remove from each other; and yet Christians, as Paneloux understands their calling, must appropriate this disparity in all its forms. Indeed, we may see here the absurd raised to its highest imaginable power, once nature is believed to be created and history is believed to be salvific. Christians are required, on the one hand, to live godly lives of vast hope and loving acceptance and, at the same time, to live human lives of clear-sightedness and resolute struggle against the very order of things. Paneloux argues that we must go to the very heart of what is unacceptable. We must confess and affirm the will of God even in the anguish of child victims and, with the same heart, pit our every energy against the world's pestilences. Christians long for eternal happiness without granting that everlasting bliss can make up for one moment's human suffering. For all their limitless hopes, Christians are still somehow without solace. Theirs, says Paneloux, is a hard faith.

Once Paneloux joins the plague-fighters his solidarity with their passions and their struggles is without seam. His sacred faith, hope, and charity seem to figure not at all and count for nothing. Only in death, wherein separation is never to be avoided, does Paneloux stand off from his fellows. In the end and only in the end when they are so weak and emptied of life that they can struggle no more, believer and nonbeliever, sacred rebel and profane rebel, appropriately part ways. Thus the priest refuses the services of the doctor and the doctor refuses the services of the priest. In death they become a mystery one to the other.

Paneloux is convinced that "priests can have no friends";[41] and here we may recall the suggestion of Euripides that those who dwell in the love of the gods have no need of human friendship. The matter is quite the opposite, however, for those who know or experience themselves to be deprived of any divine care or sharing. For them, whom Camus calls "the damned," human friendship is essential. Indeed, if there is one perfect moment in *The Plague*, one moment which simply shines, it is when Tarrou and Rieux set aside history and celebrate nature. They flee the plague and affirm what nothing, including the plague, can ever deny: their essential kinship with one another in the earth (49). Momentarily they taste a happiness that forgets nothing; momentarily all is in perfect measure. It is for the preservation of such moments that their every nerve is otherwise strained.

After their brief respite with each other, buoyed by the infinite sea, they "set their shoulders to the wheel again."[42] Again we recall Sisyphus, and this time the difference is manifestly clear. The rock, the never-ending defeat, is essentially shared. "We all have the plague . . . and one must do what one can" (50). Tarrou and Rieux leave sanctity to others and strive only for "approximations of sainthood . . . a mild benevolent diabolism."[43] "They knew now that if there is one thing one can always yearn for and sometimes attain, it is human love."[44] And here we must surely have in mind neither *eros*, erotic love, nor *charitas*, divine love, but *philia*, friendship. For friendship's sake, Rieux sets aside all regulation when Tarrou contracts the plague. He will permit no separation. Those who have no fellowship with the gods need, desperately, human friendship. Tarrou and Rieux have known these three certainties together—exile, suffering, and love. They part with these in mind. And, for a moment, we glimpse what has become of a happy death, death without solace but attended with all the care that friends can muster.

We turn now to *The Rebel* for which the central philosophical question is no longer the solipsistic question of suicide but rather the communal question of murder. Surely there would be no distortion in our recalling Tarrou's comment on society in *The Plague* and attributing those words now to Camus: "To my mind the social order around me was based on the death sentence, and by fighting the established order I'd be fighting against murder."[45] Camus clearly recognizes this centrality of death to society not only in practice but also in theory. And his own rebellious course of thought consequently stands at odds not only with modern practice but also with modern social theory. In fact, the alternative vision which he proposes is not a social theory at all but a political theory rooted in the classical Greek understanding of the city and of natural human fellowship.

Modern social theory—beginning with Machiavelli, Hobbes, Locke, and Rousseau and informing every modern Western state—represents the eclipse of political theory. The debate here is not a matter of mere semantics. What is at stake is the simple assertion that human being is essentially political, namely that each human being requires the shared presence and activity of others for his or her own natural becoming and well-being. Modern social theory, in its many diverse metamorphoses, asserts the contrary: that human beings are at essential odds with each other apart from the construction of an unnatural but relatively beneficial system called "society." In the face of this foreign yet beguiling social order, Camus' own affirmation of our political nature must be rebellious or antisocial. And, for those who would unwittingly equate social theory with political theory, Camus' thought must seem antipolitical. Indeed, Camus has been incessantly accused of irrelevance, of not taking his bearings by modern political realities. And such accusations are on the mark, except that they confuse theories for realities. Work, death, suffering, hatred, and compassion—these are realities; and Camus never takes his eyes off them. But Marxism, capitalism, anarchism, liberalism, pluralism—these are the theories not the realities of our times; and Camus' roots and convictions lie elsewhere. With any but the most parochial understanding of the political realm in mind, Camus' thought is profoundly political. In fact, it is only in confrontation with the modern denial of *l'homme politique* that Camus must speak of *l'homme révolté*; the latter is simply the stance which the former must take in our times.

Murder is not peculiar to our social order. Human beings have always, on occasion, flown at one another in rage, and, when the blinding passion left them, stared in horror at what they have just done. What Camus suggests is peculiar, indeed congenital, to our social order is logical murder, murder to which we are led not by passion but by our doctrines and their dispassionately calculated implications (51). Passion is orgasmic. It runs its course swiftly and leaves us prey to an often merciless lucidity. Ideologies are not so kind. They are capable of justifying any crime, indefinitely; for they do not so much overpower thought as destroy it. They avoid passion altogether and create a neutered language simply conducive to their purposes. Hobbes was not the first to employ self-defined, internally consistent language to tame human passion; but he is a tutor we must note. For he taught us moderns our most characteristic skill, the art of systematic lying, which begins with self-deception and only then converts others. We call each deed what it pleases us to call it and enter into a pact of silence about whatever we wish not to notice or not to think about. We practice the art of measure with a god-like vengeance, allowing our imaginations to be the gauge of reality. As a result:

> We suffocate among people who think they are absolutely right, whether in their machines or in their ideas. And for all who can live only in an atmosphere of human dialogue and sociability, this silence is the end of the world.[46]

Quite simply, Camus proposes that we examine our most suspect deed—murder—and that we do so "in the language of a common humanity."[47] He proposes no doctrine but only a path, a way of insight and integrity. For "the problem is not how to carry men away; it is essential, on the contrary, that they not be carried away but rather that they be made to understand clearly what they are doing."[48] If we look closely in *The Rebel* we will see Prometheus, the "fore-thinker," everywhere.

If suicide is incoherent, so is murder. Here *The Rebel* strikes its first roots (52). If my life is a good whose violation is unacceptable, then the same must be true of the lives of others. Here we witness the discovery of a "common good" in the classical sense, a good which is not diminished but rather enhanced in the sharing. All political life resides in *koinonia*, in communion; and communion requires something to be communed in, a common good. In the same moment of lucidity wherein murder and suicide become inseparable, so do the lives and deaths of human beings, you and I, become inseparable; and the latter insight is the more foundational of the two. Camus, as rebel, must proceed from rejection to acceptance, from the denial of suicide and murder to the affirmation of a common life which is good. The rebel's "no" contains a "yes" which grounds and supports it. When slaves deny the denial of their humanity, they affirm their humanity not as a personal prerogative but as a common possession. Throughout Camus' analysis of rebellion we must understand that two negatives make a positive. And when something essential has been denied, the denial of that denial is likewise essential. The path which Camus pursues is indirect and, indeed, backwards; to this extent he belongs to our times. He recognizes that our grasp on our most essential truths is tenuous. Some dark reminiscence allows us to reject the false without our being able to articulate the true. Yet each essential denial brings a new disclosure of its foundations. "Awareness, no matter how confused it may be, develops from every act of rebellion: the sudden, dazzling perception that there is something in man with which he can identify himself" (53). In other words, "rebellion, though apparently negative, since it creates nothing, is profoundly positive in that it reveals the part of man which must always be defended."[49] Namely, human nature, which is common and which is the appropriate measure of each individual life, word, and deed.

With this disclosure, Camus' political philosophy is grounded. Awareness is born; and it too is common. The measure is at hand. And thinking now becomes the art of measuring. Every sect or state must be measured against the natural human community which must be preserved at all costs within, in spite of, or against history. For a moment rejection yields to acceptance and Camus asserts that human fellowship is metaphysical. One might suspect that even he may have marveled at his saying this. Perhaps he wondered what he was saying, though not why he was saying it. Of Camus himself, no less than of his rebel, it may be said that "the act of rebellion carries him far beyond the point he had reached by simply refusing." [50]

The Rebel is itself an exercise in rebellion, denying what requires to be denied in our times and disclosing the affirmations implicit in its denials. In all this it is seeking above all a rule of conduct (54), a true measure, while remaining always "faithful to its first noble promise" (55), the affirmation of life as a common good. This pursuit of a common measure is expressive, at the same time, of "an aspiration to order" (56), which recognizes that only crime and disorder can result when the common human good is denied. In a world wherein Camus sees no evidence of divine providence or responsibility, it follows that whatever order or disorder there is must be the work of human beings. "Then begins," writes Camus, "the desperate effort to create, at the price of crime and murder if necessary, the dominion of man" (57). Camus sees no alternative to human sovereignty and yet wishes to retain human accountability; but on what basis? (58) Even when the divine Creator is denied, Camus cannot countenance wanton human willfulness. Even without God, human being is the measurer but not the measure. Human beings alone speak of justice but Camus would never accept that this makes them the creators of justice. The path which Camus seeks to disclose lies somewhere between the decalogue and

nihilism (59), somewhere between hatred of the Creator and hatred
of Creation (60).

In an analysis of modern theory and practice, which perhaps
seeks to be too exhaustive, Camus traces, nevertheless with striking
clarity, the "convulsive effort to control the world and to introduce
a universal rule" (61). When the human will to power knows no
limits, it refutes itself. It is one thing to overturn the throne of the
Creator and quite another to debase Creation. And yet, "by the law
of spiritual imperialism,"[51] the two become one act. When God is
no longer worshiped and obeyed, human beings become responsible for the earth; and "when nature ceases to be an object of contemplation and admiration, it can be nothing more than material
for an action that aims at transforming it."[52] The question, then,
is: how to preserve nature as an object of contemplation and admiration without worshiping God? Similarly, how are we to remain
just once all supposed divine justice has been denied? Camus
points out that, once human beings look to themselves and not to
God for justice, they themselves mostly become unjust. They grow
so obsessed with the progress of humankind as they project it that
they are willing to murder, lie, and play the tyrant so as to realize
their vision. Prometheus, once he forgets his original goodwill, all
too readily becomes Caesar (62). In *The Rebel* Camus traces two
movements, both the path of degeneration from Prometheus to
Caesar and the path of regeneration from Caesar back to Prometheus, namely, both a historical critique of modern rebellion and a
proposed return to the origins of all true rebellion.

The pivotal problem throughout *The Rebel* remains the problem
of murder, both in its active commission and in its passive acceptance. The rejection of murder is the touchstone of true rebellion,
rebellion faithful to its origins. And thus the decisive condemnation
of the would-be rebels of our century is their acquiescence in mass
murder, in retrospect and in prospect (63). Murder is "the definitive crime against man" (64), the act which literally and symboli-
cally severs the human bond and leaves us without measure, with-

out limits. Thus murder must never under any circumstance be justified and given an inoffensive euphemism. Still, murder cannot be altogether ruled out from the rebel's consideration. There may and do arise cursed circumstances in which the sparing of one life may require the acceptance of many unnecessary deaths. In such moments, dark and out of joint, one must set aside the rule and act out an intolerable exception. But there must have been no alternative; and how can one know that one has thought long enough, considered every possibility? As a rule of thumb, Camus suggests that one has taken another's life seriously when one has weighed it evenly with one's own. The murderer who is going to die with the victim will presumably not act prematurely or lightly. The bond between murder and suicide, between another's death and one's own must be maintained. Murder must be as desperate and presumably anguished an act as suicide; perhaps crazed but never convenient. In murder, above all, one must, paradoxically, be fastidious. Only so can the highly contagious disease of murder be contained. "It is the limit that can be reached but once, after which one must die . . . Beyond that frontier, contradiction and nihilism begin." [53] In short, every rebel, even the one who murders, "pleads for life" (65).

The one principle which guides Camus in his political thinking is itself not a political principle: that everything human is intrinsically limited. Every human freedom, every human power, human justice and injustice, innocence and guilt, flesh and spirit—all are relative, requiring balance and attunement (66). So unsteady and compromised are all human undertakings, so uncertain their outcome, that the means must be attended to as carefully as the end (67). One word gathers these concerns together: moderation (68). Nothing in excess. No password is more Greek, which is not to say that the Greeks were a moderate people. If they were, they would not likely have been so impressed with the need for moderation. The same may be said of Camus and of our times. To live in moderation is to live in constant tension, checking, bending back, drawing together would-be absolute passions and projects. Like the tips of a massive bow, nature and history must be drawn back by a will that is taunt and strong, spun of many fibers (69). In the end Prometheus is intransigent if nothing else in his rejection of divinity and in his love of humankind. He follows the rebel's logic to the end: "to want to serve justice so as not to add to the injustice of the human condition, to insist on plain language so as not to increase the universal falsehood, and to wager, in spite of human misery, for happiness."[54] And, Camus insists, we must imagine Prometheus and his fellows happy, participant in a common joy born of struggle and sharing a modest human hope for less dark times.

Camus' plays of this period, *State of Siege* and *The Just Assassins*, are transparent to the concerns and the commitments of *The Rebel*. In *State of Siege*, set in Spain, the appropriateness of which Camus explicitly defended,[55] a city is overtaken by a deadly plague. The plague, however, is no witless, random microbe on the loose but rather a neatly organized state of terror established by a few logical murders in the right places. The new administration, whose claim to legitimacy rests upon the divine right of murderers, promises three things: "order, silence, total justice" (70). If successful, it will represent "the triumph of death and silence" (71). Death, in the new role of secretary to the Plague, is no longer natural death, the ancient reaper, irrational yet mostly rhythmical in his visitations, but murder, always calculated and logically justified (72). Death, now a human power, claims divine sovereignty, claims to be the only real power there is (73). Fear is once again proclaimed to be the beginning of wisdom. But these pretensions shatter when a young rebel, Diego, refuses either to fear or to hate. He chooses justice but forgets love (74) in its simplest, most immediate expression. His love becomes a mere abstraction, a flight of soul, an idea, which could not breathe and sustain itself. "Love is injustice," writes Camus in his *Notebooks*, "but justice is not enough."[56]

In conclusion of these reflections on Promethean rebellion and fellowship, we turn to *The Just Assassins*, Camus' dramatic recreation of the assassination of the Grand Duke Sergei by Kaliayev in Moscow, 1905. These terrorists, whom Camus labeled "the fastidious assassins,"[57] exemplify rebellion true to its origins as well as its destiny. They were indeed absurd rebels, contradicted to their core. "Necessary and inexcusable—that is how murder appeared to them."[58] These were, Camus assures us, "men of the highest principles . . .

> History offers few examples of fanatics who have suffered from scruples, even in action. But the men of 1905 were always prey to doubts. The greatest homage we can pay them is to say that we would not be able, in 1950, to ask them one question that they had not already asked and that, in their life or by their death, they had not partially answered.[59]

In speaking of the rebels of 1905 and of all those who would take up common cause with them, Camus suggests that it must be understood "that they correct one another and that a limit, under the sun, shall curb them all."[60] In *The Just Assassins*, particularly in the argument over Kaliayev's refusal to kill children (75) and in Dora's challenging Kaliayev to a love more warm and selfish than the love of justice (76), we glimpse what this mutual correction might mean in practice. Perhaps it is true that "there is no justice—but there are limits."[61] In any event, justice is a lethal idea, judging by the vast injustice done in its name. History is a treacherous sea and, morally, we can boast of no more than the simplest rigging to make our way in it. We tack our way to our dreams. Nothing more frustrating could be imagined than the struggles of human beings to better themselves. The task is endless (77) and we will surely forget both the past and the future, both our modest origins and our modest hopes without one another to remind us of them. Alone we are dangerous, and joyless, condemned to a solitary hell which can only be of our own making.

NOTES

1. Aeschylus, *Prometheus Bound*, 209–213, tr. E. A. Havelock, in *Prometheus*, E. A. Havelock, Seattle: University of Washington, 1950.

2. Hesiod, *Theogony*, 513, tr. Richmond Lattimore, in *Hesiod*, Ann Arbor: University of Michigan Press, 1959.

3. Aeschylus, *Prometheus Bound*, *op. cit.*, 230–232.

4. *Ibid.*, 444.

5. Aeschylus, *Prometheus Bound*, 513–514, tr. David Grene, University of Chicago Press, 1942.

6. Cf. *ibid.*, 11, 28.

7. Cf. *ibid.*, 123.

8. Aeschylus, *Prometheus Bound*, 274–275, tr. E. A. Havelock, *op. cit.*

9. *Ibid.*, 1067–1070.

10. *Ibid.*, 309–310.

11. *Ibid.*, 998.

12. Cf. *ibid.*, 1001.

13. Camus, *Death*, p. 84.

14. *Ibid.*, p. 128.

15. *Ibid.*, p. 7.

16. Plato, *Phaedo*, 83c, tr. Hugh Tredennick, in *Collected Dialogues*, *op. cit.*

17. Cf. Plato, *Protagoras*, 356c, ff., in *Collected Dialogues*, *op. cit.*

18. Cf. Plato, *Crito*, 47a, in *Collected Dialogues*, *op. cit.*

19. Cf. Camus, *Neither*, p. 8.

20. *Ibid.*, p. 18.

21. *Ibid.*, p. 14.

22. *Ibid.*, p. 18.

23. Cf. *ibid.*, p. 3.

24. Cf. *ibid.*, p. 5.

25. Cf. *ibid.*, p. 4.

26. Camus, *Plague*, p. 4.

27. *Ibid.*

28. *Ibid.*, p. 15.

29. *Ibid.*, p. 34.

30. *Ibid.*, p. 67.

31. *Ibid.*, p. 229.

32. *Ibid.*, p. 277.

33. Camus, *Myth*, p. 149.

34. Camus, *Plague*, p. 27.
35. *Ibid.*, p. 121.
36. *Ibid.*, p. 230.
37. *Ibid.*, p. 150.
38. *Ibid.*, p. 229.
39. *Ibid.*, pp. 230–231.
40. *Ibid.*, p. 265.
41. *Ibid.*, p. 210.
42. *Ibid.*, p. 233.
43. *Ibid.*, p. 248.
44. *Ibid.*, p. 271.
45. *Ibid.*, p. 226.
46. Camus, *Neither*, p. 2.
47. *Ibid.*, p. 1.
48. *Ibid.*, p. 17.
49. Camus, *Rebel*, p. 19.
50. *Ibid.*, p. 14.
51. *Ibid.*, p. 103.
52. *Ibid.*, p. 299.
53. *Ibid.*, p. 282.
54. *Ibid.*, p. 285.
55. Cf. Camus, "Why Spain?" in *Resistance*, pp. 57–62.
56. Camus, *Notebooks II*, p. 250.
57. Cf. Camus, *Rebel*, pp. 164–173.
58. *Ibid.*, p. 169.
59. *Ibid.*, p. 167.
60. *Ibid.*, p. 306.
61. Camus, *Plays*, p. 231.

Readings

1

Everything is decided. It is simple and straightforward. But then human suffering intervenes, and alters our plans.

(*Notebooks I*, 198)

~

2

To grow old is to move from passion to compassion.

(*Notebooks II*, 254)

~

3

The Mediterranean sun has something tragic about it, quite different from the tragedy of fogs. Certain evenings at the base of the seaside mountains, night falls over the flawless curve of a little bay, and there rises from the silent waters a sense of anguished fulfillment. In such spots one can understand that if the Greeks knew despair, they always did so through beauty and its stifling quality. In that gilded calamity, tragedy reaches its highest point. Our time, on the other hand, has fed its despair on ugliness and convulsions. This is why Europe would be vile, if suffering could ever be so.

We have exiled beauty; the Greeks took up arms for her. First difference, but one that has a history. Greek thought always took refuge behind the conception of limits. It never carried anything to

extremes, neither the sacred nor reason, because it negated nothing, neither the sacred nor reason. It took everything into consideration, balancing shadow with light. Our Europe, on the other
hand, off in the pursuit of totality, is the child of disproportion.
She negates beauty, as she negates whatever she does not glorify.
And, through all her diverse ways, she glorifies but one thing,
which is the future rule of reason. In her madness she extends the
eternal limits, and at that very moment dark Erinyes fall upon her
and tear her to pieces. Nemesis, the goddess of measure and not of
revenge, keeps watch. All those who overstep the limit are pitilessly
punished by her.

The Greeks, who for centuries questioned themselves as to what
is just, could understand nothing of our idea of justice. For them
equity implied a limit, whereas our whole continent is convulsed in
its search for a justice that must be total. At the dawn of Greek
thought Heraclitus was already imagining that justice sets limits for
the physical universe itself: "The sun will not overstep his measures; if he does, the Erinyes, the handmaids of justice, will find
him out."* We who have cast the universe and spirit out of our
sphere laugh at that threat. In a drunken sky we light up the suns
we want. But nonetheless the boundaries exist, and we know it. In
our wildest aberrations we dream of an equilibrium we have left
behind, which we naïvely expect to find at the end of our errors.
Childish presumption which justifies the fact that child-nations,
inheriting our follies, are now directing our history.

A fragment attributed to the same Heraclitus simply states: "Presumption, regression of progress." And, many centuries after the
man of Ephesus, Socrates, facing the threat of being condemned to
death, acknowledged only this one superiority in himself: what he
did not know he did not claim to know. The most exemplary life
and thought of those centuries close on a proud confession of ignorance. Forgetting that, we have forgotten our virility. We have

* Bywater's translation. [*Translator's note.*]

preferred the power that apes greatness, first Alexander and then the Roman conquerors whom the authors of our schoolbooks, through some incomparable vulgarity, teach us to admire. We, too, have conquered, moved boundaries, mastered heaven and earth. Our reason has driven all away. Alone at last, we end up by ruling over a desert. What imagination could we have left for that higher equilibrium in which nature balanced history, beauty, virtue, and which applied the music of numbers even to blood-tragedy? We turn our backs on nature; we are ashamed of beauty. Our wretched tragedies have a smell of the office clinging to them, and the blood that trickles from them is the color of printer's ink.

This is why it is improper to proclaim today that we are the sons of Greece. Or else we are the renegade sons. Placing history on the throne of God, we are progressing toward theocracy like those whom the Greeks called Barbarians and whom they fought to death in the waters of Salamis. In order to realize how we differ, one must turn to him among our philosophers who is the true rival of Plato. "Only the modern city," Hegel dares write, "offers the mind a field in which it can become aware of itself." We are thus living in the period of big cities. Deliberately, the world has been amputated of all that constitutes its permanence: nature, the sea, hilltops, evening meditation. Consciousness is to be found only in the streets, because history is to be found only in the streets—this is the edict. And consequently our most significant works show the same bias. Landscapes are not be found in great European literature since Dostoevsky. History explains neither the natural universe that existed before it nor the beauty that exists above it. Hence it chose to be ignorant of them. Whereas Plato contained everything—nonsense, reason, and myth—our philosophers contain nothing but nonsense or reason because they have closed their eyes to the rest. The mole is meditating.

It is Christianity that began substituting the tragedy of the soul for contemplation of the world. But, at least, Christianity referred to a spiritual nature and thereby preserved a certain fixity. With God dead, there remains only history and power. For some time the entire effort of our philosophers has aimed solely at replacing the notion of human nature with that of situation, and replacing ancient harmony with the disorderly advance of chance or reason's pitiless progress. Whereas the Greeks gave to will the boundaries of reason, we have come to put the will's impulse in the very center of reason, which has, as a result, become deadly. For the Greeks, values pre-existed all action, of which they definitely set the limits. Modern philosophy places its values at the end of action. They *are* not but *are becoming*, and we shall know them fully only at the completion of history. With values, all limit disappears, and since conceptions differ as to what they will be, since all struggles, without the brake of those same values, spread indefinitely, today's Messianisms confront one another and their clamors mingle in the clash of empires. Disproportion is a conflagration, according to Heraclitus. The conflagration is spreading; Nietzsche is outdistanced. Europe no longer philosophizes by striking a hammer, but by shooting a cannon.

Nature is still there, however. She contrasts her calm skies and her reasons with the madness of men. Until the atom too catches fire and history ends in the triumph of reason and the agony of the species. But the Greeks never said that the limit could not be overstepped. They said it existed and that whoever dared to exceed it was mercilessly struck down. Nothing in present history can contradict them.

The historical spirit and the artist both want to remake the world. But the artist, through an obligation of his nature, knows his limits, which the historical spirit fails to recognize. This is why the latter's aim is tyranny whereas the former's passion is freedom. All those who are struggling for freedom today are ultimately fighting for beauty. Of course, it is not a question of defending beauty for itself. Beauty cannot do without man, and we shall not give our era its nobility and serenity unless we follow it in its misfortune. Never again shall we be hermits. But it is no less true that man cannot do without beauty, and this is what our era pretends to want to disregard. It steels itself to attain the absolute and authority; it wants to transfigure the world before having exhausted it, to set it to rights before having understood it. Whatever it may say, our era is deserting this world. Ulysses can choose at Calypso's bidding between immortality and the land of his fathers. He chooses the land, and death with it. Such simple nobility is foreign to us today. Others will say that we lack humility; but, all things considered, this word is ambiguous. Like Dostoevsky's fools who boast of everything, soar to heaven, and end up flaunting their shame in any public place, we merely lack man's pride, which is fidelity to his limits, lucid love of his condition.

"I hate my time," Saint-Exupéry wrote shortly before his death, for reasons not far removed from those I have spoken of. But, however upsetting that exclamation, coming from him who loved men for their admirable qualities, we shall not accept responsibility for it. Yet what a temptation, at certain moments, to turn one's back on this bleak, fleshless world! But this time is ours, and we cannot live hating ourselves. It has fallen so low only through the excess of its virtues as well as through the extent of its vices. We shall fight for the virtue that has a history. What virtue? The horses of Patroclus weep for their master killed in battle. All is lost. But Achilles resumes the fight, and victory is the outcome, because friendship has just been assassinated: friendship is a virtue.

Admission of ignorance, rejection of fanaticism, the limits of the world and of man, the beloved face, and finally beauty—this is where we shall be on the side of the Greeks. In a certain sense, the direction history will take is not the one we think. It lies in the struggle between creation and inquisition. Despite the price which artists will pay for their empty hands, we may hope for their victory. Once more the philosophy of darkness will break and fade away over the dazzling sea. O midday thought, the Trojan war is being fought far from the battlefields! Once more the dreadful walls of the modern city will fall to deliver up—"soul serene as the ocean's calm"—the beauty of Helen.

(*Myth*, 134–138)

4

The whole question: the antithesis between history and nature.

(*Notebooks I*, 81)

5

I cannot live without beauty. That's what makes me weak in the face of certain people.

(*Notebooks II*, 71)

6

Little bay before Tenès, at the foot of the chains of mountains. Perfect half-circle. As evening falls, a ripeness full of anguish hangs over the silent waters. Then one realizes that if the Greeks formed the idea of despair and tragedy they always did so *through* beauty and its oppressive quality. It's a tragedy that culminates. Whereas the modern mind based its despair on ugliness and mediocrity.

What Char means probably. For the Greeks, beauty is a point of departure. For a European, it is an end, rarely achieved. I am not modern.

(*Notebooks II*, 188)

7

Saint-Etienne and its suburbs. Such a sight is the condemnation of the civilization that produced it. A world in which there is no more place for the human being, for joy, for active leisure, is a world that must die. No group of people can live devoid of beauty. They can go on living for a time and that's all. And the Europe that presents one of its most characteristic faces here is progressively get-

ting away from beauty. That is why it is going through convulsions
and that's why it will die if peace does not signify for it a return to
beauty and love's return to its rightful place.

(*Notebooks II*, 69–70)

8

Yet I obscurely missed something during all those years. When one
has once had the good luck to love intensely, life is spent in trying
to recapture that ardor and that illumination. Forsaking beauty and
the sensual happiness attached to it, exclusively serving misfortune,
calls for a nobility I lack. But, after all, nothing is true that forces
one to exclude. Isolated beauty ends up simpering; solitary justice
ends up oppressing. Whoever aims to serve one exclusive of the
other serves no one, not even himself, and eventually serves injustice twice. A day comes when, thanks to rigidity, nothing causes
wonder any more, everything is known, and life is spent in beginning over again. These are the days of exile, of desiccated life, of
dead souls. To come alive again, one needs a special grace, self-
forgetfulness, or a homeland. Certain mornings, on turning a corner, a delightful dew falls on the heart and then evaporates. But its
coolness remains, and this is what the heart requires always. I had
to set out again. . . .

At noon on the half-sandy slopes covered with heliotropes like a
foam left by the furious waves of the last few days as they withdrew,
I watched the sea barely swelling at that hour with an exhausted
motion, and I satisfied the two thirsts one cannot long neglect
without drying up—I mean loving and admiring. For there is
merely bad luck in not being loved; there is misfortune in not loving. All of us, today, are dying of this misfortune. For violence and
hatred dry up the heart itself; the long fight for justice exhausts the
love that nevertheless gave birth to it. In the clamor in which we
live, love is impossible and justice does not suffice. This is why

Europe hates daylight and is only able to set injustice up against injustice. But in order to keep justice from shriveling up like a beautiful orange fruit containing nothing but a bitter, dry pulp, I discovered once more at Tipasa that one must keep intact in oneself a freshness, a cool wellspring of joy, love the day that escapes injustice, and return to combat having won that light. Here I recaptured the former beauty, a young sky, and I measured my luck, realizing at last that in the worst years of our madness the memory of that sky had never left me. This was what in the end had kept me from despairing. I had always known that the ruins of Tipasa were younger than our new constructions or our bomb damage. There the world began over again every day in an ever new light. O light! This is the cry of all the characters of ancient drama brought face to face with their fate. This last resort was ours, too, and I knew it now. In the middle of winter I at last discovered that there was in me an invincible summer.

I have again left Tipasa; I have returned to Europe and its struggles. But the memory of that day still uplifts me and helps me to welcome equally what delights and what crushes. In the difficult hour we are living, what else can I desire than to exclude nothing and to learn how to braid with white thread and black thread a single cord stretched to the breaking-point? In everything I have done or said up to now, I seem to recognize these two forces, even when they work at cross-purposes. I have not been able to disown the light into which I was born and yet I have not wanted to reject the servitudes of this time. It would be too easy to contrast here with the sweet name of Tipasa other more sonorous and crueler names. For men of today there is an inner way, which I know well from having taken it in both directions, leading from the spiritual hilltops to the capitals of crime. And doubtless one can always rest, fall asleep on the hilltop or board with crime. But if one forgoes a part of what is, one must forgo being onself; one must forgo living or loving otherwise than by proxy. There is thus a will to live without rejecting anything of life, which is the virtue I honor most in this world. From time to time, at least, it is true that I should like to have practiced it. Inasmuch as few epochs require as much as ours that one should be equal to the best as to the worst, I should like, indeed, to shirk nothing and to keep faithfully a double memory. Yes, there is beauty and there are the humiliated. Whatever may be the difficulties of the undertaking, I should like never to be unfaithful either to one or to the others.

(*Myth*, 141, 143–145)

9

Like all men of my age, I grew up to the sound of the drums of the First World War, and our history since that time has remained murder, injustice, or violence. But real pessimism, which does exist, lies in outbidding all this cruelty and shame. For my part, I have never ceased fighting against this dishonor, and I hate only the cruel. I have sought only reasons to transcend our darkest nihilism. Not, I would add, through virtue, nor because of some rare elevation of the spirit, but from an instinctive fidelity to a light in which I was born, and in which for thousands of years men have learned to welcome life even in suffering. Aeschylus is often heartbreaking; yet he radiates light and warmth. At the center of his universe, we find not fleshless nonsense but an enigma, that is to say, a meaning which is difficult to decipher because it dazzles us. Likewise, to the unworthy but nonetheless stubborn sons of Greece who still survive in this emaciated century, the scorching heat of our history may seem unendurable, but they endure it in the last analysis because they want to understand it. In the center of our work, dark though it may be, shines an inexhaustible sun, the same sun that shouts today across the hills and plain.

After this, the flaxen fire can burn; who cares what we appear to be and what we usurp? What we are, what we have to be, are enough to fill our lives and occupy our strength. Paris is a won-drous cave, and its inhabitants, seeing their own shadows reflected on the far wall, take them for the only reality there is. The same is true of the strange, fleeting renown this town dispenses. But we have learned, far from Paris, that there is a light behind us, that we must turn around and cast off our chains in order to face it directly, and that our task before we die is to seek through any words to identify it.

(*Lyrical*, 160–161)

~~~

10

Misfortune of this age. Not so long ago, bad deeds called for jus-tification, but today it's good deeds.

(*Notebooks II*, 165)

~~~

11

Grenier.* Concerning the good use of freedom. "Modern man has ceased to believe in a God to be obeyed (Hebrew and Christian), a society to be respected (Hindu and Chinese), a nature to be fol-lowed (Greek and Roman)."

Id. "Whoever greatly loves a value is thereby an enemy of free-dom. Whoever loves freedom above all either negates values or else adopts them only temporarily. (Tolerance coming from the decay of values.)"

"If we stop (on the path of negation), this is less to spare others than to spare ourselves." (No for oneself, yes for others!)

(*Notebooks II*, 164)

---

* Jean Grenier, Camus' teacher of philosophy in Algiers, greatly influenced his thought. *The Rebel* is dedicated to him, as are other works by Camus.

~~⌣~~

12

Existentialism kept Hegelianism's basic error, which consists in reducing man to history. But it did not keep the consequence, which is to refuse in fact any liberty to man.

(*Notebooks II*, 141)

~~⌣~~

13

Id. The whole effort of German thought has been to substitute for the notion of human nature that of human situation and hence to substitute history for God and modern tragedy for ancient equilibrium. Modern existentialism carries that effort even further and introduces into the idea of situation the same uncertainty as in the idea of nature. Nothing remains but a motion. But like the Greeks I believe in nature.

(*Notebooks II*, 136)

~~⌣~~

14

For Christians, Revelation stands at the beginning of history. For Marxists, it stands at the end. Two religions.

(*Notebooks II*, 188)

~~⌣~~

15

To begin with, this proves that they reject at the present moment what we all are: those humanists are accusers of man. How can we be surprised that such a claim should have developed in the world of court trials? They reject the man of today in the name of the man of the future. That claim is religious in nature. Why should it be more justified than the one which announces the kingdom of heaven to come? In reality the end of history cannot have, within the limits of our condition, any definable significance.

(*Myth*, 1948)

16

We are asked to choose between God and history. Whence this dreadful longing to choose the earth, the world, and trees, if I were not absolutely sure that all mankind does not coincide with history.

(*Notebooks II*, 122)

17

Mad nature of sacrifice: the fellow who dies for something *he will not see*.

(*Notebooks II*, 95)

18

The mad thing about love is that one wants to hurry and *lose* the interim. In this way one wants to get closer to the end. In this way love in one of its aspects coincides with death.

(*Notebooks II*, 255)

19

We are in a world in which we must choose between being a victim or an executioner—and nothing else. Such a choice is not easy.

(*Notebooks II*, 109)

20

Historical materialism, absolute determinism, the negation of all liberty, that frightful world of courage and silence—these are the most legitimate consequences of a philosophy without God. This is where Parain is right. If God does not exist, nothing is permitted. Christianity alone is strong in this regard. For to the divinization of history it will always raise the objection of the creation of history; it will inquire of the existentialist situation whence its origin, etc. But its replies do not come from reasoning; they come from mythology that calls for faith.

What to do between the two? Something in me tells me, convinces me that I cannot detach myself from my era without cowardice, without accepting slavery, without denying my mother and my truth. I could not do so, or accept a commitment that was both sincere and relative, unless I were a Christian. Not a Christian, I must go on to the end. But going on to the end means choosing history absolutely, and with it the murder of man if the murder of man is necessary to history. Otherwise, I am but a witness. That is the question: can I be merely a witness? In other words: have I the right to be merely an artist? I cannot believe so. If I do not choose both against God and against history, I am the witness of pure liberty whose fate in history is to be put to death. In the present state of things, my situation lies in silence or death. If I choose to do violence to myself and to believe in history, my situation will be falsehood and murder. Outside that, religion. I understand that a man can hurl himself into religion blindly to escape this madness and this painful (yes, really painful) laceration. But I cannot do it.

Consequence: Have I the right, as an artist still attached to liberty, to accept the advantages in money and consideration that are linked to that attitude? The reply for me would be simple. It is in poverty that I have found and shall always find the conditions essential to keep my culpability, if it exists, from being shameful at least and to keep it proud. But must I reduce my children to poverty, refuse even the very modest comfort I am preparing for them? And in these conditions, was I wrong to accept the simplest human tasks and duties, such as having children? In the end, has one the right to have children, to assume the human condition* when one doesn't believe in God (add the intermediary arguments)?

(*Notebooks II*, 120–121)

21

Understand this: we can despair of the meaning of life in general, but not of the particular form that it takes; we can despair of existence, for we have no power over it, but not of history, where the individual can do everything. It is individuals who are killing us today. Why should not individuals manage to give the world peace? We must simply begin without thinking of grandiose aims. You must realize that men make war as much with the enthusiasm of those who want it as with the despair of those who reject it with all their soul.

(*Notebooks I*, 151–152)

22

By what right would a Communist or a Christian (to take only the respectable forms of modern thought) blame me for being a pessimist? *I* didn't invent human misery or the terrible formulas of divine malediction. *I* didn't say that man was incapable of saving himself alone and that from the depths in which he wallows he had no definitive hope save in the grace of God. As for the famous Marxist optimism, allow me to laugh. Few men have carried fur-

---

* Moreover, did I really assume it when I felt such hesitation and still have trouble doing so? Does not this inconstant heart deserve such a contradiction? [*Author's note.*]

ther distrust of their fellow men. Marxists do not believe in persuasion or in dialogue. A workman cannot be made out of a bourgeois, and economic conditions are in their world more terrible fatalities than divine whims.

As for M. Herriot and the subscribers to *Les Annales!* *

Communists and Christians will tell me that their optimism looks further ahead, that it is superior to all the rest, and that God or history, according to the case, is the satisfactory aim of their dialectic. I have the same reasoning to make. If Christianity is pessimistic as to man, it is optimistic as to human destiny. Marxism, pessimistic as to destiny, pessimistic as to human nature, is optimistic as to the progress of history (its contradiction!). *I* shall say that, pessimistic as to the human condition, I am optimistic as to mankind.

(*Notebooks II*, 123–124)

23

Why refuse denunciation, police, etc. . . . if we are neither Christians nor Marxists? We have no value for that. Until we have found a basis for those values, we are condemned to choose the good (when we do choose it) in an unjustifiable way. Virtue will always be illegitimate until that time.

(*Notebooks II*, 210)

24

But if there is a human nature, where does it come from?

Obvious that I ought to give up all creative activity so long as I don't know.

(*Notebooks II*, 144)

---

* Edouard Herriot (1872–1957), several times premier of France, sponsored the conservative and popular periodical of this name.

25

Meaning of my work: So many men are deprived of grace. How can one live without grace? One has to try it and do what Christianity never did: be concerned with the damned.

(*Notebooks II*, 99)

26

The only fraternity which is now possible, which is offered or allowed to us, is the sordid and sticky fraternity in the face of battle.

(*Notebooks I*, 93)

27

But in order to speak about all and to all, one has to speak of what all know and of the reality common to us all. The sea, rains, necessity, desire, the struggle against death—these are the things that unite us all. We resemble one another in what we see together, in what we suffer together. Dreams change from individual to individual, but the reality of the world is common to us all. Striving toward realism is therefore legitimate, for it is basically related to the artistic adventure.

(*Resistance*, 258)

28

If I have tried to define something, it is, on the contrary, simply the common existence of history and of man, everyday life with the most possible light thrown upon it, the dogged struggle against one's own degradation and that of others.

(*Myth*, 148)

29

The community of suffering, struggle, and death exists; it alone lays the foundation of the hope for a community of joy and reconciliation. He who accepts membership in the first community finds in it a nobility, a faithfulness, a reason for accepting his doubts; and if he is an artist he finds the deep wellsprings of his art. Here man learns, in one confused and unhappy moment, that it is not true he must die alone. All men die when he dies, and with the same violence. How, then, can he cut himself off from a single one of them, how can he ever refuse him that higher life, which the artist can restore through forgiveness and man can restore through justice.

(*Lyrical*, 287)

30

Justification of art: the true work of art helps sincerity, strengthens the complicity of mankind, etc. . . .

(*Notebooks II*, 97)

31

We had to overcome our weakness for mankind, the image we had formed of a peaceful destiny, that deep-rooted conviction of ours that no victory ever pays, whereas any mutilation of mankind is irrevocable. We had to give up all at once our knowledge and our hope, the reasons we had for loving and the loathing we had for all war. To put it in a word that I suppose you will understand when it comes from me whom you counted as a friend, we had to stifle our passion for friendship.

Now we have done that. We had to make a long detour, and we

are far behind. It is a detour that regard for truth imposes on intelligence, that regard for friendship imposes on the heart. It is a detour that safeguarded justice and put truth on the side of those who questioned themselves. And, without a doubt, we paid very dearly for it. We paid for it with humiliations and silences, with bitter experiences, with prison sentences, with executions at dawn, with desertions and separations, with daily pangs of hunger, with emaciated children, and, above all, with humiliation of our human dignity. But that was natural. It took us all that time to find out if we had the right to kill men, if we were allowed to add to the frightful misery of this world. And because of that time lost and recaptured, our defeat accepted and surmounted, those scruples paid for with blood, we French have the right to think today that we entered this war with hands clean—clean as victims and the condemned are—and that we are going to come out of it with hands clean—but clean this time with a great victory won against injustice and against ourselves.

For we shall be victorious, you may be sure. But we shall be victorious thanks to that very defeat, to that long, slow progress during which we found our justification, to that suffering which, in all its injustice, taught us a lesson. It taught us the secret of any victory, and if we don't lose the secret, we shall know final victory. It taught us that, contrary to what we sometimes used to think, the spirit is of no avail against the sword, but that the spirit together with the sword will always win out over the sword alone. That is why we have now accepted the sword, after making sure that the spirit was on our side. We had first to see people die and to run the risk of dying ourselves. We had to see a French workman walking toward the guillotine at dawn down the prison corridors and exhorting his comrades from cell to cell to show their courage. Finally, to possess ourselves of the spirit, we had to endure torture of our flesh. One really possesses only what one has paid for. We have paid dearly, and we have not finished paying. But we have our certainties, our justifications, our justice; your defeat is inevitable.

I have never believed in the power of truth in itself. But it is at least worth knowing that when expressed forcefully truth wins out over falsehood. This is the difficult equilibrium we have reached. This is the distinction that gives us strength as we fight today. And I am tempted to tell you that it so happens that we are fighting for fine distinctions, but the kind of distinctions that are as important as man himself. We are fighting for the distinction between sacrifice and mysticism, between energy and violence, between strength and cruelty, for that even finer distinction between the true and the false, between the man of the future and the cowardly gods you revere.

(*Resistance*, 8–10)

~~~~~~

32

You never believed in the meaning of this world, and you therefore deduced the idea that everything was equivalent and that good and evil could be defined according to one's wishes. You supposed that in the absence of any human or divine code the only values were those of the animal world—in other words, violence and cunning. Hence you concluded that man was negligible and that his soul could be killed, that in the maddest of histories the only pursuit for the individual was the adventure of power and his only morality, the realism of conquests. And, to tell the truth, I, believing I thought as you did, saw no valid argument to answer you except a fierce love of justice which, after all, seemed to me as unreasonable as the most sudden passion.

Where lay the difference? Simply that you readily accepted despair and I never yielded to it. Simply that you saw the injustice of our condition to the point of being willing to add to it, whereas it seemed to me that man must exalt justice in order to fight against eternal injustice, create happiness in order to protest against the universe of unhappiness. Because you turned your despair into intoxication, because you freed yourself from it by making a principle of it, you were willing to destroy man's works and to fight him in order to add to his basic misery. Meanwhile, refusing to accept that despair and that tortured world, I merely wanted men to rediscover their solidarity in order to wage war against their revolting fate.

(*Resistance*, 27–28)

33

I, on the contrary, chose justice in order to remain faithful to the world. I continue to believe that this world has no ultimate meaning. But I know that something in it has a meaning and that is man, because he is the only creature to insist on having one. This world has at least the truth of man, and our task is to provide its justifications against fate itself. And it has no justification but man; hence he must be saved if we want to save the idea we have of life. With your scornful smile you will ask me: what do you mean by saving man? And with all my being I shout to you that I mean not mutilating him and yet giving a chance to the justice that man alone can conceive.

This is why we are fighting. This is why we first had to follow you on a path we didn't want and why at the end of that path we met defeat. For your despair constituted your strength. The moment despair is alone, pure, sure of itself, pitiless in its consequences, it has a merciless power. That is what crushed us while we were hesitating with our eyes still fixed on happy images. We thought that happiness was the greatest of conquests, a victory over the fate imposed upon us. Even in defeat this longing did not leave us.

But you did what was necessary, and we went down in history. And for five years it was no longer possible to enjoy the call of birds in the cool of the evening. We were forced to despair. We were cut off from the world because to each moment of the world clung a whole mass of mortal images. For five years the earth has not seen a single morning without death agonies, a single evening without prisons, a single noon without slaughters. Yes, we had to follow you. But our difficult achievement consisted in following you into war without forgetting happiness.

(*Resistance*, 28–29)

~{~

34

"Do you know, Fontanes, what most amazes me in the world? The inability of force to maintain anything at all. There are only two powers in the world: the sword and the mind. In the long run, the sword is always defeated by the mind."

—Napoleon

(*Notebooks I*, 156)

~{~

35

Revolt. Beginning: "The only really serious moral problem is murder. The rest comes after. But to find out whether or not I can kill this person in my presence, or agree to his being killed, to find that I know nothing before finding out whether or not I can cause death, that is what must be learned."

(*Notebooks II*, 134)

~{~

36

People always want to push us in the direction of *their* consequences. If they judge us, they always do so with their principles in mind. But *I* don't care what they think. What matters to me is to find out whether or not I can kill. Because you have reached the frontiers where all thought stumbles, they begin rubbing their

hands. "And now, what is he going to do?" And they have their
truth all ready. But I think I don't care if I am in a state of contradiction; I don't want to be a philosophical genius. I don't even want
to be a genius at all, for I have enough trouble just being a man. I
want to find an agreement, and, knowing that I cannot kill myself,
to find out whether I can kill or let others be killed and, knowing it,
to draw all the conclusions from it even if that is to leave me in a
state of contradiction.

(*Notebooks II*, 134–135)

37

I am not made for politics because I am incapable of wanting or accepting the death of the adversary.

(*Notebooks II*, 119)

38

It requires bucketsful of blood and centuries of history to lead to an
imperceptible modification in the human condition. Such is the
law. For years heads fall like hail. Terror reigns, Revolution is tou-
ted, and one ends up by substituting constitutional monarchy for
legitimate monarchy.

(*Notebooks II*, 119)

39

Push no one to rebel. We must be sparing of other people's blood
and liberty.

(*Notebooks I*, 151)

40

Before he died in combat in the last war, Richard Hilary found the phrase that sums up this dilemma: "We were fighting a lie in the name of a half-truth." He thought he was expressing a very pessimistic idea. But one may even have to fight a lie in the name of a quarter-truth. This is our situation at present. However, the quarter-truth contained in Western society is called liberty. And liberty is the way, and the only way, of perfectibility. Without liberty heavy industry can be perfected, but not justice or truth. Our most recent history, from Berlin to Budapest, ought to convince us of this. In any case, it is the reason for my choice. I have said in this very place that none of the evils totalitarianism claims to remedy is worse than totalitarianism itself. I have not changed my mind. On the contrary, after twenty years of our harsh history, during which I have tried to accept every experience it offered, liberty ultimately seems to me, for societies and for individuals, for labor and for culture, the supreme good that governs all others.

(*Resistance*, 247–248)

41

When oppression wins out, as we all know here, those who nevertheless believe that their cause is just suffer from a sort of astonishment upon discovering the apparent impotence of justice. Then come the hours of exile and solitude that we have all known. Yet I should like to tell you that, in my opinion, the worst thing that can happen in the world we live in is for one of those men of freedom and courage I have described to stagger under the weight of isolation and prolonged adversity, to doubt himself and what he represents. And it seems to me that at such a moment those who are like him must come toward him (forgetting his titles and all devices of the official orator) to tell him straight from the heart that he is not alone and that his action is not futile, that there always comes a day when the palaces of oppression crumble, when exile comes to an end, when liberty catches fire. Such calm hope justifies your action. If, after all, men cannot always make history have a meaning, they can always act so that their own lives have one. Believe me when I tell you that across thousands of miles, all the way from far-off Colombia, you and your collaborators have shown us a part of the difficult road we must travel together toward liberty. And allow me, in the name of the faithful and grateful friends receiving you here, to greet fraternally in you and your collaborators the great companions of our common liberation.

(*Resistance*, 106–107)

42

And on the Sunday of the sermon a huge congregation filled the nave, overflowing on to the steps and precincts. The sky had clouded up on the previous day, and now it was raining heavily. Those in the open unfurled umbrellas. The air inside the Cathedral was heavy with fumes of incense and the smell of wet clothes when Father Paneloux stepped into the pulpit.

He was a stockily built man, of medium height. When he leaned on the edge of the pulpit, grasping the woodwork with his big hands, all one saw was a black, massive torso and, above it, two rosy cheeks overhung by steel-rimmed spectacles. He had a powerful, rather emotional delivery, which carried to a great distance, and when he launched at the congregation his opening phrase in clear, emphatic tones: "Calamity has come on you, my brethren, and, my brethren, you deserved it," there was a flutter that extended to the crowd massed in the rain outside the porch.

In strict logic what came next did not seem to follow from this dramatic opening. Only as the sermon proceeded did it become apparent to the congregation that, by a skillful oratorical device, Father Paneloux had launched at them, like a fisticuff, the gist of his whole discourse. After launching it he went on at once to quote a text from Exodus relating to the plague of Egypt, and said: "The first time this scourge appears in history, it was wielded to strike down the enemies of God. Pharaoh set himself up against the divine will, and the plague beat him to his knees. Thus from the dawn of recorded history the scourge of God has humbled the proud of heart and laid low those who hardened themselves against Him. Ponder this well, my friends, and fall on your knees."

The downpour had increased in violence, and these words, striking through a silence intensified by the drumming of raindrops on the chancel windows, carried such conviction that, after a momentary hesitation, some of the worshipers slipped forward from their seats on to their knees. Others felt it right to follow their example, and the movement gradually spread until presently everyone was kneeling, from end to end of the cathedral. No sound, except an occasional creak of chairs, accompanied the movement. Then Paneloux drew himself up to his full height, took a deep breath, and continued his sermon in a voice that gathered strength as it proceeded.

"If today the plague is in your midst, that is because the hour has struck for taking thought. The just man need have no fear, but the evildoer has good cause to tremble. For plague is the flail of God and the world His threshing-floor, and implacably He will thresh out His harvest until the wheat is separated from the chaff. There will be more chaff than wheat, few chosen of the many called. Yet this calamity was not willed by God. Too long this world of ours has connived at evil, too long has it counted on the divine mercy, on God's forgiveness. Repentance was enough, men thought; nothing was forbidden. Everyone felt comfortably assured; when the day came, he would surely turn from his sins and repent. Pending that day, the easiest course was to surrender all along the line; divine compassion would do the rest. For a long while God gazed down on this town with eyes of compassion; but He grew weary of waiting, His eternal hope was too long deferred, and now He has turned His face away from us. And so, God's light withdrawn, we walk in darkness, in the thick darkness of this plague."

Someone in the congregation gave a little snort, like that of a restive horse. After a short silence the preacher continued in a lower tone.

"We read in the *Golden Legend* that in the time of King Umberto Italy was swept by plague and its greatest ravages took place in Rome and Pavia. So dreadful were these that the living hardly sufficed to bury the dead. And a good angel was made visible to human eyes, giving his orders to an evil angel who bore a great hunting-spear, and bidding him strike the houses; and as many strokes as he dealt a house, so many dead were carried out of it."

Here Paneloux stretched forth his two short arms toward the open porch, as if pointing to something behind the tumbling curtain of the rain.

"My brothers," he cried, "that fatal hunt is up, and harrying our streets today. See him there, that angel of the pestilence, comely as Lucifer, shining like Evil's very self! He is hovering above your roofs with his great spear in his right hand, poised to strike, while his left hand is stretched toward one or other of your houses. Maybe at this very moment his finger is pointing to your door, the red spear crashing on its panels, and even now the plague is entering your home and settling down in your bedroom to await your return. Patient and watchful, ineluctable as the order of the scheme of things, it bides its time. No earthly power, nay, not even—mark me well—the vaunted might of human science can avail you to avert that hand once it is stretched toward you. And winnowed like corn on the blood-stained threshing-floor of suffering, you will be cast away with the chaff."

At this point the Father reverted with heightened eloquence to the symbol of the flail. He bade his hearers picture a huge wooden bar whirling above the town, striking at random, swinging up again in a shower of drops of blood, and spreading carnage and suffering on earth, "for the seedtime that shall prepare the harvest of the truth."

At the end of his long phrase Father Paneloux paused; his hair was straggling over his forehead, his body shaken by tremors that his hands communicated to the pulpit. When he spoke again, his voice was lower, but vibrant with accusation.

"Yes, the hour has come for serious thought. You fondly imagined it was enough to visit God on Sundays, and thus you could make free of your weekdays. You believed some brief formalities, some bendings of the knee, would recompense Him well enough for your criminal indifference. But God is not mocked. These brief encounters could not sate the fierce hunger of His love. He wished to see you longer and more often; that is His manner of loving and, indeed, it is the only manner of loving. And this is why, wearied of waiting for you to come to Him, He loosed on you this visitation; as He has visited all the cities that offended against Him since the dawn of history. Now you are learning your lesson, the lesson that was learned by Cain and his offspring, by the people of Sodom and Gomorrah, by Job and Pharaoh, by all that hardened their hearts against Him. And like them you have been beholding mankind and all creation with new eyes, since the gates of this city closed on you and on the pestilence. Now, at last, you know the hour has struck to bend your thoughts to first and last things."

A wet wind was sweeping up the nave, making the candleflames bend and flicker. The pungency of burning wax, coughs, a stifled sneeze, rose toward Father Paneloux, who, reverting to his exordium with a subtlety that was much appreciated, went on in a calm, almost matter-of-fact voice: "Many of you are wondering, I know, what I am leading up to. I wish to lead you to the truth and teach you to rejoice, yes, rejoice—in spite of all that I have been telling you. For the time is past when a helping hand or mere words of good advice could set you on the right path. Today the truth is a command. It is a red spear sternly pointing to the narrow path, the one way of salvation. And thus, my brothers, at last it is revealed to you, the divine compassion which has ordained good and evil in everything; wrath and pity, the plague and your salvation. This same pestilence which is slaying you works for your good and points your path.

"Many centuries ago the Christians of Abyssinia saw in the plague a sure and God-sent means of winning eternal life. Those who were not yet stricken wrapped round them sheets in which men had died of plague, so as to make sure of their death. I grant you such a frenzied quest of salvation was not to be commended. It shows an overhaste—indeed, a presumptuousness, which we can but deplore. No man should seek to force God's hand or to hurry on the appointed hour, and from a practice that aims at speeding up the order of events which God has ordained unalterably from all time, it is but a step to heresy. Yet we can learn a salutary lesson from the zeal, excessive though it was, of those Abyssinian Christians. Much of it is alien to our more enlightened spirits, and yet it gives us a glimpse of that radiant eternal light which glows, a small still flame, in the dark core of human suffering. And this light, too, illuminates the shadowed paths that lead towards deliverance. It reveals the will of God in action, unfailingly transforming evil into good. And once again today it is leading us through the dark valley of fears and groans towards the holy silence, the well-spring of all life. This, my friends, is the vast consolation I would hold out to you, so that when you leave this house of God you will carry away with you not only words of wrath, but a message, too, of comfort for your hearts."

Everyone supposed that the sermon had ended. Outside, the rain had ceased and watery sunshine was yellowing the Cathedral square. Vague sounds of voices came from the streets, and a low hum of traffic, the speech of an awakening town. Discreetly, with a subdued rustling, the congregation gathered together their belongings. However, the Father had a few more words to say. He told

them that after having made it clear that this plague came from
God for the punishment of their sins, he would not have recourse,
in concluding, to an eloquence that, considering the tragic nature
of the occasion, would be out of keeping. He hoped and believed
that all of them now saw their position in its true light. But, before
leaving the pulpit, he would like to tell them of something he had
been reading in an old chronicle of the Black Death at Marseille.
In it Mathieu Marais, the chronicler, laments his lot; he says he
has been cast into hell to languish without succor and without
hope. Well, Mathieu Marais was blind! Never more intensely than
today had he, Father Paneloux, felt the immanence of divine succor and Christian hope granted to all alike. He hoped against hope
that, despite all the horrors of these dark days, despite the groans of
men and women in agony, our fellow citizens would offer up to
heaven that one prayer which is truly Christian, a prayer of love.
And God would see to the rest.

(*Plague*, 86–91)

43

Tarrou's gray eyes met the doctor's gaze serenely.

"What did you think of Paneloux's sermon, doctor?"

The question was asked in a quite ordinary tone, and Rieux answered in the same tone.

"I've seen too much of hospitals to relish any idea of collective
punishment. But, as you know, Christians sometimes say that sort
of thing without really thinking it. They're better than they seem."

"However, you think, like Paneloux, that the plague has its good
side; it opens men's eyes and forces them to take thought?"

The doctor tossed his head impatiently.

"So does every ill that flesh is heir to. What's true of all the evils
in the world is true of plague as well. It helps men to rise above
themselves. All the same, when you see the misery it brings, you'd

need to be a madman, or a coward, or stone blind, to give in tamely to the plague."

Rieux had hardly raised his voice at all; but Tarrou made a slight gesture as if to calm him. He was smiling.

"Yes." Rieux shrugged his shoulders. "But you haven't answered my question yet. Have you weighed the consequences?"

Tarrou squared his shoulders against the back of the chair, then moved his head forward into the light.

"Do you believe in God, doctor?"

Again the question was put in an ordinary tone. But this time Rieux took longer to find his answer.

"No—but what does that really mean? I'm fumbling in the dark, struggling to make something out. But I've long ceased finding that original."

"Isn't that it—the gulf between Paneloux and you?"

"I doubt it. Paneloux is a man of learning, a scholar. He hasn't come in contact with death; that's why he can speak with such assurance of the truth—with a capital T. But every country priest who visits his parishioners and has heard a man gasping for breath on his deathbed thinks as I do. He'd try to relieve human suffering before trying to point out its excellence." Rieux stood up; his face was now in shadow. "Let's drop the subject," he said, "as you won't answer."

Tarrou remained seated in his chair; he was smiling again.

"Suppose I answer with a question."

The doctor now smiled, too.

"You like being mysterious, don't you? Yes, fire away."

"My question's this," said Tarrou. "Why do you yourself show such devotion, considering you don't believe in God? I suspect your answer may help me to mine."

His face still in shadow, Rieux said that he'd already answered: that if he believed in an all-powerful God he would cease curing the sick and leave that to Him. But no one in the world believed in a God of that sort; no, not even Paneloux, who believed that he believed in such a God. And this was proved by the fact that no one ever threw himself on Providence completely. Anyhow, in this respect Rieux believed himself to be on the right road—in fighting against creation as he found it.

"Ah," Tarrou remarked. "So that's the idea you have of your profession?"

"More or less." The doctor came back into the light.

Tarrou made a faint whistling noise with his lips, and the doctor gazed at him.

"Yes, you're thinking it calls for pride to feel that way. But I assure you I've no more than the pride that's needed to keep me going. I have no idea what's awaiting me, or what will happen when all this ends. For the moment I know this; there are sick people and they need curing. Later on, perhaps, they'll think things over; and so shall I. But what's wanted now is to make them well. I defend them as best I can, that's all."

"Against whom?"

Rieux turned to the window. A shadow-line on the horizon told of the presence of the sea. He was conscious only of his exhaustion, and at the same time was struggling against a sudden, irrational impulse to unburden himself a little more to his companion; an eccentric, perhaps, but who, he guessed, was one of his own kind.

"I haven't a notion, Tarrou; I assure you I haven't a notion. When I entered this profession, I did it 'abstractedly,' so to speak; because I had a desire for it, because it meant a career like another, one that young men often aspire to. Perhaps, too, because it was particularly difficult for a workman's son, like myself. And then I had to see people die. Do you know that there are some who *refuse* to die? Have you ever heard a woman scream 'Never!' with her last gasp? Well, I have. And then I saw that I could never get hardened to it. I was young then, and I was outraged by the whole scheme of things, or so I thought. Subsequently I grew more modest. Only, I've never managed to get used to seeing people die. That's all I know. Yet after all—"

Rieux fell silent and sat down. He felt his mouth dry.

"After all—?" Tarrou prompted softly.

"After all," the doctor repeated, then hesitated again, fixing his eyes on Tarrou, "it's something that a man of your sort can understand most likely, but, since the order of the world is shaped by death, mightn't it be better for God if we refuse to believe in Him and struggle with all our might against death, without raising our eyes toward the heaven where He sits in silence."

Tarrou nodded.

"Yes. But your victories will never be lasting; that's all."

Rieux's face darkened.

"Yes, I know that. But it's no reason for giving up the struggle."

"No reason, I agree. Only, I now can picture what this plague must mean for you."

"Yes. A never ending defeat."

Tarrou stared at the doctor for a moment, then turned and tramped heavily toward the door. Rieux followed him and was almost at his side when Tarrou, who was staring at the floor, suddenly said:

"Who taught you all this, doctor?"

The reply came promptly:

"Suffering."

(*Plague*, 115–118)

44

The evil that is in the world always comes of ignorance, and good intentions may do as much harm as malevolence, if they lack understanding. On the whole, men are more good than bad; that, however, isn't the real point. But they are more or less ignorant, and it is this that we call vice or virtue; the most incorrigible vice being that of an ignorance that fancies it knows everything and therefore claims for itself the right to kill. The soul of the murderer is blind; and there can be no true goodness nor true love without the utmost clear-sightedness.

Hence the sanitary groups, whose creation was entirely Tarrou's work, should be considered with objectivity as well as with approval. And this is why the narrator declines to vaunt in over-glowing terms a courage and a devotion to which he attributes only a relative and reasonable importance. But he will continue being the chronicler of the troubled, rebellious hearts of our townspeople under the impact of the plague.

Those who enrolled in the "sanitary squads," as they were called, had, indeed, no such great merit in doing as they did, since they knew it was the only thing to do, and the unthinkable thing would then have been not to have brought themselves to do it. These groups enabled our townsfolk to come to grips with the disease and convinced them that, now that plague was among us, it was up to them to do whatever could be done to fight it. Since plague became in this way some men's duty, it revealed itself as what it really was; that is, the concern of all.

(*Plague*, 120–121)

~⌣~

45

"Doctor," Rambert said, "I'm not going. I want to stay with you."

Tarrou made no movement; he went on driving. Rieux seemed unable to shake off his fatigue.

"And what about *her*?" His voice was hardly audible.

Rambert said he'd thought it over very carefully, and his views hadn't changed, but if he went away, he would feel ashamed of himself, and that would embarrass his relations with the woman he loved.

Showing more animation, Rieux told him that was sheer nonsense; there was nothing shameful in preferring happiness.

"Certainly," Rambert replied. "But it may be shameful to be happy by oneself."

Tarrou, who had not spoken so far, now remarked, without turning his head, that if Rambert wished to take a share in other people's unhappiness, he'd have no time left for happiness. So the choice had to be made.

"That's not it," Rambert rejoined. "Until now I always felt a stranger in this town, and that I'd no concern with you people. But now that I've seen what I have seen, I know that I belong here whether I want it or not. This business is everybody's business." When there was no reply from either of the others, Rambert seemed to grow annoyed. "But you know that as well as I do, damn it! Or else what are you up to in that hospital of yours? Have *you* made a definite choice and turned down happiness?"

Rieux and Tarrou still said nothing, and the silence lasted until they were at the doctor's home. Then Rambert repeated his last question in a yet more emphatic tone.

Only then Rieux turned toward him, raising himself with an effort from the cushion.

"Forgive me, Rambert, only—well, I simply don't know. But stay with us if you want to." A swerve of the car made him break off. Then, looking straight in front of him, he said: "For nothing in the world is it worth turning one's back on what one loves. Yet that is what I'm doing, though why I do not know." He sank back on the cushion. "That's how it is," he added wearily, "and there's nothing to be done about it. So let's recognize the fact and draw the conclusions."

"What conclusions?"

"Ah," Rieux said, "a man can't cure and know at the same time. So let's cure as quickly as we can. That's the more urgent job."

At midnight Tarrou and Rieux were giving Rambert the map of the district he was to keep under surveillance. Tarrou glanced at his watch. Looking up, he met Rambert's gaze.

"Have you let them know?" he asked.

The journalist looked away.

"I'd sent them a note"—he spoke with an effort—"before coming to see you."

(*Plague,* 188–189)

~⌒~

46

"Come, doctor," he began.

Rieux swung round on him fiercely.

"Ah! That child, anyhow, was innocent, and you know it as well as I do!"

He strode on, brushing past Paneloux, and walked across the school playground. Sitting on a wooden bench under the dingy, stunted trees, he wiped off the sweat that was beginning to run into his eyes. He felt like shouting imprecations—anything to loosen the stranglehold lashing his heart with steel. Heat was flooding down between the branches of the fig trees. A white haze, spreading rapidly over the blue of the morning sky, made the air yet more stifling. Rieux lay back wearily on the bench. Gazing up at the ragged branches, the shimmering sky, he slowly got back his breath and fought down his fatigue.

He heard a voice behind him. "Why was there that anger in your voice just now? What we'd been seeing was as unbearable to me as it was to you."

Rieux turned toward Paneloux.

"I know. I'm sorry. But weariness is a kind of madness. And there are times when the only feeling I have is one of mad revolt."

"I understand," Paneloux said in a low voice. "That sort of thing is revolting because it passes our human understanding. But perhaps we should love what we cannot understand."

Rieux straightened up slowly. He gazed at Paneloux, summoning to his gaze all the strength and fervor he could muster against his weariness. Then he shook his head.

"No, Father. I've a very different idea of love. And until my dying day I shall refuse to love a scheme of things in which children are put to torture."

A shade of disquietude crossed the priest's face. "Ah, doctor," he said sadly, "I've just realized what is meant by 'grace.' "

Rieux had sunk back again on the bench. His lassitude had returned and from its depths he spoke, more gently:

"It's something I haven't got; that I know. But I'd rather not discuss that with you. We're working side by side for something that unites us—beyond blasphemy and prayers. And it's the only thing that matters."

Paneloux sat down beside Rieux. It was obvious that he was deeply moved.

"Yes, yes," he said, "you, too, are working for man's salvation."

Rieux tried to smile.

"Salvation's much too big a word for me. I don't aim so high. I'm concerned with man's health; and for me his health comes first."

Paneloux seemed to hesitate. "Doctor—" he began, then fell silent. Down his face, too, sweat was trickling. Murmuring: "Good-by for the present," he rose. His eyes were moist. When he turned to go, Rieux, who had seemed lost in thought, suddenly rose and took a step toward him.

"Again, please forgive me. I can promise there won't be another outburst of that kind."

Paneloux held out his hand, saying regretfully:

"And yet—I haven't convinced you!"

"What does it matter? What I hate is death and disease, as you well know. And whether you wish it or not, we're allies, facing them and fighting them together." Rieux was still holding Paneloux's hand. "So you see"—but he refrained from meeting the priest's eyes—"God Himself can't part us now."

(*Plague*, 196–197)

47

Since joining Rieux's band of workers Paneloux had spent his entire time in hospitals and places where he came in contact with plague. He had elected for the place among his fellow workers that he judged incumbent on him—in the forefront of the fight. And constantly since then he had rubbed shoulders with death. Though theoretically immunized by periodical inoculations, he was well aware that at any moment death might claim him too, and he had given thought to this. Outwardly he had lost nothing of his serenity. But from the day on which he saw a child die, something seemed to change in him. And his face bore traces of the rising tension of his thoughts. When one day he told Rieux with a smile that he was working on a short essay entitled "Is a Priest Justified in Consulting a Doctor?" Rieux had gathered that something graver lay behind the question than the priest's tone seemed to imply. On the doctor's saying he would greatly like to have a look at the essay, Paneloux informed him that he would shortly be preaching at a Mass for men, and his sermon would convey some at least of his considered opinions on the question.

"I hope you'll come, doctor. The subject will interest you."

A high wind was blowing on the day Father Paneloux preached his second sermon.

(*Plague*, 198)

~⌣~

48

And it was in a cold, silent church, surrounded by a congregation of men exclusively, that Rieux watched the Father climb into the pulpit. He spoke in a gentler, more thoughtful tone than on the previous occasion, and several times was noticed to be stumbling over his words. A yet more noteworthy change was that instead of saying "you" he now said "we."

However, his voice grew gradually firmer as he proceeded. He started by recalling that for many a long month plague had been in our midst, and we now knew it better, after having seen it often seated at our tables or at the bedsides of those we loved. We had

seen it walking at our side, or waiting for our coming at the places
where we worked. Thus we were now, perhaps, better able to
comprehend what it was telling us unceasingly; a message to
which, in the first shock of the visitation, we might not have listened with due heed. What he, Father Paneloux, had said in his
first sermon still held good—such, anyhow, was his belief. And yet,
perhaps, as may befall any one of us (here he struck his breast), his
words and thoughts had lacked in charity. However this might be,
one thing was not to be gainsaid; a fact that always, under all circumstances, we should bear in mind. Appearances notwithstanding, all trials, however cruel, worked together for good to the Christian. And, indeed, what a Christian should always seek in his hour
of trial was to discern that good, in what it consisted and how best
he could turn it to account. . . . There was no doubt as to the existence of good and evil and, as a rule, it was easy to see the difference between them. The difficulty began when we looked into
the nature of evil, and among things evil he included human suffering. Thus we had apparently needful pain, and apparently needless pain; we had Don Juan cast into hell, and a child's death. For
while it is right that a libertine should be struck down, we see no
reason for a child's suffering. And, truth to tell, nothing was more
important on earth than a child's suffering, the horror it inspires in
us, and the reasons we must find to account for it. In other mani-
festations of life God made things easy for us and, thus far, our
religion had no merit. But in this respect He put us, so to speak,
with our backs to the wall. Indeed, we all were up against the wall
that plague had built around us, and in its lethal shadow we must
work out our salvation. He, Father Paneloux, refused to have recourse to simple devices enabling him to scale that wall. Thus he
might easily have assured them that the child's sufferings would be
compensated for by an eternity of bliss awaiting him. But how
could he give that assurance when, to tell the truth, he knew
nothing about it? For who would dare to assert that eternal happiness can compensate for a single moment's human suffering? He

who asserted that would not be a true Christian, a follower of the Master who knew all the pangs of suffering in his body and his soul. No, he, Father Paneloux, would keep faith with that great symbol of all suffering, the tortured body on the Cross; he would stand fast, his back to the wall, and face honestly the terrible problem of a child's agony. And he would boldly say to those who listened to his words today: "My brothers, a time of testing has come for us all. We must believe everything or deny everything. And who among you, I ask, would dare to deny everything?"

It crossed Rieux's mind that Father Paneloux was dallying with heresy in speaking thus, but he had no time to follow up the thought. The preacher was declaring vehemently that this uncompromising duty laid on the Christian was at once his ruling virtue and his privilege. He was well aware that certain minds, schooled to a more indulgent and conventional morality, might well be dismayed, not to say outraged, by the seemingly excessive standard of Christian virtue about which he was going to speak. But religion in a time of plague could not be the religion of every day. While God might accept and even desire that the soul should take its ease and rejoice in happier times, in periods of extreme calamity He laid extreme demands on it. Thus today God had vouchsafed to His creatures an ordeal such that they must acquire and practice the greatest of all virtues: that of the All or Nothing.

Many centuries previously a profane writer had claimed to reveal a secret of the Church by declaring that purgatory did not exist. He wished to convey that there could be no half measures, there was only the alternative between heaven and hell; you were either saved or damned. That, according to Paneloux, was a heresy that could spring only from a blind, disordered soul. Nevertheless, there may well have been periods of history when purgatory could not be hoped for; periods when it was impossible to speak of venial sin. Every sin was deadly, and any indifference criminal. It was all or it was nothing.

The preacher paused, and Rieux heard more clearly the whistling of the wind outside; judging by the sounds that came in below the closed doors, it had risen to storm pitch. Then he heard Father Paneloux's voice again. He was saying that the total acceptance of which he had been speaking was not to be taken in the limited sense usually given to the words; he was not thinking of mere resignation or even of that harder virtue, humility. It involved humiliation, but a humiliation to which the person humiliated gave full assent. True, the agony of a child was humiliating to the heart and to the mind. But that was why we had to come to terms with it. And that, too, was why—and here Paneloux assured those present that it was not easy to say what he was about to say—since it was God's will, we, too, should will it. Thus and thus only the Christian could face the problem squarely and, scorning subterfuge, pierce to the heart of the supreme issue, the essential choice. And his choice would be to believe everything, so as not to be forced into denying everything. Like those worthy women who, after learning that buboes were the natural issues through which the body cast out infection, went to their church and prayed: "Please, God, give him buboes," thus the Christian should yield himself wholly to the divine will, even though it passed his understanding. It was wrong to say: "*This* I understand, but *that* I cannot accept"; we must go straight to the heart of that which is unacceptable, precisely because it is thus that we are constrained to make our choice. The sufferings of children were our bread of affliction, but without this bread our souls would die of spiritual hunger.

The shuffling sounds which usually followed the moment when the preacher paused were beginning to make themselves heard when, unexpectedly, he raised his voice, making as if to put himself in his hearers' place and ask what then was the proper course to follow. He made no doubt that the ugly word "fatalism" would be applied to what he said. Well, he would not boggle at the word, provided he were allowed to qualify it with the adjective "active." Needless to say, there was no question of imitating the Abyssinian Christians of whom he had spoken previously. Nor should one even think of acting like those Persians who in time of plague threw their infected garments on the Christian sanitary workers and loudly called on Heaven to give the plague to these infidels who were trying to avert a pestilence sent by God. But, on the other hand, it would be no less wrong to imitate the monks at Cairo who, when plague was raging in the town, distributed the Host with pincers at the Mass, so as to avoid contact with wet, warm mouths in which infection might be latent. The plague-stricken Persians and the monks were equally at fault. For the former a child's agony did not count; with the latter, on the contrary, the natural dread of suffering ranked highest in their conduct. In both cases the real problem had been shirked; they had closed their ears to God's voice.

But, Paneloux continued, there were other precedents of which he would now remind them. If the chronicles of the Black Death at Marseille were to be trusted, only four of the eighty-one monks in the Mercy Monastery survived the epidemic. And of these four three took to flight. Thus far the chronicler, and it was not his task to tell us more than the bare facts. But when he read that chronicle, Father Paneloux had found his thoughts fixed on that monk who stayed on by himself, despite the death of his seventy-seven companions, and, above all, despite the example of his three brothers who had fled. And, bringing down his fist on the edge of the pulpit, Father Paneloux cried in a ringing voice: "My brothers, each one of us must be the one who stays!"

There was no question of not taking precautions or failing to comply with the orders wisely promulgated for the public weal in the disorders of a pestilence. Nor should we listen to certain moralists who told us to sink on our knees and give up the struggle. No, we should go forward, groping our way through the darkness, stumbling perhaps at times, and try to do what good lay in our power. As for the rest, we must hold fast, trusting in the divine goodness, even as to the deaths of little children, and not seeking personal respite.

At this point Father Paneloux evoked the august figure of Bishop Belzunce during the Marseille plague. He reminded his hearers how, toward the close of the epidemic, the Bishop, having done all that it behooved him, shut himself up in his palace, behind high walls, after laying in a stock of food and drink. With a sudden revulsion of feeling, such as often comes in times of extreme tribulation, the inhabitants of Marseille, who had idolized him hitherto, now turned against him, piled up corpses round his house in order to infect it, and even flung bodies over the walls to make sure of his death. Thus in a moment of weakness the Bishop had proposed to isolate himself from the outside world—and, lo and behold, corpses rained down on his head! This had a lesson for us all; we must convince ourselves that there is no island of escape in time of plague. No, there was no middle course. We must accept the dilemma and choose either to hate God or to love God. And who would dare to choose to hate Him?

"My brothers"—the preacher's tone showed he was nearing the conclusion of his sermon—"the love of God is a hard love. It demands total self-surrender, disdain of our human personality. And yet it alone can reconcile us to suffering and the deaths of children, it alone can justify them, since we cannot understand them, and we can only make God's will ours. That is the hard lesson I would share with you today. That is the faith, cruel in men's eyes, and crucial in God's, which we must ever strive to compass. We must aspire beyond ourselves toward that high and fearful vision. And on that lofty plane all will fall into place, all discords be resolved, and truth flash forth from the dark cloud of seeming injustice."

(*Plague*, 200–206)

49

"Rieux," Tarrou said in a quite ordinary tone, "do you realize that you've never tried to find out anything about me—the man I am? Can I regard you as a friend?"

"Yes, of course, we're friends; only so far we haven't had much time to show it."

"Good. That gives me confidence. Suppose we now take an hour off—for friendship?"

Rieux smiled by way of answer.

"Well, here goes!"

.   .   .

"Do you know," he said, "what we now should do for friendship's sake?"

"Anything you like, Tarrou."

"Go for a swim. It's one of these harmless pleasures that even a saint-to-be can indulge in, don't you agree?" Rieux smiled again, and Tarrou continued: "With our passes, we can get out on the pier. Really, it's too damn silly living only in and for the plague. Of course, a man should fight for the victims, but if he ceases caring for anything outside that, what's the use of his fighting?"

"Right," Rieux said. "Let's go."

Some minutes later the car drew up at the harbor gates. The moon had risen and a milk-white radiance, dappled with shadows, lay around them. Behind them rose the town, tier on tier, and from it came warm, fetid breaths of air that urged them toward the sea. After showing their passes to a guard, who inspected them minutely, they crossed some open ground littered with casks, and headed toward the pier. The air here reeked of stale wine and fish. Just before they reached the pier a smell of iodine and seaweed announced the nearness of the sea and they clearly heard the sound of waves breaking gently on the big stone blocks.

Once they were on the pier they saw the sea spread out before them, a gently heaving expanse of deep-piled velvet, supple and sleek as a creature of the wild. They sat down on a boulder facing the open. Slowly the waters rose and sank, and with their tranquil breathing sudden oily glints formed and flickered over the surface in a haze of broken lights. Before them the darkness stretched out into infinity. Rieux could feel under his hand the gnarled, weather-worn visage of the rocks, and a strange happiness possessed him. Turning to Tarrou, he caught a glimpse on his friend's face of the same happiness, a happiness that forgot nothing, not even murder.

They undressed, and Rieux dived in first. After the first shock of cold had passed and he came back to the surface the water seemed tepid. When he had taken a few strokes he found that the sea was warm that night with the warmth of autumn seas that borrow from the shore the accumulated heat of the long days of summer. The movement of his feet left a foaming wake as he swam steadily ahead, and the water slipped along his arms to close in tightly on his legs. A loud splash told him that Tarrou had dived. Rieux lay on his back and stayed motionless, gazing up at the dome of sky lit by the stars and moon. He drew a deep breath. Then he heard a sound of beaten water, louder and louder, amazingly clear in the hollow silence of the night. Tarrou was coming up with him, he now could hear his breathing.

Rieux turned and swam level with his friend, timing his stroke to Tarrou's. But Tarrou was the stronger swimmer and Rieux had to put on speed to keep up with him. For some minutes they swam side by side, with the same zest, in the same rhythm, isolated from the world, at last free of the town and of the plague. Rieux was the first to stop and they swam back slowly, except at one point, where unexpectedly they found themselves caught in an ice-cold current. Their energy whipped up by this trap the sea had sprung on them, both struck out more vigorously.

They dressed and started back. Neither had said a word, but they were conscious of being perfectly at one, and the memory of this night would be cherished by them both. When they caught sight of the plague watchman, Rieux guessed that Tarrou, like himself, was thinking that the disease had given them a respite, and this was good, but now they must set their shoulders to the wheel again.

(*Plague*, 221, 231–233)

～

50

"To make things simpler, Rieux, let me begin by saying I had plague already, long before I came to this town and encountered it here. Which is tantamount to saying I'm like everybody else. Only there are some people who don't know it, or feel at ease in that condition; others know and want to get out of it. Personally, I've always wanted to get out of it.

.   .   .

"I have realized that we all have plague, and I have lost my peace. And today I am still trying to find it; still trying to understand all those others and not to be the mortal enemy of anyone. I only know that one must do what one can to cease being plague-stricken, and that's the only way in which we can hope for some peace or, failing that, a decent death. This, and only this, can bring relief to men and, if not save them, at least do them the least harm possible and even, sometimes, a little good. So that is why I resolved to have no truck with anything which, directly or indirectly, for good reasons or for bad, brings death to anyone or justifies others' putting him to death.

"That, too, is why this epidemic has taught me nothing new, except that I must fight it at your side. I know positively—yes, Rieux, I can say I know the world inside out, as you may see—that each of us has the plague within him; no one, no one on earth is free from it. And I know, too, that we must keep endless watch on ourselves lest in a careless moment we breathe in somebody's face and fasten the infection on him. What's natural is the microbe. All the rest —health, integrity, purity (if you like)—is a product of the human will, of a vigilance that must never falter. The good man, the man who infects hardly anyone, is the man who has the fewest lapses of attention. And it needs tremendous will-power, a never ending tension of the mind, to avoid such lapses. Yes, Rieux, it's a wearying business, being plague-stricken. But it's still more wearying to refuse to be it. That's why everybody in the world today looks so tired; everyone is more or less sick of plague. But that is also why some of us, those who want to get the plague out of their systems, feel such desperate weariness, a weariness from which nothing remains to set us free except death.

"Pending that release, I know I have no place in the world of today; once I'd definitely refused to kill, I doomed myself to an exile that can never end. I leave it to others to make history."

(*Plague*, 222, 228–229)

51

There are crimes of passion and crimes of logic. The boundary between them is not clearly defined. But the Penal Code makes the convenient distinction of premeditation. We are living in the era of premeditation and the perfect crime. Our criminals are no longer helpless children who could plead love as their excuse. On the contrary, they are adults and they have a perfect alibi: philosophy, which can be used for any purpose—even for transforming murderers into judges.

Heathcliff, in *Wuthering Heights*, would kill everybody on earth in order to possess Cathy, but it would never occur to him to say that murder is reasonable or theoretically defensible. He would commit it, and there his convictions end. This implies the power of love, and also strength of character. Since intense love is rare, murder remains an exception and preserves its aspect of infraction. But as soon as a man, through lack of character, takes refuge in doctrine, as soon as crime reasons about itself, it multiplies like reason itself and assumes all the aspects of the syllogism. Once crime was as solitary as a cry of protest; now it is as universal as science. Yesterday it was put on trial; today it determines the law.

This is not the place for indignation. The purpose of this essay is once again to face the reality of the present, which is logical crime, and to examine meticulously the arguments by which it is justified; it is an attempt to understand the times in which we live. One might think that a period which, in a space of fifty years, uproots, enslaves, or kills seventy million human beings should be condemned out of hand. But its culpability must still be understood. In more ingenuous times, when the tyrant razed cities for his own greater glory, when the slave chained to the conqueror's chariot was dragged through the rejoicing streets, when enemies were thrown to the wild beasts in front of the assembled people, the mind did not reel before such unabashed crimes, and judgment remained unclouded. But slave camps under the flag of freedom, massacres justified by philanthropy or by a taste for the superhuman, in one sense cripple judgment. On the day when crime dons the apparel of innocence—through a curious transposition peculiar to our times—it is innocence that is called upon to justify itself. The ambition of this essay is to accept and examine this strange challenge.

Our purpose is to find out whether innocence, the moment it becomes involved in action, can avoid committing murder. We can act only in terms of our own time, among the people who surround us. We shall know nothing until we know whether we have the right to kill our fellow men, or the right to let them be killed. In that every action today leads to murder, direct or indirect, we cannot act until we know whether or why we have the right to kill.

The important thing, therefore, is not, as yet, to go to the root of things, but, the world being what it is, to know how to live in it. In the age of negation, it was of some avail to examine one's position concerning suicide. In the age of ideologies, we must examine our position in relation to murder. If murder has rational foundations, then our period and we ourselves are rationally consequent. If it has no rational foundations, then we are insane and there is no alternative but to find some justification or to avert our faces. It is incumbent upon us, at all events, to give a definite answer to the question implicit in the blood and strife of this century. For we are being put to the rack. Thirty years ago, before reaching a decision to kill, people denied many things, to the point of denying themselves by suicide. God is deceitful; the whole world (myself included) is deceitful; therefore I choose to die: suicide was the problem then. Ideology today is concerned only with the denial of other human beings, who alone bear the responsibility of deceit. It is then that we kill. Each day at dawn, assassins in judges' robes slip into some cell: murder is the problem today.

The two arguments are inextricably bound together. Or rather they bind us, and so firmly that we can no longer choose our own problems. They choose us, one after another, and we have no alternative but to accept their choice. This essay proposes, in the face of murder and rebellion, to pursue a train of thought which began with suicide and the idea of the absurd.

(*Rebel*, 3–5)

52

The final conclusion of absurdist reasoning is, in fact, the repudiation of suicide and the acceptance of the desperate encounter between human inquiry and the silence of the universe. Suicide would mean the end of this encounter, and absurdist reasoning considers that it could not consent to this without negating its own premises. According to absurdist reasoning, such a solution would be the equivalent of flight or deliverance. But it is obvious that absurdism hereby admits that human life is the only necessary good since it is precisely life that makes this encounter possible and since, without life, the absurdist wager would have no basis. To say that life is absurd, the conscience must be alive. How is it possible, without making remarkable concessions to one's desire for comfort, to preserve exclusively for oneself the benefits of such a process of reasoning? From the moment that life is recognized as good, it becomes good for all men. Murder cannot be made coherent when suicide is not considered coherent. A mind imbued with the idea of the absurd will undoubtedly accept fatalistic murder; but it would never accept calculated murder. In terms of the encounter between human inquiry and the silence of the universe, murder and suicide are one and the same thing, and must be accepted or rejected together.

(*Rebel*, 6)

<p style="text-align:center">~~~♦~~~</p>

53

What is a rebel? A man who says no, but whose refusal does not imply a renunciation. He is also a man who says yes, from the moment he makes his first gesture of rebellion. A slave who has taken orders all his life suddenly decides that he cannot obey some new command. What does he mean by saying "no"?

He means, for example, that "this has been going on too long," "up to this point yes, beyond it no," "you are going too far," or, again, "there is a limit beyond which you shall not go." In other words, his no affirms the existence of a borderline. The same concept is to be found in the rebel's feeling that the other person "is exaggerating," that he is exerting his authority beyond a limit where he begins to infringe on the rights of others. Thus the movement of rebellion is founded simultaneously on the categorical rejection of an intrusion that is considered intolerable and on the confused conviction of an absolute right which, in the rebel's mind, is more precisely the impression that he "has the right to . . ." Rebellion cannot exist without the feeling that, somewhere and somehow, one is right. It is in this way that the rebel slave says yes and no simultaneously. He affirms that there are limits and also that he suspects—and wishes to preserve—the existence of certain things on this side of the borderline. He demonstrates, with obstinacy, that there is something in him which "is worth while . . ." and which must be taken into consideration. In a certain way, he confronts an order of things which oppresses him with the insistence on a kind of right not to be oppressed beyond the limit that he can tolerate.

In every act of rebellion, the rebel simultaneously experiences a feeling of revulsion at the infringement of his rights and a complete and spontaneous loyalty to certain aspects of himself. Thus he implicitly brings into play a standard of values so far from being gratuitous that he is prepared to support it no matter what the risks. Up to this point he has at least remained silent and has abandoned himself to the form of despair in which a condition is accepted even though it is considered unjust. To remain silent is to give the impression that one has no opinions, that one wants nothing, and in certain cases it really amounts to wanting nothing. Despair, like the absurd, has opinions and desires about everything in general and nothing in particular. Silence expresses this attitude very well. But from the moment that the rebel finds his voice—even though he says nothing but "no"—he begins to desire and to judge. The rebel, in the etymological sense, does a complete turnabout. He acted under the lash of his master's whip. Suddenly he turns and faces him. He opposes what is preferable to what is not. Not every value entails rebellion, but every act of rebellion tacitly invokes a value. Or is it really a question of values?

Awareness, no matter how confused it may be, develops from every act of rebellion: the sudden, dazzling perception that there is something in man with which he can identify himself, even if only for a moment. Up to now this identification was never really experienced. Before he rebelled, the slave accepted all the demands made upon him. Very often he even took orders, without reacting against them, which were far more conducive to insurrection than the one at which he balks. He accepted them patiently, though he may have protested inwardly, but in that he remained silent he was more concerned with his own immediate interests than as yet aware of his own rights. But with loss of patience—with impatience—a reaction begins which can extend to everything that he previously accepted, and which is almost always retroactive. The very moment the slave refuses to obey the humiliating orders of his master, he simultaneously rejects the condition of slavery. The act of rebellion carries him far beyond the point he had reached by simply refusing.

He exceeds the bounds that he fixed for his antagonist, and now
demands to be treated as an equal. What was at first the man's ob-
stinate resistance now becomes the whole man, who is identified
with and summed up in this resistance. The part of himself that he
wanted to be respected he proceeds to place above everything else
and proclaims it preferable to everything, even to life itself. It
becomes for him the supreme good. Having up to now been willing
to compromise, the slave suddenly adopts ("because this is how it
must be . . .") an attitude of All or Nothing. With rebellion,
awareness is born.

. . .

The sudden appearance of the concept of "All or Nothing" demonstrates that rebellion, contrary to current opinion, and though it
springs from everything that is most strictly individualistic in man,
questions the very idea of the individual. If the individual, in fact,
accepts death and happens to die as a consequence of his act of
rebellion, he demonstrates by doing so that he is willing to sacrifice
himself for the sake of a common good which he considers more
important than his own destiny. If he prefers the risk of death to the
negation of the rights that he defends, it is because he considers
these rights more important than himself. Therefore he is acting in
the name of certain values which are still indeterminate but which
he feels are common to himself and to all men. We see that the affirmation implicit in every act of rebellion is extended to something
that transcends the individual in so far as it withdraws him from his
supposed solitude and provides him with a reason to act. But it is
already worth noting that this concept of values as pre-existent to
any kind of action contradicts the purely historical philosophies, in
which values are acquired (if they are ever acquired) after the action
has been completed. Analysis of rebellion leads at least to the suspi-
cion that, contrary to the postulates of contemporary thought, a
human nature does exist, as the Greeks believed. Why rebel if
there is nothing permanent in oneself worth preserving? It is for the

sake of everyone in the world that the slave asserts himself when he comes to the conclusion that a command has infringed on something in him which does not belong to him alone, but which is common ground where all men—even the man who insults and oppresses him—have a natural community.*

Two observations will support this argument. First, we can see that an act of rebellion is not, essentially, an egoistic act. Of course, it can have egoistic motives. But one can rebel equally well against lies as against oppression. Moreover, the rebel—once he has accepted the motives and at the moment of his greatest impetus—preserves nothing in that he risks everything. He demands respect for himself, of course, but only in so far as he identifies himself with a natural community.

Then we note that rebellion does not arise only, and necessarily, among the oppressed, but that it can also be caused by the mere spectacle of oppression of which someone else is the victim. In such cases there is feeling of identification with another individual. And it must be pointed out that this is not a question of psychological identification—a mere subterfuge by which the individual imagines that it is he himself who has been offended. On the contrary, it can often happen that we cannot bear to see offenses done to others which we ourselves have accepted without rebelling. The suicides of the Russian terrorists in Siberia as a protest against their comrades' being whipped is a case in point. Nor is it a question of the feeling of a community of interests. Injustices done to men whom we consider enemies can, actually, be profoundly repugnant to us. There is only identification of one's destiny with that of others and a choice of sides. Therefore the individual is not, in himself alone, the embodiment of the values he wishes to defend. It needs all humanity, at least, to comprise them. When he rebels, a man identifies himself with other men and so surpasses himself,

* The community of victims is the same as that which unites victim and executioner. But the executioner does not know this.

and from this point of view human solidarity is metaphysical. But
for the moment we are only talking of the kind of solidarity that is
born in chains.

(*Rebel*, 13–17)

~~{~~

54

We live in an unsacrosanct moment in history. Insurrection is certainly not the sum total of human experience. But history today,
with all its storm and strife, compels us to say that rebellion is one
of the essential dimensions of man. It is our historic reality. Unless
we choose to ignore reality, we must find our values in it. Is it possible to find a rule of conduct outside the realm of religion and its
absolute values? That is the question raised by rebellion.

(*Rebel*, 21)

~~{~~

55

Man's solidarity is founded upon rebellion, and rebellion, in its
turn, can only find its justification in this solidarity. We have,
then, the right to say that any rebellion which claims the right to
deny or destroy this solidarity loses simultaneously its right to be
called rebellion and becomes in reality an acquiescence in murder.
In the same way, this solidarity, except in so far as religion is concerned, comes to life only on the level of rebellion. And so the real
drama of revolutionary thought is announced. In order to exist,
man must rebel, but rebellion must respect the limit it discovers in
itself—a limit where minds meet and, in meeting, begin to exist.
Rebellious thought, therefore, cannot dispense with memory: it is a
perpetual state of tension. In studying its actions and its results, we
shall have to say, each time, whether it remains faithful to its first
noble promise or if, through indolence or folly, it forgets its origi-

nal purpose and plunges into a mire of tyranny or servitude.

Meanwhile, we can sum up the initial progress that the spirit of rebellion provokes in a mind that is originally imbued with the absurdity and apparent sterility of the world. In absurdist experience, suffering is individual. But from the moment when a movement of rebellion begins, suffering is seen as a collective experience. Therefore the first progressive step for a mind overwhelmed by the strangeness of things is to realize that this feeling of strangeness is shared with all men and that human reality, in its entirety, suffers from the distance which separates it from the rest of the universe. The malady experienced by a single man becomes a mass plague. In our daily trials rebellion plays the same role as does the *"cogito"* in the realm of thought: it is the first piece of evidence. But this evidence lures the individual from his solitude. It founds its first value on the whole human race. I rebel—therefore we exist.

(*Rebel*, 22)

56

Metaphysical rebellion is the movement by which man protests against his condition and against the whole of creation. It is metaphysical because it contests the ends of man and of creation. The slave protests against the condition in which he finds himself within his state of slavery; the metaphysical rebel protests against the condition in which he finds himself as a man. The rebel slave affirms that there is something in him that will not tolerate the manner in which his master treats him; the metaphysical rebel declares that he is frustrated by the universe. For both of them, it is not only a question of pure and simple negation. In both cases, in fact, we find a value judgment in the name of which the rebel refuses to approve the condition in which he finds himself.

The slave who opposes his master is not concerned, let us note, with repudiating his master as a human being. He repudiates him as a master. He denies that he has the right to deny him, a slave, on grounds of necessity. The master is discredited to the exact extent that he fails to respond to a demand which he ignores. If men cannot refer to a common value, recognized by all as existing in each one, then man is incomprehensible to man. The rebel demands that this value should be clearly recognized in himself because he knows or suspects that, without this principle, crime and disorder would reign throughout the world. An act of rebellion on his part seems like a demand for clarity and unity. The most elementary form of rebellion, paradoxically, expresses an aspiration to order.

(*Rebel*, 23)

57

When the throne of God is overturned, the rebel realizes that it is now his own responsibility to create the justice, order, and unity that he sought in vain within his own condition, and in this way to justify the fall of God. Then begins the desperate effort to create, at the price of crime and murder if necessary, the dominion of man. This will not come about without terrible consequences, of which we are so far only aware of a few. But these consequences are in no way due to rebellion itself, or at least they only occur to the extent that the rebel forgets his original purpose, tires of the tremendous tension created by refusing to give a positive or negative answer, and finally abandons himself to complete negation or total submission. Metaphysical insurrection, in its first stages, offers us the same positive content as the slave's rebellion. Our task will be to examine what becomes of this positive content of rebellion in the actions that claim to originate from it and to explain where the fidelity or infidelity of the rebel to the origins of his revolt finally leads him.

(*Rebel*, 25)

58

From the moment that man submits God to moral judgment, he kills Him in his own heart. And then what is the basis of morality? God is denied in the name of justice, but can the idea of justice be understood without the idea of God?

(*Rebel*, 62)

59

One hundred and fifty years of metaphysical rebellion and of nihilism have witnessed the persistent reappearance, under different guises, of the same ravaged countenance, the face of human protest. All of them, decrying the human condition and its creator, have affirmed the solitude of man and the nonexistence of any kind of morality. But at the same time they have all tried to construct a purely terrestrial kingdom where their chosen principles will hold sway. As rivals of the Creator, they have inescapably been led to the point of reconstructing creation according to their own concepts.

(*Rebel*, 100)

60

Each time that it deifies the total rejection, the absolute negation, of what exists, it destroys. Each time that it blindly accepts what exists and gives voice to absolute assent, it destroys again. Hatred of the creator can turn to hatred of creation or to exclusive and defiant love of what exists. But in both cases it ends in murder and loses the right to be called rebellion.

(*Rebel*, 101)

61

We must now embark on the subject of this convulsive effort to control the world and to introduce a universal rule. We have arrived at the moment when rebellion, rejecting every aspect of servitude, attempts to annex all creation. Every time it experiences a setback, we have already seen that the political solution, the solution of conquest, is formulated. Henceforth, with the introduction of moral nihilism, it will retain, of all its acquisitions, only the will to power. In principle, the rebel only wanted to conquer his own existence and to maintain it in the face of God. But he forgets his origins and, by the law of spiritual imperialism, he sets out in search of world conquest by way of an infinitely multiplied series of murders.

(*Rebel*, 103)

62

Here ends Prometheus' surprising itinerary. Proclaiming his hatred of the gods and his love of mankind, he turns away from Zeus with scorn and approaches mortal men in order to lead them in an assault against the heavens. But men are weak and cowardly; they must be organized. They love pleasure and immediate happiness; they must be taught to refuse, in order to grow up, immediate rewards. Thus Prometheus, in his turn, becomes a master who first teaches and then commands. Men doubt that they can safely attack the city of light and are even uncertain whether the city exists. They must be saved from themselves. The hero then tells them that he, and he alone, knows the city. Those who doubt his word will be thrown into the desert, chained to a rock, offered to the vultures. The others will march henceforth in darkness, behind the pensive and solitary master. Prometheus alone has become god and reigns over the solitude of men. But from Zeus he has gained only solitude and cruelty; he is no longer Prometheus, he is Caesar. The real, the eternal Prometheus has now assumed the aspect of one of his victims. The same cry, springing from the depths of the past, rings forever through the Scythian desert.

(*Rebel*, 244–245)

63

Far from this source of life, however, Europe and the revolution are being shaken to the core by a spectacular convulsion. During the last century, man cast off the fetters of religion. Hardly was he free, however, when he created new and utterly intolerable chains. Virtue dies but is born again, more exacting than ever. It preaches an ear-splitting sermon on charity to all comers and a kind of love for the future which makes a mockery of contemporary humanism. When it has reached this point of stability, it can only wreak havoc. A day arrives when it becomes bitter, immediately adopts police methods, and, for the salvation of mankind, assumes the ignoble aspect of an inquisition. At the climax of contemporary tragedy, we therefore become intimates of crime. The sources of life and of creation seem exhausted. Fear paralyzes a Europe peopled with phantoms and machines. Between two holocausts, scaffolds are installed in underground caverns where humanist executioners celebrate their new cult in silence. What cry would ever trouble them? The poets themselves, confronted with the murder of their fellow men, proudly declare that their hands are clean. The whole world absentmindedly turns its back on these crimes; the victims have reached the extremity of their disgrace: they are a bore. In ancient times the blood of murder at least produced a religious horror and in this way sanctified the value of life. The real condemnation of the period we live in is, on the contrary, that it leads us to think that it is not bloodthirsty enough. Blood is no longer visible; it does not bespatter the faces of our pharisees visibly enough. This is the extreme of nihilism; blind and savage murder becomes an oasis, and the imbecile criminal seems positively refreshing in comparison with our highly intelligent executioners.

Having believed for a long time that it could fight against God with all humanity as its ally, the European mind then perceived that it must also, if it did not want to die, fight against men. The rebels who, united against death, wanted to construct, on the foundation of the human species, a savage immortality are terrified at the prospect of being obliged to kill in their turn. Nevertheless, if they retreat they must accept death; if they advance they must accept murder. Rebellion, cut off from its origins and cynically travestied, oscillates, on all levels, between sacrifice and murder.

(*Rebel*, 279–280)

64

Can the "We are" contained in the movement of rebellion, without shame and without subterfuge, be reconciled with murder? In assigning oppression a limit within which begins the dignity common to all men, rebellion defined a primary value. It put in the first rank of its frame of reference an obvious complicity among men, a common texture, the solidarity of chains, a communication between human being and human being which makes men both similar and united. In this way, it compelled the mind to take a first step in defiance of an absurd world. By this progress it rendered still more acute the problem that it must now solve in regard to murder. On the level of the absurd, in fact, murder would only give rise to logical contradictions; on the level of rebellion it is mental laceration. For it is now a question of deciding if it is possible to kill someone whose resemblance to ourselves we have at last recognized and whose identity we have just sanctified. When we have only just conquered solitude, must we then re-establish it

definitively by legitimizing the act that isolates everything? To force
solitude on a man who has just come to understand that he is not
alone, is that not the definitive crime against man?

Logically, one should reply that murder and rebellion are contradictory. If a single master should, in fact, be killed, the rebel, in a
certain way, is no longer justified in using the term *community of
men* from which he derived his justification. If this world has no
higher meaning, if man is only responsible to man, it suffices for a
man to remove one single human being from the society of the living to automatically exclude himself from it. When Cain kills
Abel, he flees to the desert. And if murderers are legion, then this
legion lives in the desert and in that other kind of solitude called
promiscuity.

From the moment that he strikes, the rebel cuts the world in
two. He rebelled in the name of the identity of man with man and
he sacrifices this identity by consecrating the difference in blood.
His only existence, in the midst of suffering and oppression, was
contained in this identity. The same movement, which intended to
affirm him, thus brings an end to his existence. He can claim that
some, or even almost all, are with him. But if one single human
being is missing in the irreplaceable world of fraternity, then this
world is immediately depopulated. If we are not, then I am not and
this explains the infinite sadness of Kaliayev and the silence of
Saint-Just. The rebels, who have decided to gain their ends through
violence and murder, have in vain replaced, in order to preserve
the hope of existing, "We are" by the "We shall be." When the
murderer and the victim have disappeared, the community will
provide its own justification without them. The exception having
lasted its appointed time, the rule will once more become possible.
On the level of history, as in individual life, murder is thus a desperate exception or it is nothing. The disturbance that it brings to
the order of things offers no hope of a future; it is an exception and
therefore it can be neither utilitarian nor systematic as the purely
historical attitude would have it. It is the limit that can be reached

but once, after which one must die. The rebel has only one way of reconciling himself with his act of murder if he allows himself to be led into performing it: to accept his own death and sacrifice. He kills and dies so that it shall be clear that murder is impossible. He demonstrates that, in reality, he prefers the "We are" to the "We shall be." The calm happiness of Kaliayev in his prison, the serenity of Saint-Just when he walks toward the scaffold, are explained in their turn. Beyond that farthest frontier, contradiction and nihilism begin.

(*Rebel*, 281–282)

65

Every rebel, solely by the movement that sets him in opposition to the oppressor, therefore pleads for life, undertakes to struggle against servitude, falsehood, and terror, and affirms, in a flash, that these three afflictions are the cause of silence between men, that they obscure them from one another and prevent them from rediscovering themselves in the only value that can save them from nihilism—the long complicity of men at grips with their destiny.

In a flash—but that is time enough to say, provisionally, that the most extreme form of freedom, the freedom to kill, is not compatible with the sense of rebellion. Rebellion is in no way the demand for total freedom. On the contrary, rebellion puts total freedom up for trial. It specifically attacks the unlimited power that authorizes a superior to violate the forbidden frontier. Far from demanding general independence, the rebel wants it to be recognized that freedom has its limits everywhere that a human being is to be found—the limit being precisely that human being's power to rebel. The most profound reason for rebellious intransigence is to be found here. The more aware rebellion is of demanding a just limit, the more inflexible it becomes. The rebel undoubtedly demands a certain degree of freedom for himself; but in no case, if he is consistent, does he demand the right to destroy the existence and the freedom of others. He humiliates no one. The freedom he claims, he claims for all; the freedom he refuses, he forbids everyone to enjoy. He is not only the slave against the master, but also man against the world of master and slave. Therefore, thanks to rebellion, there is something more in history than the relation between mastery and servitude. Unlimited power is not the only law. It is in the name of another value that the rebel affirms the impossibility of total freedom while he claims for himself the relative freedom necessary to recognize this impossibility. Every human freedom, at its very roots, is therefore relative. Absolute freedom, which is the freedom to kill, is the only one which does not claim, at the same time as itself, the things that limit and obliterate it. Thus it cuts itself off from its roots and—abstract and malevolent shade—wanders haphazardly until such time as it imagines that it has found substance in some ideology.

It is then possible to say that rebellion, when it develops into destruction, is illogical. Claiming the unity of the human condition, it is a force of life, not of death. Its most profound logic is not the logic of destruction; it is the logic of creation. Its movement, in order to remain authentic, must never abandon any of the terms of the contradiction that sustains it. It must be faithful to the *yes* that it contains as well as to the *no* that nihilistic interpretations isolate in rebellion. The logic of the rebel is to want to serve justice so as not to add to the injustice of the human condition, to insist on plain language so as not to increase the universal falsehood, and to wager, in spite of human misery, for happiness. Nihilistic passion, adding to falsehood and injustice, destroys in its fury its original demands and thus deprives rebellion of its most cogent reasons. It kills in the fond conviction that this world is dedicated to death. The consequence of rebellion, on the contrary, is to refuse to legitimize murder because rebellion, in principle, is a protest against death.

But if man were capable of introducing unity into the world entirely on his own, if he could establish the reign, by his own decree, of sincerity, innocence, and justice, he would be God Himself. Equally, if he could accomplish all this, there would be no more reasons for rebellion. If rebellion exists, it is because falsehood, injustice, and violence are part of the rebel's condition. He cannot, therefore, absolutely claim not to kill or lie, without renouncing his rebellion and accepting, once and for all, evil and murder. But no more can he agree to kill and lie, since the inverse reasoning which would justify murder and violence would also destroy the reasons for his insurrection. Thus the rebel can never find peace. He knows what is good and, despite himself, does evil. The value that supports him is never given to him once and for all; he must fight to uphold it, unceasingly. Again the existence he achieves collapses if rebellion does not support it. In any case, if he is not always able not to kill, either directly or indirectly, he can put his conviction and passion to work at diminishing the chances of murder around him. His only virtue will lie in never yielding to the impulse to allow himself to be engulfed in the shadows that surround him and in obstinately dragging the chains of evil, with which he is bound, toward the light of good. If he finally kills himself, he will accept death. Faithful to his origins, the rebel demonstrates by sacrifice that his real freedom is not freedom from murder but freedom from his own death. At the same time, he achieves honor in metaphysical terms. Thus Kaliayev climbs the gallows and visibly designates to all his fellow men the exact limit where man's honor begins and ends.

Rebellion also deploys itself in history, which demands not only exemplary choices, but also efficacious attitudes. Rational murder runs the risk of finding itself justified by history. The contradiction of rebellion, then, is reflected in an apparently insoluble contradiction, of which the two counterparts in politics are on the one hand the opposition between violence and nonviolence, and on the other hand the opposition between justice and freedom. Let us try to define them in the terms of their paradox.

The positive value contained in the initial movement of rebellion supposes the renunciation of violence committed on principle. It consequently entails the impossibility of stabilizing a revolution. Rebellion is, incessantly, prey to this contradiction. On the level of history it becomes even more insoluble. If I renounce the project of making human identity respected, I abdicate in favor of oppression, I renounce rebellion and fall back on an attitude of nihilistic consent. Then nihilism becomes conservative. If I insist that human identity should be recognized as existing, then I engage in an action which, to succeed, supposes a cynical attitude toward violence and denies this identity and rebellion itself. To extend the contradiction still farther, if the unity of the world cannot come from on high, man must construct it on his own level, in history. History without a value to transfigure it, is controlled by the law of expediency. Historical materialism, determinism, violence, negation of every form of freedom which does not coincide with expediency and the world of courage and of silence, are the highly legitimate consequences of a pure philosophy of history. In the world today, only a philosophy of eternity could justify nonviolence. To absolute worship of history it would make the objection of the creation of history and of the historical situation it would ask whence it had sprung. Finally, it would put the responsibility for justice in God's hands, thus consecrating injustice. Equally, its answers, in their turn, would insist on faith. The objection will be raised of evil, and of the paradox of an all-powerful and malevolent, or benevolent and sterile, God. The choice will remain open between grace and history, God or the sword.

What, then, should be the attitude of the rebel? He cannot turn away from the world and from history without denying the very principle of his rebellion, nor can he choose eternal life without resigning himself, in one sense, to evil. If, for example, he is not a Christian, he should go to the bitter end. But to the bitter end means to choose history absolutely and with it murder, if murder is essential to history: to accept the justification of murder is again to

deny his origins. If the rebel makes no choice, he chooses the
silence and slavery of others. If, in a moment of despair, he declares that he opts both against God and against history, he is the
witness of pure freedom; in other words, of nothing. In our period
of history and in the impossible condition in which he finds himself, of being unable to affirm a superior motive that does not have
its limits in evil, his apparent dilemma is silence or murder—in either case, a surrender.

(*Rebel*, 284–287)

66

The revolution of the twentieth century has arbitrarily separated,
for overambitious ends of conquest, two inseparable ideas. Absolute
freedom mocks at justice. Absolute justice denies freedom. To be
fruitful, the two ideas must find their limits in each other. No man
considers that his condition is free if it is not at the same time just,
nor just unless it is free. Freedom, precisely, cannot even be
imagined without the power of saying clearly what is just and what
is unjust, of claiming all existence in the name of a small part of
existence which refuses to die. Finally there is a justice, though a
very different kind of justice, in restoring freedom, which is the
only imperishable value of history. Men are never really willing to
die except for the sake of freedom: therefore they do not believe in
dying completely.

(*Rebel*, 291)

67

Authentic arts of rebellion will only consent to take up arms for institutions that limit violence, not for those which codify it. A revolution is not worth dying for unless it assures the immediate sup-
pression of the death penalty; not worth going to prison for unless it

refuses in advance to pass sentence without fixed terms. If rebel violence employs itself in the establishment of these institutions, announcing its aims as often as it can, it is the only way in which it can be really provisional. When the end is absolute, historically speaking, and when it is believed certain of realization, it is possible to go so far as to sacrifice others. When it is not, only oneself can be sacrificed, in the hazards of a struggle for the common dignity of man. Does the end justify the means? That is possible. But what will justify the end? To that question, which historical thought leaves pending, rebellion replies: the means.

(*Rebel*, 292)

68

Moderation . . . teaches us that at least one part of realism is necessary to every ethic: pure and unadulterated virtue is homicidal. And one part of ethics is necessary to all realism: cynicism is homicidal. That is why humanitarian cant has no more basis than cynical provocation. Finally, man is not entirely to blame; it was not he who started history; nor is he entirely innocent, since he continues it. Those who go beyond this limit and affirm his total innocence end in the insanity of definitive culpability. Rebellion, on the contrary, sets us on the path of calculated culpability. Its sole but invincible hope is incarnated, in the final analysis, in innocent murderers.

At this limit, the "We are" paradoxically defines a new form of individualism. "We are" in terms of history, and history must reckon with this "We are," which must in its turn keep its place in history. I have need of others who have need of me and of each other. Every collective action, every form of society, supposes a discipline, and the individual, without this discipline, is only a stranger, bowed down under the weight of an inimical collectivity. But society and discipline lose their direction if they deny the "We are." I alone, in one sense, support the common dignity that I cannot allow either myself or others to debase. This individualism is in no sense pleasure; it is perpetual struggle, and, sometimes, unparalleled joy when it reaches the heights of proud compassion.

(*Rebel*, 297)

69

There does exist for man, therefore, a way of acting and of thinking which is possible on the level of moderation to which he belongs. Every undertaking that is more ambitious than this proves to be contradictory. The absolute is not attained nor, above all, created through history. Politics is not religion, or if it is, then it is nothing but the Inquisition. How would society define an absolute? Perhaps everyone is looking for this absolute on behalf of all. But society and politics only have the responsibility of arranging everyone's affairs so that each will have the leisure and the freedom to pursue this common search. History can then no longer be presented as an object of worship. It is only an opportunity that must be rendered fruitful by a vigilant rebellion.

"Obsession with the harvest and indifference to history," writes René Char admirably, "are the two extremities of my bow." If the duration of history is not synonymous with the duration of the harvest, then history, in effect, is no more than a fleeting and cruel shadow in which man has no more part. He who dedicates himself to this history dedicates himself to nothing and, in his turn, is nothing. But he who dedicates himself to the duration of his life, to the house he builds, to the dignity of mankind, dedicates himself to the earth and reaps from it the harvest that sows its seed and sustains the world again and again. Finally, it is those who know how to rebel, at the appropriate moment, against history who really advance its interests. To rebel against it supposes an interminable tension and the agonized serenity of which René Char also speaks. But

the true life is present in the heart of this dichotomy. Life is this dichotomy itself, the mind soaring over volcanoes of light, the
madness of justice, the extenuating intransigence of moderation.
The words that reverberate for us at the confines of this long adventure of rebellion are not formulas for optimism, for which we have
no possible use in the extremities of our unhappiness, but words of
courage and intelligence which, on the shores of the eternal seas,
even have the qualities of virtue.

No possible form of wisdom today can claim to give more. Rebellion indefatigably confronts evil, from which it can only derive a
new impetus. Man can master in himself everything that should be
mastered. He should rectify in creation everything that can be rec-
tified. And after he has done so, children will still die unjustly even
in a perfect society. Even by his greatest effort man can only propose to diminish arithmetically the sufferings of the world. But the
injustice and the suffering of the world will remain and, no matter
how limited they are, they will not cease to be an outrage. Dimitri
Karamazov's cry of "Why?" will continue to resound; art and rebellion will die only with the last man.

There is an evil, undoubtedly, which men accumulate in their
frantic desire for unity. But yet another evil lies at the roots of this
inordinate movement. Confronted with this evil, confronted with
death, man from the very depths of his soul cries out for justice.
Historical Christianity has only replied to this protest against evil by
the annunciation of the kingdom and then of eternal life, which
demands faith. But suffering exhausts hope and faith and then is
left alone and unexplained. The toiling masses, worn out with suffering and death, are masses without God. Our place is henceforth
at their side, far from teachers, old or new. Historical Christianity
postpones to a point beyond the span of history the cure of evil and
murder, which are nevertheless experienced within the span of history. Contemporary materialism also believes that it can answer all
questions. But, as a slave to history, it increases the domain of historic murder and at the same time leaves it without any justifica-

tion, except in the future—which again demands faith. In both cases one must wait, and meanwhile the innocent continue to die. For twenty centuries the sum total of evil has not diminished in the world. No paradise, whether divine or revolutionary, has been realized. An injustice remains inextricably bound to all suffering, even the most deserved in the eyes of men. The long silence of Prometheus before the powers that overwhelmed him still cries out in protest. But Prometheus, meanwhile, has seen men rail and turn against him. Crushed between human evil and destiny, between terror and the arbitrary, all that remains to him is his power to rebel in order to save from murder him who can still be saved, without surrendering to the arrogance of blasphemy.

Then we understand that rebellion cannot exist without a strange form of love. Those who find no rest in God or in history are condemned to live for those who, like themselves, cannot live: in fact, for the humiliated. The most pure form of the movement of rebellion is thus crowned with the heart-rending cry of Karamazov: if all are not saved, what good is the salvation of one only? Thus Catholic prisoners, in the prison cells of Spain, refuse communion today because the priests of the regime have made it obligatory in certain prisons. These lonely witnesses to the crucifixion of innocence also refuse salvation if it must be paid for by injustice and oppression. This insane generosity is the generosity of rebellion, which unhesitatingly gives the strength of its love and without a moment's delay refuses injustice. Its merit lies in making no calculations, distributing everything it possesses to life and to living men. It is thus that it is prodigal in its gifts to men to come. Real generosity toward the future lies in giving all to the present.

Rebellion proves in this way that it is the very movement of life and that it cannot be denied without renouncing life. Its purest outburst, on each occasion, gives birth to existence. Thus it is love and fecundity or it is nothing at all. Revolution without honor, calculated revolution which, in preferring an abstract concept of man to a man of flesh and blood, denies existence as many times as is necessary, puts resentment in the place of love. Immediately rebellion, forgetful of its generous origins, allows itself to be contaminated by resentment; it denies life, dashes toward destruction, and raises up the grimacing cohorts of petty rebels, embryo slaves all of them, who end by offering themselves for sale, today, in all the market-places of Europe, to no matter what form of servitude. It is no longer either revolution or rebellion but rancor, malice, and tyr-anny. Then, when revolution in the name of power and of history becomes a murderous and immoderate mechanism, a new rebel-lion is consecrated in the name of moderation and of life. We are at the extremity now. At the end of this tunnel of darkness, how-ever, there is inevitably a light, which we already divine and for which we only have to fight to ensure its coming. All of us, among the ruins, are preparing a renaissance beyond the limits of nihilism. But few of us know it.

Already, in fact, rebellion, without claiming to solve everything, can at least confront its problems. From this moment high noon is borne away on the fast-moving stream of history. Around the de-vouring flames, shadows writhe in mortal combat for an instant of time and then as suddenly disappear, and the blind, fingering their eyelids, cry out that this is history. The men of Europe, abandoned to the shadows, have turned their backs upon the fixed and radiant point of the present. They forget the present for the future, the fate of humanity for the delusion of power, the misery of the slums for the mirage of the eternal city, ordinary justice for an empty prom-ised land. They despair of personal freedom and dream of a strange freedom of the species; reject solitary death and give the name of immortality to a vast collective agony. They no longer believe in the things that exist in the world and in living man; the secret of Europe is that it no longer loves life. Its blind men entertain the puerile belief that to love one single day of life amounts to justify-ing whole centuries of oppression. That is why they wanted to ef-face joy from the world and to postpone it until a much later date. Impatience with limits, the rejection of their double life, despair at being a man, have finally driven them to inhuman excesses. Denying the real grandeur of life, they have had to stake all of their own excellence. For want of something better to do, they deified themselves and their misfortunes began; these gods have had their eyes put out. Kaliayev, and his brothers throughout the entire world, refuse, on the contrary, to be deified in that they refuse the unlimited power to inflict death. They choose, and give us as an example the only original rule of life today: to learn to live and to die, and, in order to be a man, to refuse to be a god.

At this meridian of thought, the rebel thus rejects divinity in order to share in the struggles and destiny of all men. We shall choose Ithaca, the faithful land, frugal and audacious thought, lucid action, and the generosity of the man who understands. In the light, the earth remains our first and our last love. Our brothers are breathing under the same sky as we; justice is a living thing. Now is born that strange joy which helps one live and die, and which we shall never again postpone to a later time. On the sorrowing earth it is the unresting thorn, the bitter brew, the harsh wind off the sea, the old and the new dawn. With this joy, through long struggle, we shall remake the soul of our time, and a Europe which will exclude nothing. Not even that phantom Nietzsche, who for twelve years after his downfall was continually invoked by the West as the blasted image of its loftiest knowledge and its nihilism; nor the prophet of justice without mercy who lies, by mistake, in the unbelievers' plot at Highgate Cemetery; nor the deified mummy of the man of action in his glass coffin; nor any part of what the intelligence and energy of Europe have ceaselessly furnished to the pride of a contemptible period. All may indeed live again, side by side with the martyrs of 1905, but on condition that it is understood that they correct one another, and that a limit, under the sun, shall curb them all. Each tells the other that he is not God; this is the end of romanticism. At this moment, when each of us must fit an arrow to his bow and enter the lists anew, to reconquer, within history and in spite of it, that which he owns already, the thin yield of his fields, the brief love of this earth, at this moment when at last a man is born, it is time to forsake our age and its adolescent furies. The bow bends; the wood complains. At the moment of supreme tension, there will leap into flight an unswerving arrow, a shaft that is inflexible and free.

(*Rebel*, 302–306)

70

THE PLAGUE: I am the ruler here; this is a fact, therefore it is a right. A right that admits of no discussion; a fact you must accept.

In any case, make no mistake; when I say I rule you, I rule in a rather special way—it would be more correct to say I function. You Spaniards always have a tendency to be romantic, and I'm sure you'd like to see me as a sort of black king or some monstrous, gaudy insect. That would satisfy your dramatic instincts, of which we've heard so much. Well, they won't be satisfied this time. I don't wield a sceptor or anything like that; in fact I prefer to look like a quite ordinary person, let's say a sergeant or a corporal. That's one of my ways of vexing you, and being vexed will do you good; you still have much to learn. So now your king has black nails and a drab uniform. He doesn't sit on a throne, but in an office chair. His palace is a barracks and his hunting-lodge a courthouse. You are living in a stage of siege.

That is why when I step in all sentiment goes by the board. So take good notice, sentiment is banned, and so are other imbecilities, such as the fuss you make about your precious happiness, the maudlin look on lovers' faces, your selfish habit of contemplating landscapes, and the crime of irony. Instead of these I give you organization. That will worry you a bit to start with, but very soon you'll realize that good organization is better than cheap emotion. By way of illustration of this excellent precept I shall begin by segregating the men from the women. This order will have the force of law. [*The Guards promptly carry out the order.*]

Your monkey-tricks have had their day; the time has come for realizing that life is earnest.

I take it you have grasped my meaning. As from today you are going to learn to die in an orderly manner. Until now you died in the Spanish manner, haphazard—when you felt like it, so to say. You died because the weather suddenly turned cold, or a mule stumbled; because the skyline of the Pyrenees was blue and the river Guadalquivir has a fascination for the lonely man in springtime. Or else it was because there are always brawling fools ready to kill for money or for honor— when it's so much more elegant to kill for the delight of being logical. Yes, you muffed your deaths. A dead man here, a dead man there, one in his bed, another in the bull ring— what could be more slovenly? But, happily for you, I shall impose order on all that. There will be no more dying as the fancy takes you. Lists will be kept up—what admirable things lists are!—and we shall fix the order of your going. Fate has learned wisdom and will keep its records. You will figure in statistics, so at last you'll serve some purpose. For, I was forgetting to tell you, you will die, that goes without saying, but then—if not before—you will be packed off to the incinerator. Nothing could be more hygienic and efficient, and it fits in with our program. Spain first!

So line up for a decent death, that's your first duty. On these terms you will enjoy my favor. But take care that you don't indulge in nonsensical ideas, or righteous indignation, or in any of those little gusts of petulance which lead to big revolts. I have suppressed these mental luxuries and put logic in their stead, for I can't bear untidiness and irrationality. So from this day on you are going to be rational and tidy; the wearing of badges will be compulsory. Besides the mark on your groins you will have the plague star under your armpits, for all to see—meaning that you are marked down for elimination. So the others, people who think these marks are no concern of theirs and line up cheerfully for the bullfight every Sunday, will treat you as suspects and edge away from you. But you need not feel aggrieved; these marks concern them also, they're all down on our lists and nobody is overlooked. In fact all are suspects—that's the long and the short of it.

Don't take all this to mean I haven't any feelings. As a matter of fact I like birds, the first violets of the year, the cool lips of girls. Once in a while it's refreshing, that sort of thing. Also, I'm an idealist. My heart. . . . No, I fear I am getting sentimental—that's enough for today. Just a word more, by way of summing up. I bring you order, silence, total justice. I don't ask you to thank me for this; it's only natural, what I am doing here for you. Only, I must insist on your collaboration. My administration has begun.

(*Plays*, 170–173)

71

We want to fix things up in such a way that nobody understands a word of what his neighbor says. And, let me tell you, we are steadily nearing that perfect moment when nothing anybody says will rouse the least echo in another's mind; when the two languages that are fighting it out here will exterminate each other so thoroughly that we shall be well on the way to that ideal consummation—the triumph of death and silence.

(*Plays*, 186)

72

THE PLAGUE: What authority have you to question my orders?
THE SECRETARY: The authority of memory. For I have not forgotten what I was before you came. Then I was free, an ally of the

accidental. No one hated me. I was the visitant who checks
the march of time, shapes, destinies, and stabilizes loves. I
stood for the permanent. But you have made me the hand-
maid of logic, rules, and regulations. And I have lost the
knack I had of sometimes being helpful.

THE PLAGUE: Who wants your help?

THE SECRETARY: Those who are not big enough to face a sea of
troubles. Nearly everyone, that is to say. Quite often I could
work in a sort of harmony with them: I existed, in my fashion.
Today I do violence to them, and one and all they curse me
with their last breath. Perhaps that's why I like this man whom
you are telling me to kill. He chose me freely, and, in his
way, he pitied me. Yes, I like people who meet me halfway.

(*Plays*, 225)

73

Look at me! Look for a last time at the only power in the world,
acclaim your one true monarch, and learn to fear. [*Laughs.*] In
the old days you professed to fear God and his caprices. But your
God was an anarchist who played fast and loose with logic. He
thought He could be both autocratic and kindhearted at the same
time—but that was obviously wishful thinking, if I may put it so. *I*,
anyhow, know better. I stand for power and power alone. Yes, I
have chosen domination which, as you have learned, can be more
formidable than Hell itself.

For thousands and thousands of years I have strewn your fields
and cities with dead bodies. My victims have fertilized the sands of
Libya and black Ethiopia, the soil of Persia still is fat with the sweat
of my corpses. I filled Athens with the fires of purification, kindled
on her beaches thousands of funeral pyres, and spread the seas of
Greece so thick with ashes that their blue turned gray. The gods,
yes, even the poor gods were revolted by my doings. Then, when
the temples gave place to cathedrals, my black horsemen filled

them with howling mobs. For years untold, on all five continents, I
have been killing without respite and without compunction.

As systems go, mine was not a bad one. There was a sound idea
behind it. Nevertheless, that idea was somewhat narrow. If you
want to know the way I feel about it, I'll say a dead man is refreshing enough, but he's not remunerative. Not nearly so rewarding as
a slave. So the great thing is to secure a majority of slaves by means
of a minority of well-selected deaths. And, thanks to our improved
technique, we now can bring this off. That's why, after having
killed or humiliated the requisite number of persons, we shall have
whole nations on their knees. No form of beauty or grandeur will
stand up to us, and we shall triumph over everything. . . .

(*Plays*, 226–227)

<hr />

74

VICTORIA: No, you should have chosen me, though all the powers
of heaven forbade you. You should have preferred me to the
whole earth.

DIEGO: I have squared up accounts with death—there lies my
strength. But it is an all-devouring strength; happiness has no
place in it.

VICTORIA: What did your strength matter to me? It was you—the
man you were—that I loved.

DIEGO: I have burned myself out in the struggle. I am no longer a
man and it is right that I should die.

VICTORIA [*flinging herself on him*]: Then take me with you.

DIEGO: No, this world needs you. It needs our women to teach it
how to live. We men have never been capable of anything but
dying.

VICTORIA: Ah, it was too simple, wasn't it, to love each other in
silence and to endure together whatever had to be endured? I
preferred your fear, Diego.

DIEGO [*gazing at* VICTORIA]: I loved you with my whole soul.

VICTORIA [*passionately*]: But that wasn't enough! No, even that was not enough! You loved me with your soul, perhaps, but I wanted more than that, far more.

[*The* SECRETARY *stretches her hand toward* DIEGO. *The death agony begins, while the women hasten toward* VICTORIA *and gather round her.*]

CHORUS OF WOMEN: Our curse on him! Our curse on all who forsake our bodies! And pity on us, most of all, who are forsaken and must endure year after year this world which men in their pride are ever aspiring to transform! Surely, since everything may not be saved, we should learn at least to safeguard the home where love is. Then, come war, come pestilence, we could bravely see them through with you beside us. Thus, instead of this solitary death, haunted by foolish dreams and nourished with words, your last end would be shared by us, we would die united in an all-consuming flame of love. But no! Men go whoring after ideas, a man runs away from his mother, forsakes his love, and starts rushing upon adventure, wounded without a scar, slain without a dagger, a hunter of shadows or a lonely singer who invokes some impossible reunion under a silent sky, and makes his way from solitude to solitude, toward the final isolation, a death in the desert.

(*Plays*, 228–229)

75

STEPAN: I wonder if you people realize what this decision means? Two solid months of shadowing, of hairbreadth escapes—two wasted months! Egor arrested to no purpose. Rikov hanged to no purpose. Must we start that all over again? Weeks and weeks of harrowing suspense without a break; of sleepless nights, of plotting and scheming, before another opportunity like this comes our way. Have you all gone crazy?

ANNENKOV: In two days' time, as you know quite well, the Grand
Duke will be going to the theater again.

STEPAN: Two days during which we run the risk of being caught at
any moment; why, you've said so yourself!

KALIAYEV: I'm off!

DORA: No, wait. [To STEPAN] You, Stepan, could you fire point
blank on a child, with your eyes open?

STEPAN: I could, if the group ordered it.

DORA: Why did you shut your eyes then?

STEPAN: What? Did I shut my eyes?

DORA: Yes.

STEPAN: Then it must have been because I wanted to picture . . .
what you describe, more vividly, and to make sure my answer
was the true one.

DORA: Open your eyes, Stepan, and try to realize that the group
would lose all its driving force, were it to tolerate, even for a
moment, the idea of children's being blown to pieces by our
bombs.

STEPAN: Sorry, but I don't suffer from a tender heart; that sort of
nonsense cuts no ice with *me*. . . . Not until the day comes
when we stop sentimentalizing about children will the revolution triumph, and we be masters of the world.

DORA: When that day comes, the revolution will be loathed by the
whole human race.

STEPAN: What matter, if we love it enough to force our revolution
on it; to rescue humanity from itself and from its bondage?

DORA: And suppose mankind at large doesn't want the revolution?
Suppose the masses for whom you are fighting won't stand for
the killing of their children? What then? Would you strike at
the masses, too?

STEPAN: Yes, if it were necessary, and I would go on striking at
them until they understood. . . . No, don't misunderstand
me; I, too, love the people.

DORA: Love, you call it. That's not how love shows itself.

STEPAN: Why says so?

DORA: *I* say it.

STEPAN: You're a woman, and your idea of love is . . . well, let's say, unsound.

DORA [*passionately*]: Anyhow, I've a very sound idea of what shame means.

STEPAN: Once, and once only, in my life I felt ashamed of myself. It was when I was flogged. Yes, I was flogged. The knout— you know what that is, don't you? Vera was there beside me and she killed herself, as a protest. But I . . . I went on living. So why should I be ashamed of anything, now?

ANNENKOV: Stepan, all of us love you and respect you. But whatever private reasons you may have for feeling as you do, I can't allow you to say that everything's permissible. Thousands of our brothers have died to make it known that everything is *not* allowed.

STEPAN: Nothing that can serve our cause should be ruled out.

ANNENKOV [*angrily*]: Is it permissible for one of us to join the police and play a double game, as Evno proposed to do? Would *you* do it?

STEPAN: Yes, if I felt it necessary.

ANNENKOV [*rising to his feet*]: Stepan, we will forget what you've just said, for the sake of all that you have done for us and with us. . . . Now, let's keep to the matter in hand. The question is whether, presently, we are to throw bombs at those two children.

STEPAN: Children! There you go, always talking about children! Cannot you realize what is at stake? Just because Yanek couldn't bring himself to kill those two, thousands of Russian children will go on dying of starvation for years to come. Have you ever seen children dying of starvation? I have. And to be killed by a bomb is a pleasant death compared with that. But Yanek never saw children starving to death. He saw only the Grand Duke's pair of darling little lapdogs. Aren't you sentient human beings? Or are you living like animals for the moment only? In that case by all means indulge in charity and cure each petty suffering that meets your eye; but don't meddle with the revolution, for its task is to cure all sufferings present and to come.

DORA: Yanek's ready to kill the Grand Duke because his death may help to bring nearer the time when Russian children will no longer die of hunger. That in itself is none too easy for him. But the death of the Grand Duke's niece and nephew won't prevent any child from dying of hunger. Even in destruction there's a right way and a wrong way—and there are limits.

STEPAN [*vehemently*]: There are no limits! The truth is that you don't believe in the revolution, any of you. [*All, except* KALIAYEV, *rise to their feet.*] No, you don't believe in it. If you did believe in it sincerely, with all your hearts; if you felt sure that, by dint of our struggles and sacrifices, some day we shall build up a new Russia, redeemed from despotism, a land of freedom that will gradually spread out over the whole earth; and if you felt convinced that then and only then, freed from his masters and his superstitions, man will at last look up toward the sky, a god in his own right—how, I ask you, could the deaths of two children be weighed in the balance against such a faith? Surely you would claim for yourselves the right to do anything and everything that might bring that great day nearer! So now, if you draw the line at killing these two children, well, it simply means you are not sure you have that right. So, I repeat, you do *not* believe in the revolution. [*There is a short silence.* KALIAYEV, *too, rises to his feet.*]

KALIAYEV: Stepan, I am ashamed of myself—yet I cannot let you continue. I am ready to shed blood, so as to overthrow the present despotism. But, behind your words, I see the threat of another despotism which, if ever it comes into power, will make of me a murderer—and what I want to be is a doer of justice, not a man of blood.

STEPAN: Provided justice is done—even if it's done by assassins— what does it matter which you are? You and I are negligible quantities.

KALIAYEV: We are not, and you know it as well as anyone; in fact it's pride, just pride, that makes you talk as you are doing now.

STEPAN: My pride is my concern alone. But men's pride, their rebellion, the injustice that is done them—these are the concern of all of us.

KALIAYEV: Men do not live by justice alone.

STEPAN: When their bread is stolen, what else have they to live by?

KALIAYEV: By justice, and, don't forget, by innocence.

STEPAN: Innocence? Yes, maybe I know what that means. But I prefer to shut my eyes to it—and to shut others' eyes to it, for the time being—so that one day it may have a world-wide meaning.

KALIAYEV: Well, you must feel very sure that day is coming if you repudiate everything that makes life worth living today, on its account.

STEPAN: I am certain that that day is coming.

KALIAYEV: No, you can't be as sure as that. . . . Before it can be known which of us, you or I, is right, perhaps three generations will have to be sacrificed; there will have been bloody wars, and no less bloody revolutions. And by the time that all this blood has dried off the earth, you and I will long since have turned to dust.

STEPAN: Then others will come—and I hail them as my brothers.

KALIAYEV [excitedly, raising his voice]: Others, you say! Quite likely you are right. But those I love are the men who are alive today, and walk this same earth. It's they whom I hail, it is for them I am fighting, for them I am ready to lay down my life. But I shall not strike my brothers in the face for the sake of some far-off city, which, for all I know, may not exist. I refuse to add to the living injustice all around me for the sake of a dead justice. [*In a lower voice, but firmly*] Brothers, I want to speak to you quite frankly and to tell you something that even the simplest peasant in our backwoods would say if you asked him his opinion. Killing children is a crime against a man's honor. And if one day the revolution thinks fit to break with honor, well, I'm through with the revolution. If you decide that I must do it, well and good; I will go to the theater when they're due to come out—but I'll fling myself under the horses' feet.

STEPAN: Honor is a luxury reserved for people who have carriages-and-pairs.

KALIAYEV: No. It's the one wealth left to a poor man. You know it, and you also know that the revolution has its code of honor. It's what we all are ready to die for. It's what made you hold your head up, Stepan, when they flogged you, and it's behind what you have been saying to us today.

STEPAN [*shrilly*]: Keep quiet! I forbid you to speak of that!

KALIAYEV [*angrily*]: Why must I keep quiet? I took it lying down when you said I didn't believe in the revolution. Which was as good as telling me that I was ready to kill the Grand Duke for nothing; that I was a common murderer. I let you say that—and somehow I kept my hands off you!

ANNENKOV: Yanek!

STEPAN: It's killing for nothing, sometimes, not to kill enough.

ANNENKOV: Stepan, none of us here agrees with you. And we have made our decision.

STEPAN: Then I bow to it. Only, let me tell you once again that squeamishness is out of place in work like ours. We're murderers, and we have chosen to be murderers.

KALIAYEV [*losing all self-control*]: That's a lie! I have chosen death so as to prevent murder from triumphing in the world. I've chosen to be innocent.

ANNENKOV: Yanek! Stepan! That's enough of it. The group has

decided that the slaughter of these children would serve no purpose. We must start again from the beginning, and be ready for another try at it in two days' time.

STEPAN: And supposing the children are there again?

KALIAYEV: Then we shall await another opportunity.

STEPAN: And supposing the Grand Duchess is with the Duke?

KALIAYEV: *Her* I shall not spare.

(*Plays*, 256–271)

～✦～

76

DORA: It's not your fault.

KALIAYEV: I've hurt him, hurt him cruelly. Do you know what he said to me the other day?

DORA: He was always saying how happy he was.

KALIAYEV: Yes. But he told me there was no happiness for him outside our comradeship. This is what he said: "We—the organization—stand for all that matters in the world today. It's like an order of chivalry come back to earth." Oh, Dora, what a shame this has happened!

DORA: He'll come back.

KALIAYEV: No. I can picture how I'd feel if I were in his position. I'd be heartbroken.

DORA: And now? Aren't you heartbroken?

KALIAYEV: Now? But I'm with you all, and I am happy—as he was happy.

DORA [*musingly*]: Yes, it's a great happiness.

KALIAYEV: None greater. Don't you feel as I do?

DORA: Yes . . . But why then are you so depressed? Two days ago you looked so cheerful. Like a schoolboy going on vacation. But today . . .

KALIAYEV [*rising to his feet; with a rush of bitterness*]: Today I know something I did *not* know then. You were right, Dora; it's not so simple as it seems. I thought it was quite easy to kill, provided one has courage and he is buoyed up by an ideal. But now I've lost my wings. I have realized that hatred brings no happiness. I can see the vileness in myself, and in the others, too. Murderous instincts, cowardice, injustice. I've got to kill—there are no two ways about it. But I shall see it through to the end. I shall go beyond hatred.

DORA: Beyond? There's nothing beyond.

KALIAYEV: Yes. There is love.

DORA: Love? No, that's not what is needed.

KALIAYEV: Oh, Dora, how can you say that? You of all people, you whose heart I know so well!

DORA: Too much blood, too much brutal violence—there's no escape for us. Those whose hearts are set on justice have no right to love. They're on their toes, as I am, holding their heads up, their eyes fixed on the heights. What room for love is there in such proud hearts? Love bows heads, gently, compassionately. We, Yanek, are stiff-necked.

KALIAYEV: But we love our fellow men.

DORA: Yes, we love them—in our fashion. With a vast love that has nothing to shore it up; that brings only sadness. The masses? We live so far away from them, shut up in our thoughts. And do they love us? Do they even guess we love them? No, they hold their peace. Ah, that silence, that unresponsive silence!

KALIAYEV: But surely that's precisely what love means—sacrificing everything without expecting anything in return?

DORA: Perhaps. Yes, I know that love, an absolute, ideal love, a pure and solitary joy—and I feel it burning in my heart. Yet there are times when I wonder if love isn't something else; something more than a lonely voice, a monologue, and if there isn't sometimes a response. And then I see a picture floating up before my eyes. The sun is shining, pride dies from the heart, one bows one's head gently, almost shyly, and every barrier is down! Oh, Yanek, if only we could forget, even for an hour, the ugliness and misery of this world we live in, and let ourselves go—at last! One little hour or so of thinking of ourselves, just you and me, for a change. Can you see what I mean?

KALIAYEV: Yes, Dora, I can; it's what is called love—in the simple, human sense.

DORA: Yes, darling, you've guessed what I mean—but does that kind of love mean anything to you, really? Do you love justice with that kind of love? [KALIAYEV *is silent.*] Do you love our Russian people with that love—all tenderness and gentleness and self-forgetting? [KALIAYEV *still says nothing.*] You see. [*She goes toward him. Her voice is very low.*] And how about *me*, Yanek? Do you love me—as a lover?

KALIAYEV [*after gazing at her in silence for some moments*]: No one will ever love you as I love you.

DORA: I know. But wouldn't it be better to love—like an ordinary person?

KALIAYEV: I'm not an ordinary person. Such as I am, I love you.

DORA: Do you love me more than justice, more than the organization?

KALIAYEV: For me, you, justice, the organization are inseparable. I don't distinguish between you.

DORA: Yes. But do, please, answer me. Do you love me all for yourself . . . selfishly . . . possessively?—oh, you know what I mean! Would you love me if I were unjust?

KALIAYEV: If you were unjust and I could love you, it wouldn't be you I loved.

DORA: That's no answer. Tell me only this; would you love me if I didn't belong to the organization?

KALIAYEV: Then what would you belong to?

DORA: I remember the time when I was a student. I was pretty then. I used to spend hours walking about the town, dreaming all sorts of silly daydreams. I was always laughing. Would you love me if I were like that now—carefree, gay, like a young girl?

KALIAYEV [*hesitantly, in a very low voice*]: I'm longing, oh, how I'm longing to say Yes.

DORA [*eagerly*]: Then say Yes, darling—if you mean it, if it's true. In spite of everything: of justice, of our suffering fellow men, of human bondage. Do try to forget for a moment all those horrors—the scaffold, the agony of little children, of men who are flogged to death.

KALIAYEV: Dora! Please!

DORA: No, surely for once we can let our hearts take charge. I'm waiting for you to say the word, to tell me you want me—Dora, the living woman—and I mean more to you than this world, this foully unjust world around us.

KALIAYEV [*brutally*]: Keep quiet! My heart yearns for you, and you alone. . . . But, a few minutes hence I'll need a clear head and a steady hand.

DORA [*wildly*]: A few minutes hence? Ah, yes, I was forgetting. [*Laughing and sobbing at once*] No, darling, I'll do as you want. Don't be angry with me—I was talking nonsense. I promise to be sensible. I'm overtired, that's all. I, too, I couldn't have said—what I wanted you to say. I love you with the same love as yours: a love that's half frozen, because it's rooted in justice and reared in prison cells. . . . Summer, Yanek, can you remember what that's like, a real summer's day? But—no, it's never-ending winter here. We don't belong to the world of men. We are the just ones. And outside there is warmth and light; but not for us, never for us! [*Averting her eyes.*] Ah, pity on the just!

KALIAYEV [*gazing at her with despair in his eyes*]: Yes, that's our lot on earth; love is . . . impossible. But I shall kill the Grand Duke, and then at last there will be peace for you and me.

DORA: Peace? When shall we find peace?

KALIAYEV [*violently*]: The next day.

[ANNENKOV *and* STEPAN *enter.* DORA *and* KALIAYEV *move away from each other.*]

ANNENKOV: Yanek!

KALIAYEV: I'm ready. [*Draws a deep breath.*] At last! At last!

STEPAN [*going up to him*]: Brother, I'm with you.

KALIAYEV: Good-by, Stepan. [*Turning to* DORA] Good-by, Dora.

[DORA *comes toward him. They are standing very close, but neither touches the other.*]

DORA: No, not good-by. *Au revoir. Au revoir, mon chéri.* We shall meet again.

[*They gaze at each other in silence for some moments.*]

KALIAYEV: *Au revoir,* Dora. I . . . I . . . . Russia will be free.

DORA [*weeping*]: Russia will be free.

[KALIAYEV *crosses himself as he passes the icon; then walks out of the room with* ANNENKOV. STEPAN *goes to the window.* DORA *remains statue-still, staring at the door.*]

STEPAN: How straight he's walking! Yes, I was wrong not to feel confidence in Yanek. But his enthusiasm was too . . . too romantic for my liking. Did you notice how he crossed himself just now? Is he religious?

DORA: Well, he's not a churchgoer.

STEPAN: Still, he has leanings toward religion. That's why we didn't hit it off. I'm more bitter than he. For people like me, who don't believe in a God, there is no alternative between total justice and utter despair.

DORA: To Yanek's mind there's an element of despair in justice itself.

STEPAN: Yes, he has a weak soul. But happily he's better than his soul, his arm won't falter. Yanek will kill the Grand Duke, I'd swear to it. And it will be a good day's work, a very good day's work. Destruction, that's what's wanted. But you're not saying anything. [*Scans her face attentively.*] Are you in love with him?

DORA: Love calls for time, and we have hardly time enough for— justice.

STEPAN: You are right. There's so much still to do; we must smash

this world we live in, blast it to smithereens! And after that
. . . [*Looks down into the street.*] They're out of sight. They
must have reached their posts by now.

DORA: Yes? "After that," you said. What will happen after that?

STEPAN: After that we shall love each other.

DORA: If we are still alive.

STEPAN: Then others will love each other. Which comes to the
same thing.

DORA: Stepan, say *hatred*.

STEPAN: What?

DORA: I just want you to utter that word: *hatred*.

STEPAN: Hatred.

DORA: Yes, that's right. Yanek could never say it well.

(*Plays*, 268–273)

~⌣~

77

The task is endless, it's true. But we are here to pursue it. I do not
have enough faith in reason to subscribe to a belief in progress or to
any philosophy of history. I do believe at least that man's awareness
of his destiny has never ceased to advance. We have not overcome
our condition, and yet we know it better. We know that we live in
contradiction, but we also know that we must refuse this contradiction and do what is needed to reduce it. Our task as men is to
find the few principles that will calm the infinite anguish of free
souls. We must mend what has been torn apart, make justice imaginable again in a world so obviously unjust, give happiness a meaning once more to peoples poisoned by the misery of the century.
Naturally, it is a superhuman task. But superhuman is the term for
tasks men take a long time to accomplish, that's all.

(*Lyrical*, 135)

THREE

Nemesis

Some were dreadfully insulted, and quite seriously, to have held up as a model such an immoral character as A *Hero of Our Time;* others shrewdly noticed that the author had portrayed himself and his acquaintances. . . . A *Hero of Our Time,* gentlemen, is in fact a portrait, but not of an individual; it is the aggregate of the vices of our whole generation in their fullest expression.

—Lermontov
(frontispiece to *The Fall*)

The completion of *The Rebel* in 1951 was to mark a point of turning for Camus. Having endeavored to do conceptual justice to his times and to their peculiar demands, Camus hoped now for "free creation," in which he would be able to speak openly and directly his own heart and mind (1). The times, the importunities of history, were not, however, prepared to release their grip upon him. Camus was to continue to live in dark times, far from the magically brilliant Mediterranean skies and even further from the irretrievable innocence of youth (2). His earlier work had reached toward a redefinition of heroism and sanctity, toward the discernment of an order of human perfection neither eternal nor revealed (3). He plied the fibers of human instinct and energy in search of a common sense of right, a shared, innate striving for quality and excellence of life. And Camus sought to embody that striving not only in his thoughts but in his deeds as well. One might imagine that no desire in him was more fierce than the desire one day to say with the aged Nestor: "But once I shone among the young heroes." [1] He tried with all his strength to be moral in his thinking and in his life; but morality, his and morality itself, has its limits (4). The dark times crept within, as they always do. Camus saw his own spirit to be increasingly shadowed. The sun and the warm rich landscapes falling to the sea as to infinity began to recede even in his imagination (5). If Camus' new creation was to be free, each day it would have to wrestle dogged cynicism to the ground (6).

In the final place was to be the saint, living without God, without grace, and without reward. Yet we find nothing so shining or clairvoyant as a saint in Camus' later writings. Instead, we are presented with a vision of lucidly acknowledged human evil. Camus' later writings are situated within a conscious state of radical imperfection, a hell of sorts wherein no slight nor massive flaw escapes its appropriate judgment and undoing. Camus had suggested in his earlier writings that we can do no better then to act out a mild, benevolent diabolism. The human will is flawed, irremediably so. Thus Camus respects the terrible honesty of Augustine's *Nemo bonus* ("There is no one who is good") (7). Indeed, Camus would have us look to the Christian Gospels for a clear recognition both of human impurity and of the rightful precedence of forgiveness over judgment (8). It is not within our power to be other than diabolic, as proud and willful as would-be gods; but it does lie within our power to become mild and benevolent. We may perhaps hope for purgatory, though never for heaven, once we are finally tamed and filled with goodwill, one for the other. But first we must be broken.

Human beings desire to be gods, gifted with divine, that is absolute, freedom and power. The happiness which they seek is unqualified and undying. This desire for a happiness beyond limits is surely what Camus had in mind when he wrote in his *Notebooks:*

> So long as man has not dominated desire, he has dominated nothing. And he almost never dominates it.[2]

If human happiness is to be perfect, then "no one can be happy without causing harm to others."[3] One human being is, in this case, another's inevitable undoing. In their willful flights of fantasy, human beings crash into one another like so many disinherited and doomed gods. We cannot always have our way where we should not. There may be no perfect justice; but there are limits to the appropriate exercise of human freedom and power (9). And those who cross over those limits are necessarily brought low. Even so, the human will must try itself if it is to discover itself, its proper scale and measure. Human freedom is of the nature of a venture, a chance, a possibility (10). It cannot know its own proper limit until it strains against that limit and is bent back. Human being must be untamed before it can be tamed, unbridled before it can be broken; and so it is.

"When the human limit finally has a meaning," writes Camus, "then the problem of God will arise. But not before then, never before the possibility has been fully experienced."[4] Running the gamut of human experience would seem to mean above all else desiring happiness and learning that it is not to be had. We learn this in part from one another. We inevitably resist and frustrate the tyranny of each other's desires. However, Camus suggests that we are finally broken by a force far more implacable than any we might wield. There is no one of us so effectively indignant at human presumption as is Nemesis, the goddess of measure, whom Camus perceived to be the patroness of his next development of thought (11).

When the human limit is reached and overstepped, it is a goddess who strikes down the overweening will. The vigilant Nemesis never blinks. As sure as the sun rises, night falls. Nemesis is, in Greek tradition, the daughter of Night. "And she, destructive Night," writes Hesiod, "bore Nemesis, who gives much pain to mortals."[5] Nemesis, as the etymology of her name suggests (from *nemein:* to distribute, to allot), is the virgin goddess of measure, the personification of fateful retribution. When the rightful order of things has been violated, she restores due proportion and balance. She stands as a check upon extravagant favors and wanton recklessness. The gods, we are told, are jealous of their prerogatives and resent mortals who mimic them. Should human presumption and arrogance elude every other leveling blow, there is no escape from Nemesis, sometimes winged, sometimes borne in a chariot drawn by griffins, bridle in one hand and scourge in the other. When Nemesis visits the lives of mortals she brings much suffering and leaves them forsaken of hope.

> and at last Nemesis and Aides, Decency and Respect,
> shrouding

> their bright forms in pale mantles, shall go
>   from the wide-wayed
> earth back on their way to Olympos,
>   forsaking the whole race
> of mortal men, and all that will be left by them
>   to mankind
> will be wretched pain. And there shall be no defense
>   against evil.[6]

Camus is no theologian, much less a theologian of Greek deities. His thoughts do not presume to cross the boundaries which Nemesis patrols. Born of Night, Nemesis strikes from out of an impenetrable darkness; mortals know well her fatal stroke but never her face. Like necessity, she has no altars nor festivals whereat she might be placated or wooed. Nemesis cannot be bought. The borders which mortals transgress either not at all or only at their sure peril are, in the end, mysteries.

> The limits. Thus I shall say that there are mysteries it is suitable to enumerate and to meditate. Nothing more.[7]

Indeed Camus' last works may be seen as meditations upon these limits whose source is as unknowable as night and yet whose edge is honed and ruthless. We may recall Dionysos' charges flung at Pentheus: You do not know the limits of your power; you do not know what you do or who you are. Nemesis, in short, teaches all three in the only way in which mortals tend to learn such truths, against their will. We may call her fate or necessity or whatever; she answers to none of our names. There is never any answer, whence the darkness which Camus' last works confront.

Camus' last works tread a border edged on the far side by darkness and mystery. And Christianity bears somehow upon both. This is not to say that Camus was considering conversion to Christian faith. On the contrary, in the last years of his life, he seems to have been no nearer to belief than at any earlier time. Nevertheless, his last completed works, as their very titles suggest (*The Fall* and *Exile and the Kingdom*), are deeply informed by Christian thought. His own journey back to Greek thought, a journey which aimed at what Heidegger has called the repetition or retrieval (*Wiederholung*) of a lost possibility, necessarily led him to an encounter with Christian thought (12). In the modern despair of both faith and reason, Camus perceived the eclipse of the human spirit; and his own flight from nihilism required that he return first to Christian truth and then to Greek truth (13). The latter, he was convinced, had room for everything (14). Christian truth, however, as Camus understood it, already represented a reduction, an abstraction, the beginning of the fall.

In such reflections as these, one must be cautious and tentative; for Camus' last works are frequently and finally silent concerning the source of the measure and of the love which he sought so singlemindedly and singleheartedly. Camus followed the tuggings of his mind toward truth very much like those who yet allow a crooked stick to lead them to water. How either works is indeed a mystery. It is enough, and indeed all we can do, to follow Camus' last movements of thought without knowing precisely where or how they were leading him. And we ought always to respect his many silences and, most particularly, that final silence which he never chose but which chose him so out of season.

In Camus' last works one reality and concern threatens to preside: human evil or sin. And it is not surprising that his understanding of sin was guided by two of his first and foremost spiritual mentors: Plotinus and Augustine. For both of these ancient thinkers, all sin is a matter of abstraction. And abstraction is what invariably occurs when human beings pretend to a knowledge which they do not, in fact, possess. All sin is, therefore, born of would-be knowledge. Knowledge of a part is taken to be knowledge of the whole; limited insight is acted upon as if it were full comprehension. Reality is reduced to what in any given moment one wishes to regard as real. Human being and, even further, individual human beings presume to be themselves the measure of the real. Most often this presumption expresses itself in what Camus calls "judgment," which is both the root and the result of all evil. And judgment breeds judgment. A person commits a crime and the person as well as the deed are judged to be criminal. Capital punishment is founded upon such a leap in judgment, as is war. Once an individual or a state is judged to be criminal or inimical, the rest is easy (15). Here we may fruitfully recall Nietzsche's comments upon the fact that all states are now ranged against each other:

> They presuppose their neighbor's bad disposition and their own good disposition. This presupposition, however, is *inhumane*, as bad as war and worse. At bottom, indeed, it is itself the challenge and the cause of wars. . . .[8]

Camus, with considerable assistance from Augustine, traced human hostility and arrogance, as well as all human evil, to the imperious will, the would-be divine presumption to know enough to pass judgment. When human beings look through the eyes of God (16), they turn against creator and creature alike (17) and become incorrigibly cruel and indifferent. Unable to create, they destroy. Unable to utter the first all-evoking word, they set their hearts upon having the last word, the word that silences, the word of final judgment which leaves the judged without recourse. History, like a petri dish, breeds judges; and nowhere are they more secure and inaccessible than behind the robes and flags and metal-case desks of modern states. Whether in face of terrorist slaughter of "the innocent" (18) or legal execution of "the guilty" (19), Camus fought and begged for compassion and for a simple presumption in favor of life. He would not give in to the murderous fatality of our times; instead, he wrote and lived against the death penalty, insisting too that we must "refuse either to practice or to suffer terror."[9] Today's victims dwell in an illusion of impotence while our executioners dwell in an illusion of omnipotence. The former claim to understand nothing of what is happening, while the latter pretend to understand it all. Nemesis, in due time, brings lucid reversal, if nothing else, to both.

Under the patronage of Nemesis, Camus now sets out in pursuit of just such an unmasking lucidity. "The task of men of culture and faith, in any case," writes Camus, "is not to desert historical struggles nor to serve the cruel and inhuman elements in those struggles." [10] And it is precisely these "cruel and inhuman elements" which Camus now endeavors to isolate and to analyze close up. In *The Fall*, Camus performs a moral autopsy on a society which has about it the unmistakable stench of death, physical and spiritual. On the face of it, *The Fall* describes the path of but one man decidedly given to extremes. But this is no ordinary individual. Jean-Baptiste Clamence, the hero of *The Fall*, is indeed a hero of our time, a persona whose resemblance to us all is too striking to disdain. In Clamence, we find ourselves distilled and essentially disclosed. We live in dark times whose darkness may be traced to our own misdeeds. We are, it seems, to be known best by our failings. Thus Camus proposes to us a hero who is "the aggregate of the vices of our whole generation in their fullest expression." In short, Clamence is Camus' Satan, the prince of darkness, unalloyed evil.

We must make no mistake here. In *The Fall* we are in hell, all apparent pleasantries notwithstanding. Clamence leaves us with no illusions regarding our neighborhood:

> For we are at the heart of things here. Have you noticed that Amsterdam's concentric canals resemble the circles of hell? The middle-class hell, of course, peopled with bad dreams. When one comes from the outside, as one gradually goes through those circles, life—and hence its crimes—becomes denser, darker. Here we are in the last circle. The circle of the . . . [11]

The imaginative geography which Camus has in mind here is clearly that of Dante's *Inferno*; and from that magnificent poem we know how to complete Clamence's allusion. We have fallen into the circle of the betrayers and, preeminently, those who betrayed their guests, their lords, and their friends. We must recall that the deepest abyss of Dante's hell is a sea not of flames but of ice. Of the existence in that most forsaken of all places, Dante explains: "This was not life, and yet it was not death." [12] Camus, and the ancient Greeks, would say the same of exile: exile from the sun, exile from the warm care of friends, exile from the passion of one's own heart. As we enter this city of desolation, it seems that we too must "lay down all hope." [13]

The Fall, like *The Stranger*, is a monologue. However, those two solitary voices—the voice of Clamence and that of Meursault—speak from directly opposite extremes of consciousness and will. Meursault, at least initially, dwells in an innocent immediacy, shy and unknowing of human fellowship, whereas Clamence dwells in guilt-ridden abstraction, despairing of the human bond. The gulf between them comes finally to this: Meursault is judged while Clamence judges. Judgment, generically understood, lies at the center of *The Fall*; for in the act of judgment Camus claims to have isolated the plague bacillus, the cause of our spiritual degeneration or, in Augustinian terms, the cause of "second death," the eternal death of the soul to which some or most are doomed in the Last Judgment. Yet, "don't wait for the Last Judgment," Clamence advises us, "it takes place every day." [14]

Judgment rests upon the assumption or the assertion that one's own perception is definitive. In passing judgment, I claim either to have seen all or to have seen enough to act. In so doing, I willfully impose the limits of my own knowing upon the known. By my own personal fiat, reality must conform to one peculiar appearance: its appearance to me. If others appear good or evil, innocent or guilty, to me, then they really are such and must be treated accordingly. If others strike me as gifted or dull, tall or short, useful or useless, then that is how they are to be regarded, not only by me but by everyone else, including themselves. I thus become the sliding, self-styled measure of all things. This is the presumption of the judge: to enforce one's will—however informed, uninformed, or misinformed one's will may be—as though it were constitutive of the very character and being of its objects. Under the influence of a

most often quite subtle arrogance, the will moves from discernment to determination, from inquiry to creation. And Camus, in
perfect accord here with Augustine, sees in this movement the
primordial movement of sin. For Augustine, sin is mimicry of
God. The sinful act is not an act unworthy of God; rather, it is an
act of which God alone is worthy. And a mere change of mood is
required to speak of Camus' understanding of human misdeeds as
acts of which God alone would be worthy, if there were a God.

In focusing upon the imperious human and individual will,
Camus has disclosed the center of the long-standing quarrel between the ancients and the moderns, presaged in the quarrel between Sokrates and Thrasymachos in *The Republic*, and rehearsed
in the garden. The issue is ancient and, it would seem, indigenous;
what is peculiarly modern and western is the consentual resolution
which we seem to have reached: that not only the human will but,
more exactly, the individual human will is the only appropriate
measure of all things. Camus recognizes that this is no joyful wisdom. Such a claim—once reserved for dreams, whether of tyrants,
or of children, or of the crazed, or of us all as we sleep—now
becomes the waking preoccupation of nearly everyone. Such a
calling consigns us to hell, a hell necessitated, as Sartre has made
clear, by the sheer presence of other people, others like ourselves
with the airs and ambitions of gods who must have the last word.
With a vengeance, we practice the task assigned to Adam, the giving of names to things and to one another, myriad diverse and
conflicting names. "Yes," writes Camus, "hell must be like that:
streets filled with shop signs and no way of explaining oneself. One
is classified once and for all." [15] Polytheism can't be expected to
work, particularly when the gods are not gods.

The Fall, however, offers no historical development nor philosophical critique of the concept of judgment. Instead, we are lowered into the tangle and mire of one preeminent judge's mind. *The
Fall* undertakes an autobiography of judgment, a psychic phenome-
nology of our common character. Judgment, we must understand,

rests upon a comprehensive illusion of one's own utter centrality and power; and the sustaining of that illusion is a consuming and consummate art. Clamence demonstrates that art to perfection. We must notice not only the purport of his words but their pace, their slick, mesmerizing fluidity. We misunderstand him if we fail to notice that he is casting a spell. Indeed, Clamence is as deft and effective as a spider as he winds his victims in a sticky web of words. His doctrine is straightforward and familiar: the human vocation is to rule, to exercise control (20). What is unique and intriguing is the perfectly subtle yet pedestrian path by which he ascends to power. He is, one might say, the Picasso of this most perversely human art of dominating. Machiavelli, like the great masters, required a proper canvas and a princely subject; Clamence's art uses everything it finds. The possibilities for personal power and subtle control lie everywhere once one develops an eye for them. To be sure, Clamence will gladly sharpen our eyes and turn them too to his own advantage.

Clamence's ambitions are indeed vast. He wishes the people in his world—anyone his eyes meet or whose eyes meet him—to behave as if they were his very own creatures (21), inhabiting a world of his construction. Whatever truth this vision or dream may acquire will quite obviously be not literal but symbolic and subtle. What is essential is that he have a claim, a determinative influence, upon others, without others having the slightest claim upon him. His maneuvers to this end are too numerous and intricate to detail here. One example may suffice, the example of his sexual liaisons. He explains that he preferred to go to bed with mysteries, beings of his moments without recognized pasts and futures of their own. "Sometimes," Clamence confesses:

> I went so far as to make them swear not to give themselves to any other man, in order to quiet my worries once and for all on that score. My heart, however, played no part in that worry, nor even my imagination. A certain type of pretension was in fact so personified

in me that it was hard for me to imagine, despite the facts, that a woman who had once been mine could ever belong to another. But the oath they swore to me liberated me while it bound them. As soon as I knew they would never belong to anyone, I could make up my mind to break off—which otherwise was almost always impossible for me. As far as they were concerned, I had proved my point once and for all and assured my power for a long time. Strange, isn't it? But that's the way it was, *mon cher compatriote*. Some cry: "Love me!" Others: "Don't leave me!" But a certain genus, the worst and the most unhappy, cries: "Don't love me and be faithful to me!" [16]

In this one account, the perverse art which Clamence practices with every breath becomes transparently clear. He is bent upon controlling the uncontrollable; and it is, indeed, a hapless and hopeless passion which moves him. He has the most success in small spaces with as few variables as possible. To be alone with one companion indoors serves his purpose to the letter. Islands are easier to control, he tells us. And love affairs are natural islands, where we would expect his art to triumph. "The moment I was loved and my partner forgotten, I shone, I was at the top of my form, I became likable." [17] On several occasions, Clamence likens fornicating to reading the newspapers. And the point of this proposal would appear to be that in both of these activities we may enjoy and even convey the illusion of intimate engagement and intense care and yet remain at a safe, indifferent, almost infinite remove from it all. "A single sentence," suggests Clamence, "will suffice for modern man: he fornicated and read the papers." [18] And he tells us what he means by such a suggestion:

Fundamentally, nothing mattered. War, suicide, love, poverty got my attention, of course, when circumstances forced me, but a courteous, superficial attention. At times, I would pretend to get excited about some cause foreign to my daily life. But basically I didn't really take part in it except, of course, when my freedom was thwarted. How can I express it? Everything slid off—yes, just rolled off me. [19]

Clamence's triumphs are, in fact, by his own account few. There are many seams in his delusion. Daily Clamence patrols the walls of his willful fantasies which have been raised as dikes against the sea.

> I lived consequently without any other continuity than that, from day to day, of I, I, I. From day to day women, from day to day virtue or vice, from day to day, like dogs—but every day secure at my post. Thus I progressed on the surface of life, in the realm of words as it were, never in reality.[20]

Clamence, the would-be last Adam, giving names and identities to creatures as if they were his own—their pasts voided by his oblivion and their futures determined by his delusions—is finally comical. Not to himself, not ever to himself. But one day the otherness which is supposed to be his construct and under his control, finds voice and laughs aloud at this consummate fool. Laughter is, indeed, the perfect metaphor of resistance to and freedom from Clamence's all-embracing pretense. Clamence hears laughter within and laughter without, in his heart and outdoors. Once, he collapses in public (22). He utterly loses control of a circumstance and is made to play the fool that he is. His own idea, his picture, of himself doesn't hold up. The impatient sea breaks in.

Even more decisively is the self-containment of Clamence shattered by a cry in the night, a cry of abandonment and ultimate need (23). He feels himself claimed, confronted with desire and demand beyond his own making and control. To respond is to leap, to release his very heart and soul into what his dream has never contained: other people, free and willful and needy like himself. Not to respond is to be judged; and this Clamence cannot endure. His evil genius now takes its grandest and most foolish steps. He is bent upon denying and destroying the human bond. He strives for the perfection of evil and, like his ancient namesake, John the Baptist, he goes into the desert. His is truly a voice crying in the wilderness (*vox clamantis in deserto, Is.*, 40.3; *Mt.*, 3.3; *Mk.*, 1.3; *Lk.*, 3.4; *Jn.*, 1.23, whence *Clamence*).

> Well, what do you think of it? Isn't it the most beautiful negative landscape? Just see on the left that pile of ashes they call a dune here, the gray dike on the right, the livid beach at our feet, and in front of us, the sea the color of a weak lye-solution with the vast sky reflecting the colorless waters. A soggy hell, indeed! Everything horizontal, no relief; space is colorless, and life dead. Is it not universal obliteration, everlasting nothingness made visible? No human beings, above all, no human beings! You and I alone facing the planet at last deserted![21]

In this context we may recall the desperate self-isolating denials of Kreon in the *Antigone*. He refuses the claims of his wife and son and daughter-in-law-to-be and his citizens, asking: Should a husband hearken to his wife? Should father hearken to his son, a man to a woman, or a king to his subjects? He waits for no answer; for he has resolved the matter in his heart, as has Clamence, who also prefers lofty places, far above the human consortium. Thus we may address to Clamence the harsh words hurled at Kreon: "You'd rule a desert beautifully alone."[22]

In one word, Clamence must deny and destroy friendship, the human bond of compassion and care. No one leaps. No one reaches out without grabbing. All love is self-love in the most cynical sense possible (24). Distrust reigns. And Clamence informs us of the outcome of any exception to this rule:

> I knew a pure heart who rejected distrust. He was a pacifist and libertarian and loved all humanity and the animals with an equal love. An exceptional soul, that's certain. Well, during the last wars of religion in Europe he had retired to the country. He had written on his threshold: "Wherever you come from, come in and be welcome." Who do you think answered that noble invitation? The militia, who made themselves at home and disemboweled him.[23]

So much, it seems, for hospitality and friendship. No one is innocent; all are guilty (25). Even Jesus, a murderer like the rest of us (26). He knew himself to be responsible for the Slaughter of the Innocents; and like the rest of us, he died unforgiven. Yes, Clamence assures his *compatriote* in this hell of theirs, we are alone.

This "we" is decisive. With its assertion, Clamence, the judge-penitent, has played out his double nature and calling. He confesses his own utter sinfulness, awakening the bad conscience of his companion, until the "we" emerges. Then, in his most perverse and practical sleight of hand, Clamence slips loose of this bond. The first among sinners becomes the first among judges. He gains his edge, such as it is. Indeed, his scale has become so slight that he seems to himself to have become God the Father, no less, in this movement. "Don't laugh," he pleads, as well we might (27). Clamence confesses, even from his throne, off the record, as it were, that he still doubts, that he still hears laughter. Human being, the being gifted with speech, is in Clamence reduced to sheer technique, the art of lying. And nothing is so open, so pitiful, so devoid of resource as a lie once found out. We might, in fact, leave Clamence, with this in mind, as he goes back to bed. "To be sure," as he admits, "my solution is not the ideal." [24]

In giving us Clamence as the proper hero for our times, Camus clearly does not commend Clamence to us; rather, Camus commends to us the self-recognition which our encounter with Clamence is sure to occasion. With Clamence we have touched "point-zero" again; this time at polar remove from the innocence and immediacy of Meursault. Clamence represents sheer abstraction, and thus radical evil. Camus was fond of the saying of Pascal to the effect that we reveal our greatness not by embracing an extreme but by touching two extremes at once. Indeed, this is what Camus sought to do, to abandon neither Meursault nor Clamence, neither immediacy nor abstraction, neither innocence nor guilt, neither love nor hate. In doing so, he hoped to embrace humanity, his own and ours, spread as we are between these extremes of our own nature. Above all else he wished to affirm and reaffirm the essential human consortium which binds us all. It is night, and we must not sleep (28). It is ours to be vigilant on each other's behalf, refusing even happiness until there is enough of it to go around (29). And if there is a happiness beyond what eyes have seen or ears heard or beyond the heart's imagining, perhaps we must be holy yet live in sin out of solidarity with the damned (30). Such are Camus' thoughts and images as he pursues a hero, a story, or a myth that will contain it all.

As Camus began what was, in prospect, to be "free creation," his heart was, it seems, fixed upon that admittedly exceptional "true love" which Clamence dismisses out of hand. Once or twice a century, Clamence assures us.[25] Negligible. So it must seem in hell. Unlike Clamence, Camus was prepared to give decisive weight to the exception. Unlike Clamence, Camus was prepared to leap. Indeed, we may discern the voice of Camus in the question posed by "The Adulterous Woman": "Is there another love than that of darkness?"[26] Is there a love that overcomes Nemesis, daughter of Night? One senses in this question a radical turning, a movement at the core of Camus' thought. We may well recall here the words of the weary Philoktetes: "I look for something new."[27]

In the closing tale of what proved to be his last published work, *Exile and the Kingdom*, Camus presents us with an image of precisely this: a man looking for something new. On the face of it, D'Arrast, in "The Growing Stone" (31), is looking for nothing. Instead, he descends like Prometheus with modern civilization and its arts as his own beneficent gifts to a benighted people unable to ward off the forces of nature. D'Arrast, whose profession it is "to command the waters and dominate rivers,"[28] brings a power and a preoccupation which define us all—engineering—the engineers of worlds and of lives. In one word: control. This dream of power and of control, however, cannot withstand the vast and wild tangle of the Brazilian forest which D'Arrast has entered. It is a dream for offices and not for rainforests. And when it fades, it leaves him with a solitude and a helplessness reserved for the once omnipotent.

D'Arrast comes as a demigod and becomes a stranger, an exile. He begins with the pretension of being slightly more than human and comes to see that he is, in fact, less. He now longs for a fellowship and a communion which he has never tasted and which is yet commonplace in this primitive, one might almost say "original," community into which he has stumbled. There is no purpose, however, to our extracting from this splendid tale each symbol and its meaning. Camus cannot have known that this would be the last story he would tell; and yet there is a brilliant summary of Camus' vision to be found herein. We encounter again a stranger, Sisyphus and his rock, Prometheus and his well-meaning forethought, and, above all, a Night of lucidity and wonder when D'Arrast witnesses festivity: a love, a release, and an affirmation beyond control. That night reveals itself as a mysterious source of healing and of renewal. The stone grows, the waters rise, bonds are broken, borders overstepped. D'Arrast is filled "with a tumultuous happiness."[29] True, there is perhaps no more sad nor telling moment in all of Camus' work than the moment when D'Arrast must confess that in his land no one dances. Then we hear laughter, the same resounding laughter which hounded Clamence. Not possible, not possible not to dance. Rebellion cannot suffice. Our hearts must keep a festival and they do not know how. Whether directed at D'Arrast, or at us, or at Camus himself, the response is an inept and unknowing silence to the invitation of Socrates: "Stay with us."[30] It would seem that there is no staying, no dancing. Camus leads us no further. But very few have led this far. We know ourselves now as strangers and as invited guests. Without the heart to dance, we may yet know something of compassion. After all, it is a miracle not only that the rock grows but also that it is borne freely on one another's behalf. Those who have known too much of history and its demands as well as those who have known nothing of these—rebel and native—in the end sit down together to await the night and its mysteries. And we must imagine them happy.

NOTES

1. Homer, *The Iliad*, XXIII.645, tr. Richmond Lattimore, University of Chicago Press, 1951.

2. Camus, *Notebooks II*, p. 210.

3. Camus, *Plays*, p. 221.

4. Camus, *Notebooks II*, pp. 118–119.

5. Hesiod, *Theogony*, 223, in *Hesiod. op. cit.*

6. Hesiod, *The Works and Days*, 197–201, in *Hesiod, op. cit.*

7. Camus, *Notebooks II*, p. 126.

8. Friedrich Nietzsche, *The Wanderer and His Shadow*, #284, in *The Portable Nietzsche*, tr. Walter Kaufmann, New York: Viking, 1954, p. 72.

9. Camus, *Resistance*, p. 106.

10. *Ibid.*

11. Camus, *Fall*, p. 14.

12. Dante Alighieri, *The Divine Comedy 1, Hell*, Canto XXXIV, 25, tr. Dorothy L. Sayers, Baltimore: Penguin, 1949.

13. *Ibid.*, Canto III, 9.

14. Camus, *Fall*, p. 111.

15. *Ibid.*, p. 47.

16. *Ibid.*, pp. 62–63.

17. *Ibid.*, p. 67.

18. *Ibid.*, pp. 6–7.

19. *Ibid.*, p. 49.

20. *Ibid.*, p. 50.

21. *Ibid.*, pp. 72–73.

22. Sophokles, *Antigone*, 739, tr. Elizabeth Wyckoff, University of Chicago Press, 1954.

23. Camus, *Fall*, pp. 11–12.

24. *Ibid.*, p. 144.

25. *Ibid.*, p. 57.

26. Camus, *Exile*, p. 28.

27. Sophokles, *Philoktetes*, 784, tr. David Grene, University of Chicago Press, 1957.

28. Camus, *Exile*, p. 170.

29. *Ibid.*, p. 212.

30. *Ibid.*, p. 200.

Readings

1

First Cycle. From my first books (*Noces*) to *La Corde* and *The Rebel*, my whole effort has been in reality to depersonalize myself (each time in a different tone). Later on, I shall be able to speak in my own name.

(*Notebooks II*, 210)

After *The Rebel*, free creation.

(*Notebooks II*, 254)

Finished the first writing of *The Rebel*. With this book the first two cycles come to an end. Thirty-seven years old. And now, can creation be free?

(*Notebooks II*, 270)

2

I lived my whole youth with the idea of my innocence, in other words with no idea at all. Today . . .

(*Notebooks II*, 119)

3

"What am I thinking that is greater than I and that I experience without being able to define it? A sort of arduous progress toward a sanctity of negation—a heroism without God—man alone, in short. All human virtues, including solitude in regard to God.

"What constitutes the *exemplary* superiority (the only one) of Christianity? Christ and his saints; pursuit of a *style of life*. My work will count as many forms as it has stages on the way to an unrewarded perfection. *The Stranger* is the zero point. Likewise *The Myth of Sisyphus*. *The Plague* is a progress, not from zero toward the infinite, but toward a deeper complexity that remains to be defined. The last point will be the saint, but he will have his arithmetical value, measurable like man."

(*Notebooks II*, 20)

4

I have tried with all my strength, knowing my weakness, to be a man of morality. Morality kills.

(*Notebooks II*, 200)

5

I have read over all these notebooks—beginning with the first. This was obvious to me: landscapes gradually disappear. The modern cancer is gnawing me too.

(*Notebooks II*, 162)

6

My most constant temptation, the one against which I have never ceased fighting to the point of exhaustion: cynicism.

(*Notebooks II*, 249)

7

The only great Christian mind that *faced* the problem of evil was
St. Augustine. He drew from it the terrible "Nemo Bonus." Since
then Christianity has striven to give the problem temporary solu-
tions.

The result is evident. For it is the result. Men took their time,
but today they are poisoned by an intoxication that has been going
on for two thousand years. They are fed up with evil or resigned,
and this comes to the same thing. At least they can no longer accept lies on the subject.

(*Notebooks II*, 140)

8

In short, the Gospel is realistic, whereas people think it impossible
to put into practice. It knows that man cannot be pure. But he can
make the effort of recognizing his impurity; in other words, of par-
doning. Criminals are always judges . . . The only ones who can
condemn absolutely are those who are absolutely innocent . . .
This is why God must be absolutely innocent.

(*Notebooks II*, 213)

9

There is no justice; there are only limits.

(*Notebooks II*, 185)

10

Man's most natural inclination is to ruin himself and everyone with
him. What exceptional efforts he must make to be merely normal!

And what an even greater effort for anyone who has an ambition to dominate himself and to dominate the mind. Man is nothing in himself. He is but an infinite chance. But he is infinitely responsible for that chance. By himself, man is inclined to water himself down. But the moment his will, his conscience, his spirit of adventure dominates, chance begins to increase. No one can say that he has reached the limit of man. The five years we have just lived through taught me that. From the animal to the martyr, from the spirit of evil to hopeless sacrifice, every testimony was staggering. Each of us has the responsibility of exploiting in himself man's greatest chance, his definitive virtue. When the human limit finally has a meaning, then the problem of God will arise. But not before then, never before the possibility has been fully experienced. There is but one possible aim for great deeds and that is human productiveness. *But first of all make oneself master of oneself.*

(*Notebooks II*, 118–119)

11

Nemesis—the goddess of measure. All those who have overstepped the limit will be pitilessly destroyed.

(*Notebooks II*, 156)

12

Go back to the passage from Hellenism to Christianity, the true and only turning point in history. Essay on fate (Nemesis?).

(*Notebooks II*, 267)

13

If, to outgrow nihilism, one must return to Christianity, one may well follow the impulse and outgrow Christianity in Hellenism.

(*Notebooks II*, 183)

~⌣~

14

It seems that I still have to find a humanism. I have nothing against humanism, of course. I just find it inadequate. And Greek thought, for example, was quite different from a humanism. It was a thought that had room for everything.

(*Notebooks II*, 135)

~⌣~

15

Polemics—as an element of abstraction. Every time you have decided to consider a man as an enemy, you make him abstract. You set him at a distance; you don't want to know that he has a hearty laugh. He has become a *silhouette*.

Etc., etc.

(*Notebooks II*, 182)

~⌣~

16

Paris—Algiers. The airplane as one of the elements of modern negation and abstraction. There is no more nature; the deep gorge, true relief, the impassable mountain stream, everything disappears. There remains *a diagram*—a map.

Man, in short, looks through the eyes of God. And he perceives then that God can have but an abstract view. This is not a good thing.

(*Notebooks II*, 182)

~⌣~

17

Who can tell the anguish of the man who sided with the creature against the creator and who, losing the idea of his own innocence, and that of others, judges the creature, and himself, to be as criminal as the creator.

(*Notebooks II*, 221–222)

~❦~

18

If I had the power to give a voice to the solitude and anguish in each of us, that is the voice with which I should address you. As for me, I have passionately loved this land where I was born, I drew from it whatever I am, and in forming friendships I have never made any distinction among the men who live here, whatever their race. Although I have known and shared every form of poverty in which this country abounds, it is for me the land of happiness, of energy, and of creation. And I cannot bear to see it become a land of suffering and hatred.

I know that the great tragedies of history often fascinate men with approaching horror. Paralyzed, they cannot make up their minds to do anything but wait. So they wait, and one day the Gorgon devours them. But I should like to convince you that the spell can be broken, that there is only an illusion of impotence, that strength of heart, intelligence, and courage are enough to stop fate and sometimes reverse it. One has merely to will this, not blindly, but with a firm and reasoned will.

People are too readily resigned to fatality. They are too ready to believe that, after all, nothing but bloodshed makes history progress and that the stronger always progresses at the expense of the weaker. Such fatality exists perhaps. But man's task is not to accept it or to bow to its laws. If he had accepted it in the earliest ages, we should still be living in prehistoric times. The task of men of culture and faith, in any case, is not to desert historical struggles nor to serve the cruel and inhuman elements in those struggles. It is rather to remain what they are, to help man against what is oppressing him, to favor freedom against the fatalities that close in upon it.

That is the condition under which history really progresses, innovates—in a word, creates. In everything else it repeats itself, like a bleeding mouth that merely vomits forth a wild stammering. Today we are at the stage of stammering, and yet the broadest perspectives are opening up for our century. We are at the stage of a duel with daggers, or almost, while the world is progressing at the speed of supersonic planes. The same day that our newspapers print the dreadful story of our provincial squabbles, they announce the European atomic pool. Tomorrow, if only Europe can come to an internal agreement, floods of riches will cover the continent and, overflowing even to us, will make our problems out of date and our hatreds null and void.

For that still unimaginable but not so distant future we must organize and stand together. The absurd and heart-breaking aspect of the tragedy we are living through comes out in the fact that, in order someday to reach those world-wide perspectives, we must now gather together in paltry fashion to beg merely, without making any other claims yet, that on a single spot of the globe a handful of innocent victims be spared. But since that is our task, however obscure and ungrateful it may be, we must tackle it decisively in order to deserve living someday as free men—in other words, as men who refuse either to practice or to suffer terror.

(*Resistance*, 140–142)

19

In relation to crime, how can our civilization be defined? The reply is easy: for thirty years now, State crimes have been far more numerous than individual crimes. I am not even speaking of wars, general or localized, although bloodshed too is an alcohol that eventually intoxicates like the headiest of wines. But the number of individuals killed directly by the State has assumed astronomical proportions and infinitely outnumbers private murders. There are fewer and fewer condemned by common law and more and more condemned for political reasons. The proof is that each of us, how-ever honorable he may be, can foresee the possibility of being someday condemned to death, whereas that eventuality would have seemed ridiculous at the beginning of the century. Alphonse Karr's witty remark: "Let the noble assassins begin" has no meaning now. Those who cause the most blood to flow are the same ones who believe they have right, logic, and history on their side.

Hence our society must now defend herself not so much against the individual as against the State. It may be that the proportions will be reversed in another thirty years. But, for the moment, our self-defense must be aimed at the State first and foremost. Justice and expediency command the law to protect the individual against a State given over to the follies of sectarianism or of pride. "Let the State begin and abolish the death penalty" ought to be our rallying cry today.

Bloodthirsty laws, it has been said, make bloodthirsty customs. But any society eventually reaches a state of ignominy in which, despite every disorder, the customs never manage to be as blood-thirsty as the laws. Half of Europe knows that condition. We French knew it in the past and may again know it. Those executed during the Occupation led to those executed at the time of the Lib-eration, whose friends now dream of revenge. Elsewhere States laden with too many crimes are getting ready to drown their guilt in even greater massacres. One kills for a nation or a class that has been granted divine status. One kills for a future society that has likewise been given divine status. Whoever thinks he has omni-science imagines he has omnipotence. Temporal idols demanding an absolute faith tirelessly decree absolute punishments. And re-ligions devoid of transcendence kill great numbers of condemned men devoid of hope.

How can European society of the mid-century survive unless it decides to defend individuals by every means against the State's oppression? Forbidding a man's execution would amount to pro-claiming publicly that society and the State are not absolute values, that nothing authorizes them to legislate definitively or to bring about the irreparable. Without the death penalty, Gabriel Péri and Brasillach would perhaps be among us. We could then judge them according to our opinion and proudly proclaim our judgment, whereas now they judge us and we keep silent. Without the death penalty Rajk's corpse would not poison Hungary; Germany, with less guilt on her conscience, would be more favorably looked upon by Europe; the Russian Revolution would not be agonizing in shame; and Algerian blood would weigh less heavily on our consciences. Without the death penalty, Europe would not be infected by the corpses accumulated for the last twenty years in its tired soil. On our continent, all values are upset by fear and hatred between individuals and between nations. In the conflict of ideas the weapons are the cord and the guillotine. A natural and human society exercising her right of repression has given way to a dominant ideology that requires human sacrifices. "The example of the gallows," it has been written, "is that a man's life ceases to be sacred when it is thought useful to kill him." Apparently it is becoming ever more useful; the example is being copied; the contagion is spreading everywhere. And together with it, the disorder of nihilism. Hence we must call a spectacular halt and proclaim, in our principles and institutions, that the individual is above the State. And any measure that decreases the pressure of social forces upon the individual will help to relieve the congestion of a Europe suffering from a rush of blood, allowing us to think more clearly and to start on the way toward health. Europe's malady consists in believing nothing and claiming to know everything. But Europe is far from knowing everything, and, judging from the revolt and hope we feel, she believes in something: she believes that the extreme of man's wretchedness, on some mysterious limit, borders on the extreme of his greatness. For the majority of Europeans, faith is lost. And with it, the justifications faith provided in the domain of punishment. But the majority of Europeans also reject the State idolatry that aimed to take the place of faith. Henceforth in mid-

course, both certain and uncertain, having made up our minds
never to submit and never to oppress, we should admit at one and
the same time our hope and our ignorance, we should refuse absolute law and the irreparable judgment. We know enough to say that
this or that major criminal deserves hard labor for life. But we don't
know enough to decree that he be shorn of his future—in other
words, of the chance we all have of making amends. Because of
what I have just said, in the unified Europe of the future the solemn abolition of the death penalty ought to be the first article of
the European Code we all hope for.

(*Resistance*, 227–230)

20

I am well aware that one can't get along without domineering or
being served. Every man needs slaves as he needs fresh air. Com-
manding is breathing—you agree with me? And even the most de-
stitute manage to breathe. The lowest man in the social scale still
has his wife or his child. If he's unmarried, a dog. The essential
thing, after all, is being able to get angry with someone who has no
right to talk back. "One doesn't talk back to one's father"—you
know the expression? In one way it is very odd. To whom should
one talk back in this world if not to what one loves? In another
way, it is convincing. Somebody has to have the last word. Otherwise, every reason can be answered with another one and there
would never be an end to it. Power, on the other hand, settles
everything. It took time, but we finally realized that. For instance,
you must have noticed that our old Europe at last philosophizes in
the right way. We no longer say as in simple times: "This is the
way I think. What are your objections?" We have become lucid.
For the dialogue we have substituted the communiqué: "This is the
truth," we say. "You can discuss it as much as you want; we aren't
interested. But in a few years there'll be the police who will show
you we are right."

Ah, this dear old planet! All is clear now. We know ourselves, we
now know of what we are capable.

(*Fall*, 44–45)

~~~

21

On my own admission, I could live happily only on condition that
all the individuals on earth, or the greatest possible number, were
turned toward me, eternally in suspense, devoid of independent life
and ready to answer my call at any moment, doomed in short to
sterility until the day I should deign to favor them. In short, for me
to live happily it was essential for the creatures I chose not to live at
all. They must receive their life, sporadically, only at my bidding.

(*Fall*, 68)

~~~

22

One day in my car when I was slow in making a getaway at the
green light while our patient fellow citizens immediately began
honking furiously behind me, I suddenly remembered another occasion set in similar circumstances. A motorcycle ridden by a spare
little man wearing spectacles and plus fours had gone around me
and planted itself in front of me at the red light. As he came to a
stop the little man had stalled his motor and was vainly striving to
revive it. When the light changed, I asked him with my usual courtesy to take his motorcycle out of my way so I might pass. The little
man was getting irritable over his wheezy motor. Hence he replied,
according to the rules of Parisian courtesy, that I could go climb a
tree. I insisted, still polite, but with a slight shade of impatience in
my voice. I was immediately told that in any case I could go
straight to hell. Meanwhile several horns began to be heard behind
me. With greater firmness I begged my interlocutor to be polite and
to realize that he was blocking traffic. The irascible character, probably exasperated by the now evident ill will of his motor, informed

me that if I wanted what he called a thorough dusting off he would gladly give it to me. Such cynicism filled me with a healthy rage and I got out of my car with the intention of thrashing this coarse individual. I don't think I am cowardly (but what doesn't one think!); I was a head taller than my adversary and my muscles have always been reliable. I still believe the dusting off would have been received rather than given. But I had hardly set foot on the pavement when from the gathering crowd a man stepped forth, rushed at me, assured me that I was the lowest of the low and that he would not allow me to strike a man who had a motorcycle between his legs and hence was at a disadvantage. I turned toward this musketeer and, in truth, didn't even see him. Indeed, hardly had I turned my head when, almost simultaneously, I heard the motorcycle begin popping again and received a violent blow on the ear. Before I had the time to register what had happened, the motorcycle rode away. Dazed, I mechanically walked toward d'Artagnan when, at the same moment, an exasperated concert of horns rose from the now considerable line of vehicles. The light was changing to green. Then, still somewhat bewildered, instead of giving a drubbing to the idiot who had addressed me, I docilely returned to my car and drove off. As I passed, the idiot greeted me with a "poor dope" that I still recall.

A totally insignificant story, in your opinion? Probably. Still it took me some time to forget it, and that's what counts. Yet I had excuses. I had let myself be beaten without replying, but I could not be accused of cowardice. Taken by surprise, addressed from both sides, I had mixed everything up and the horns had put the finishing touch to my embarrassment. Yet I was unhappy about this as if I had violated the code of honor. I could see myself getting back into my car without a reaction, under the ironic gaze of a crowd especially delighted because, as I recall, I was wearing a very elegant blue suit. I could hear the "poor dope" which, in spite of everything, struck me as justified. In short, I had collapsed in public. As a result of a series of circumstances, to be sure, but there are always circumstances. As an afterthought I clearly saw what I should have done. I saw myself felling d'Artagnan with a good hook to the jaw, getting back into my car, pursuing the monkey who had struck me, overtaking him, jamming his machine against the curb, taking him aside, and giving him the licking he had fully deserved. With a few variants, I ran off this little film a hundred times in my imagination. But it was too late, and for several days I chewed a bitter resentment.

Why, it's raining again. Let's stop, shall we, under this portico? Good. Where was I? Oh, yes, honor! Well, when I recovered the recollection of that episode, I realized what it meant. After all, my dream had not stood up to facts.

(*Fall*, 51–54)

~

23

That particular night in November, two or three years before the evening when I thought I heard laughter behind me, I was returning to the Left Bank and my home by way of the Pont Royal. It was an hour past midnight, a fine rain was falling, a drizzle rather, that scattered the few people on the streets. I had just left a mistress, who was surely already asleep. I was enjoying that walk, a little numbed, my body calmed and irrigated by a flow of blood gentle as the falling rain. On the bridge I passed behind a figure leaning over the railing and seeming to stare at the river. On closer view, I made out a slim young woman dressed in black. The back of her neck, cool and damp between her dark hair and coat collar, stirred me. But I went on after a moment's hesitation. At the end of the bridge I followed the quays toward Saint-Michel, where I lived. I had already gone some fifty yards when I heard the sound—which, despite the distance, seemed dreadfully loud in the midnight silence—of a body striking the water. I stopped short, but without turning around. Almost at once I heard a cry, repeated several times, which was going downstream; then it suddenly ceased. The silence that followed, as the night suddenly stood still, seemed in-

terminable. I wanted to run and yet didn't stir. I was trembling, I
believe from cold and shock. I told myself that I had to be quick
and I felt an irresistible weakness steal over me. I have forgotten
what I thought then. "Too late, too far . . ." or something of the
sort. I was still listening as I stood motionless. Then, slowly under
the rain, I went away. I informed no one.

(*Fall*, 69–70)

~◆~

24

Friendship is less simple. It is long and hard to obtain, but when
one has it there's no getting rid of it; one simply has to cope with it.
Don't think for a minute that your friends will telephone you every
evening, as they ought to, in order to find out if this doesn't happen
to be the evening when you are deciding to commit suicide, or
simply whether you don't need company, whether you are not in a
mood to go out. No, don't worry, they'll ring up the evening you
are not alone, when life is beautiful. As for suicide, they would be
more likely to push you to it, by virtue of what you owe to yourself,
according to them. May heaven protect us, *cher monsieur*, from
being set on a pedestal by our friends! Those whose duty is to love
us—I mean relatives and connections (what an expression!)—are
another matter. They find the right word, all right, and it hits the
bull's-eye; they telephone as if shooting a rifle. And they know how
to aim. Oh, the Bazaines!

What? What evening? I'll get to it, be patient with me. In a certain way I *am* sticking to my subject with all that about friends and
connections. You see, I've heard of a man whose friend had been
imprisoned and who slept on the floor of his room every night in
order not to enjoy a comfort of which his friend had been deprived.
Who, *cher monsieur*, will sleep on the floor for us? Whether I am
capable of it myself? Look, I'd like to be and I shall be. Yes, we
shall all be capable of it one day, and that will be salvation. But it's
not easy, for friendship is absent-minded or at least unavailing. It is

incapable of achieving what it wants. Maybe, after all, it doesn't want it enough? Maybe we don't love life enough? Have you noticed that death alone awakens our feelings? How we love the friends who have just left us? How we admire those of our teachers who have ceased to speak, their mouths filled with earth! Then the expression of admiration springs forth naturally, that admiration they were perhaps expecting from us all their lives. But do you know why we are always more just and more generous toward the dead? The reason is simple. With them there is no obligation. They leave us free and we can take our time, fit the testimonial in between a cocktail party and a nice little mistress, in our spare time, in short. If they forced us to anything, it would be to remembering, and we have a short memory. No, it is the recently dead we love among our friends, the painful dead, our emotion, ourselves after all!

For instance, I had a friend I generally avoided. He rather bored me, and, besides, he was something of a moralist. But when he was on his deathbed, I was there—don't worry. I never missed a day. He died satisfied with me, holding both my hands. A woman who used to chase after me, and in vain, had the good sense to die young. What room in my heart at once! And when, in addition, it's a suicide! Lord, what a delightful commotion! One's telephone rings, one's heart overflows, and the intentionally short sentences yet heavy with implications, one's restrained suffering and even, yes, a bit of self-accusation!

That's the way man is, *cher monsieur*. He has two faces: he can't love without self-love.

(*Fall*, 31–34)

～◦～

25

Moreover, we cannot assert the innocence of anyone, whereas we can state with certainty the guilt of all. Every man testifies to the crime of all the others—that is my faith and my hope.

Believe me, religions are on the wrong track the moment they moralize and fulminate commandments. God is not needed to create guilt or to punish. Our fellow men suffice, aided by ourselves. You were speaking of the Last Judgment. Allow me to laugh respectfully. I shall wait for it resolutely, for I have known what is worse, the judgment of men. For them, no extenuating circumstances; even the good intention is ascribed to crime. Have you at least heard of the spitting-cell, which a nation recently thought up to prove itself the greatest on earth? A walled-up box in which the prisoner can stand without moving. The solid door that locks him in his cement shell stops at chin level. Hence only his face is visible, and every passing jailer spits copiously on it. The prisoner, wedged into his cell, cannot wipe his face, though he is allowed, it is true, to close his eyes. Well, that, *mon cher*, is a human invention. They didn't need God for that little masterpiece.

What of it? Well, God's sole usefulness would be to guarantee innocence, and I am inclined to see religion rather as a huge laundering venture—as it was once but briefly, for exactly three years, and it wasn't called religion. Since then, soap has been lacking, our faces are dirty, and we wipe one another's noses. All dunces, all punished, let's all spit on one another and—hurry! to the little-ease! Each tries to spit first, that's all. I'll tell you a big secret, *mon cher*. Don't wait for the Last Judgment. It takes place every day.

(*Fall*, 110–111)

26

Say, do you know why he was crucified—the one you are perhaps thinking of at this moment? Well, there were heaps of reasons for that. There are always reasons for murdering a man. On the contrary, it is impossible to justify his living. That's why crime always finds lawyers, and innocence only rarely. But, beside the reasons that have been very well explained to us for the past two thousand years, there was a major one for that terrible agony, and I don't know why it has been so carefully hidden. The real reason is that *he* knew he was not altogether innocent. If he did not bear the weight of the crime he was accused of, he had committed others— even though he didn't know which ones. Did he really not know them? He was at the source, after all; he must have heard of a certain Slaughter of the Innocents. The children of Judea massacred while his parents were taking him to a safe place—why did they die if not because of him? Those blood-spattered soldiers, those infants cut in two filled him with horror. But given the man he was, I am sure he could not forget them. And as for that sadness that can be felt in his every act, wasn't it the incurable melancholy of a man who heard night after night the voice of Rachel weeping for her children and refusing all comfort? The lamentation would rend the night, Rachel would call her children who had been killed for him, and he was still alive!

Knowing what he knew, familiar with everything about man—ah, who would have believed that crime consists less in making others die than in not dying oneself!—brought face to face day and night with his innocent crime, he found it too hard for him to hold on and continue. It was better to have done with it, not to defend himself, to die, in order not to be the only one to live, and to go elsewhere where perhaps he would be upheld. He was not upheld, he complained, and as a last straw, he was censored. Yes, it was the third evangelist, I believe, who first suppressed his complaint. "Why hast thou forsaken me?"—it was a seditious cry, wasn't it? Well, then, the scissors! Mind you, if Luke had suppressed nothing, the matter would hardly have been noticed; in any case, it would not have assumed such importance. Thus the censor shouts aloud what he proscribes. The world's order likewise is ambiguous.

Nonetheless, the censored one was unable to carry on. And I know, *cher*, whereof I speak. There was a time when I didn't at any minute have the slightest idea how I could reach the next one. Yes, one can wage war in this world, ape love, torture one's fellow man, or merely say evil of one's neighbor while knitting. But, in certain cases, carrying on, merely continuing, is superhuman. And he was not superhuman, you can take my word for it. He cried aloud his agony and that's why I love him, my friend who died without knowing.

The unfortunate thing is that he left us alone, to carry on, whatever happens, even when we are lodged in the little-ease, knowing in turn what he knew, but incapable of doing what he did and of dying like him. People naturally tried to get some help from his death. After all, it was a stroke of genius to tell us: "You're not a very pretty sight, that's certain! Well, we won't go into the details! We'll just liquidate it all at once, on the cross!" But too many people now climb onto the cross merely to be seen from a greater distance, even if they have to trample somewhat on the one who has been there so long. Too many people have decided to do without generosity in order to practice charity. Oh, the injustice, the rank injustice that has been done him! It wrings my heart!

Good heavens, the habit has seized me again and I'm on the point of making a speech to the court. Forgive me and realize that I have my reasons. Why, a few streets from here there is a museum called "Our Lord in the Attic." At the time, they had the catacombs in the attic. After all, the cellars are flooded here. But today—set your mind at rest—their Lord is neither in the attic nor in the cellar. They have hoisted him onto a judge's bench in the secret of their hearts, and they smite, they judge above all, they judge in his name. He spoke softly to the adulteress: "Neither do I condemn thee!" but that doesn't matter; they condemn without absolving anyone. In the name of the Lord, here is what you deserve. Lord? He, my friend, didn't expect so much. He simply wanted to be loved, nothing more.

(*Fall*, 111–115)

27

Inasmuch as one couldn't condemn others without immediately judging oneself, one had to overwhelm oneself to have the right to judge others. Inasmuch as every judge some day ends up as a penitent, one had to travel the road in the opposite direction and practice the profession of penitent to be able to end up as a judge. You follow me? Good. But to make myself even clearer, I'll tell you how I operate.

First I closed my law office, left Paris, traveled. I aimed to set up under another name in some place where I shouldn't lack for a practice. There are many in the world, but chance, convenience, irony, and also the necessity for a certain mortification made me choose a capital of waters and fogs, girdled by canals, particularly crowded, and visited by men from all corners of the earth. I set up my office in a bar in the sailors' quarter. The clientele of a porttown is varied. The poor don't go into the luxury districts, whereas eventually the gentlefolk always wind up at least once, as you have seen, in the disreputable places. I lie in wait particularly for the bourgeois, and the straying bourgeois at that; it's with him that I get my best results. Like a virtuoso with a rare violin, I draw my subtlest sounds from him.

So I have been practicing my useful profession at *Mexico City* for some time. It consists to begin with, as you know from experience, in indulging in public confession as often as possible. I accuse myself up and down. It's not hard, for I now have acquired a memory. But let me point out that I don't accuse myself crudely, beating my breast. No, I navigate skillfully, multiplying distinctions and digressions, too—in short I adapt my words to my listener and lead him to go me one better. I mingle what concerns me and what concerns others. I choose the features we have in common, the experiences we have endured together, the failings we share—good form, in other words, the man of the hour as he is rife in me and in others. With all that I construct a portrait which is the image of all and of no one. A mask, in short, rather like those carnival masks which are both lifelike and stylized, so that they make people say: "Why, surely I've met him!" When the portrait is finished, as it is this evening, I show it with great sorrow: "This, alas, is what I am!" The prosecutor's charge is finished. But at the same time the portrait I hold out to my contemporaries becomes a mirror.

Covered with ashes, tearing my hair, my face scored by clawing, but with piercing eyes, I stand before all humanity recapitulating my shames without losing sight of the effect I am producing, and saying: "I was the lowest of the low." Then imperceptibly I pass from the "I" to the "we." When I get to "This is what we are," the trick has been played and I can tell them off. I am like them, to be sure; we are in the soup together. However, I have a superiority in that I know it and this gives me the right to speak. You see the advantage, I am sure. The more I accuse myself, the more I have a right to judge you. Even better, I provoke you into judging yourself, and this relieves me of that much of the burden. Ah, *mon cher*, we are odd, wretched creatures, and if we merely look back over our lives, there's no lack of occasions to amaze and horrify ourselves. Just try, I shall listen, you may be sure, to your own confession with a great feeling of fraternity.

Don't laugh! Yes, you are a difficult client; I saw that at once. But you'll come to it inevitably. Most of the others are more sentimental than intelligent; they are disconcerted at once. With the intelligent ones it takes time. It is enough to explain the method fully to them. They don't forget it; they reflect. Sooner or later, half as a game and half out of emotional upset, they give up and tell all. *You* are not only intelligent, you look polished by use. Admit, however, that today you feel less pleased with yourself than you felt five days ago? Now I shall wait for you to write me or come back. For you will come back, I am sure! You'll find me unchanged. And why should I change, since I have found the happiness that suits me? I have accepted duplicity instead of being upset about it.

On the contrary, I have settled into it and found there the comfort I was looking for throughout life. I was wrong, after all, to tell you that the essential was to avoid judgment. The essential is being able to permit oneself everything, even if, from time to time, one has to profess vociferously one's own infamy. I permit myself everything again, and without the laughter this time. I haven't changed my way of life; I continue to love myself and to make use of others. Only, the confession of my crimes allows me to begin again lighter in heart and to taste a double enjoyment, first of my nature and secondly of a charming repentance.

Since finding my solution, I yield to everything, to women, to pride, to boredom, to resentment, and even to the fever that I feel delightfully rising at this moment. I dominate at last, but forever. Once more I have found a height to which I am the only one to climb and from which I can judge everybody. At long intervals, on a really beautiful night I occasionally hear a distant laugh and again I doubt. But quickly I crush everything, people and things, under the weight of my own infirmity, and at once I perk up.

So I shall await your respects at *Mexico City* as long as necessary. But remove this blanket; I want to breathe. You will come, won't you? I'll show you the details of my technique, for I feel a sort of affection for you. You will see me teaching them night after night that they are vile. This very evening, moreover, I shall resume. I can't do without it or deny myself those moments when one of them collapses, with the help of alcohol, and beats his breast. Then I grow taller, *très cher*, I grow taller, I breathe freely, I am on the mountain, the plain stretches before my eyes. How intoxicating to feel like God the Father and to hand out definitive testimonials of bad character and habits. I sit enthroned among my bad angels at the summit of the Dutch heaven and I watch ascending toward me, as they issue from the fogs and the water, the multitude of the Last Judgment. They rise slowly; I already see the first of them arriving. On his bewildered face, half hidden by his hand, I read the melancholy of the common condition and the despair of not being able to escape it. And as for me, I pity without absolving, I understand without forgiving, and above all, I feel at last that I am being adored!

(*Fall*, 138–143)

28

There was a night in the history of humanity when a man weighed down with all his destiny looked at his sleeping companions and, alone in a silent world, declared that no one must sleep, but that all must watch to the end of time. We are still living in times like these.

(*Soir-Républicain*, January 1, 1940, cf. *Notebooks I*, 174)

29

. . . "I do not want the happiness that is allotted to me unless I am first reassured as to each of my blood brothers, bone of my bone and flesh of my flesh . . ."

(*Notebooks II*, 177)

30

A man (a Frenchman?), a holy man who has lived his whole life in sin (never partaking of Communion, not marrying the woman with whom he lived) because, unable to endure the idea that a single soul was damned, he wanted to be damned too.

"It involved the love that is greater than all: the love of the man who gives his soul for a friend."

(*Notebooks II*, 166)

31

The automobile swung clumsily around the curve in the red sand-stone trail, now a mass of mud. The headlights suddenly picked out in the night—first on one side of the road, then on the other—two wooden huts with sheet-metal roofs. On the right near the second one, a tower of coarse beams could be made out in the light fog. From the top of the tower a metal cable, invisible at its starting-point, shone as it sloped down into the light from the car before disappearing behind the embankment that blocked the road. The car slowed down and stopped a few yards from the huts.

The man who emerged from the seat to the right of the driver labored to extricate himself from the car. As he stood up, his huge, broad frame lurched a little. In the shadow beside the car, solidly planted on the ground and weighed down by fatigue, he seemed to be listening to the idling motor. Then he walked in the direction of the embankment and entered the cone of light from the headlights. He stopped at the top of the slope, his broad back outlined against the darkness. After a moment he turned around. In the light from the dashboard he could see the chauffeur's black face, smiling. The man signaled and the chauffeur turned off the motor. At once a vast cool silence fell over the trail and the forest. Then the sound of the water could be heard.

The man looked at the river below him, visible solely as a broad dark motion, flecked with occasional shimmers. A denser motion-less darkness, far beyond, must be the other bank. By looking fix-edly, however, one could see on that still bank a yellowish light like an oil lamp in the distance. The big man turned back toward the car and nodded. The chauffeur switched off the lights, turned them on again, then blinked them regularly. On the embankment the man appeared and disappeared, taller and more massive each time he came back to life. Suddenly, on the other bank of the river, a lantern held up by an invisible arm swung back and forth several times. At a final signal from the lookout, the chauffeur turned off his lights once and for all. The car and the man disappeared into the night. With the lights out, the river was almost visible—or at least a few of its long liquid muscles shining intermittently. On each side of the road, the dark masses of forest foliage stood out against the sky and seemed very near. The fine rain that had soaked the trail an hour earlier was still hovering in the warm air, intensifying the silence and immobility of this broad clearing in the virgin forest. In the black sky misty stars flickered.

But from the other bank rose sounds of chains and muffled plashings. Above the hut on the right of the man still waiting there, the cable stretched taut. A dull creaking began to run along it, just as there rose from the river a faint yet quite audible sound of stirred-up water. The creaking became more regular, the sound of water spread farther and then became localized, as the lantern grew larger. Now its yellowish halo could be clearly seen. The halo gradually expanded and again contracted while the lantern shone through the mist and began to light up from beneath a sort of square roof of dried palms supported by thick bamboos. This crude shelter, around which vague shadows were moving, was slowly approaching the bank. When it was about in the middle of the river, three little men, almost black, were distinctly outlined in the yellow light, naked from the waist up and wearing conical hats. They stood still with feet apart, leaning somewhat to offset the strong drift of the river pressing with all its invisible water against the side of a big crude raft that eventually emerged from the darkness. When the ferry came still closer, the man could see behind the shelter on the downstream side two tall Negroes likewise wearing nothing but broad straw hats and cotton trousers. Side by side they weighed with all their might on long poles that sank slowly into the river toward the stern while the Negroes, with the same slow motion, bent over the water as far as their balance would allow. In the bow the three mulattoes, still and silent, watched the bank approach without raising their eyes toward the man waiting for them.

The ferry suddenly bumped against something. And the lantern swaying from the shock lighted up a pier jutting into the water. The tall Negroes stood still with hands above their heads gripping the ends of the poles, which were barely stuck in the bottom, but their taut muscles rippled constantly with a motion that seemed to come from the very thrust of the water. The other ferrymen looped chains over the posts on the dock, leaped onto the boards, and lowered a sort of gangplank that covered the bow of the raft with its inclined plane.

The man returned to the car and slid in while the chauffeur stepped on the starter. The car slowly climbed the embankment, pointed its hood toward the sky, and then lowered it toward the river as it tackled the downward slope. With brakes on, it rolled forward, slipped somewhat on the mud, stopped, started up again. It rolled onto the pier with a noise of bouncing planks, reached the end, where the mulattoes, still silent, were standing on either side, and plunged slowly toward the raft. The raft ducked its nose in the water as soon as the front wheels struck it and almost immediately bobbed back to receive the car's full weight. Then the chauffeur ran the vehicle to the stern, in front of the square roof where the lantern was hanging. At once the mulattoes swung the inclined plane back onto the pier and jumped simultaneously onto the ferry, pushing it off from the muddy bank. The river strained under the raft and raised it on the surface of the water, where it drifted slowly at the end of the long drawbar running along the cable overhead. The tall Negroes relaxed their effort and drew in their poles. The man and the chauffeur got out of the car and came over to stand on the edge of the raft facing upstream. No one had spoken during the maneuver, and even now each remained in his place, motionless and quiet except for one of the tall Negroes who was rolling a cigarette in coarse paper.

The man was looking at the gap through which the river sprang from the vast Brazilian forest and swept down toward them. Several hundred yards wide at that point, the muddy, silky waters of the river pressed against the side of the ferry and then, unimpeded at the two ends of the raft, sheered off and again spread out in a single powerful flood gently flowing through the dark forest toward the sea and the night. A stale smell, come from the water or the spongy sky, hung in the air. Now the slapping of the water under the ferry could be heard, and at intervals the calls of bullfrogs from the two banks or the strange cries of birds. The big man approached the small, thin chauffeur, who was leaning against one of the bamboos with his hands in the pockets of his dungarees, once blue but now covered with the same red dust that had been blowing in their faces all day long. A smile spread over his face, all wrinkled in spite of his youth. Without really seeing them, he was staring at the faint stars still swimming in the damp sky.

But the birds' cries became sharper, unfamiliar chatterings mingled with them, and almost at once the cable began to creak. The tall Negroes plunged their poles into the water and groped blindly for the bottom. The man turned around toward the shore they had just left. Now that shore was obscured by the darkness and the water, vast and savage like the continent of trees stretching beyond it for thousands of kilometers. Between the near-by ocean and this sea of vegetation, the handful of men drifting at that moment on a wild river seemed lost. When the raft bumped the new pier it was as if, having cast off all moorings, they were landing on an island in the darkness after days of frightened sailing.

Once on land, the men's voices were at last heard. The chauffeur had just paid them and, with voices that sounded strangely gay in the heavy night, they were saying farewell in Portuguese as the car started up again.

"They said sixty, the kilometers to Iguape. Three hours more and it'll be over. Socrates is happy," the chauffeur announced.

The man laughed with a warm, hearty laugh that resembled him.

"Me too, Socrates, I'm happy too. The trail is hard."

"Too heavy, Mr. D'Arrast, you too heavy," and the chauffeur laughed too as if he would never stop.

The car had taken on a little speed. It was advancing between high walls of trees and inextricable vegetation, amidst a soft, sweetish smell. Fireflies on the wing constantly crisscrossed in the darkness of the forest, and every once in a while red-eyed birds would bump against the windshield. At times a strange, savage sound would reach them from the depths of the night and the chauffeur would roll his eyes comically as he looked at his passenger.

The road kept turning and crossed little streams on bridges of wobbly boards. After an hour the fog began to thicken. A fine drizzle began to fall, dimming the car's lights. Despite the jolts, D'Arrast was half asleep. He was no longer riding in the damp forest but on the roads of the Serra that they had taken in the morning as they left São Paulo. From those dirt trails constantly rose the red dust which they could still taste, and on both sides, as far as the eye could see, it covered the sparse vegetation of the plains. The harsh sun, the pale mountains full of ravines, the starved zebus encountered along the roads, with a tired flight of ragged urubus as their only escort, the long, endless crossing of an endless desert . . . He gave a start. The car had stopped. Now they were in Japan: fragile houses on both sides of the road and, in the houses, furtive kimonos. The chauffeur was talking to a Japanese wearing soiled dungarees and a Brazilian straw hat. Then the car started up again.

"He said only forty kilometers."

"Where were we? In Tokyo?"

"No. Registro. In Brazil all the Japanese come here."

"Why?"

"Don't know. They're yellow, you know, Mr. D'Arrast."

But the forest was gradually thinning out, and the road was becoming easier, though slippery. The car was skidding on sand. The window let in a warm, damp breeze that was rather sour.

"You smell it?" the chauffeur asked, smacking his lips. "That's the good old sea. Soon, Iguape."

"If we have enough gas," D'Arrast said. And he went back to sleep peacefully.

Sitting up in bed early in the morning, D'Arrast looked in amazement at the huge room in which he had just awakened. The lower half of the big walls was newly painted brown. Higher up, they had once been painted white, and patches of yellowish paint covered them up to the ceiling. Two rows of beds faced each other. D'Arrast saw only one bed unmade at the end of his row and that bed was empty. But he heard a noise on his left and turned toward the door, where Socrates, a bottle of mineral water in each hand, stood laughing, "Happy memory!" he said. D'Arrast shook himself. Yes, the hospital in which the Mayor had lodged them the night before was named "Happy Memory." "Sure memory," Socrates continued. "They told me first build hospital, later build water. Meanwhile, happy memory, take fizz water to wash." He disappeared, laughing and singing, not at all exhausted apparently by the cataclysmic sneezes that had shaken him all night long and kept D'Arrast from closing an eye.

Now D'Arrast was completely awake. Through the iron-latticed window he could see a little red-earth courtyard soaked by the rain that was noiselessly pouring down on a clump of tall aloes. A woman passed holding a yellow scarf over her head. D'Arrast lay back in bed, then sat up at once and got out of the bed, which creaked under his weight. Socrates came in at that moment: "For you, Mr. D'Arrast. The Mayor is waiting outside." But, seeing the look on D'Arrast's face, he added: "Don't worry; he never in a hurry."

After shaving with the mineral water, D'Arrast went out under the portico of the building. The Mayor—who had the proportions and, under his gold-rimmed glasses, the look of a nice little weasel—seemed lost in dull contemplation of the rain. But a charming smile transfigured him as soon as he saw D'Arrast. Holding his little body erect, he rushed up and tried to stretch his arms around the engineer. At that moment an automobile drove up in front of them on the other side of the low wall, skidded in the wet clay, and came to a stop on an angle. "The Judge!" said the Mayor.

Like the Mayor, the Judge was dressed in navy blue. But he was much younger, or at least seemed so because of his elegant figure and his look of a startled adolescent. Now he was crossing the courtyard in their direction, gracefully avoiding the puddles. A few steps from D'Arrast, he was already holding out his arms and welcoming him. He was proud to greet the noble engineer who was honoring their poor village; he was delighted by the priceless service the noble engineer was going to do Iguape by building that little jetty to prevent the periodic flooding of the lower quarters of town. What a noble profession, to command the waters and dominate rivers! Ah, surely the poor people of Iguape would long remember the noble engineer's name and many years from now would still mention it in their prayers. D'Arrast, captivated by such charm and eloquence, thanked him and didn't dare wonder what possible connection a judge could have with a jetty. Besides, according to the Mayor, it was time to go to the club, where the leading citizens wanted to receive the noble engineer appropriately before going to inspect the poorer quarters. Who were the leading citizens?

"Well," the Mayor said, "myself as Mayor, Mr. Carvalho here, the Harbor Captain, and a few others less important. Besides, you won't have to pay much attention to them, for they don't speak French."

D'Arrast called Socrates and told him he would meet him when the morning was over.

"All right," Socrates said, "I'll go to the Garden of the Fountain."

"The Garden?"

"Yes, everybody knows. Have no fear, Mr. D'Arrast."

The hospital, D'Arrast noticed as he left it, was built on the edge of the forest, and the heavy foliage almost hung over the roofs. Over the whole surface of the trees was falling a sheet of fine rain which the dense forest was noiselessly absorbing like a huge sponge. The town, some hundred houses roofed with faded tiles, extended between the forest and the river, and the water's distant murmur reached the hospital. The car entered drenched streets and almost at once came out on a rather large rectangular square which showed, among numerous puddles in its red clay, the marks of tires, iron wheels, and horseshoes. All around, brightly plastered low houses closed off the square, behind which could be seen the two round towers of a blue-and-white church of colonial style. A smell of salt water coming from the estuary dominated this bare setting. In the center of the square a few wet silhouettes were wandering. Along the houses a motley crowd of gauchos, Japanese, half-breed Indians, and elegant leading citizens, whose dark suits looked exotic here, were sauntering with slow gestures. They stepped aside with dignity to make way for the car, then stopped and watched it. When the car stopped in front of one of the houses on the square, a circle of wet gauchos silently formed around it.

At the club—a sort of small bar on the second floor furnished with a bamboo counter and iron café tables—the leading citizens were numerous. Sugar-cane alcohol was drunk in honor of D'Arrast after the Mayor, glass in hand, had wished him welcome and all the happiness in the world. But while D'Arrast was drinking near the window, a huge lout of a fellow in riding-breeches and leggings came over and, staggering somewhat, delivered himself of a rapid and obscure speech in which the engineer recognized solely the word "passport." He hesitated and then took out the document, which the fellow seized greedily. After having thumbed through the passport, he manifested obvious displeasure. He resumed his speech, shaking the document under the nose of the engineer, who, without getting excited, merely looked at the angry man. Whereupon the Judge, with a smile, came over and asked what was the matter. For a moment the drunk scrutinized the frail creature who dared to interrupt him and then, staggering even more dangerously, shook the passport in the face of his new interlocutor. D'Arrast sat peacefully beside a café table and waited. The dialogue became very lively, and suddenly the Judge broke out in a deafening voice that one would never have suspected in him. Without

any forewarning, the lout suddenly backed down like a child caught
in the act. At a final order from the Judge, he sidled toward the
door like a punished schoolboy and disappeared.

The Judge immediately came over to explain to D'Arrast, in a
voice that had become harmonious again, that the uncouth individual who had just left was the Chief of Police, that he had dared
to claim the passport was not in order, and that he would be
punished for his outburst. Judge Carvalho then addressed himself
to the leading citizens, who stood in a circle around him, and
seemed to be questioning them. After a brief discussion, the Judge
expressed solemn excuses to D'Arrast, asked him to agree that nothing but drunkenness could explain such forgetfulness of the sen-
timents of respect and gratitude that the whole town of Iguape owed
him, and, finally, asked him to decide himself on the punishment
to be inflicted on the wretched individual. D'Arrast said that he
didn't want any punishment, that it was a trivial incident, and that
he was particularly eager to go to the river. Then the Mayor spoke
up to assert with much simple good-humor that a punishment was
really mandatory, that the guilty man would remain incarcerated,
and that they would all wait until their distinguished visitor decided
on his fate. No protest could soften that smiling severity, and D'Arrast had to promise that he would think the matter over. Then they
agreed to visit the poorer quarters of the town.

The river was already spreading its yellowish waters over the low,
slippery banks. They had left behind them the last houses of Iguape
and stood between the river and a high, steep embankment to
which clung huts made of clay and branches. In front of them, at
the end of the embankment, the forest began abruptly, as on the
other bank. But the gap made by the water rapidly widened between the trees until reaching a vague grayish line that marked the
beginning of the sea. Without saying a word, D'Arrast walked toward the slope, where the various flood levels had left marks that
were still fresh. A muddy path climbed toward the huts. In front of
them, Negroes stood silently staring at the newcomers. Several

couples were holding hands, and on the edge of the mound, in front of the adults, a row of black children with bulging bellies and spindly legs were gaping with round eyes.

When he arrived in front of the huts, D'Arrast beckoned to the Harbor Captain. He was a fat, laughing Negro wearing a white uniform. D'Arrast asked him in Spanish if it were possible to visit a hut. The Captain was sure it was, he even thought it a good idea, and the noble engineer would see very interesting things. He harrangued the Negroes at length, pointing to D'Arrast and to the river. They listened without saying a word. When the Captain had finished, no one stirred. He spoke again, in an impatient voice. Then he called upon one of the men, who shook his head. Whereupon the Captain said a few brief words in a tone of command. The man stepped forth from the group, faced D'Arrast, and with a gesture showed him the way. But his look was hostile. He was an elderly man with short, graying hair and a thin, wizened face; yet his body was still young, with hard wiry shoulders and muscles visible through his cotton pants and torn shirt. They went ahead, followed by the Captain and the crowd of Negroes, and climbed a new, steeper embankment where the huts made of clay, tin, and reeds clung to the ground with such difficulty that they had to be strengthened at the base with heavy stones. They met a woman going down the path, sometimes slipping in her bare feet, who was carrying on her head an iron drum full of water. Then they reached a small irregular square bordered by three huts. The man walked toward one of them and pushed open a bamboo door on hinges made of tropical liana. He stood aside without saying a word, staring at the engineer with the same impassive look. In the hut, D'Arrast saw nothing at first but a dying fire built right on the ground in the exact center of the room. Then in a back corner he made out a brass bed with a bare, broken mattress, a table in the other corner covered with earthenware dishes, and, between the two, a sort of stand supporting a color print representing Saint George. Nothing else but a pile of rags to the right of the entrance and, hanging from the ceiling, a few lioncloths of various colors drying over the fire. Standing still, D'Arrast breathed in the smell of smoke and poverty that rose from the ground and choked him. Behind him, the Captain clapped his hands. The engineer turned around and, against the light, saw the graceful silhouette of a black girl approach and hold out something to him. He took a glass and drank the thick sugar-cane alcohol. The girl held out her tray to receive the empty glass and went out with such a supple motion that D'Arrast suddenly wanted to hold her back. But on following her out he didn't recognize her in the crowd of Negroes and leading citizens gathered around the hut. He thanked the old man, who bowed without a word. Then he left. The Captain, behind him, resumed his explanations and asked when the French company from Rio could begin work and whether or not the jetty could be built before the rainy season. D'Arrast didn't know; to tell the truth, he wasn't thinking of that. He went down toward the cool river under the fine mist. He was still listening to that great pervasive sound he had been hearing continually since his arrival, which might have been made by the rustling of either the water or the trees, he could not tell. Having reached the bank, he looked out in the distance at the vague line of the sea, the thousands of kilometers of solitary waters leading to Africa and, beyond, his native Europe.

"Captain," he asked, "what do these people we have just seen live on?"

"They work when they're needed," the Captain said. "We are poor."

"Are they the poorest?"

"They are the poorest."

The Judge, who arrived at that moment, slipping somewhat in his best shoes, said they already loved the noble engineer who was going to give them work.

"And, you know, they dance and sing every day."

Then, without transition, he asked D'Arrast if he had thought of the punishment.

"What punishment?"

"Why, our Chief of Police."

"Let him go." The Judge said that this was not possible; there had to be a punishment. D'Arrast was already walking toward Iguape.

In the little Garden of the Fountain, mysterious and pleasant under the fine rain, clusters of exotic flowers hung down along the lianas among the banana trees and pandanus. Piles of wet stones marked the intersection of paths on which a motley crowd was strolling. Half-breeds, mulattoes, a few gauchos were chatting in low voices or sauntering along the bamboo paths to the point where groves and bush became thicker and more impenetrable. There, the forest began abruptly.

D'Arrast was looking for Socrates in the crowd when Socrates suddenly bumped him from behind.

"It's holiday," he said, laughing, and clung to D'Arrast's tall shoulders to jump up and down.

"What holiday?"

"Why, you not know?" Socrates said in surprise as he faced D'Arrast. "The feast of good Jesus. Each year they all come to the grotto with a hammer."

Socrates pointed out, not a grotto, but a group that seemed to be waiting in a corner of the garden.

"You see? One day the good statue of Jesus, it came upstream from the sea. Some fishermen found it. How beautiful! How beautiful! Then they washed it here in the grotto. And now a stone grew up in the grotto. Every year it's the feast. With the hammer you break, you break off pieces for blessed happiness. And then it keeps growing and you keep breaking. It's the miracle!"

They had reached the grotto and could see its low entrance beyond the waiting men. Inside, in the darkness studded with the flickering flames of candles, a squatting figure was pounding with a hammer. The man, a thin gaucho with a long mustache, got up and came out holding in his open palm, so that all might see, a small piece of moist schist, over which he soon closed his hand carefully before going away. Another man then stooped down and entered the grotto.

D'Arrast turned around. On all sides pilgrims were waiting, without looking at him, impassive under the water dripping from the trees in thin sheets. He too was waiting in front of the grotto under the same film of water, and he didn't know for what. He had been waiting constantly, to tell the truth, for a month since he had arrived in this country. He had been waiting—in the red heat of humid days, under the little stars of night, despite the tasks to be accomplished, the jetties to be built, the roads to be cut through— as if the work he had come to do here were merely a pretext for a surprise or for an encounter he did not even imagine but which had been waiting patiently for him at the end of the world. He shook himself, walked away without anyone in the little group paying attention to him, and went toward the exit. He had to go back to the river and go to work.

But Socrates was waiting for him at the gate, lost in voluble conversation with a short, fat, strapping man whose skin was yellow rather than black. His head, completely shaved, gave even more sweep to a considerable forehead. On the other hand, his broad, smooth face was adorned with a very black beard, trimmed square.

"He's champion!" Socrates said by way of introduction. "Tomorrow he's in the procession."

The man, wearing a sailor's outfit of heavy serge, a blue-and-white jersey under the pea jacket, was examining D'Arrast attentively with his calm black eyes. At the same time he was smiling, showing all his very white teeth between his full, shiny lips.

"He speaks Spanish," Socrates said and, turning toward the stranger, added: "Tell Mr. D'Arrast." Then he danced off toward another group. The man ceased to smile and looked at D'Arrast with outright curiosity.

"You are interested, Captain?"

"I'm not a captain," D'Arrast said.

"That doesn't matter. But you're a noble. Socrates told me."

"Not I. But my grandfather was. His father too and all those before his father. Now there is no more nobility in our country."

"Ah!" the Negro said, laughing. "I understand; everybody is a noble."

"No, that's not it. There are neither noblemen nor common people."

The fellow reflected; then he made up his mind.

"No one works? No one suffers?"

"Yes, millions of men."

"Then that's the common people."

"In that way, yes, there is a common people. But the masters are policemen or merchants."

The mulatto's kindly face closed in a frown. Then he grumbled: "Humph! Buying and selling, eh! What filth! And with the police, dogs command."

Suddenly, he burst out laughing.

"You, you don't sell?"

"Hardly at all. I make bridges, roads."

"That's good. Me, I'm a ship's cook. If you wish, I'll make you our dish of black beans."

"All right."

The cook came closer to D'Arrast and took his arm.

"Listen, I like what you tell. I'm going to tell you too. Maybe you will like."

He drew him over near the gate to a damp wooden bench beneath a clump of bamboos.

"I was at sea, off Iguape, on a small coastwise tanker that supplies the harbors along here. It caught fire on board. Not by my

fault! I know my job! No, just bad luck. We were able to launch
the lifeboats. During the night, the sea got rough; it capsized the
boat and I went down. When I came up, I hit the boat with my
head. I drifted. The night was dark, the waters are vast, and besides, I don't swim well; I was afraid. Just then I saw a light in the
distance and recognized the church of the good Jesus in Iguape. So
I told the good Jesus that at his procession I would carry a hundred-
pound stone on my head if he saved me. You don't have to believe
me, but the waters became calm and my heart too. I swam slowly,
I was happy, and I reached the shore. Tomorrow I'll keep my
promise."

He looked at D'Arrast in a suddenly suspicious manner.

"You're not laughing?"

"No, I'm not laughing. A man has to do what he has promised."

The fellow clapped him on the back.

"Now, come to my brother's, near the river. I'll cook you some
beans."

"No," D'Arrast said, "I have things to do. This evening, if you
wish."

"Good. But tonight there's dancing and praying in the big hut.
It's the feast for Saint George." D'Arrast asked him if he danced
too. The cook's face hardened suddenly; for the first time his eyes
became shifty.

"No, no, I won't dance. Tomorrow I must carry the stone. It is
heavy. I'll go this evening to celebrate the saint. And then I'll leave
early."

"Does it last long?"

"All night and a little into the morning."

He looked at D'Arrast with a vaguely shameful look.

"Come to the dance. You can take me home afterward. Otherwise, I'll stay and dance. I probably won't be able to keep from it."

"You like to dance?"

"Oh, yes! I like. Besides, there are cigars, saints, women. You
forget everything and you don't obey any more."

"There are women too? All the women of the town?"

"Not of the town, but of the huts."

The ship's cook resumed his smile. "Come. The Captain I'll obey. And you will help me keep my promise tomorrow."

D'Arrast felt slightly annoyed. What did that absurd promise mean to him? But he looked at the handsome frank face smiling trustingly at him, its dark skin gleaming with health and vitality.

"I'll come," he said. "Now I'll walk along with you a little."

Without knowing why, he had a vision at the same time of the black girl offering him the drink of welcome.

They went out of the garden, walked along several muddy streets, and reached the bumpy square, which looked even larger because of the low structures surrounding it. The humidity was now dripping down the plastered walls, although the rain had not increased. Through the spongy expanse of the sky, the sound of the river and of the trees reached them somewhat muted. They were walking in step, D'Arrast heavily and the cook with elastic tread. From time to time the latter would raise his head and smile at his companion. They went in the direction of the church, which could be seen above the houses, reached the end of the square, walked along other muddy streets now filled with aggressive smells of cooking. From time to time a woman, holding a plate or kitchen utensil, would peer out inquisitively from one of the doors and then disappear at once. They passed in front of the church, plunged into an old section of similar low houses, and suddenly came out on the sound of the invisible river behind the area of the huts that D'Arrast recognized.

"Good. I'll leave you. See you this evening," he said.

"Yes, in front of the church."

But the cook did not let go of D'Arrast's hand. He hesitated. Finally he made up his mind.

"And you, have you never called out, made a promise?"

"Yes, once, I believe."

"In a shipwreck?"

"If you wish." And D'Arrast pulled his hand away roughly. But as he was about to turn on his heels, he met the cook's eyes. He hesitated, and then smiled.

"I can tell you, although it was unimportant. Someone was about to die through my fault. It seems to me that I called out."

"Did you promise?"

"No. I should have liked to promise."

"Long ago?"

"Not long before coming here."

The cook seized his beard with both hands. His eyes were shining.

"You are a captain," he said. "My house is yours. Besides, you are going to help me keep my promise, and it's as if you had made it yourself. That will help you too."

D'Arrast smiled, saying: "I don't think so."

"You are proud, Captain."

"I used to be proud; now I'm alone. But just tell me: has your good Jesus always answered you?"

"Always . . . no, Captain!"

"Well, then?"

The cook burst out with a gay, childlike laugh.

"Well," he said, "he's free, isn't he?"

At the club, where D'Arrast lunched with the leading citizens, the Mayor told him he must sign the town's guest-book so that some trace would remain of the great event of his coming to Iguape. The Judge found two or three new expressions to praise, besides their guest's virtues and talents, the simplicity with which he represented among them the great country to which he had the honor to belong. D'Arrast simply said that it was indeed an honor to him and an advantage to his firm to have been awarded the allocation of this long construction job. Whereupon the Judge expressed his admiration for such humility. "By the way," he asked, "have you thought of what should be done to the Chief of Police?" D'Arrast smiled at him and said: "Yes, I have a solution."

He would consider it a personal favor and an exceptional grace if the foolish man could be forgiven in his name so that his stay here in Iguape, where he so much enjoyed knowing the beautiful town and generous inhabitants, could begin in a climate of peace and friendship. The Judge, attentive and smiling, nodded his head. For a moment he meditated on the wording as an expert, then called on those present to applaud the magnanimous traditions of the great French nation and, turning again toward D'Arrast, declared himself satisfied. "Since that's the way it is," he concluded, "we shall dine this evening with the Chief." But D'Arrast said that he was invited by friends to the ceremony of the dances in the huts. "Ah, yes!" said the Judge. "I am glad you are going. You'll see, one can't resist loving our people."

That evening, D'Arrast, the ship's cook, and his brother were seated around the ashes of a fire in the center of the hut the engineer had already visited in the morning. The brother had not seemed surprised to see him return. He spoke Spanish hardly at all and most of the time merely nodded his head. As for the cook, he had shown interest in cathedrals and then had explained at length on the black bean soup. Now night had almost fallen and, although D'Arrast could still see the cook and his brother, he could scarcely make out in the back of the hut the squatting figures of an old woman and of the same girl who had served him. Down below, he could hear the monotonous river.

The cook rose, saying: "It's time." They got up, but the women did not stir. The men went out alone, D'Arrast hesitated, then joined the others. Night had now fallen and the rain had stopped. The pale-black sky still seemed liquid. In its transparent dark water, stars began to light up, low on the horizon. Almost at once they flickered out, falling one by one into the river as if the last lights were trickling from the sky. The heavy air smelled of water and smoke. Near by the sound of the huge forest could be heard too, though it was motionless. Suddenly drums and singing broke out in the distance, at first muffled and then distinct, approaching closer and closer and finally stopping. Soon after, one could see a procession of black girls wearing low-waisted white dresses of coarse silk. In a tight-fitting red jacket adorned with a necklace of varicolored teeth, a tall Negro followed them and, behind him, a disorderly crowd of men in white pajamas and musicians carrying triangles and broad, short drums. The cook said they should follow the men.

The hut, which they reached by following the river a few hundred yards beyond the last huts, was large, empty, and relatively comfortable, with plastered walls. It had a dirt floor, a roof of thatch and reeds supported by a central pole, and bare walls. On a little palm-clad altar at the end, covered with candles that scarcely lighted half the hall, there was a magnificent colored print in which Saint George, with alluring grace, was getting the better of a bewhiskered dragon. Under the altar a sort of niche decorated with rococo paper sheltered a little statue of red-painted clay representing a horned god, standing between a candle and a bowl of water. With a fierce look the god was brandishing an oversized knife made of silver paper.

The cook led D'Arrast to a corner, where they stood against the wall near the door. "This way," he whispered, "we can leave without disturbing." Indeed, the hut was packed tight with men and women. Already the heat was rising. The musicians took their places on both sides of the little altar. The men and women dancers separated into two concentric circles with the men inside. In the very center the black leader in the red jacket took his stand. D'Arrast leaned against the wall, folding his arms.

But the leader, elbowing his way through the circle of dancers, came toward them and, in a solemn way, said a few words to the cook. "Unfold your arms, Captain," the cook said. "You are hugging yourself and keeping the saint's spirit from descending." Obediently D'Arrast let his arms fall to his sides. Still leaning against the wall, with his long, heavy limbs and his big face already shiny with sweat, D'Arrast himself looked like some bestial and kindly god. The tall Negro looked at them and, satisfied, went back to his place. At once, in a resounding voice, he intoned the opening notes of a song that all picked up in chorus, accompanied by the drums. Then the circles began to turn in opposite directions in a sort of heavy, insistent dance rather like stamping, slightly emphasized by the double line of swaying hips.

The heat had increased. Yet the pauses gradually diminished, the stops became less frequent, and the dance speeded up. Without any slowing of the others' rhythm, without ceasing to dance himself, the tall Negro again elbowed his way through the circles to go toward the altar. He came back with a glass of water and a lighted candle that he stuck in the ground in the center of the hut. He poured the water around the candle in two concentric circles and, again erect, turned maddened eyes toward the roof. His whole body taut and still, he was waiting. "Saint George is coming. Look! Look!" whispered the cook, whose eyes were popping.

Indeed, some dancers now showed signs of being in a trance, but a rigid trance with hands on hips, step stiff, eyes staring and vacant. Others quickened their rhythm, bent convulsively backward, and began to utter inarticulate cries. The cries gradually rose higher, and when they fused in a collective shriek, the leader, with eyes still raised, uttered a long, barely phrased outcry at the top of his lungs. In it the same words kept recurring. "You see," said the cook, "he says he is the god's field of battle." Struck by the change in his voice, D'Arrast looked at the cook, who, leaning forward with fists clenched and eyes staring, was mimicking the others' measured stamping without moving from his place. Then he noticed that he himself, though without moving his feet, had for some little time been dancing with his whole weight.

But all at once the drums began to beat violently and suddenly the big devil in red broke loose. His eyes flashing, his four limbs whirling around him, he hopped with bent knee on one leg after the other, speeding up his rhythm until it seemed that he must eventually fly to pieces. But abruptly he stopped on the verge of one leap to stare at those around him with a proud and terrible look while the drums thundered on. Immediately a dancer sprang from a dark corner, knelt down, and held out a short saber to the man possessed of the spirit. The tall Negro took the saber without ceasing to look around him and then whirled it above his head. At that moment D'Arrast noticed the cook dancing among the others. The engineer had not seen him leave his side.

In the reddish, uncertain light a stifling dust rose from the ground, making the air even thicker and sticking to one's skin. D'Arrast felt gradually overcome by fatigue and breathed with ever greater difficulty. He did not even see how the dancers had got hold of the huge cigars they were now smoking while still dancing; their strange smell filled the hut and rather made his head swim. He merely saw the cook passing near him, still dancing and puffing on a cigar. "Don't smoke," he said. The cook grunted without losing the beat, staring at the central pole with the expression of a boxer about to collapse, his spine constantly twitching in a long shudder. Beside him a heavy Negress, rolling her animal face from side to side, kept barking. But the young Negresses especially went into the most frightful trance, their feet glued to the floor and their bodies shaken from feet to head by convulsive motions that became more violent upon reaching the shoulders. Their heads would wag backward and forward, literally separated from a decapitated body. At the same time all began to howl incessantly with a long collective and toneless howl, apparently not pausing to breathe or to introduce modulations—as if the bodies were tightly knotted, muscles and nerves, in a single exhausting outburst, at last giving voice in each of them to a creature that had until then been absolutely silent. And, still howling, the women began to fall one by one. The black leader knelt by each one and quickly and convulsively pressed her temples with his huge, black-muscled hand. Then they would get up, staggering, return to the dance, and resume their howls, at first feebly and then louder and faster, before falling again, and getting up again, and beginning over again, and for a long time more, until the general howl decreased, changed, and degenerated into a sort of coarse barking which shook them with gasps. D'Arrast, exhausted, his muscles taut from his long dance as he stood still, choked by his own silence, felt himself stagger. The heat, the dust, the smoke of the cigars, the smell of bodies now made the air almost unbreathable. He looked for the cook, who had disappeared. D'Arrast let himself slide down along the wall and squatted, holding back his nausea.

When he opened his eyes, the air was still as stifling but the noise had stopped. The drums alone were beating out a figured bass, and groups in every corner of the hut, covered with whitish cloths, were marking time by stamping. But in the center of the room, from which the glass and candle had now been removed, a group of black girls in a semi-hypnotic state were dancing slowly, always on the point of letting the beat get ahead of them. Their eyes closed and yet standing erect, they were swaying lightly on their toes, almost in the same spot. Two of them, fat ones, had their faces covered with a curtain of raffia. They surrounded another girl, tall, thin, and wearing a fancy costume. D'Arrast suddenly recognized her as the daughter of his host. In a green dress and a huntress's hat of blue gauze turned up in front and adorned with plumes, she held in her hand a green-and-yellow bow with an arrow on the tip of which was spitted a multicolored bird. On her slim body her pretty head swayed slowly, tipped backward a little, and her sleeping face reflected an innocent melancholy. At the pauses in the music she staggered as if only half awake. Yet the intensified beat of the drums provided her with a sort of invisible support around which to entwine her languid arabesques until, stopping again together with the music, tottering on the edge of equilibrium, she uttered a strange bird cry, shrill and yet melodious.

D'Arrast, bewitched by the slow dance, was watching the black Diana when the cook suddenly loomed up before him, his smooth face now distorted. The kindness had disappeared from his eyes, revealing nothing but a sort of unsuspected avidity. Coldly, as if speaking to a stranger, he said: "It's late, Captain. They are going to dance all night long, but they don't want you to stay now." With head heavy, D'Arrast got up and followed the cook, who went along the wall toward the door. On the threshold the cook stood aside, holding the bamboo door, and D'Arrast went out. He turned back and looked at the cook, who had not moved. "Come. In a little while you'll have to carry the stone."

"I'm staying," the cook said with a set expression.

"And your promise?"

Without replying, the cook gradually pushed against the door that D'Arrast was holding open with one hand. They remained this way for a second until D'Arrast gave in, shrugging his shoulders. He went away.

The night was full of fresh aromatic scents. Above the forest the few stars in the austral sky, blurred by an invisible haze, were shining dimly. The humid air was heavy. Yet it seemed delightfully cool on coming out of the hut. D'Arrast climbed the slippery slope, staggering like a drunken man in the potholes. The forest, near by, rumbled slightly. The sound of the river increased. The whole continent was emerging from the night, and loathing overcame D'Arrast. It seemed to him that he would have liked to spew forth this whole country, the melancholy of its vast expanses, the glaucous light of its forests, and the nocturnal lapping of its big deserted rivers. This land was too vast, blood and seasons mingled here, and time liquefied. Life here was flush with the soil, and, to identify with it, one had to lie down and sleep for years on the muddy or dried-up ground itself. Yonder, in Europe, there was shame and wrath. Here, exile or solitude, among these listless and convulsive madmen who danced to die. But through the humid night, heavy with vegetable scents, the wounded bird's outlandish cry, uttered by the beautiful sleeping girl, still reached his ears.

When D'Arrast, his head in the vise of a crushing migraine, had awakened after a bad sleep, a humid heat was weighing upon the town and the still forest. He was waiting now under the hospital

portico, looking at his watch, which had stopped, uncertain of the
time, surprised by the broad daylight and the silence of the town.
The almost clear blue sky hung low over the first dull roofs. Yellowish urubus, transfixed by the heat, were sleeping on the house
across from the hospital. One of them suddenly fluttered, opened
his beak, ostensibly got ready to fly away, flapped his dusty wings
twice against his body, rose a few inches above the roof, fell back,
and went to sleep almost at once.

The engineer went down toward the town. The main square was
empty, like the streets through which he had just walked. In the
distance, and on both sides of the river, a low mist hung over the
forest. The heat fell vertically, and D'Arrast looked for a shady spot.
At that moment, under the overhang on one of the houses, he saw
a little man gesturing to him. As he came closer, he recognized
Socrates.

"Well, Mr. D'Arrast, you like the ceremony?"

D'Arrast said that it was too hot in the hut and that he preferred
the sky and the night air.

"Yes," Socrates said, "in your country there's only the Mass. No
one dances." He rubbed his hands, jumped on one foot, whirled
about, laughed uproariously. "Not possible, they're not possible."
Then he looked at D'Arrast inquisitively. "And you, are you going
to Mass?"

"No."

"Then, where are you going?"

"Nowhere. I don't know."

Socrates laughed again. "Not possible! A noble without a
church, without anything!"

D'Arrast laughed likewise. "Yes, you see, I never found my
place. So I left."

"Stay with us, Mr. D'Arrast, I love you."

"I'd like to, Socrates, but I don't know how to dance." Their
laughter echoed in the silence of the empty town.

"Ah," Socrates said, "I forget. The Mayor wants to see you. He is lunching at the club." And without warning he started off in the direction of the hospital.

"Where are you going?" D'Arrast shouted.

Socrates imitated a snore. "Sleep. Soon the procession." And, half running, he resumed his snores.

The Mayor simply wanted to give D'Arrast a place of honor to see the procession. He explained it to the engineer while sharing with him a dish of meat and rice such as would miraculously cure a paralytic. First they would take their places on a balcony of the Judge's house, opposite the church, to see the procession come out. Then they would go to the town hall in the main street leading to the church, which the penitents would take on their way back. The Judge and the Chief of Police would accompany D'Arrast, the Mayor being obliged to take part in the ceremony. The Chief of Police was in fact in the clubroom and kept paying court to D'Arrast with an indefatigable smile, lavishing upon him incomprehensible but obviously well-meaning speeches. When D'Arrast left, the Chief of Police hastened to make a way for him, holding all the doors open before him.

Under the burning sun, in the still empty town, the two men walked toward the Judge's house. Their steps were the only sound heard in the silence. But all of a sudden a firecracker exploded in a neighboring street and flushed on every roof the heavy, awkward flocks of bald-necked urubus. Almost at once dozens of firecrackers went off in all directions, doors opened, and people began to emerge from the houses and fill the narrow streets.

The Judge told D'Arrast how proud he was to receive him in his unworthy house and led him up a handsome baroque staircase painted chalky blue. On the landing, as D'Arrast passed, doors opened and children's dark heads popped out and disappeared at once with smothered laughter. The main room, beautiful in architecture, contained nothing but rattan furniture and large cages filled with squawking birds. The balcony on which the Judge and D'Arrast settled overlooked the little square in front of the church.

The crowd was now beginning to fill it, strangely silent, motionless under the heat that came down from the sky in almost visible waves. Only the children ran around the square, stopping abruptly to light firecrackers, and sharp reports followed one another in rapid succession. Seen from the balcony, the church with its plaster walls, its dozen blue steps, its blue-and-gold towers, looked smaller.

Suddenly the organ burst forth within the church. The crowd, turned toward the portico, drew over to the sides of the square. The men took off their hats and the women knelt down. The distant organ played at length something like marches. Then an odd sound of wings came from the forest. A tiny airplane with transparent wings and frail fuselage, out of place in this ageless world, came in sight over the trees, swooped a little above the square, and, with the clacking of a big rattle, passed over the heads raised toward it. Then the plane turned and disappeared in the direction of the estuary.

But in the shadow of the church a vague bustle again attracted attention. The organ had stopped, replaced now by brasses and drums, invisible under the portico. Black-surpliced penitents came out of the church one by one, formed groups outside the doors, and began to descend the steps. Behind them came white penitents bearing red-and-blue banners, then a little group of boys dressed up as angels, sodalities of Children of Mary with little black and serious faces. Finally, on a multicolored shrine borne by leading citizens sweating in their dark suits, came the effigy of the good Jesus himself, a reed in his hand and his head crowned with thorns, bleeding and tottering above the crowd that lined the steps.

When the shrine reached the bottom of the steps, there was a pause during which the penitents tried to line up in a semblance of order. Then it was that D'Arrast saw the ship's cook. Bare from the waist up, he had just come out under the portico carrying on his bearded head an enormous rectangular block set on a cork mat. With steady tread he came down the church steps, the stone perfectly balanced in the arch formed by his short, muscular arms. As soon as he fell in behind the shrine, the procession moved. From

the portico burst the musicians, wearing bright-colored coats and
blowing into beribboned brasses. To the beat of a quick march, the
penitents hastened their step and reached one of the streets opening
off the square. When the shrine had disappeared behind them,
nothing could be seen but the cook and the last of the musicians.
Behind them, the crowd got in motion amidst exploding firecrackers, while the plane, with a great rattle of its engine, flew back over
the groups trailing behind. D'Arrast was looking exclusively at the
cook, who was disappearing into the street now and whose
shoulders he suddenly thought he saw sag. But at that distance he
couldn't see well.

Through the empty streets, between closed shops and bolted
doors, the Judge, the Chief of Police, and D'Arrast reached the
town hall. As they got away from the band and the firecrackers,
silence again enveloped the town and already a few urubus returned to the places on the roofs that they seemed to have occupied
for all time. The town hall stood in a long, narrow street leading
from one of the outlying sections to the church square. For the
moment, the street was empty. From the balcony could be seen, as
far as the eye could reach, nothing but a pavement full of potholes,
in which the recent rain had left puddles. The sun, now slightly
lower, was still nibbling at the windowless façades of the houses
across the street.

They waited a long time, so long that D'Arrast, from staring at
the reverberation of the sun on the opposite wall, felt his fatigue
and dizziness returning. The empty street with its deserted houses
attracted and repelled him at one and the same time. Once again
he wanted to get away from this country; at the same time he
thought of that huge stone; he would have liked that trial to be
over. He was about to suggest going down to find out something
when the church bells began to peal forth loudly. Simultaneously,
from the other end of the street on their left, a clamor burst out and
a seething crowd appeared. From a distance the people could be
seen swarming around the shrine, pilgrims and penitents mingled,

and they were advancing, amidst firecrackers and shouts of joy, along the narrow street. In a few seconds they filled it to the edges, advancing toward the town hall in an indescribable disorder—ages, races, and costumes fused in a motley mass full of gaping eyes and yelling mouths. From the crowd emerged an army of tapers like lances with flames fading into the burning sunlight. But when they were close and the crowd was so thick under the balcony that it seemed to rise up along the walls, D'Arrast saw that the ship's cook was not there.

Quick as lightning, without excusing himself, he left the balcony and the room, dashed down the staircase, and stood in the street under the deafening sound of the bells and firecrackers. There he had to struggle against the crowd of merrymakers, the taper-bearers, the shocked penitents. But, bucking the human tide with all his weight, he cut a path in such an impetuous way that he staggered and almost fell when he was eventually free, beyond the crowd, at the end of the street. Leaning against the burning-hot wall, he waited until he had caught his breath. Then he resumed his way. At that moment a group of men emerged into the street. The ones in front were walking backward, and D'Arrast saw that they surrounded the cook.

He was obviously dead tired. He would stop, then, bent under the huge stone, run a little with the hasty step of stevedores and coolies—the rapid, flat-footed trot of drudgery. Gathered about him, penitents in surplices soiled with dust and candle-drippings encouraged him when he stopped. On his left his brother was walking or running in silence. It seemed to D'Arrast that they took an interminable time to cover the space separating them from him. Having almost reached him, the cook stopped again and glanced around with dull eyes. When he saw D'Arrast—yet without appearing to recognize him—he stood still, turned toward him. An oily, dirty sweat covered his face, which had gone gray; his beard was full of threads of saliva; and a brown, dry froth glued his lips together. He tried to smile. But, motionless under his load, his whole body was trembling except for the shoulders, where the muscles were obviously caught in a sort of cramp. The brother, who had recognized D'Arrast, said to him simply: "He already fell." And Socrates, popping up from nowhere, whispered in his ear: "Dance too much, Mr. D'Arrast, all night long. He's tired."

The cook advanced again with his jerky trot, not like a man who wants to progress but as if he were fleeing the crushing load, as if he hoped to lighten it through motion. Without knowing how, D'Arrast found himself at his right. He laid his hand lightly on the cook's back and walked beside him with hasty, heavy steps. At the other end of the street the shrine had disappeared, and the crowd, which probably now filled the square, did not seem to advance any more. For several seconds, the cook, between his brother and D'Arrast, made progress. Soon a mere space of some twenty yards separated him from the group gathered in front of the town hall to see him pass. Again, however, he stopped. D'Arrast's hand became heavier. "Come on, cook, just a little more," he said. The man trembled; the saliva began to trickle from his mouth again, while the sweat literally spurted from all over his body. He tried to breathe deeply and stopped short. He started off again, took three steps, and tottered. And suddenly the stone slipped onto his shoulder, gashing it, and then forward onto the ground, while the cook, losing his balance, toppled over on his side. Those who were preceding him and urging him on jumped back with loud shouts. One of them seized the cork mat while the others took hold of the stone to load it on him again.

Leaning over him, D'Arrast with his bare hand wiped the blood and dust from his shoulder, while the little man, his face against the ground, panted. He heard nothing and did not stir. His mouth opened avidly as if each breath were his last. D'Arrast grasped him around the waist and raised him up as easily as if he had been a child. Holding him upright in a tight clasp with his full height leaning over him, D'Arrast spoke into his face as if to breathe his own strength into him. After a moment, the cook, bloody and

caked with earth, detached himself with a haggard expression on
his face. He staggered toward the stone, which the others were raising a little. But he stopped, looked at the stone with a vacant stare,
and shook his head. Then he let his arms fall at his sides and
turned toward D'Arrast. Huge tears flowed silently down his
ravaged face. He wanted to speak, he was speaking, but his mouth
hardly formed the syllables. "I promised," he was saying. And then:
"Oh, Captain! Oh, Captain!" and the tears drowned his voice. His
brother suddenly appeared behind him, threw his arms around
him, and the cook, weeping, collapsed against him, defeated, with
his head thrown back.

D'Arrast looked at him, not knowing what to say. He turned
toward the crowd in the distance, now shouting again. Suddenly he
tore the cork mat from the hands holding it and walked toward the
stone. He gestured to the others to hold it up and then he loaded it
almost effortlessly. His head pressed down under the weight of the
stone, his shoulders hunched, and breathing rather hard, he
looked down at his feet as he listened to the cook's sobs. Then with
vigorous tread he started off on his own, without flagging covered
the space separating him from the crowd at the end of the street,
and energetically forced his way through the first rows, which stood
aside as he approached. In the hubbub of bells and firecrackers he
entered the square between two solid masses of onlookers, suddenly
silent and gaping at him in amazement. He advanced with the
same impetuous pace, and the crowd opened a path for him to the
church. Despite the weight which was beginning to crush his head
and neck, he saw the church and the shrine, which seemed to be
waiting for him at the door. He had already gone beyond the center
of the square in that direction when brutally, without knowing
why, he veered off to the left and turned away from the church,
forcing the pilgrims to face him. Behind him, he heard someone
running. In front of him mouths opened on all sides. He didn't understand what they were shouting, although he seemed to recognize
the one Portuguese word that was being constantly hurled at him.

Suddenly Socrates appeared before him, rolling startled eyes, speaking incoherently and pointing out the way to the church behind him. "To the church! To the church!" was what Socrates and the crowd were shouting at him. Yet D'Arrast continued in the direction in which he was launched. And Socrates stood aside, his arms raised in the air comically, while the crowd gradually fell silent. When D'Arrast entered the first street, which he had already taken with the cook and therefore knew it led to the river section, the square had become but a confused murmur behind him.

The stone weighed painfully on his head now and he needed all the strength of his long arms to lighten it. His shoulders were already stiffening when he reached the first streets on the slippery slope. He stopped and listened. He was alone. He settled the stone firmly on its cork base and went down with a cautious but still steady tread toward the huts. When he reached them, his breath was beginning to fail, his arms were trembling under the stone. He hastened his pace, finally reached the little square where the cook's hut stood, ran to it, kicked the door open, and brusquely hurled the stone onto the still glowing fire in the center of the room. And there, straightening up until he was suddenly enormous, drinking in with desperate gulps the familiar smell of poverty and ashes, he felt rising within him a surge of obscure and panting joy that he was powerless to name.

When the inhabitants of the hut arrived, they found D'Arrast standing with his shoulders against the back wall and eyes closed. In the center of the room, in the place of the hearth, the stone was half buried in ashes and earth. They stood in the doorway without advancing and looked at D'Arrast in silence as if questioning him. But he didn't speak. Whereupon the brother led the cook up to the stone, where he dropped on the ground. The brother sat down too, beckoning to the others. The old woman joined him, then the girl of the night before, but no one looked at D'Arrast. They were squatting in a silent circle around the stone. No sound but the murmur of the river reached them through the heavy air. Standing in the darkness, D'Arrast listened without seeing anything, and the sound of the waters filled him with a tumultuous happiness. With eyes closed, he joyfully acclaimed his own strength; he acclaimed, once again, a fresh beginning in life. At that moment, a firecracker went off that seemed very close. The brother moved a little away from the cook and, half turning toward D'Arrast but without looking at him, pointed to the empty place and said: "Sit down with us."

(*Exile*, 159–213)

Conclusion

"To lie," wrote Camus, "is not simply to say what is not the case. It is also, and even more so, to say more than is the case and, in matters which concern the human heart, to say more than one feels."[1] Indeed, Camus struggled never to lie, never to speak falsehood and never to say too much. And, for this latter caution and reticence which so characterized him, Camus received misunderstanding and abuse from those to whom grand and intransigent words came all too easily. Some thought him self-righteous while others thought him nihilistic. In fact, he was only careful. And honest, impeccably so. If we must give his thought a name, there may be some revealing sense in saying that it is minimalist. In suggesting this title, I have in mind minimal art which strives after the simplest, most pedestrian materials, gestures, and expressions with a view toward our learning to wonder at and delight in the beauty which edges us all around. And herein we may find the most telling bond of all between Camus and the Greek tradition.

The outspoken purpose of this volume has been to suggest a deep and pervasive synergism between Camus' thought and that of classical Greece. By now the case for such a suggestion has either been made or not. However, one remaining and perhaps conclusive link might well be drawn here. I wish to reflect briefly upon the figure of Sokrates, so paradigmatic for the Greek tradition. More specifically yet, it is the irony of Sokrates by which I wish to take my bearings in these concluding comments. Sokrates proclaimed his own ranging ignorance and yet he refuted one falsehood after another.

Instead of unfolding a positive teaching of his own, he withheld himself and disenchanted his companions from their own and others' false opinions. He taught by denial rather than by profession; or so it seemed. And, in doing so, he claimed to know next to nothing. Nevertheless, one might envy with cause the ignorance of one who knew enough to stand back from every false opinion. Indeed, never to have embraced falsehood would seem to constitute unparalleled knowledge. Similarly, when Sokrates explained that a daimonic power stayed his hand and heart from ever committing an evil deed, he was laying claim to a virtue all but beyond our imagination.

Nonetheless, it is one thing to steel oneself against error and evil and quite another to announce the truth and to enact virtue. Ironically, they are not at all the same. Camus knew this fact well; and so must we if we are to understand him. Still, we insist, even a confessedly nocturnal mind which makes its way among shadows knows something of light. Surely even a cautious mind may once risk saying too much for fear of saying too little. And here we may recall Sokrates and his last dialogue recounted in the *Phaido*. Among friends, his death imminent, his struggle against falsehood and evil at an end, Sokrates permitted himself to sing of all that filled his heart, whether or not his heart might mislead him. There is, it seems, a time to imagine and to hope and to speak unguardedly and without one's most cautious counsels. Even irony gives way in the end to what may be called a sublime humor.

Camus knew no such release. His sudden and unprovided death left him unprivileged with the period of grace which Sokrates and, for that matter, Camus' own Meursault put to such wondrous use. Further, unlike Sokrates, Camus has no Plato to follow him and to speak into God knows how many silences. Not since he wrote *Melusina's Book* as a gift to his bride, Simone Hié, on their first Christmas together when he was twenty-one had Camus forgotten the rigors of responsible speech and let his mind dance as Sokrates' did in the *Phaido*. To be sure, there are moments of festivity, moments of grace in his writings; and, finally, an imponderable night sky which we know is more than the absence of day. How much more, Camus has never fully told us. It may contain more suns than we can count.

NOTE

1. From Camus' own preface to *L'Etranger*, ed. Germaine Brée and Carlos Lynes, Jr., New York: Appleton-Century-Crofts, 1955, p. vii, translation mine.

Bibliography

OEUVRES D'ALBERT CAMUS

(Par ordre chronologique, dans chaques catégorie)

RECITS ET ROMANS

L'Etranger (Paris: Gallimard, 1942)
La Peste (Paris: Gallimard, 1947)
La Chute (Paris: Gallimard, 1956)
L'Exile et le royaume (Paris: Gallimard, 1957)
La Mort heureuse (Paris: Gallimard, 1971), *Cahiers Albert Camus I*

THEATRE

Révolte dans les Asturies: Essai de création collective (Alger: Charlot, 1936)
Le Malentendu (Paris: Gallimard, 1944)
Caligula (Paris: Gallimard, 1944)
L'Etat de siège (Paris: Gallimard, 1948)
Les Justes (Paris: Gallimard, 1950)

ESSAIS

L'Envers et l'endroit (Alger: Charlot, 1937; Paris: Gallimard, 1957 et 1958)
Noces (Alger: Charlot, 1938; Paris: Gallimard, 1947)
Le Mythe de Sisyphe (Paris: Gallimard, 1942)
Lettres à un ami allemand (Paris: Gallimard, 1945)
"Remarque sur la révolte," dans *L'Existence* (Paris: Gallimard, 1945, pp. 2–23)

Prométhée aux enfers (Paris: Palimugre, 1947)

Actuelles I, chroniques 1944–1948 (Paris: Gallimard, 1950)

L'Homme révolté (Paris: Gallimard, 1951)

Actuelles II, chroniques 1948–1953 (Paris: Gallimard, 1953)

L'Eté (Paris: Gallimard, 1954)

"Discours de Suède" et "L'Artiste et son temps" (Paris: Gallimard, 1958)

Actuelles III, chroniques algériennes 1939–1958 (Paris: Gallimard, 1958)

L'Intelligence et l'échafaud (Liège: Dynamo, 1960), Collection: "Brimborions," #59

Méditation sur le théâtre et la vie (Liège: Dynamo, 1961), Collection: "Brimborions," #75

Lettre à Bernanos (Paris: Minard, 1963), Collection: "Bulletin de la Société des Amis de Bernanos," #45

Le premier Camus, par Paul Viallaneix, suivi des Ecrits de jeunesse d'Albert Camus (Paris: Gallimard, 1973), *Cahiers Albert Camus II*

CARNETS

Carnets I, mai 1935–fév. 1942 (Paris: Gallimard, 1962)

Carnets II, jan. 1942–mars 1951 (Paris: Gallimard, 1964)

EN COLLABORATION

Désert vivant: Images en couleurs de Walt Disney. Textes de Marcel Aymé, Louis Bromfield, Albert Camus, *et al.* (Paris: Société française du livre, 1954)

Réflexions sur la peine capitale: Introduction et étude de Jean Bloch-Michel, par Arthur Koestler et Albert Camus (Paris: Calmann-Lévy, 1957)

PREFACES

Chamfort, Sébastien, *Maximes et anecdotes* (Monaco: Duc, 1944)

Salvet, André, *Le Combat silencieux* (Paris: Ed. France-Empire, Collection Le Portulan, 1945)

Camp, Jean, et Cassou, Jean, *L'Espagne libre* (Paris: Calmann-Lévy, 1946)

Char, René, *Feuillet d'Hypnos* (Paris: Gallimard, 1946)

Clairin, Pierre-Eugène, *Dix Estampes originales, présentées par Albert Camus* (Paris: Rombaldi, 1946)

Leynaud, René, *Poésies posthumes* (Paris: Gallimard, 1947)

Méry, J., *Laissez-passer mon peuple* (Paris: Ed. du Seuil, 1947)

Héon-Canonne, Jeanne, *Devant la mort* (Anger: Siraudeau, 1951; Paris: Amiot-Dumont, 1953)

Char, René, *Das brautiche Antlitz*, tr. Johannes Hübner und Lothar Klünner (Frankfurt: K. O. Gotz, 1952); *René Char's Poetry*, tr. David Paul (Rome: Ed. de Luca, 1956)

Mauroc, Daniel, *Contre-Amour* (Paris: Ed. de Minuit, 1952)

Wilde, Oscar, *La Ballade de la geôle de Reading* (Paris: Falaize, 1952)

Guilloux, Louis, *La Maison de peuple* (Paris: Grasset, 1953)

Rosmer, Alfred, *Moscou sous Lénine: Les Origines du Communisme* (Paris: Ed. Flore, Pierre Horay, 1953)

Bieber, Konrad, *L'Allemagne vue par les écrivains de la Résistance française* (Genève: Droz, 1954)

Targuebayre, Claire, *Cordes-en-Albigeois* (Toulouse: E. Privat, 1954)

Camus, Albert, *L'Etranger*, ed. Germaine Brée and Carlos Lynes, Jr. (New York: Appleton-Century-Crofts, 1955)

Martin du Gard, Roger, *Oeuvres complètes* (Paris: Bibliotheque de la Pléiade, Gallimard, 1955)

Faulkner, William, *Requiem pour une nonne*, tr. M. E. Coindreau (Paris: Gallimard, 1957)

La Vérité sur l'affaire Nagy: Les Faits, les documents, les temoignages internationaux (Paris: Plon, 1958)

Grenier, Jean, *Les Iles* (Paris: *La Nouvelle Revue Française*, 1959)

TRADUCTIONS

Thurber, James, *La Dernière Fleur* (Paris: Gallimard, 1952)

Caldéron de la Barca, Pedro, *La Dévotion à la croix* (Paris: Gallimard, 1953)

Buzzati, Dino, *Un Cas intéressant* (Paris: L'Avant-scène, 1955)

Vega Carpio, Lope de, *Le Chevalier d'Olmedo* (Paris: Gallimard, 1957)

ADAPTATIONS

de Larivey, Pierre, *Les Esprits* (Paris: Gallimard, 1953)
Faulkner, William, *Requiem pour une nonne* (Paris: Gallimard, 1957)
Dostoevsky, Féodor, *Les Possédés* (Paris: Gallimard, 1959)

ŒUVRES GROUPÉES

Œuvres complètes (Paris: Bibliothèque de la Pléiade, Gallimard)
  I: *Théâtre, récits, nouvelles,* ed. Roger Quilliot, 1962
  II: *Essais,* ed. R. Quilliot et L. Faucon, 1965
Œuvres complètes (Paris: Imprimerie nationale Sauret)
  I: *Récits et romans,* 1961
  II: *Essais littéraires,* 1962
  III: *Essais philosophiques,* 1962
  IV: *Essais politiques,* 1962
  V: *Théâtre,* 1962
  VI: *Adaptations et traductions,* 1962

WORKS IN ENGLISH TRANSLATIONS

The Stranger, tr. Stuart Gilbert (New York: Knopf, 1946)
The Plague, tr. Stuart Gilbert (New York: Knopf, 1948)
"*Caligula*" and "*Cross-Purpose,*" tr. Stuart Gilbert (Norfolk, Conn.: New
      Directions, 1948)
The Rebel, tr. Anthony Bower (New York: Knopf, 1954)
The Myth of Sisyphus and Other Essays, tr. Justin O'Brien (New York:
      Knopf, 1955)
The Fall, tr. Justin O'Brien (New York: Knopf, 1957)
"*Caligula*" *and Three Other Plays,* tr. Stuart Gilbert; preface by Camus [tr.
      Justin O'Brien] (New York: Knopf, 1958)
Exile and the Kingdom, tr. Justin O'Brien (New York: Knopf, 1958)
Speech of Acceptance upon the Award of the Nobel Prize for Literature, tr.
      Justin O'Brien (New York: Knopf, 1958); also in *The Atlantic
      Monthly* [May, 1958, pp. 33–34]

The Possessed, Adaptation, tr. Justin O'Brien; foreword by Camus (New York: Knopf, 1960)

Resistance, Rebellion and Death, tr. Justin O'Brien (New York: Knopf, 1961)

Neither Victims Nor Executioners, tr. Dwight Macdonald (Berkeley: World Without War Publications, 1968)

Lyrical and Critical Essays, ed. Philip Thody; tr. Ellen Conroy Kennedy (New York: Knopf, 1968)

Youthful Writings, tr. Ellen Conroy Kennedy; introductory essay by Paul Viallaneix (New York: Knopf, 1976)

BIBLIOGRAPHIES

Bollinger, Renate, *Albert Camus: Eine Bibliographie der Literatur über ihn und sein Werk* (Köln: Greven Verlag, 1957)

Crépin, Simone, *Albert Camus: Essai de bibliographie* (Bruxelles: Commission Belge de Bibliographie, 1960)

Fitch, Brian T., *Calepins de bibliographie*, Albert Camus, 1937–1962 (Paris: Minard, Lettres Modernes, 1965)

Roeming, Robert F., *Camus: A Bibliography* (Madison: The University of Wisconsin Press, 1968)

SELECTED STUDIES IN ENGLISH

Archambault, Paul, *Camus' Hellenic Sources* (Chapel Hill: University of North Carolina Press, 1972)

Braun, Lev, *Witness of Decline—Albert Camus: Moralist of the Absurd* (Cranbury, N.J.: Fairleigh Dickinson, 1974)

Brée, Germaine, *Camus* (New Brunswick: Rutgers University Press, 1961; New York: Harcourt, Brace, and World, 1964)

———, ed., *Camus: A Collection of Critical Essays* (Englewood Cliffs, N.J.: Prentice-Hall, 1962)

———, *Camus and Sartre: Crisis and Commitment* (New York: Dell, 1972)

Burnier, Michel-Antoine, *Choice of Action: The French Existentialists on the Political Front Line*, tr. Bernard Murchland, with essay by translator: "Sartre and Camus—The Anatomy of a Quarrel" (New York: Random House, 1968)

Champigny, Robert, *Pagan Hero: An Interpretation of Meursault in Camus' The Stranger*, tr. Rowe Portis (Philadelphia: University of Pennsylvania Press, 1970)

Cruickshank, John, *Albert Camus and the Literature of Revolt* (New York: Oxford University Press, 1960)

Freeman, Edward, *The Theatre of Albert Camus: A Critical Study* (London: Methuen, 1971)

Hanna, Thomas, *The Thought and Art of Albert Camus* (Chicago: Regnery, 1958)

King, Adele, *Camus* (New York: Putnam, 1971)

Lazere, Donald, *The Unique Creation of Albert Camus* (New Haven: Yale University Press, 1973)

Lebesque, Morvan, *Portrait of Camus*, tr. T. C. Sharman (New York: Herder and Herder, 1971)

Luppé, Robert de, *Albert Camus*, tr. John Cumming and J. Hargreaves (London: Merlin, 1967)

Maquet, Albert, *Albert Camus: The Invincible Summer*, tr. Herma Briffault (New York: George Braziller, 1958)

Merton, Thomas, *Albert Camus' The Plague* (New York: Seabury, 1968)

O'Brien, Conor Cruse, *Albert Camus of Europe and North Africa* (New York: Viking, 1970)

Onimus, Jean, *Albert Camus and Christianity* (Tuscaloosa: University of Alabama Press, 1970)

Parker, Emmett, *Albert Camus: The Artist in the Arena* (Madison: University of Wisconsin Press, 1965)

Peterson, Carol, *Albert Camus*, tr. Alexander Gode (New York: Frederick Ungar, 1969)

Pollman, Leo, *Sartre and Camus: Literature of Existence*, tr. Helen & Gregor Sebba (New York: Frederick Ungar, 1976)

Quilliot, Roger, *Sea and Prisons: A Commentary on the Life and Thought of Albert Camus,* tr. Emmett Parker (University: University of Alabama Press, 1970)

Rhein, Philip H., *Albert Camus* (Boston: Twayne, 1969)

Scott, Nathan, *Albert Camus* (New York: Hillary House, 1962; 2nd rev. ed., London: Bowes, 1969)

Thody, Philip, *Albert Camus: 1913–1960* (London: Hamish Hamilton, 1961), a revision of *Albert Camus: A Study of His Work* (New York: Macmillan, 1957; Grove, 1959)

Willhoite, Fred H., Jr., *Beyond Nihilism: Albert Camus' Contribution to Political Thought* (Baton Rouge: Louisiana State University Press, 1968)

Woelfel, James W., *Camus: A Theological Perspective* (Nashville: Abingdon, 1975)

SELECTED STUDIES IN ENGLISH CONTAINING SECTIONS ON CAMUS

Barrett, William, *Irrational Man: A Study in Existential Philosophy* (New York: Doubleday, 1958)

————, *Time of Need: Forms of Imagination in the Twentieth Century* (New York: Harper & Row, 1972)

Brée, Germaine, and Guiton, Margaret, *An Age of Fiction* (London: Chatto and Windus, 1958)

Collins, James, *The Existentialists: A Critical Study* (Chicago: Regnery, 1952)

Cruickshank, John, ed., *The Novelist as Philosopher: Studies in French Fiction 1935–60* (London: Oxford University Press, 1962)

Falk, Eugene H., *Types of Thematic Structure* (Chicago: University of Chicago Press, 1967)

Fowlie, Wallace, *Dionysus in Paris* (New York: Meridian, 1960)

Friedman, Maurice, *Problematic Rebel: Melville, Dostoievsky, Kafka, Camus* (Chicago: University of Chicago Press, 1970)

Hanna, Thomas, *The Lyrical Existentialists* (New York: Atheneum, 1962)

Jacobson, Norman, *Pride and Solace: The Functions and Limits of Political Theory* (Berkeley: University of California Press, 1978)

Lerner, Max, *Actions and Passions: Notes on the Multiple Revolutions of Our Times* (New York: Simon and Schuster, 1949)

Lewis, Wyndham, *The Writer and the Absolute* (London: Methuen, 1952)

Rhein, Philip H., *Urge to Live: A Comparative Study of Franz Kafka's* Der Prozess *and Albert Camus'* L'Etranger (Chapel Hill: University of North Carolina Press, 1964)

Sartre, Jean-Paul, *Literary and Philosophical Essays*, tr. Annette Michelson (New York: Criterion, 1955)

Wilson, Colin, *The Outsider* (London: Gollancz, 1956)

Index

317